MAX ABADDON AND THE PURITY LAW

A Max Abaddon Novel. Book 2

Justin S. Leslie

J.S.L

Copyright © 2020 Justin S. Leslie

All rights reserved

This book or any portion thereof may not be reproduced or used in any manner whatsoever without the express written permission of the publisher except for the use of brief quotations in a book review.

This is a work of fiction. Names, characters, places, and incidents either are the products of the author's imagination or are used fictitiously. Any resemblance to actual persons, living or dead, events, or locales is entirely coincidental. Or I had too much to drink while writing and just forgot.

Hardcover ISBN 978-1-7353035-0-5
Paperback ISBN: 978-1-7331873-5-0
E-book ISBN: 978-1-7331873-4-3

Contact Information

Email: Abaddonbooks@hotmail.com

Facebook: @Maxabaddonbooks

Website: www.JustinLeslie.com

The fire you kindle for your enemy often burns you more.
—Proverb

A candle factory once burned down. Everyone just stood around singing
"Happy Birthday."
—Steven Wright

CHAPTER 1

Can We Talk This Over?

"I know it smells in here," I said, looking over at Petro as he flew to the reception desk with a trail of dust coming off his wings. The odor was a mix of decaying flesh, sulfur, and general death all coming together at the wrong place and time.

Petro, as of twelve months ago, had become my partner, owing me what he called a life debt. He was also an eight-inch-tall overly brave Pixie from a place called the Plane.

Today was our turn to work at the newly mandated Transitions Office. It also happened to be one of the few times someone walked in, making the hair on the back of my neck stand up. Maybe it was the smell or the fact that it looked like something was moving under his skin that was putting us on edge.

"Hey, Max, I think he's looking at me!" Petro said in his high-pitched voice, taking position hovering over my shoulder. This was his normal spot when he was sizing up something or someone who had come into the office. Petro was brave and smart; however, he had a tendency to rush into things. That's why Ed had locked Petro in the break room freezer before Phil and I found him, letting Petro out after getting a few drinks in us.

Me? I was standing there trying to figure out who—or what, exactly—the rather mysteriously dressed man in front of us was. He was hovering over the pamphlet table that Dr. Simmons, better known to her friends as Jenny, had set up in the entrance. I ran my hands through my recently grown-out hair.

"He either wants to chat or eat us," I said to no one under my breath, stopping my mind from wandering as the tall man started to creep toward the desk.

He was roughly six feet tall and had an odd build. There was too much oddly positioned muscle; however, he was thin at the same time. His face looked sunburnt, almost red, with strong lines leading to his mouth and eyes. The hair was my favorite. It looked like he had poured a can of motor oil in it, slicking it back. Topping it off was on an odd pair of round black sunglasses covering his eyes.

His clothes, I would guess, were from sometime in the mideighteenth century—a suit made of what looked to be crushed velvet covering a neatly cut dress shirt that you would see in an old movie. The style would have worked on Halloween. Too bad that was last month.

"He's coming over here, and man, that smell." Petro chirped louder than needed, causing the man to pause.

"Gods and graves, he's big, dressed like it's Halloween, and smells bad. It reminds me of someone. Get Phil," I said to Petro as he landed on the desk, pushing the buttons on the tablet sitting there at blazing speed. I looked down to see he had typed *S.O.S.*

"Great." I thought to myself, *I'm not the only one feeling a little nervous.*

The Transitions Office had been created six months ago after our little adventure under the Bridge of Lions in St. Augustine, Florida, and the subsequent destruction of the actual Fountain of Youth. Yeah, about that—sorry.

It was a medium-size shop that used to be a bookstore catering to the magical crowd. The space was trimmed in dark wood and had shelves lining the walls that sat bare at the moment. We planned to fill it up with some of the lesser books from the Atheneum, with Ed's permission, after they had been digitized.

The entrance windows were glass with slats forming crosses. The floor was covered in rich, dark-patterned carpet that looked like it was from a hotel of some sort. Walking in on the left was a desk full of pamphlets on "How to integrate the easy way" and a set of sitting chairs in front of the reception desk halfway through the room. Scents of lemon, old books, and rich mahogany hung in the air. I contributed this to the deep cleaning of the wood and the overall amount of the stuff. Wood was special to the magical community. It could be manipulated and was easy to work spells with.

There was an upstairs apartment; however, the leasing agent hadn't opened it yet for access. Something about it needing to be unwarded.

Since our little adventure dealing with the Fountain of Youth, a date had been set for what had been coined "the Balance." Basically, the magical community had decided to come out to the real world. I, as of twelve months ago…well, I was now part of that world. I only found out after my Gramps passed away that when I hit the ripe old age of thirty, I was going to become a Mage, or at least start the process to become one.

In his will, Gramps left me a few notable things, one being this job and his house attached to the Atheneum, a facility that was half library and half home to a group of particularly gifted magical detectives. At least that's what I had interpreted the team as, and I was now part of it.

Earthborn Mages and Wizards, not to mention other random creatures people would find generally scary, had been the driving force behind the initiative to integrate into civilized society.

Not everyone was on the same page, however. Others from a place called the Plane were a harder sell. Better known as Ethereals. Pure Fae, Demigods, and the like. While most supported the great joining of civilizations, a few saw it as a threat to the things and people from the Plane.

The Thule Society was recently identified as one of those syndicates working to stop the two groups from integrating, thus ensuring their ability to keep relevant, not allowing the combined group to tip the scales or in the least work to overtake the process to gain power.

The lines were blurry, and stipulations had been imposed by the civilian governments, including the creation of the Transitions Office, which was basically a registration office for all things considered not "completely human." Some of my favorite questions:

1. Can you do magic, and if so, what type?
2. Have you ever killed another person, Mage, Ethereal, or other?
3. Do you consider yourself violent?
4. Are you Earthborn, and have you ever been to the Plane?
5. What do you do for a living?
6. Do you own any weapons? Magical, charmed, blended, or natural?
7. What do you consider yourself?

I wasn't the most dialed-in person, being new to this world; however, I could tell the indignation of some of the visitors to the office. That being said, if you wanted to be part of the big show, you had to be registered and sanctioned to use whatever gift—or curse, for that matter—you may possess.

Vampires, or V's, as I had learned to call them, had the most fun when they came in. Yup, those are real half-Earthborn, half-cursed Fae that actually have a great sense of humor. I had to keep reminding them that their devilishly good looks and charm were not considered a deadly weapon. They got a kick out of that. I bet the joke had gotten around, seeing that the Magical and Ethereal communities on Earth was not in actuality that large. Thing is, that was changing with more people and things having abilities manifest that in the past wouldn't have. Or—as I had a feeling—in front of us, just showing up from who knows where.

The First Coast area of northeast Florida was a hotspot for people traveling through. I learned it was due to St. Augustine being the oldest city in the United States. There was a kind of magic in the air, so to speak. It was a central hub for coming in and out of the country through connecting gates. That's the way most magic types traveled. Jenny had explained it to me as "Significantly easier to get to and work magic in than, say, Kansas City."

Ed, the fearless leader of our team working out of the Atheneum, set us up to have an office located close to the main facility. There were four others in the United States: in New York, Chicago, Los Angeles, and Dallas. These were manned by other Mages working for the NCTS, an acronym for the National Council of Traditional Sciences.

The thought dissipated as the man pushed forward, seeming to melt through the two chairs in front of the desk. We had set up a code to send out to the group if trouble walked in. Ed and Phil had also taken the time to set up a gate in the main room just in case. This gate opened directly behind the reception desk.

Phil was another member of the Atheneum team. When there was trouble, you called Phil. If he couldn't figure it out, he would at least be able to bash it into submission. Or, as he did on occasion, drink it under the table.

The creature was roughly ten feet away from the desk as we backed up; I reached into my shoulder holster, putting my hand on the grip of Durundle but not pulling it out. Durundle is a mythical sword, which for some reason had taken a shining to the hellfire that I was apparently good at using. Well, I wouldn't say good, but I had at least figured out how to not burn the house down.

Before I could speak, the gate behind us shimmered to life, as Phil came out holding a shotgun with a barrel magazine hanging off the bottom, an unlit cigarette dangling out of his mouth.

Phil looked much like a hipster who worked out too much. Beard, neatly sculpted short hair, tattoos on his neck, and he wore skinny jeans, a pair of jet-black combat boots with a button-down shirt, and a formfitting vest to wrap it all up. I highly recommended to people not to call him a hipster for their personal well-being.

Boredom had struck Phil over the past few months by way of things being quiet, and you could tell he was ready for some action as he walked up behind us.

"Bruther, what the hell," Phil said as he spit his cigarette out on the floor, slightly lowering the barrel of his shotgun.

"Hey, man, nice to see you too. Think you could hold that thing back up?" I said, feeling the castor on my wrist start to warm up with energy that I was on the verge of releasing into the sword. I had received the castor on my re-birthday. It was a dive watch that also doubled as a small holding tank for Etherium.

"That's a demon," Phil said as I looked back at him, finally taking my eyes off the creature. "It say anything yet?" he asked in his thickest Irish, mixing with the southern Texas drawl he had inherited from his mother. Phil was half Fae, half human.

Petro interjected, "Not yet, just creeping around the shop smelling bad."

The demon had stopped moving and stood there taking on a harder, more solid stance as we watched.

Phil, much to my surprise, walked to the other side of the desk, squaring off in front of the demon. "Can we help you?" Phil asked, not letting it know he was nervous. Hell, if I had that shotgun, I would be the same. I also bet he had some of his nefarious special ammo in it, the kind purchased off the black market that would have drastic effects on Ethereal and magical types.

"I'm here to take part in the registration," the demon said with a smoother voice than the only other demon I had ever met spoke in.

Belm, your friendly neighborhood demon, was the son of Devin, who I am fairly sure is the devil. Belm was with us when our team finally ran into the bad guys last year at the Blue House. To be clear he impaled the two bad guys with his spiked tail and laughed about it afterward. He even joined us for drinks when it was all said and done. Told you, it's been a crazy year so far.

The Blue House is an exclusive eating establishment owned by Marlow Goolsby. I was banned from there for setting it mostly on fire and the following round of dismembering crafts. Crafts are nothing more than human-looking drones being controlled by someone through magic, and not to mention expensive.

He was the known leader of the Order Society, more or less a shifty organization that rode the line between law abiding and not so much. Even more Mr. Goolsby was now the

CEO of Mags-Tech, one of the largest companies no one has ever heard of. They made everyday items that Mages and the like could use without blowing themselves, or others, up.

His brother Ezra was one of the people murdered by the Thule Society, leaving Marlow the company. Rumor had it he was selling the company to get back to his other less visible responsibilities.

The building was supposed to be warded to avoid things like demons from wondering in. Demons are not on the registration list and in general are not supposed to be on Earth, from what I had gathered. I don't even think there's a space for them to check on the forms. *Got to love the government*, I thought, putting a smirk on my face. You know…Caucasian, Asian, African American, Native American, Hispanic, Mage, Wizard, Vampire, Fae…nope, no spot for demon.

Phil did the most Phil thing he could and reached out his hand in a shaking gesture while still holding the shotgun level with his chest.

That's when things went sideways. The demon reached out with his opposite arm and smashed the shotgun out of Phil's other hand, trailing up to his chest, shoving him over the desk, and landing him in the space Petro and I had created by backing up in one graceful motion.

On instinct, I pulled the sword completely out and yelled "*Ignis*," turning the blade into a dark, glowing red instrument of death. I carried the sword in a modified shoulder holster due to the fact that when I sheathed the blade, it disappeared into the holder, making the length of the blade immaterial and hidden. Still couldn't figure that little trick out; something about spatial magic.

Petro flew to the other side of the room behind the demon as the words left my mouth.

The demon started to walk forward, resolute in his

movement. "It's not nice to point a shotgun at someone when you're trying to shake hands," the demon said, raising an eyebrow from behind his glasses. I was quite sure the desk wouldn't stop him. Phil was shuffling around to get up as his shotgun was on the floor out of reach.

Petro threw what looked like a small blended charm, setting loose a spell on the backside of our guest. Much to his—and now, my—surprise, the small round sphere dissolved into his body and dissipated.

By now the demon had effectively started to cut himself in half as his upper torso slid across the top of the reception desk heading toward Phil and me, leaving his bottom half standing in place. As his body started to move across the surface, he put his hands down, dragging his upper body forward, leaving a trail of viscous black slime in his wake. The smell by that point was multiplied, leaving me standing there staring at the figure.

Just to think—it was only noon, and I already needed a drink. Good thing the office was in the same building as the trusty Fallen Angel, FA's for short and one of the best supernatural bars on the planet.

As the demon reached the end of the desk still holding his perfect posture, Phil had gotten back up and was standing beside me. Then a thought crossed my mind. This thing hadn't really tried to hurt us until we reached out to it holding a shotgun or threw a charm at it.

Phil pulled out a solid black knife from his waist, flexing his strength. You could hear the leather castor on his wrist stretching.

"Hang on," I said as I whispered, "*Desino*," putting out the blade's glow.

As soon as the blade's hellfire dissipated, the demon reached out his hand palm up, leaning his head in a polite gesture. "Ah, a gentleman," came the smooth voice.

"Bruther, it moves; I'm going at it," Phil said as I let the demon's hand touch my outreached fingers in some old-timey limp handshake.

"I don't mean you gentlemen any harm. Belm sent me. I do believe you are all acquaintances. I thought you would all be scarier, to be honest," the demon said, lightly licking his lips.

Phil looked over, raising an eyebrow and seeing the look on my face.

Working with Ed, being the full-blown Wizard that he was, had taught me one thing. You can return the favor and use your manners. "What's your name? I'm Max" was all I could muster.

The demon stood still for a moment before the charm Petro had thrown at him dropped out of his hand into mine. "Boegosh."

I froze in place for a second before Petro spoke up, now back over my shoulder. "How the hell did you do that?" Petro asked him as he looked over at the charm in my hand.

"Really?" Boegosh said in a low, smoky voice. "I'm a demon, not a baby."

"Boegosh, are you alone?" Phil asked as he set his posture and started scanning around the front of the building, obviously looking for a fast way to get to his shotgun just in case.

"Of course. Some of my associates are not as civilized as I am. Belm, a friend of mine, told me I could come here…well, sort of. Well, none of us are really friends, but that's beside the point," Boegosh said, backing up, sliding from the table, and making himself whole again. The noise was nauseating, not to mention the smell. He was doing this little trick on purpose. I bet it was an illusion.

"I only thought that Mages and the like needed to register here," Phil said. I could tell that Boegosh had pissed Phil off, and things were about to go south again as he continued. "Not sure about demons. In some ways it would be like getting your dog a driver's license…"

It was too late. Boegosh sent a small pile of black oil-looking goo loose on the desk he had occupied prior, followed by a light chuckle.

Before Phil could react, I let out a light chuckle as well. I guess it was contagious, as Petro joined in. The black goo formed a small terrier-looking dog that, after wagging its little black-oil puppy tail, had chuffed and jumped off the table, and was proceeding to piss black oil on Phil's shined combat boots.

You see, the one thing I learned from Belm is that if a demon hasn't tried to eat you or is not actively trying to kill you, then he either wants something you have, or he has something for you. Phil knew this and let his ego take a back seat to common sense.

"To hell with you," Phil said as he opened his palm, letting out a casting and dissipating the small black-goo dog.

"It is nice this time of year back home," Boegosh countered, handing Phil his shotgun. "See, we can be civil. Where do I register?"

Boegosh was either crazy or didn't care if he had tipped Phil over the edge. The thing I like about Phil is that he can take a joke. Not today though. Phil grabbed his shotgun, turned, and gated out of the room, letting out a flurry of Irish curse words that trailed off as the gate closed,

leaving Petro and me to deal with our guest.

"Guess your friend didn't like my little pet. I have plenty. You can call me Bo," the demon said.

"Well, I guess that answers that. Here, fill this out. Just put 'demon.' There's not a box for it, and just take a stab at the rest," I said, using a little humor I had picked up from Belm.

I stood there, fully knowing the Council's stance on demons and understanding this would likely cause an issue. For some reason I didn't care.

Working at the Transitions Office had seemed exciting at first and had in fact been rather dull. Today was the exception. While I enjoyed meeting new people or whatever, the entire process seemed pointless. Not to mention all the excitement from last year had pretty much come to an abrupt halt.

Even though the day was young, we had seen enough excitement for now, plus I didn't think I could stand the smell until we aired out the room; it was time to call it a day.

What I didn't realize was that by submitting Bo's registration, I had set off a series of ill-fated events, both positive and negative, that would further affect my newly found friends and family.

CHAPTER 2

The Fallen Angel

"So let me get this straight," Kim said as she took a sip from an overly poured glass of red wine. "Then the demon—"

"Bo," I interjected, also taking a pull from my favorite beer, Vamp Amber.

"Bo created a puppy made of e-core, and it proceeded to relieve itself on Phil's boots," Kim said as Petro and I both shook our heads to reaffirm our story from earlier in the day.

Kim Kimber, resident regular federal marshal and general badass, let out a howl of laughter, splashing some of her wine on the bar top.

The marshal was what the Mage community called a regular, someone who doesn't have any magical abilities. It was a slang term, and if used in front of the wrong person, such as Kim, you may just be picking your teeth up off the floor.

She, up until recently, had spent most of her time making sure I knew I was out of my league both professionally and in the relationship department, mainly thanks to my last dip into the dating pool almost getting us all killed. Kim had a way of making a guy feel that way. A fighter through and through. Not to mention she had dealt with her fair share of things that went bump in the night.

Kim was given cases that were flagged OTN, or "other than natural," by regular law enforcement of various sorts. She was one of two marshals assigned to the NCTS. While she had access to the regular marshal field force, she had additionally been given a rather flexible range of responsibilities. With the civilian governments agreeing to the terms of the Balance, Kim had become quite popular recently, much to her dislike.

She was five and half feet tall. Muscular, blond, and she only recently stopped always using that stern look on her face when she talked to me. Kim was pretty in a strong way that lent itself to endless hours of training.

The scents of vanilla and honey radiated from her body, both deliberate and subtle at the same time. The way she dressed screamed normal federal agent: bland, dark jeans with a blouse and usually a light jacket on to cover her service pistol. She looked good and only recently started to loosen up around me.

"Hey, boss, your phone's buzzing," Petro said, sipping rum from a small glass.

"Damn, it's Jenny. She's on the warpath about the Council ball in a few days and is calling a meeting to go over last-minute details tonight," I choked out, taking a finishing pull from my beer.

Trish appeared and leaned down on the bar in front of us, talking in her smooth voice. "Sounds like you all are in for a long night. Jenny was in here earlier talking about some unique catering items she wants me to get."

Trish was the proprietor and bar keep of the Fallen Angel. FA's my favorite place on the face of Earth. She was, from my best guess, not fully human and from northern Africa. I assumed this due to her dark, smooth brown skin and slight accent. Trish was always there and constantly working. Highly respected and mysterious was about the best way to explain her.

Like most barkeeps she seemed to know the answer to just about anything. From what I had gathered, she had known Gramps and Ed for well over a hundred years.

While not all Mages or the like age slowly, that group just happened to. My mother, for example, was a witch. News to me last year. She aged just like the rest of us. I had been told I would more than likely hit the brakes soon as the whole aging thing was more dominant with the second generation.

The Fallen Angel itself was an homage to the several generations it had been there for. Dark wood, rich red leather chairs, and yellow ambient lighting that radiated from the solid copper printed-tile ceiling set the mood. From the kitchen the smell of earthy wood tones and buttered steak on a grill lingered in the air. The bar was a large horseshoe that divided itself from the rest of the place, keeping dinner conversations and that of the bar patrons generally separated.

"Well, looks like I'll catch up with you boys later. Have fun with your party planning committee," Kim said, putting down her glass with a clink and walking out again, leaving me with the tab as I watched her retreat.

"Hmm..." I said, looking at Trish and Petro with a raised eyebrow, biting my bottom lip. "That's the first time she hasn't insisted on paying for her own drink."

Trish let out a light snicker, picking up my empty bottle. "Drink up, lover boy. Good luck with that one. You better get going."

"I'm not sure what you mean," I said, obviously hiding my interest in Kim's exit without picking up her tab.

"Max, just because a woman does something doesn't mean it has to have meaning. Anyways, did you hear who's coming to the ball?" Trish said, lighting up the room with her smile.

"You got me Santa?" I said with a smirk.

"Planes Drifter is playing a set. It's supposed to be a surprise performance, but I overheard one of their road crew in here talking about it. Can you believe it?" Trish said as a smile forced its way onto my face.

Planes Drifter is one of the best rock/metal acts on the face of the Earth. Well, at least my Earth. It wasn't until recently that I had figured out why I was so drawn to them. They were a band of Mages that just happened to play heavy metal.

"You have to be shitting me!" I said as I stood up, grinning, playing a lick on the old air guitar and finishing up with a weak kick of my foot in true rock star fashion.

Every year the Ethereal Council holds a themed ball for the power players in the Mage, regular, and Ethereal communities alike. Consisting mostly of politicians and Council members, the ball was a big deal. With all the excitement last year, we had been given the honor of hosting the event at the Atheneum.

Those events included chasing a murderous cult around the world and destroying the Fountain of Youth. In that mix was the betrayal of someone I had grown close to and fond of, Chloe. She worked for the Dunn, our sister location in London. We worked together on my first assignment dealing with the world of magic. She had betrayed not only me, but the team as well.

Chloe was responsible for the deaths of several people, and I was there beside her not knowing a thing. I spent most of last year researching the Thule Society, the organization she worked for, in order to find her and get answers. It was a touchy subject and one the rest of the team also wanted closure on.

One of the last visions I had of Chloe was her holding a pistol to Jayal's head, pulling the trigger at point-blank range, ending his life. Every time I thought of her, it felt like someone plopped a scoop of ice cream on my head, letting it slowly melt in the sun, electrifying my senses.

"I have a feeling Jenny will let the cat out of the bag tonight and maybe a few other surprises. Have fun and text me if you find anything out," Trish said as she wiped up the spilled wine Kim had left, looking down at it and letting her smile fade slightly.

Petro and I went through our normal round of exiting banter with Trish before heading out to the Black Beast, my old Dodge truck.

On the ride home, Petro and I reflected on our day and chalked it up to bad luck. We did, however, decide that a conversation with Belm was in order.

"Petro, text Jamison and see if he can meet us, and tell him to bring Belm. I'm sure Ed would want us to talk to him as well. When that registration gets processed, everyone will have questions. Hell, I have questions," I said, looking over at Petro leaning back in the cupholder and thinking I may have made a mistake.

Jamison was Ned's son, half Fae, half human. Ned, on the other hand, was a full-on Fae and just happened to be my sponsor. Yes, I know, cliché—I was an apprentice, and he was…well, since the word *master* was no longer politically correct, my sponsor. Political correctness had found its way into the magical community. That didn't hold true for the pure Ethereals from the Plane, however.

Petro picked up his small phone and started pecking out

the text at lightning speed. His phone chimed back almost immediately.

"Hey, boss, looks like they're coming in. I think Jamison was expecting us," Petro said with a slight drawl in his voice.

Pixies were notorious for not being able to handle their drink.

"Well, that settles it. Either Bo and Belm are acquaintances, or we have a problem," I said.

Demons were known for their scary ability to not lie, much like the Fae. Leave out important details, sure. Tell a flat-out lie, not so much. Either way it was something that would keep us occupied and hopefully give Phil something to do.

CHAPTER 4

Party Planners Unite

"Phil, stop dripping ranch dressing on your folder," Dr. Simmons—or, as we call her, Jenny—barked, standing with her arms crossed and looking disheveled. She was tall, curvy in all the right places, blond, and looked like a librarian who would, in fact, take your head off if you took a book out of the library without a proper checkout. Jenny also, as I had noticed, was close to Ed in a way that I had yet to figure out.

"Damn," Phil said as he put the soaked chicken wing down on the clinking plate, detecting the ranch also dripping from his long, well-groomed beard onto the table. He was an Earth Mage capable of extreme feats of strength; however, he always leaned on the massive amount of firepower he could carry in most cases.

"A few announcements first," Jenny said as she walked around the room, her shoes making loud clicks on the dark marble floor.

The whole group was present. Phil, Ed, Kim, Angel, Frank, and Dr. Freeman, who had recently also joined the team.

Sitting at the small table in the center was, of course, the Pixie crew: Petro, Macey, Lacey, and Cacey. Jamison and Belm, while ever present, really didn't fall into the core group that worked out of the Atheneum on a day-to-day basis. Plus, after today I had a feeling those two were doing some damage control. Ned, as the main Council representative for the region, thought himself above party planning.

"Planes Drifter is playing the ball," Jenny continued as Phil and I let out catcall whistles, even though I knew it was still exciting to hear. "Next, as you all know, the theme is the Roaring Twenties, 1923 to be exact, the last year a dragon was ever recorded to have been alive. We captured a few other important milestones from that year to build on the theme. Harry Houdini demonstrated magic to the world, and no one really cared, him ending up an entertainer. The last dragon was buried in Dawson, New Mexico. While causing many deaths, it was a symbol to our community of great change after the war. Much like Houdini, the 'Hollywoodland' sign was erected, now known as 'Hollywood,' starting the slow presentation of our world to the general public through ignored films. Lastly and my favorite is Howard Carter opening Tutankhamun's tomb that year, and we all know how that turned out. We are just using that as the theme for the food."

I really didn't know what most of that meant, but the rest of the room did, nodding in genuine approval. While the timeframe had been set, the actual reason behind 1923 was a mystery to me. I just thought it was going to be another Great Gatsby party. I finally figured out it was a year when the magical community did make itself known, just to be counted as entertainment. The dragon and mummy, on the other hand, I would ask about later.

"Next," Jenny said without giving the group any time to respond, "the folder in front of you has a list of duties you will be performing during the party. I also have a timeline that will allow everyone to enjoy the party. Day two, as we know, are the meetings, and we will all be working with the security detail as support."

I opened the folder, making a shuffling noise to see my schedule with the words "check-in" next to my name. "Excuse me. What does check-in mean?" I said, hearing Phil chuckle and Ed sigh.

"Bruther, you're taking people's coats and giving them tickets," Phil said as he flipped me off, raising an eyebrow that was only to be followed by a frown as he opened his folder and looked.

Ed let out a light chuckle. "Right, Phil, I'm sure you will like escorting duties for the Council members."

"It says valet lead," Phil guffawed as he closed the folder. "Parking spoiled, rich-ass politician's cars." He trailed off with a shake of his head.

"Look," Ed said, "Ned wants to show off Max, and he, at the end of the day, calls the shots. The important thing is the safety of our guests. There will be regulars here who have never met a Mage or Ethereal before. This is the first time some of the civilian governments will interact with the Council. We need to keep focused. We put you in places where we thought you could keep an eye on things. Max, I need you to track who is accompanying the lead guests and enter it into the system to see if it pings. Phil, I need to you check the vehicles out." Ed paused, expecting a comment from Phil that was, in turn, a death stare.

"Dr. Freeman, as you have remained silent, it seems you are content with staff registration duty, ensuring there are no issues there working with Max. Frank and Angel will be on the floor with the guests running interior security. Petro, you and your crew will be courting the Pixie delegation. We all know what some on the Council think and would rather have a host for that group, and please make sure everyone keeps their clothes on," Ed said, letting out a sigh because he knew the habits of Pixies all too well.

Ed looked at Petro, who simply shrugged while making hip gyrations. Leaning over to chat with Phil, I almost jumped out of my seat, seeing Leshya appear from behind the tapestry directly behind us.

"Good afternoon," Leshya said in a hollow yet eerily beautiful voice. "Will I need to be cooking for the event?" she asked, cocking her head to one side. She had a ghostly splendor, one that did not need much to catch your attention. She had the type of face that was innocent and full of curiosity. Leshya dressed plainly yet elegantly. She was a craft, a creature that was made by a Mage or Ethereal to go out and do work on their behalf or, as Phil put it, be a slave.

It was a dividing topic in the new world I had been introduced to. She was Tom's—or, as I knew him, Gramps's, to be more specific. They had been a team for more than one hundred years, according to Ed. Incongruously enough, whenever I brought her up to Ed, he became distant and didn't want to talk about it.

It was a mystery how she was there and who was in control of her. What we did know, however, is that she was different, something special, and she had a connection with the Atheneum that was more than simple. Most importantly, as Phil often reminded me, we never, ever ate her cooking.

"No, we will be able to get that handled," Jenny said, wearing a fake smile. Some people didn't like the idea of crafts, and Jenny was one. "If you would like, you can ensure the stacks are secured during the event. Let me know if someone is not where they're supposed to be."

"All right," Leshya said as she maneuvered out of the room, closing the door behind her with a light whoosh of air.

The room remained silent as she left, only to be disturbed by Phil starting back up and slurping the chicken wing on his plate.

We discussed the details for the following two hours with the group before Ed finally concluded the meeting. "Right, before we all go, Max, Phil, and Petro, we need to go over what happened today. If you would like, we can meet in your office, Max. I think we can all use a drink," Ed dictated as the rest of the team split up.

You wouldn't have thought a huge party would take place in two days, but apparently, due to the newfound world I was living in, getting things set up was much easier than I had experienced in my past.

"What's the poison for the evening?" I asked, walking over to the glass and wooden bar, lifting an eyebrow directed toward the group.

Petro buzzed over, landing on my shoulder casually whispering, "Rum" in my ear, letting it drawl out.

"Rum it is, gents," I said as I pulled out three short glasses and a plastic bottle cap for Petro.

Petro had grown very fond of spiced rum—to be more specific, Captain Morgan's. It was to the point I had to have a talk with him a few weeks ago when I woke up finding him chatting up a horse-shaped bookend on a shelf in the office. This evening it would be the classic rum and Coke.

I finished pouring the drink, seeing the team sitting around the large leather chairs in front of the out-of-place Florida fireplace wearing genuine smiles. Petro was already buzzing over, taking a pull from his drink.

"Bruther, Jenny is on fire. Tomorrow will be no easy task," Phil said, taking a slow, gulping pull, letting out a sigh and relaxing his posture in the red leather chair.

Ed followed suit, letting the group also know his reservations in dealing with the good doctor over the next two days. "Last time she organized a party, it about killed me. Literally."

"What happened?" Petro asked, smoothing the cola foam off his newly grown mustache. He had decided to grow it out in order to make him look more distinguished, just like his newfound hero, Magnum PI.

"She set the building on fire. I'll just leave it at that," Ed said, reflectively shaking his head and taking another sip.

The team obviously knew more about Mage parties and was already dreading the next few days.

"Any word on what Ned is going to have me truly doing?" I asked, not having talked to him over the past week. As my sponsor and also a full-blooded Fae, I can say Ned was more interested in showing me off, pawning my training off on others. It made sense in a weird way, reminding me of my time in the army. Truth be told he had introduced me to some interesting people—or, well, things. I was Tom's grandson and could "reportedly," use hellfire, making me a person of interest.

"Not as of today. I will say you need to be careful what you say around some of these people," Ed replied, tapping his finger on his chin. "Some of the individuals who will be present are the independent type. Fantasy books and movies like to call them 'Dark Mages' or 'Dark Ethereals.' Even some of our own kind do. End of the day, they truly fall under the self-governing, independent crowd. No rules and all that. There's a few on the Council calling themselves the *Tenebris* party. Latin, if you're asking."

"I've been reading up on the Thule Society. It seemed the two were at one point tied together," I said, showing off the fact of actually doing the reading assignments Ned had given me.

"Correct. Things split after the war, and the lines blurred.

Not everyone was as bad as the team we ran into. Scholars, engineers, and the like. Mags-Tech even came out of some of those people, and as you may not know, Ezra was, in fact, an independent Mage, not bound to any party, including the Tenebris," Ed said, in point of fact enjoying the intellectual conversation.

Phil let out a belch, interrupting the scholarly exchange, obviously not in the mood for a history lesson.

"Right, back to it. I got a call about the sensors going off reporting a demon. In our town, to be specific. Considering this is the only other one that has shown up on Earth in several years, at least detected—minus our new friend Belm—inquiring minds want to know. With the ball in two days and it showing up here, it's set off more than a few alarms, and that's why we're getting some extra security and wards," Ed finished, looking over at me directly.

Over the next five minutes, Petro and I walked through our heroic story up to the part where Phil cut us off.

"That arse took my shotgun, made an e-core dog, and let it take a whizzer on my boot," Phil said, downing the rest of his drink and ignoring Ed's light snort.

"Then I let him register as a reward," I said, putting a bow on the event.

Phil and Ed both let out a cough as Petro buzzed out of hands' reach. I had a feeling that he also knew something was up.

Ed straightened up, sitting his drink down. "You registered the demo—"

"Bo," I inserted.

"Bo, and you didn't think of the ramifications or to tell anyone?" Ed said, standing up.

"So… that's not good," I asked in the form of a statement.

Phil was sitting there acting like he wasn't in the room. "I tried to shoot the damn thing," he said, shaking his head.

"You didn't have a shotgun there, big guy. The big bad demon took it from you, and you gated out," Petro countered as the team started to point fingers. Ed was silent in thought.

"Enough. I don't know how to put this, but I need to do some research. You may have just signed a contract with a demon. Or one of some type. Look, we need to keep this fairly contained. I need to talk with Ned," Ed said as he looked down at his buzzing phone. "It's Jenny. She needs help with a vendor. This week will be the death of me."

For some reason I felt a sinking feeling in my stomach. Had I just done something terribly bad and not been aware? Or had I been? Petro, the more that I thought about it, was oddly silent on the topic and only really cared about his story of attempting to spell Bo.

"Shit," I let out in a hushed tone as the group started to leave the office as the once-loud group was now silent. *Was it that bad?* I thought.

We all said our good nights, planning on meeting in the morning to start preparations for the ball. Petro flew back as the door closed and landed on the desk.

"Hey, boss," he said, taking a deep breath. "Ed's right. This may be bad news. If they get that paperwork, you could be in some trouble. Worse—bound to a demon."

"Why didn't you say anything?" I asked, looking over at Petro. I realized he had left while I was filing out the paperwork as I gated it to the "home office," wherever that was. The office had a gate box that literally took the documents to some type of Council office for processing.

"I didn't mean that," I said as Petro looked up, concerned, petting his mustache. "The paperwork's already gone. It's not your fault. I wish I knew all these damn rules. Ed didn't even look that concerned when he was fighting Pearl."

Ed and I had grown closer over the past few months. I had finally told him about Gramps still being alive, and we had both concluded that bit of information was not to get out. We even took a potion, much like Gramps had given Dr. Freeman, to where we could only talk about it with each other. He was so excited he even hugged me. I could swear he teared up turning away. In my opinion he already knew. I felt everyone sort of knew he was alive somewhere.

I decided sleep wasn't an option after seeing the concern on Ed's and Phil's faces. Clicking the lever under the desk, I headed down to the lab to work on the staff.

CHAPTER 3

The Way Things Are

Getting back to the Atheneum and going through to the house, I headed up to Gramps's old office, finally dropping into the large leather chair and thudding my boots up on the desk that supposedly once belonged to King Arthur. I sat there for a few minutes, taking deep breaths reflectively scanning the room.

Everyone was busy, and I hadn't run into a soul on the way in. Petro had taken off to hang out with his fiancée, Cacey, and I was alone for once.

Gramps had left me his old out-of-place house attached to the Atheneum in his will. It was rustic, full of interesting relics telling the story of his travels and, most importantly, his bar. It was much like Ed's law office downtown: covered with wooden walls, Persian rugs, and large overly ornate furniture that had obviously seen centuries of wear. The bookshelves were also lined with, of course, old musty-smelling books.

The bar was to my left as I sat in the chair facing the door. It was mirrored and filled with exotic, rare liquors sitting on an oddly always stocked ice bin with beer in it. Leshya—Tom's old craft that no one knew anything about other than not to eat her cooking; as Phil puts it, "She creeps me out but rocks"—must have kept it full.

With the flick of a switch under the desk, the bar would open, revealing a staircase leading down to my laboratory. Yes, it's as eclectic as it sounds. Even stranger was the fact that the office was on the second floor, and I gave up trying to figure out how the laboratory fit between the two.

Over the past year, my newfound introduction to the world of magic and everything in it had been curiously normal minus the whole bit about destroying the Fountain of Youth. Coffee was still the same, at least the kind I got from the local gas station, and the burgers at McDonald's still tasted as they always had.

I had also taken up the sport of serious people watching. In the touristy section of St. Augustine, there's a wine bar that sits at the intersection of a walkway and drivable road called Sangrias. On the second floor, they have a balcony that lets you overlook the crowd as you drink well... sangria. Phil did get kicked out one time; however, I had started going there almost every other week to people watch. I tried to pick out persons and things that were normal and those that were not so much.

I had even run into a redheaded Irish girl there who insisted I take her out on the town. It didn't take long to figure out what she really was, and after we established that I knew she was a Fae, we proceeded to drink at every dive bar we could find. Too bad she was on vacation from somewhere up north and had to leave the next day, or it might have led to another date—supposing it was a date in the first place. I shuffled the thoughts of the night out of my mind and landed on texting Aslynn later. After all, it had been two months. I might want to at least say hi.

The magic and Ethereal communities honestly didn't categorically hide from the rest of cultured society. It was only until I was looking that I noticed it. The upcoming outing to the rest of the world, while being life changing to many, just seemed like things wouldn't really change much. I knew this wasn't the case but felt confident that my little piece of the world would be just fine.

My parents, after learning of everything, had been doing particularly well. Mom—who, unbeknownst to me, just happened to be a witch—had explained that my dad took issue with most of the stuff I was now into. He had lost most of his memory saving the lives of my mother and me before I was born. He had accepted what I was; however, he still didn't want anything to do with it.

He reminded me of Inspector Richard Holder of the Dunn, Chloe's old boss. The British version of the team I worked with. Yes, his name translates to Dick Holder. We all got that out of the way months ago, and now I just call him Dick. I thought about this meditatively, chuckling lightly in the empty room.

I looked over to my right, where the door to my small room lay. The space was ten feet wide and tall. It had a bed, nightstand, and door to a small, dark old-timey tile bathroom that had become my training ground for harnessing water. Not only was I working with hellfire, but I had also learned that I could manipulate water. While not as intensely as hellfire, I could do both; it produced an interesting combination. Apparently, this was also not normal, garnering the attention of several people.

Even more interesting was the apparent ability I had to retain small pieces of magic that I had been exposed to or used. It was like a small fragment of them stuck to me but by only a hair. I knew this was absolutely not normal and did in fact keep this to myself. Petro had figured it out the day after we destroyed the Fountain.

Taking a larger-than-needed breath, I leaned forward and pushed the latch under the desk as the mirrored wall behind the bar popped open with a rhythmic click. It was time to do some homework before the meeting.

While Petro had been an excellent instructor under the guidance of Ned, my sponsor, I found the lab to be a calming and Zen escape. I had moved a small Bluetooth radio to the space and also finally got around to at least dusting off the cobwebs.

A few days ago, I had graduated from basic potions. You know, the type that makes you awake, stronger, or in one instance, able to breathe underwater for a rather long time. I didn't really have any interest in learning more; however, what I was interested in was blending items. This meant taking something and adding an effect to it. While this is mostly a onetime deal, the combination of spelling, potions, and casting piqued my curiosity at a much higher level.

These types of items caught a hefty price on the civilian marketplace and even in the Mage community if it was good enough and done, as Jenny stated, "the right way." The issue was, however, it took a long time and solid amount of effort to make one. Trish gave me a blended item, which I account for saving our lives earlier in the year. It was one of the motivators driving my studies. Plus, there was the fact that I wanted to find Chloe and tell her just how I felt about things.

Chloe was still in my memories, even after she had turned on the team and killed Jayal. It felt like I was connected to her at times in dreams, sensing anguish, only to realize it was my feeling of guilt and betrayal. People had died, and she had blood on her hands. I had been used and still didn't understand fully why. I would do everything in my power to find out and also figure out how to earn a paycheck, learn magic, plus whatever else was thrown my way.

Entering the lab, I flicked my hand up, igniting the fireplace, which, like everything else in the room, mysteriously fit in the house. The room was old, dark, and glowing yellow from the firelight. It was filled with shelves, beakers, and tables, looking as one would imagine an old mad scientist laboratory would. Petro had some books open on the work table in the middle of the room, as I pushed them over, picking up a small wooden staff.

I had selected the short wooden staff from the stacks in the main library out of one of the display cases a few weeks ago. There was a card on the item stating it would hold a handful of spells and had once been used to cheat at sports. I thought, *Why not try to put more than one thing in it, like a Swiss army knife?*

The staff was two feet long and the width of my thumb. It bore five distinct sections, all different in design. Wood was, after all, one the most versatile materials when it came to magic and how it reacted to Etherium. Jenny had always explained it's 98 percent science and 2 percent magic. Petro denies this but refuses to talk to her about it.

My plan for the evening before I was summoned to the dining room that basically served as the Atheneum's main meeting room was to figure out what five spells I was going to add to the staff. It was about the time I had settled on one of the slots being a stunning spell that my phone chirped with a text from Phil.

Brother, it's time Demon cakes was all it read.

Shaking my head and having enjoyed the few minutes of calm after the already long day, I grabbed the charm around my neck, whispering, "Petro." The charm was a homing beacon of sorts Petro had given me as part of his life debt after saving him from being locked in a freezer for taking Ed's car apart the year prior.

"Hey, boss," Petro said from the top of the spiraling stairs leading back up to the office. "This better be good. Cacey and I were making plans for our date tomorrow. You did remember?"

I had promised to take Petro and his fiancée to the movies followed later by a trip to FA's for a drink. It still wasn't safe for them to travel out without some way of hiding. In all fairness they could handle themselves; they just couldn't do things like drive or buy movie tickets yet. Not to mention the ball was the day after. For some reason Pixies wanted to act just like regular folks. It was almost an obsession, down to their choices of clothes and music.

"Yeah, I remember. Hey, just got the text it's time for our favorite activity," I said, finally getting to the top of the stairs and clicking the door shut behind me. Petro hovered in the air in front of me, waiting for me to put my hand out so he could land on it.

"What's that? Time to bump uglies with the ladies?" Petro said, actually curious as he landed on my outstretched hand.

"Yeah, buddy, as you notice I've been batting a solid no-hitter there. No, it's time to meet Jenny and go over the final plans for the ball," I said as we both chuckled at the factual sadness of my statement.

CHAPTER 5

*The Calm before the Storm,
and Maybe Another Small Storm*

The morning started like most others. My coffeepot automatically sprang to life as I rolled over. Grabbing my castor, I immediately put it on, letting off some pressure. The castor is nothing more than a fancy watch made to store and ground out some of the extra juice I produced overnight, almost like a magic regulator. Over time I would only need it if I wanted to store a little extra gas in the tank. Jenny had a more scientific term for it, but mine also happened to be a rather nice stainless-steel dive watch.

I stood up stretching. It was 6:00 a.m., and the team was supposed to meet at seven to get started. Shuffling to the bathroom, I picked up my phone plus the cup of coffee, ready to do some reading and waste twenty minutes of my life in a steamy dark-tiled bathroom. I loved my routine.

The door clicked shut as I turned on the never-ending hot water and sat down on the closed toilet seat sipping my coffee. It was the type of bathroom that steamed up fast, and you could reach everything from the pilot's seat. The space also had the scent of fresh mint always lingering in the air. Much to my surprise, there was a group text from Jamison that came in overnight.

I'll be there around nine depending on my sidekick was all Jamison had written. Looked like we would at least get some type of break from the day's activities.

Taking stock of the day, I also realized I was supposed to take Petro and Cacey out for dinner and drinks later. I sat shaking my head, the weight of the all the recent events finally taking hold of my central nervous system.

I walked out feeling refreshed, having refilled my morning cup of coffee and wearing my favorite dark pair of jeans and latest Plains Drifter shirt showing a large sun on it. Petro was already in the office, ready to take the walk to the dining room. This, much like my shower, was a routine we had. Petro and I would spend the three-minute walk talking about our plans for later and how the rest of our prior evening had gone. His was usually more adventurous than mine, and in full disclosure, we spent most of our afternoons together anyways.

Funny thing about the Atheneum and its inhabitants is that with all its size, rooms, and grandeur, the team obviously many years before me chose the dining room as home base. Use the conference room in the modernized offices? Nope. Use the several private alcoves in the stacks? Nope. Use the private locked rooms or other specifically made to meet spaces? Nope.

The dining room was sacred. I also had the feeling it had a little more protection from prying ears around it. The table always had some type of food or meal present, now also including a small desk and table in the middle for the Pixie crew.

The dining room was well-worn, dark like the rest of the building with brown-stone walls with tapestries hanging off them. In the center was a large wooden table that could seat at least twenty people on any given Sunday.

The building was being modernized in places, and the lighting had been replaced with newer soft-yellow LEDs that you couldn't see directly. It was the only thing in the room other than a few items less than a hundred years old. I had even taken the liberty of bringing in a cushion for my chair and introduced the team to a whiteboard that sat on an aisle in the far corner. While Phil mostly used it to draw private bits to make the group laugh with various slogans and faces, I used it to brainstorm.

"So, boss, I was thinking last night," Petro started, landing on my shoulder. "If this Bo guy was bad news, I think we would have heard from him by now or something. I know demons; they're much more common on the Plane than they are here. Somebody summoned him. If I was a betting Pixie, I would say that's the person with the real issue. Folks always think they can outsmart the demon they summon. They're wrong 99 percent of the time all the time."

"I was thinking about that, but what about Belm?" I already thought I knew the answer.

"Yeah, that guy's special. He's a little more than a demon. Plus, I'm pretty sure that guy he calls Dad that brought the supercool Pixie lady with him is the devil," Petro said, leaning in and whispering, "Lucifer."

I let out a light chuckle at Petro's theatrics. He was right though; Devin wasn't normal, and this was not the first time I had heard that term thrown around.

"Let's see how this plays out. We'll talk with Belm first before your date tonight," I said, looking over at Petro lifting into the air as we rounded the corner to the main entrance hall.

The noise and bustle started immediately. There were teams of people shuffling in decorations, chairs, and tables. Jenny walked into the dining room wearing a headset and was followed by Ed as he rolled his eyes, looking at us wearing an honest-to-God black-and-white Adidas track suit probably from the '80s.

The Atheneum actually had a ballroom in what I guessed was the middle of the facility. Walking down the main hall in the entrance, we found the double doors at the end opened up into the large space. The door to the left led to the stacks. It was large, opulent, and well established.

A wide stairwell on each side on the entrance greeted patrons, leading up to a catwalk that hid sitting areas and, in some spots, rooms off to the sides, all overlooking the main floor. The space was roughly the size of a basketball court, having a large surround hiding smaller rooms with columns, also off the main area. It was eclectic. For such a large area, it felt cozy due to the number of small spaces available to escape the main floor filled with warm, rich colors. The area reminded me of a rich, deep forest; the smell of pine, earth, and cold, wet stone lingered.

Phil was already in the dining room eating a plate of eggs and bacon. Dr. Freeman was drinking tea with a plate of scones and reading the daily paper. He was one of the only people I knew who still read a newspaper besides travelers that got them for free at certain hotels.

Dr. Freeman had temporarily moved in about eight months ago, still living above the garages where Phil stayed. They were spaces like my little room off the office in Gramps's old house. I had access to other rooms, but I liked my small space.

The guest quarters, much like hotel suites, contained small kitchenettes. Ed informed me they had been built several decades ago during the war, keeping people housed who watched over the stacks and artifacts on-site. I had yet to even come close to exploring the entire facility, still having limited access to some areas.

"Morning, everyone," I exclaimed, a little more chipper than usual, trying to brighten the dull mood in the room.

Jenny looked over, obviously having been informed of the Bo situation, while letting out a breath and shaking her head. The rest of the team came walking in minus Angel and Frank. I understood those two were not exactly morning people.

"Right," Ed started as Jenny chirped orders into her headset to someone not present. "I need Dr. Freeman and Phil working on the private delegation rooms as well as the main meeting chamber. As noted, the underground range has been converted as of yesterday to a conference room. It will fit roughly fifty persons and assistants. I need you to make sure they're set up. The last of the furniture is showing up at noon, and that means we will need to sweep the furniture for bugs and spells just in case something got past the wards."

Phil looked up long enough from his meal to nod an affirmative and wink at Dr. Freeman. Thing is, it's when he doesn't wink that you more than likely have a problem on your hands.

"Max, I need you to go to FA's and help Trish. She already gated most of the provisions here; however, Trish will, like the others, need to drive onto the property to get set up and needs help running a few errands. We're closing most of the gates later today for security reasons. You can give her a ride back later. That's the only way we can make sure the local gates are not tampered with and the wards take. You already know what to do with the Postern," Ed said, taking a deep breath. Jenny handed him a clipboard with a pen hanging off tethered by a string that made a clicking sound as it bounced around.

The Postern was, in all reality, what my Gramps had left me in his will. It was a room with ten gate doors in it. Every door went somewhere different, and unlike normal gates, each had a little something extra to it. The main gate everyone knew about and could actually operate was called the Evergate.

This gate, if you took one of the gate keys from it, would transport you to or from any location it was tied to without having to create a new gate, which was a fairly tough feat unto itself. There were certain Mages that specialized in gate magic, and from what I understand, they were fairly uncommon.

The second room Jamison and I figured out how to use on the night of the First Coast Riot after getting hammered without adult supervision on the property. The First Coast Riot will forever go down in history as the time those weird folks from the library almost burned down Riverplace Tower and made Marlow Goolsby very upset. Oh, and killed a mind-eating murderer. The end.

We discovered what we called the Messenger's gate. There was an old man literally chained to a desk who would send a message to anyone at the other end of one of the thousands of gates in the massive cavelike room. Issue was, however, most of the gates no longer worked or now opened into oceans and the like. We at least figured out a way to use the space for a prank call that didn't go over well with an independent member of the Council that I would categorize as a dark Mage. There, I said it.

"One last thing, everyone. Jamison messaged earlier. That motley crew will be here around three o'clock. Everyone plan on meeting back here then," Ed stated flatly, biting his lip and turning on his heels to walk out the door.

"What about Planes Drifter?" I asked, wanting to get that job.

"They'll be setting up tomorrow before the guests arrive. I already told their tour manager to keep an eye on you and about that little shrine you keep in your office to them," Ed chuckled, walking out of the room followed by Jenny.

That was it. My chances of meeting the band were shrinking by the minute, and now I had to run errands. In all fairness running Trish around town wasn't a bad day, by any stretch of the imagination.

My pocket started buzzing with a text from Kim. *I heard Jamison and Belm are coming in, I'm planning on stopping by* was all it read. I replied with a simple *Great*.

Kim had recently taken to actually texting me without insulting my dignity or making sure that I knew she was out of my league. She was the type of person that took trust and her privacy too seriously.

"Bruther," Phil chirped as I got up from the table. "It's going to be a shit day. Call me when you're heading back. Maybe we can catch a break after Jamison gets here." Phil turned to Petro. "Big date tonight, I hear," he said, tossing a small paper ball over.

Petro caught it and dusted over to fist bump Phil. "You the man" was all he said, looking over, nodding, and flying out of the room.

"What was that?" I asked, looking at Phil sitting smugly in his chair.

"Wax for that crazy mustache of his," Phil said, letting out a chuckle. "I caught him in my medicine cabinet and saw his little handprints in my wax."

The rest of the team grumbled for a few minutes, finally heading out on their assigned duties. Since I was driving into town, I decided to grab my blazer and service pistol. I didn't make a habit of carrying the sword around all the time, even though the enchanted hilt made it nearly invisible. I was more concerned with burning buildings down.

The drive to downtown St. Augustine was relatively short. It gave me enough time to listen to a song and give my truck, the Black Beast, some words of encouragement and a light spray of air freshener. Ed had recommended I add some

Mags-Tech enhancements. I refused.

Since I was working out of the transition office, parking was much easier in town, as it was connected to the Fallen Angel. Trish stood in front of the parking spaces, leaning on a light post. I had never seen her outside of the place, and she looked stunning in the early daylight.

"Need a ride, pretty lady?" I joked with a cheesy grin as she shook her head, smirking and walking over to the passenger side. I leaned over, popping the door open, as only a southern boy could, and smacked the seat.

Trish had a way of making people feel comfortable, like they could relax and be themselves around her. She was gorgeous; however, I never looked at her that way. Initially I thought it was just the fact that she was a barkeep, and I didn't want to be that guy. Later I had landed on Trish being something more, and the mood she put people in was deliberate yet subtle.

"Of course," Trish said, sliding into the truck and lighting the space up with her smile. She smelled of lavender and lemon today. That was a far cry from the normal smell of cooking steak and copper FA's left in my mind seeing her.

"Where to?" I asked, backing out and turning Planes Drifter on in the background low enough to carry on a conversation. I already knew Trish was cool.

"Jacksonville, Saint John's Town Center, and then a quick trip to Riverplace Tower to pick something up. Don't worry; you don't have to go in," Trish said with a light giggle.

"Yes, ma'am," I replied, smiling back and reflecting on the timeline for the day. "I need to be back around three o'clock. Think we will be good? Jamison and Belm are stopping by."

"Should be. I'll ride back with you, and we can drop everything off. Is this about your little visitor? Bo, I think his name is?"

I let out a breath louder than needed. "Something like that. Hey, what do you know about demons and contracts? Ed seems worried about this whole thing. I have a feeling I might be in some kind of trouble."

Trish smirked. "Contract? Well, if you were in trouble, you would know it. The Council is not shy about things that are not in line with their vision or laws. Honestly, I think the Balance will affect them more than predicted."

"Why's that?" I asked curiously, as I had not heard Trish talk much about it and also knowing she was connected.

"Well, everyone seems to think that the regular and civilian population that doesn't know anything about our world will freak out. Really, I think the Council and everyone on our side of the fence will freak out when they realize they now have to follow civilian laws," Trish said, deadpan serious.

"I never thought about it that way. I guess you're right. They have pretty much been able to do what they want for, well…ever," I said turning onto I-95.

"That's the thing. I don't think they're truly going to stop what they are doing. You learned last year there are powerful people that think they are above the regular population. That's not going away. You will meet some of those types tomorrow. It's no secret. To put it into perspective, what do you think is going to happen when every person on Earth finds out there is a magical bar that's in several locations all at once?" Trish said. She had obviously already thought this through.

"You don't let them know," I responded.

"Precisely," Trish said as she leaned back, turning up the radio.

The next two hours were spent at Saint John's Town Center picking up items from various stores. The shopping area was massive, and much to my surprise, I could buy a normal pair of jeans, a normal iPhone, and, a few doors down in the back of another store, bottles of wine and cigarettes from the not-so-normal Plane. Ethereals and V's loved to smoke, even though it was more of a taboo these days when you saw someone light up.

We pulled out after loading up the truck, heading downtown toward Riverplace Tower in Jacksonville. Did you know Jacksonville, Florida, is the largest land-mass city in the United States? I had a feeling that was important for some reason. I thought as we drove, shelving it for later.

It was noon, and by the looks of things, we would be just in time, pending any unforeseen issues getting back, as the drive to St. Augustine and the Atheneum was about thirty minutes from downtown.

"I take it you want me to wait in the car?" I asked, pulling into the connecting parking garage.

"Probably for the best," Trish replied, throwing me a smile as she opened the door. "I still can't believe you almost burnt this place down."

Grinning sheepishly, I watched Trish walk away, taking in the manner her hips moved. It was odd; the man inside me was saying, *Stare*, but all the while, I had the feeling that I was looking at my cousin. It was magic. Had to be.

"Hello, Max!" came the smoky voice followed by the smells of decaying flesh, sulfur, and general death as I about jumped out of my seat. It was Bo.

Startled and looking over, I instinctively went for my pistol but remembered that manners had power here. I stopped.

"Bo, long time no see. How's Florida treating you?" I asked, externally keeping my cool while internally falling to pieces. I was, however, slowly reaching for my phone.

The demon let out a low, drawn-out, smooth laugh. It sounded like a disgruntled employee learning he had won the lottery and just been given a bad review at work. I had figured out demon humor over the past few months, and it was as cheesy as it came. Ever get in a fight with a demon, bust out a knock-knock joke; it will at least buy you a few seconds.

"Good. Sorry about the smell. I'm going to get that fixed later. It's better, all thanks to you," Bo said, leaning on the passenger door with the window down.

"I have to ask, why thank me?" I asked, genuinely trying to figure out if my ass was on the line and Ed's worry was justified.

"Well, some brat called me over, and without knowing who I was, he tried sending me back where I came from. When that didn't work, he had me do a few things for him. I think his daddy must have left him instructions, and he used them. I can tell you, the person that brought me here was related to someone who did so once before. Anyways, I heard through the grapevine you were reasonable or stupid. So I thought I would pay you a visit," Bo said, obviously bantering back with the one-liners as he lit up a pitch-black cigarette. It smelled like burning rubber and gas fumes. I didn't want to know.

"Who was the brat?"

"Ah…the million-dollar question. While your registration theoretically loosened the string my summoner had on me, I'm not at liberty to say. A gentleman never talks and all."

"So we aren't bound to each other? Shit, I thought I might be in some type of trouble," I countered, seeing how reasonable demons could be if you actually talked directly to them.

"Oh, trouble, yes. Bound to each other, no. Look, I'm just popping by to say hello and be on my way. Tell Belm I said hello when you see him," Bo said as he winked out of existence in a puff of black dust, his lit cigarette dropping to the ground.

Did that really happen? Or was it in my head? Who knew? What I did know is that I wasn't bound to him. That was at least one good thing. Or was I? How did he find me?

I was shaking my head as Trish walked up to the truck sniffing the air.

"Have you been smoking the cigarettes in the back?" she asked, raising an eyebrow.

"No, just sitting here," I sputtered. "Bo was just here."

"I kind of figured that out when the building security went crazy and about set the parking deck on fire with you in it," Trish stated, expressionless. "You need to get that all sorted out—and fast. You get a reputation for hanging with demons, and it's not going to end well. Belm has at least passed the smell test for some, and I stress *some*. This Bo character sounds like bad news," Trish said as she put her package in the back and jumped in.

I called Ed, Phil, and Petro to let them know what happened. They were all acting like there was something going on that I didn't know about. All the calls ended the same: "Be there in a few."

CHAPTER 6

*And Things Had Been
Going So Well*

Pulling up to the main house, I saw Jamison's red 1986 Porsche along with at least a dozen other vans and catering vehicles. The ball preparations were in full swing. Trish looked over, smiling with a shake of her head.

"Max, I forgot to mention the apartment upstairs from the Transitions Office," she said, completely changing the prior topic of discussion: my dating life. "It was cleared for occupancy yesterday, and if you're still interested, I'd be glad to lease it to you," Trish said as an afterthought.

For the past two months, I had talked to Trish about the second floor of the Transition Office. It had apparently been rented out as an apartment, and for some reason sealed off due to an "incident." I had mentioned a few times my interest in moving out of the Atheneum back to my apartment; however, the fact that it was too far away piqued my interest in the space. Phil had even mentioned being my roommate. While living in Gramps's old place was very exciting, I still needed some resemblance of normalcy in my day-to-day life.

"Sure," I said distantly, still taking in all the activity in the roundabout in front of the main entrance.

I turned off the ignition with a click and chirp. Petro came flying from the house toward the now-parked vehicle. Sliding out of the driver's seat, Petro stood on the hood, dusting the black paint. "Hey, boss, there's a bunch of people in there talking about you and this Bo guy. You better get in there," Petro said, slightly out of breath. "Oh, and everyone's in the east wing past the entrance. The smart lady opened up the doors this morning. They're all in the formal sitting room."

Odd thing is, I had never truly spent any time in that section of the facility. If you turn right in the main entrance, there was the gate that the team used to travel to New York last year and a set of double doors that, as far as I could remember, always stayed closed and locked.

The only reason I had gone to the east wing was to see someone in the guest quarters, and I always went through the garage or through the second-floor catwalk attached to the other half of the main entrance. The place was huge, and in all fairness, I hadn't been through all the stacks in the library either. At times it felt like a video game, every so often opening up a new, unexplored area full of wonders.

Trish walked over as Petro took flight, zipping off back toward the house. "Max, you need to be careful what you say in there. I'm not sure who else is here, but I'm sure your visitor earlier today will not go unnoticed, especially with you having Belm over. I get why you asked him over, but others may see it as you spending a little too much time around a sorted crowd."

She was talking about Belm and Bo with a light air of distain, as it took me a few seconds to catch on. Trish obviously didn't like demons, and I wanted to find out why.

"That's the second time someone's told me that in the past twenty-four hours," I said, raising an eyebrow while taking a deep breath.

"Ed, I bet. Tell you what. I'll get this stuff unloaded; you go figure out what's going on."

I left Trish by the truck as a burly man who had been looking her up and down walked over to lend his bulking strength, helping the damsel in distress carry in her boxes.

Walking through the door, I was almost pushed over by a group of men carrying sitting couches. "Name and identification," a voice sternly barked as I turned right to go through the east wing doors.

"Excuse me?" I asked, startled by the new security in place. The two men were strangers to me, both wearing the same black suits screaming security.

"I need your identification," the taller of the two gentleman said in a gruff voice, cocking his head to one side sizing me up.

"Max Abaddon Sand. I live here" was all I could manage, thrown off by the aggressive stance the massive, ogreish, blocky man had taken.

Out from behind the doors came the ever-trusty voice of reason. "Bruther, stop playing pattycakes with these two and get in here," Phil said, raising an eyebrow and pointing a finger at the shorter of the two guards.

The shorter guard, while not as serious as the other, flipped Phil off. This in itself was enough to make the hair on the back of my neck stack up as Phil returned the courtesy, both men smiling at each other. The taller of the two squeezed his fists, ready for a fight not liking the exchange between the two.

"Friend of yours?" I asked Phil as we walked through the doors heading down the long hallway.

"Terrence used to be. We went to the Guild together. Great

fellow. I wouldn't want to pick a fight with him, though. I saw him earlier, and we plan on catching up at some point. Plus, he still owes me twenty bucks."

The hallway was long and to my knowledge, other than the offices, one of the only other carpeted spaces in the building, not including large area rugs or private rooms.

Phil looked over at me. "Mind what you say in here. Let Ed do the talking if he cuts you off. I don't think you're going to like who's here."

Damn, another person telling me to keep my mouth shut. Was this it? Would I spend the rest of my life being told to not worry about it? While everyone had good intentions in telling me this, what it had actually done was solidify the fact that I was getting pissed off, feeling like the kid that just got dumped by his girlfriend and didn't know why.

I didn't say a word, walking into what Petro had called the formal sitting room. It was just that, looking like something out of an old '50s movie. Clumps of normal-size leather chairs were positioned around small tables. The room had bookcases scattered throughout and art deco–style paintings on the wall. Looking closer, I saw the space, while dimly lit, was bright with crisp white walls and chandeliers hanging down in random places, the crystals reflecting more light than was being given off. The sweet smell of lemons and pipe tobacco permeated the room. It was like someone had smoked a pipe, oiled the wood, and shut the door immediately after, leaving it closed for several years. It all combined together into a mellow, relaxing vibe.

"Right, Max, please take a seat," Ed said in full professional mode.

The chairs had been turned inward in a couple of places, all facing each other as a few people stood. I took stock of who was present. Jamison, Belm, Ed, Petro, Phil, Ned, and

Icupiousous, with two goons standing behind him.

Icupiousous was just as I had imagined him to be from the pictures we had pulled up on the box. The box was the main computer in the crucible room. It connected civilian and the Mags-Tech computer systems together, allowing the cross-referencing of systems.

Tall, lean, and older—close to his midsixties—with sharp edges and eyes that burned a hole all the way to your soul. He was, of course, wearing all black. See, dark Mages are real things. He had an elongated nose that, while not too obvious, would make him stick out when describing him to a stranger. I stood there taking in the room, finally sitting down in the chair that was obviously placed there for me.

"Hello, Max," Ned said in a reassuring tone. He was a politician and knew when someone was nervous. Icupiousous, on the other hand, knew when someone was scared, and you could see it in the slight movement of his predatory, thin smile.

Before I could say anything, Ed spoke up. "I appreciate the concern. We had planned on this being a smaller meeting and are glad the Council has taken an interest in our discussion. Sending someone as distinguished as yourself, Carvel, tells us this has gotten others' attention."

Ed was telling me what was going on without using his mind-reading abilities and also setting the tone for the conversation. His statement was deliberate and was aimed at keeping me on the rails. No deviation. Issue was, I was getting more aggravated by the minute, and Ed could tell. The one thing he did do that he had not done in the past hearing of my prank-call story was say his first name. *Carvel*, I thought, letting the word linger in my mind.

"Of course," Carvel replied in a snappy, tight voice, slowly turning to look at me with a smirk. "The Council is very concerned with recent events that have transpired around some of your staff and has asked me to inquire about them."

"Yes, and you will have our full cooperation," Ed said, letting his shoulders down, looking over at Ned. The two could read each other, and I could tell they didn't like Carvel being there any more than I did. Phil hadn't cracked a joke in three minutes, which was making me more uneasy than anything.

"Max," Ed said, talking directly to me. "You need to answer Carvel's questions. This pertains to the incident surrounding Bo and the occurrence today. Phil and Petro have both discussed their initial encounter with Bo. You don't need to deviate from that subject in order to keep this meeting moving so we can all get back to work before Dr. Simmons becomes upset."

He had used Jenny's formal name. This was another hint. Formal—nothing more, nothing less. I knew this game from my time in the intel community. The cat and mouse actually started to relax me. Ed, seeing I had gotten the point, held his hand out toward Carvel.

"Max," Carvel said, "I would like to hear about the registration process where you unbound a demon from its summoner and let it free to do as it pleases. Also, I am bound to inform you that these two gentlemen here are readers. They will record the conversation and will also know if you are not being completely honest."

Carvel had come out of the gate with a question in the form of an accusatory statement. You know, the type news anchors use when interviewing a political candidate they do not support, trying to convince the audience of their guilt or lack of shame.

Ed interjected politely. "Carvel, this is not a formal investigation, and with that, these readers are not necessary or required. Jamison, Belm, if you could also please step outside."

Carvel raised his hand and ushered the two out the door, Phil following behind them to make sure they left the area. "I don't need them anyways."

I spent the next five minutes reliving the rest of the events with the group. In all fairness my story hadn't changed much since the episode, minus me leaving out some of the colorful metaphors plus stopping for a drink afterward.

"Did you know what this would do to the demon or the person who summoned them?" Carvel asked. I actually didn't, and my answer came out direct and honest. I had a feeling Carvel could do just as much interpreting as his two stooges; he let out a breath of disappointment.

"No, and besides Belm, I know little to nothing about them."

"OK, what happened today in the garage?" Carvel asked, leaning forward in his seat getting close. I could finally smell him as a breeze floated past. He reeked of strong yet delicate incense. I was also finally getting a closer look at his face and, more than anything, the devious smile he wore with his thin lips.

I explained the brief encounter again, leaving out the question I asked Bo. "That was it. Trish showed up, and we headed directly here," I said, concluding on the point that we had not deviated since the encounter with Bo.

That was it. Carvel stood up again, pushing the scent of incense around the room. The rest of the group stood up, exchanging parting formalities.

The two men came back in; as he started to walk out, Carvel turned, addressing Ed directly as if I wasn't in the room. "By the way, Leon Covey went missing today shortly after Max's meeting with the creature. After their little chat in the garage, Bo, as you call him, paid Leon a visit and is now missing. You know Leon? One of the more powerful gate Mages in the US here for the ball. You mentioned this was not a formal investigation. I believe as of today it will be."

As Carvel left the room, Phil, Belm, and Jamison walked back in, the three acting like Carvel walking with a stiff cadence and making fun of his snappy voice. I looked over to see Ed and Ned, genuinely concerned.

Ned, being the politician, was probably more concerned about his reputation than my well-being.

Ed spoke first. "Dammit. Carvel is in charge; this isn't good. We all already know his opinion of Max. This also means more people have been watching him than we thought. Max, good catch on the conversation, but is there anything you left out?"

"Well, I asked him who summoned him. He just said, 'That's the million-dollar question' and shrugged it off. He implied that someone also steered him to the office," I said, reaching to remember if he said anything else important.

"Something's not passing the smell test here," Ned followed.

Belm let out a low growl, making himself heard.

"Right, Belm, we are forgetting to pull you into this, as was the original point of this meeting. Do you know who this Bo character is?" Ed asked, sitting back down.

Over the past year, Belm's appearance had actually improved. According to him it took some time to adjust to being on this side of things coming from what he called "the under." When I first met him, he was pale as a ghost, wearing all-black leather, and looking like a meth addict. Now he looked almost normal. Belm still wore leather pants and a white T-shirt that was overly bright. He had even gotten a light tan. You would have to look at his eyes and closely pay attention to the way he moved to catch the difference. After all, he was twice the size when he was in a bad mood, appearing pitch black and sporting an eight-foot-long spiked tail. Not to mention I still think his father Devin may be the devil.

"I know him. He's been on Earth before. What we would call a dweller. He likes it here and will do about anything to see that happens. We need to figure out who summoned him," Belm said in his raspy voice.

"Wait," I interjected. "You said it takes time to get yourself together when your type gets here. He was completely relaxed and looked, beside that ridiculous clothing, fine. He did smell bad."

"Interesting," Ned added. "I'll make some calls. Belm, let us know what you find."

Belm let out a cough. The two things he hadn't shaken off yet were that and his raspy voice. "He may have made a deal with someone being here for a while and still be bound. Just waiting for the right time. Sounds suspicious to me. If Bo has found a way to be here, he will take it, even if that involves behaving. In that, I mean not killing everything in sight. Kidnapping, extortion, and all that good stuff to him would not count."

Phil spoke up. "What about Leon? Max, he was in the office a few weeks ago registering. He liked you with all that Postern talk."

"Shit, that's right," I said, remembering his face and the conversation about gate creation that was above my pay grade. "Nice guy. I told him I would show him the Postern. He was invited to the ball as some type of VIP gate liaison."

"Right, Max. That little piece of information will come out if Carvel starts looking. For now, keep it between us. I'd like to see his registration and how deep Carvel's reach is. Enough of this. We have work to do. Let's get back to it," Ed relayed, obviously getting messages from Jenny.

"Max, we need to talk," Ned insisted as the rest of the group exited the room, leaving us alone. "You've been doing great this month, coming along twice as fast as any other apprentice I have ever worked with, but I need to caution you. Don't get wrapped up in this demon stuff. I would stay away from Belm for a while until this blows over. I know you're not doing this, but by the looks of it alone, from a distance it would be easy to see why others do. Don't forget Ed and I are just members of a much larger Council."

"I'll do my best," I countered. "Look, Ned, you know I'm not used to all this still. I'll take your lead here and Ed's, as it sounds like we are all on the same page, neither of you being friends of Carvel."

"True. Carvel is not a person whose bad side you want to be on, but I will say he, in most cases, is attempting to do the right thing. I believe he genuinely thinks you are the one causing this recent influx of demons. Yes…two is a big deal, in case you're wondering. They wreaked havoc on this world and the Plane in the past. Anyways, tomorrow is important. I'm going to introduce you to a few people. You may be asked to do some work in my place as a proxy of sorts. Don't agree unless I approve. You know, politicians and all. Lastly, I would stick around here for the next few days. Just in case anything else crazy happens."

Ned and I said our goodbyes as he handed me two books on wards.

I wasn't buying his statement on Carvel. I had seen Ed's face and the way he talked to him. Ned must not want me to push or dig too much. Here it goes again—everyone being overly protective of the new guy.

"So I take it date night's out, and it's dinner and a movie home style," Petro said as he buzzed over from the bookshelf, acting as if he had not been eavesdropping. Ned would have known and, as I figured, allowed it.

"Yeah, buddy, I owe you. Hey, you think I'm in trouble?" I asked, wanting his opinion.

"Yup" was all Petro said as he flew to my shoulder, hitching a ride to the main house.

Walking out the door, I saw Phil was standing there talking to the guard from earlier, both men chuckling under their breath. The two parted ways as Phil cocked his head.

"You look like you could use a drink. I just talked to Jenny. Things seem to be under control. The band doesn't set up till tomorrow, and we should be good for a while," Phil said, starting to walk in the direction of Gramps's office, obviously focused on the bar.

The main entrance was packed full of people shuffling in and out. The two security guards, now content that I wasn't a vagrant, seemed to focus on the other people moving around the space. Jenny stood there talking with Trish, holding a glass of wine tasting it.

We decided to get lost in the shuffle and passed unnoticed through the crowd. Finally reaching our destination, Phil and I landed on Magnus on the rocks with a splash of soda. Magnus was some kind of dark, superstrong liquor from the Plane. The flavor was hard to pinpoint. A mix of smoky fire and dark blackstrap rum with the bite of a strong whiskey. It came together nicely. The only issue is that consumption by the general public would probably not go over well. It had taken me up until recently to be able to stomach more than a few light sips.

"Ahh," I let out, kicking my feet up on the desk. Phil already had his up, and we looked at each other, able to read the bottoms of our boots.

"Bruther, I don't think this Carvel thing is going to go away soon. If they are looking, that means they can do about anything they want," Phil said, taking another pull of his drink, gulping more down at one time than I would probably finish.

"That's the thing. Why are they looking at me?" I asked, shaking my head.

"Over the span of the last twelve months, look at everything that's happened. It's surely not gone unnoticed. I'm actually surprised this hasn't happened sooner."

"What happened sooner?" I said, huffing in light irritation.

"Someone poking around to see what you're all about. The Council is an odd bedfellow. This may just be them seeing were your loyalties are. Or, as we heard today, you just being at the wrong place at the wrong time. With you doing hellfire and being Tom's grandson, there may be a few like Carvel out to either make you an ally or ensure you're not a roadblock. Tom, while having many friends, also had just as many enemies. So does Ed."

I took in the statement. It was probably the most sensible thing Phil had said since last year.

"OK, I get it," I said, taking another pull and deep breath. "Here's the thing. I'm going to let this play out as long as I can. I don't trust Carvel. Ned seems to want me to not go down that path. I'm going to talk with Ed in the morning if there's time and get some advice other than 'be careful what you say.' It was clear they have been and probably are watching me."

We both stopped, looking around the room, finally letting out a laugh, the joke being my preoccupation with doing and practicing magic in the bathroom.

"This isn't completely out of the norm. Let's see how the next two days go. Ed is connected, but when you get heavy hitters like Carvel involved on the head Council, things get sticky. Hell, I was in some trouble for a while when I was younger. It blew over eventually," Phil said as he finally stood up.

I hadn't noticed the time as the grandfather clock reached 9:00 p.m., chiming in affirmation.

"I almost forgot. Trish said the apartment is cleared and ready for a new occupant." I mirrored Phil, also standing up. My legs were asleep from being on the desk, making me almost fall.

"Perfect timing if you ask me. I want to get out of this nutter house. You know it's going to start getting crowded around here with the Balance coming. I saw new staffing plans are going to be discussed this week. Let's talk about it later," Phil said, walking out the door, flipping me off without looking, putting an unlit cigarette in his mouth, and letting the door close behind him.

CHAPTER 7

The Preparty

I awoke to the strong smell of coffee followed by the sweet tang of Fae honey. Was someone in my office? I really needed to get my own place. It wasn't that the company truly bothered me; it was just the open attitude everyone took toward the space. Either way I hadn't had a cup of Fae honey coffee for a few weeks, mainly due to the cost, and I wanted to see how this played out.

Walking out I found Jenny standing at the desk with a tray of the good stuff calling my name. It was then that I noticed I was in my underwear.

"Uh…good morning," I said, quickly turning around to throw on some clothes, leaving nothing to the imagination. In all fairness, over the past ten months, I had gotten in good shape. It wasn't my pride forcing me to turn around but the utter look of shock on Jenny's face. It was one of catching your child doing something inappropriate, and I felt like the kid.

Throwing on some sweatpants and a T-shirt I had flung over the nightstand, I walked back out to see Petro and Jenny laughing obviously at my old fashioned tighty-whities.

"Morning there," Jenny chirped, also texting a message out on her phone at the same time. Petro was already half done with his cap of coffee and Fae honey. "Having Trish in the house this morning has been rather nice. Fae honey?"

I tried to act cool. It never worked, and I quickly shuffled over, greedily grabbing a cup. Fae honey was extremely expensive, and for a reason. It made you feel amazing and awake—all at the cool price of three hundred bucks a cup. Like I said, I rarely got to try any, and when I did, it was at Trish's whim. "So there has to be a catch," I said, figuring this was a bribe to get something done.

"Well, yes. As you know, the band is coming in this morning. I know you were expecting to help them; however, I need you to go to the local civil airport in town and escort a group of people who are coming in early back here," Jenny said, showing her teeth through a fake smile.

"You have to be kidding me. I've been waiting for days. Any chance we can get some of Kim's folks?"

"No chance. They're all tied up in security. It's hard to make this many Council and civilian leaders fly under the radar. Especially with the gates here shut off for security," Jenny said as Petro took off in the air carrying another capful of coffee.

"Hey, boss," Petro said as he headed toward the door. "I'm taking this to Cacey, and then if you want, I'll go along for the ride."

I was crushed. "Sure" was all I could muster after the defeating news. At least I would get to see them play up close and personal later.

Jenny picked up the rest of the cups, giving me some coordinating instructions heading out the door behind Petro.

Fifteen minutes later I was ready to go. It was 8:00 a.m.,

and in all fairness, I didn't know why I was upset. The civil airport was only fifteen minutes away.

Using the charm he had given me, I called for Petro. I was able to park the Black Beast out front, and for once I actually used the front door to Gramps's place.

"How's the main house looking?" I asked, opening the doors and starting the rumbling V-8. Petro took his normal seat in the cupholder.

"They worked all night. I think they're getting close to finishing up. The rest of the food's coming in this morning, and there's a bunch of security people supposed to be here at noon," Petro said, jumping up and turning on the radio.

Petro knew most of what happened in the house. Not really sure how he knew, but he did. Plus, Pixies don't sleep much and spend a good amount of time snooping around. We had to lay down some ground rules about shower time.

"Figure this little trip won't take too long. We still might get to catch the band setting up," I said, trying to forget about the prior day's meeting with Carvel.

"We will, even if I have to make it happen."

"Thanks, man. I don't think spelling anyone will be needed. Besides this whole demon thing has me freaking out."

"About that..." Petro said, trailing off. "Ed was up late talking to Jenny about it. I think they're calling in some favors."

When the term "calling in some favors" was used, it meant seeing how many people you have on your side. I looked at Petro as he just shook his head.

The civil airport on the outskirts of St. Augustine was little more than a single short runway and flat field used by privately owned prop planes. There sat a black private jet with a limo parked in front. Leaning on the hood was the driver, drinking his cup of morning wake-up, wearing sunglasses so dark they absorbed the light. I pulled up, rolling down the window, not being able to see inside. I still had the radio up loud, the new Planes Drifter single, "Power Ride," flowing out.

"I'm Max. Jenny sent me to escort you back to the Atheneum," I said, looking at the annoyed driver.

"Yup. She said you would be in a black truck. The lady didn't say a piece of shit," the man said, walking back around to the driver's side.

I sat there, shaking my head and slowly patted the dash of the Black Beauty. "Shhh…it's OK. You're a good truck," I said. Petro just called the guy an ass and went back to listening to the radio.

It took another fifteen minutes as the plane cleared the runway, finally allowing us to head back. I didn't pay attention to the group getting off the plane, figuring it was some politician. Jenny called to see if we had linked up, and after a minute of her talking to someone else, I hung up.

We finally pulled up to the main building, as a group of staffers stood outside, looking at us driving up. "What the hell is this?" I said, making Petro take flight up to the dash.

"Might be someone important in the vehicle behind us."

We drove past the group, parking my truck in front of Tom's old house, again taking advantage of Ed not telling us to move it. I looked over at Petro. "I don't want anything to do with this. I need to get cleaned up in case PD shows up soon. I don't want to look like this." I was wearing a timeworn Planes Drifter tour shirt with holes in it, a pair of worn old jeans, and old gray sneakers that I used when outside doing work that oftentimes were accused of smelling like hot garbage.

Jenny stood there, waving us over as I cut the ignition and stood there, at least curious to see who came out of the limo from a distance.

There it was; a few yelps later, Planes Drifter emerged from the limo. "Shit" was all that I could get out as Petro took off at the speed of light.

The lead singer, Abby Normal; guitar player, Knight Raider; bassist, Kane; and drummer, Jim Smith, all piled out of the vehicle. They were rock stars through and through, from their stage names (minus Jim) to their dress. They looked like a mix between '80s glam rockers, '90s metalheads, and eclectic jazz musicians form the '20s, all coming together in some type of weird, cool circus vibe.

I finally made eye contact with Jenny, with her sticking her tongue out at me. She had lined this whole thing up. Too bad I was on the other side of the roundabout, and the band was getting mobbed.

Shaking my head, I decided to go in, get cleaned up, then go harass the band, hoping everyone else would have to get back to work under Jenny's heavy hand.

As I was showering, thoughts of the yesterday's conversation kept popping up in my head. I recently started holding water over my head until a sizable amount sat there, then let it drop in a slash of water. For some reason, I thought this might come in handy one day. It also had the ability to wash the soap out of my lengthening hair in one drop.

From the shower I could hear the phone chirping on the sink ledge. I looked to see a few texts from Jenny telling me I was good till noon. She knew I was going to go check the band out either way. The band had a room set up on the second floor overlooking the stage area, which I was betting was fairly small by their standards. That would be my first stop.

It wasn't time to put on the outfit for the evening, so I threw on my castor, a new PD T-shirt, and a trusty pair of dark jeans.

Really? I thought, hearing voices coming from the office.

For some reason it struck a nerve as I came out of my room barking orders.

"Get ou—" was all I got out. There sat Planes Drifter lead singer Abby Normal's red leather boots kicked up on my desk.

"Max, I presume," Abby said as Night handed him a drink from the bar. Normally I would get upset but figured I could make an exception for the intrusion on the bar and office today.

"Thanks for the escort. Saw your shirt. That's an old one, and those PD stickers on your truck. Those have seen some years," Abby said in a deep, smooth voice that all lead singers must have.

"I, uh...yeah, hello" was all I got out as Jim walked over, handing me a beer. He was a V; I could tell immediately.

"Hey, Max, heard a lot about you from Frank," Jim said, walking back over to where Kane stood.

"You know Frank?" I asked in the form of a statement.

"I would hope so. You may know my sister Angel," he said as he let out a light chuckle. It made sense; drummers never came out during the day and always had a way with the ladies. Were all drummers vampires?

Abby stood up. "Hey, man, we knew Tom, and Jenny called us. She actually hadn't thought about us playing the ball till you showed up. Jenny said you're a huge fan, and ohhhhhh man, we heard about all that crazy stuff you did last year. The fire sword and all that business. You heard our new song, 'Flame'?"

"Sure, I just got the new album a few weeks ago. That song's great," I said, barely containing my excitement. Was this really happening?

"Well, it's about that flaming sword man," Knight said as he sat down on one of the chairs strumming a guitar he had pulled out of nowhere.

"You wrote a song about me?" I asked, watching Petro jumping around the room.

"Yup," Kane finally spoke up, in a low bass-filled, gravelly voice. I had noticed he was not like the others and said very little. *Bassist*, I thought.

"Here you go," Knight said as he stood handing me the guitar signed in some type of gold marker by all the members. "One thing. You have to do something even more badass this year for us to write a song about."

I stood there dazed. They knew who I was and what I had done. This again proved how oblivious I was to the new world around me, betting it was my status as Tom's grandson creating the buzz.

"Deal." I was down to one-word sentences. I was like a five-year-old kid at Disney meeting his favorite character.

"Well, we got to go get set up," Abby said as the group stood up and, one by one, shook my hand with Kane just shaking his head. Abby gave me a hug as he walked out. He smelled a lot like Gramps. Burnt hickory and aged leather. It was calming and created memories, much like tasting a food you had eaten as a child after twenty years. As he pulled back, I couldn't help but notice his slight resemblance to Gramps as well. Maybe it was just my head playing tricks or the fact that I was about to have a stroke.

After a few minutes of sitting there alone, realizing I had a full beer in my hand, I sat it down and fist pumped the air, doing a little jig of excitement. Petro joined in, doing some type of finger-pointing dance.

"That was awesome," I said as Petro finally landed on the desk, inspecting the angular-shaped electric guitar.

"Yes, it was. Didn't see that coming, and I know what goes

on around here," Petro said. I figured he had been duped also.

My phone started chirping just as I actually started to enjoy myself, thinking about drinking the beer even though it was still early morning. *Damn rock stars*, I thought to myself.

"Looks like Dr. Freeman, Ed, and Phil want to go over the guest list, so we are all tracking," I said, standing up and still not fully comprehending what had just happened.

Petro and I headed toward the dining room still talking about the band. Even on the Plane, PD was a big deal.

By the time we arrived in the dining room, someone had sat out a stack of folders. These included lists and invite verification sheets.

"Right, now that we got that out of the way," Ed said as Phil looked up from the plate of kebabs he was eating. Inspector Holder—or Dick, as I was now allowed to call him—had brought some over for Phil this morning. He had actually agreed to gate into the United States the day prior and had been staying at the Casa Monaco downtown.

"The folders in front of you are the guest lists as well as picture identification. Since the wards will be fully charged, we don't suspect any issues with people coming under a glamour." Phil continued to eat loudly as Ed continued. "The security team meeting will be in the main ballroom at noon. Everyone needs to be there."

Dr. Freeman was standing beside the table with an odd look on his face.

"Hey there, doc," I said, walking over to him. "Why the long face?"

"Well, looks like I'm going to be stuck in the crucible room all night. I guess I'm not 'officially' part of the team."

Ed looked over, picking up the plate from Phil and tossing it into the trash can, obviously done with the spectacle that was his breakfast. Phil just sat there, apparently not wanting to pick a fight with Ed.

"Dr. Freeman, we intend on meeting on the subject tomorrow. I understand your frustration; however, until they figure out the Balance accords, it's best to just wait," Ed said as he pointed to the folders.

Over the past ten months, while it was clear he was part of the team, Dr. Freeman's unofficial work with Tom had gotten some pushback from the Council, leading to his onboarding with the Atheneum being stalled. I truly didn't understand why. It was probably along the lines of the whole demon situation I was going through.

Ed walked over as Phil left the room heading to direct traffic in the main drive. "Let's go look at the ballroom, shall we?"

"Sure. So you heard about the band?" I asked, as it was still front and center in my mind. We walked out, holding our folders and looking official.

Ed just let out a light sigh and snicker. "Yes, Max. Let's get focused. It's about to get busy here."

The main ballroom had been transformed walking through the double doors. The once-empty space was now covered in sheets of dark purple-and-black silks with large dark flower arrangements, and it was topped off by a large flower-covered dragon that had apparently been built around the main chandelier. The chandelier hung out of its mouth, looking as if the dragon was alive and breathing fire on the crowd. It was stunning.

The smell of roses and other strong, earthy flowers permeated the air. Looking around, I saw the stage was at the far end, almost tucked away. Jenny knew what she was doing. The alcoves all had separators jutting out into the empty dance floor area, making each space more intimate and breaking up the room. Looking up, I saw the catwalk that overlooked the basketball-court-sized floor was layered in tapestries that resembled the ones from the dining room showing various depictions of Fae castles and other gothic scenes.

Lighting in the area had been somehow muted. The large stained-glass windows in the back of the room radiated darker-than-normal colored light. Standing in the middle of the room, it almost felt as if you were underwater or something to that effect.

Ed, seeing my amazement, patted my shoulder as Petro finally zipped by. "She's good."

"She's amazing, doing all this. I've never seen anything like it. It's…well, magical," I said, finally taking a deep breath to break the trance.

"Petro," Ed said, looking over at the Pixie flying out of the dragon's mouth. "Go check on the Pixie delegation's accommodations. Second alcove to the left coming in."

"Sure thing, boss," he said, zipping off into the alcove, melting into the background.

Ed looked over. "See you at noon. Jenny told me to fill you in on your break later. Planes Drifter comes on at 9:00 p.m. The last guest arrives at eight o'clock. You should be good to break free at eight thirty. Just stay out of trouble, take it light on the drinks for once, and don't leave the property."

"Sure thing. Hey, look," I said, figuring it was a good time to talk about yesterday. "I don't want any trouble and get what you're saying. I'll make sure everything goes smoothly tonight on my end."

I was being genuine, and Ed could tell. He still had trouble reading me from time to time. With Jenny's help they had figured it was something to do with the will binding the year prior. I, on the other hand, figured it had something to do with the fact that any time someone used magic on me, I kept a small piece of it. After all he was the all-knowing mind Mage. He had even been submitted for full Wizard status and a position on the Senior Council.

"Perfect," Ed said as he patted me on the shoulder again. "I wish Tom was here to see all this. Hell, the old bastard probably will be, for all we know. Look, that's why I wanted to pull you aside. I know we discussed keeping Tom a secret. It's important that we continue to do so. No one, and I mean no one, can know he's still alive. He disappeared for a reason. Hell, probably some top-secret mission. I just wish he would call me or something. Just take it easy; look at that list. It's easy to see why. Presidents, senators, kings, queens of the Plane, Council Wizards, and the like. It will be a prime night for something to go wrong."

We parted ways as I headed toward the crucible room to look up information on Leon, the gate Mage who went missing. Leon's disappearance had generated the increase in security.

After our noon meeting, not much had changed. Kim's team, including twenty other regular marshals and agents from God knows what government agency, was on standby. The Council had also provided another two dozen Mages from the CSA defense force. Highly skilled combat Mages. My new friends from earlier—Terrence and Mouth, the large apelike man who wanted to pound me into the ground—were hanging out with me all night at check-in.

The plan had changed slightly as the missing gate Mage was to bring in several high-level dignitaries, the US president being one. Rebecca Crawford was the latest addition to the long list of dignified US presidents. She had won the election last year and was a full-blooded regular civilian. Rebecca would now be brought by special envoy via ground transport. In recent months she had enjoyed the use of a gate Mage to help her move around. Leon just happened to be that Mage and was more than likely adding to my growing pile of what I started to call complications.

CHAPTER 8

Party Time

I stood at the main entrance dressed in a boring black-and-white suit. Terrence and Mouth stood behind me as people, or whatever, started to file in. I was given a book-size tablet bearing the gleaming Mags-Tech logo on it at login, designed to scan thumbprints. A little magic and whole lot of normal tablet.

"Hey, boss," Petro said, flying up in the air. The dignitaries from the Pixie delegation were coming in. Lacey and Macey were on either side of Petro. They had become a dysfunctional family of sorts, Petro acting as the big brother while the sisters were the ones running the show.

"Petro, see you later. I'll call if I need you." I rubbed the charm he had given me. We had also made one for him. While I couldn't get to him as fast, I would know if he needed me.

I could hear a huff of disapproval come from Mouth, as I turned around to look up at the hulking man. "Hey, brother, want to make a deal?" I asked, raising an eyebrow. Terrence let out a snicker. I could see why Phil liked him.

Mouth just let out another huff. They called him Mouth due to the fact that if you made him mad, he would more than likely punch you in the mouth.

"We make it through the next three hours, and I have a bottle of Ambrosia in my office with your name on it, big guy," I said, letting out a matching huff that he could feel on his chest.

Much to my surprise, Mouth let out another light huff, raised both Neanderthal eyebrows, twisted his lip, and smiled. The smell of burnt fabric from being overironed (or lack of knowing how) was coming off his body, which I happened to be too close to.

"Seems you have his attention," Terrence said in a quick, tight voice, telling me I needed to step back. "Looks like you have a deal."

Mouth didn't say much and, to the point, not to me.

"Fair enough," I said, turning around to see a congresswoman from Florida staring wide-eyed, jaw dropped open, gawking at the group of Pixies flying away from the table.

"Ma'am? Name, and please place your thumb on the tablet," I said as she continued to stare. "I take it you haven't seen a Pixie before?"

"Uh, no, that's a Pixie?" she asked, looking at her aide.

"They're on the approved roster," the thin young man who looked as if he had spent his day blogging and fetching coffee blurted in a nasal voice.

Jenny had mentioned this was the first time some government members would meet a Mage, Ethereal, Pixie, or whatever flavor of the day one fell under outside of the regulars.

"Thank you, ma'am. Here is your welcome bag. Enjoy the ball. Down the hall through the open double doors. I highly recommend the Magnus," I threw in for good measure, not liking the way she looked at Petro. Hopefully, she tried some and had a sorted night. I was protective of the little guy and his crew. You know what? He was the same way for friends, and I guessed he would have dusted her if she had done the same to me.

Again, I could hear Mouth huff in approval. I turned around smiling to see him scowl at me. Note to self—don't push it.

From 5:00 through 8:00 p.m., the waves of people came. Much to my surprise, we only had issues with one group that turned out to be reporters from the local paper trying to find out what the party was all about. Terrence took care of that group.

I was getting anxious as 8:30 p.m. approached, and of course, I saw Carvel walking through the door. *Great,* I thought.

"Sir, name, and please place your thumb on the tablet," I said, trying to act invisible honoring my promise to Ed.

"Sir?" Carvel spat out. "You know full well who I am. Councilman Carvel Icupiousous."

"Here is your welcome bag, Councilman, enjoy the ball," I said as he lifted his thumb from the green-flashing tablet.

Carvel took his bag and stormed off. I was hoping he had calmed down, but apparently he was more irritated than yesterday.

The welcome bag he slammed into the chest of his aide included art deco '20s glasses, a map of the ball area, and other small items, including an antihangover potion labeled as an energy drink.

I noticed, as Carvel walked off, that he ushered over Mouth, whispering something to him. Mouth, not caring, stared directly at me.

"Hey, hey." The voice of Kim Kimber came from behind me as I spun around. I was so focused on the two men in front of me I had stopped listening to the background noise.

"Hello, can I help you?" I asked, my brain not catching up with the fact that Kim stood there wearing makeup, high heels, and an amazing red party dress slit to her thigh. She was stunning. I barely recognized her.

"Yeah, stop staring at my legs, and you're going to take me to see the show. Politicians creep me out. Last I heard, Phil was arguing with a driver, and Dick, well. He's being his normal chipper self this afternoon. You're stuck with me," Kim said as I watched her ruby red lips move, glancing down to the smooth, bare skin of her chest.

"Sure" was all I got out as I scrambled to recover from the gaffe. She had me dead to rights and knew it.

On cue, Mouth let out a snort this time while Terrence turned around so we wouldn't see his red face about to explode with laughter. Was I that bad at talking to women? I really don't understand why they cared, but I took it as a small victory. "It's eight thirty, and Ned's strangely the only person left to check in plus his guest. I don't think—" I was cut off as Aslynn jumped up and wrapped her arms around me in a hug.

"Max!" she exclaimed as she kissed me on the cheek, slightly pushing Kim out of the way. "Oh my God, Daddy said you would be here, and I had to come."

"Your father?" I asked as Ned walked up behind her. Of course, it all made sense now. Why she was in town. How she knew where I would be and who I was. Odd thing was, she was genuinely happy to see me.

I could feel the steam coming off Kim's shoulders as I turned to Ned, giving him and his daughter their welcome bags.

"Max, you look the part tonight. How are things holding up?" Ned asked in his calming tone that also set Kim at ease slightly.

"Good, up until Carvel came in five minutes ago," I said, looking over at Kim and raising my finger in a motion to wait.

"Yes, he has apparently been in a mood today. Anyways, good to see you. I'm heading in. Aslynn?"

Aslynn looked over at me and then back at Kim. "Max, you're taking me to see Planes Drifter. No choice, or Daddy will make you stay late for school," she said, starting to pull me from behind the table. She was pretty in a different way than the sultry Kim standing there. Aslynn was dressed in a dark-green flowing dress that, while revealing, didn't lend itself to crowd stopping as Kim's did. The funny thing was the two goons behind me were having a complete meltdown watching the sideshow.

"Max," Kim spoke up. "I'll see you later. I'm going to see what Ben's doing," she said as she walked off.

"Who's Ben?" I asked to Kim's retreating back, having visions of a burly security guard dancing with her on the floor. Why did I care? Even more, what the hell just happened?

"Girlfriend?" Aslynn asked, cocking her head and squinting her eyes.

"No." It was the truth, and she could tell as her demeanor shifted back to fun party girl.

Ned stood there shaking his head as I looked back at the goons, Terrence shooing me off. It was time to watch the show—but first, a few drinks.

Aslynn and I walked as a couple through the doors and over to the bar. It was busy and loud, so small talk wasn't needed. We both liked to people watch, and as we strolled through the crowd, we did just that.

"So where are all your friends?" Aslynn asked as I ordered two beers from the bartender. I knew she preferred pilsner from our night out on the town. Trish stood there smiling, looking like she wanted to talk but deciding that me having what looked like a date was more important.

I went to pay Trish as she put her hand up in placation, refusing.

"You are mister popular—girls, free drinks, this big house," Aslynn said as we stepped aside, both taking a pull from our Vamp Ambers before we talked further.

"Not really, just friends and work. You understand. I had no clue…" were the last words I got out of my mouth when Abby Normal's voice and Knight's guitar wailed over the loudspeakers. The crowd erupted. Fog filled the ballroom floor, making the laser lights create a visual show in itself.

There were a lot of stuffy people at the party, and either Trish had done her job getting them all smashed, or they were all actually Planes Drifter fans. I was betting on door number one.

"Hello! Are you ready to come together and rock!" Abby screamed at the top of his lungs, a slight drum spatter in the background followed by a single bass note reverberating around the room.

We both bolted for the stage on instinct to get a good view of the show. The crowd was, as expected, having a good time, but not in as much of a hurry as I was. To boot, you could tell several of the other Mages and Ethereals in the room were doing the same thing I was. The regulars mostly just stood there, enjoying the ambiance of a rock show.

The next hour was a blur of drinks being handed to me and rocking, Aslynn and I dancing and moving to the beat of the music. The show was amazing, and I was probably having a few too many drinks, finding myself holding Aslynn by the hips, pushing against her body, her head leaning on my chest as their famous love ballad "Love, Shovel, Grave" came on.

Halfway through the song, I looked around to see who else was present. Phil, check. He was the one feeding me drinks out of thin air. Petro, check. He and his crew of Pixies had buzzed over, handing me a small shot glass. Petro gave me a wink and his lesser version of a fist bump as he looked at Aslynn. Ed, check. He was standing with Jenny in the corner, both of them with a drink and watching the show. I could have sworn Ed had his hand on her lower back. Kim, not to be found. That would be something I would deal with later, the liquor was telling me. Lastly Carvel, also not to be found. I was guessing he was in the corner, or some dark hole plotting my demise after the prank Phil and I pulled on him last year. Plus, word on the street had him pegged as a complete grouch.

As the set wrapped up, the band did what rock bands do. They threw out guitar picks and drumsticks, shook hands, and told everyone to gate home responsibly.

"That was amazing," Aslynn said as the sound calmed down and the dark-purple hue of the room took back over from the stage lights. The fog and crowd calmed, settling into their buzzes.

"It was," I said, the liquor starting to kick into overdrive. "So are you," I blurted out.

Aslynn blushed, pulling me closer.

"Bruther," Phil interjected with a stern slap on the back and shove. "That was the shit! I think I peed myself a little over there in the corner," he said as he handed me a flask obviously full of Ambrosia.

"Dammit," I said, cutting him off as I remembered my promise to Face Crusher or whatever his name was. "I got to run to the office real fast. Can you keep Aslynn company?" I said, already heading out the doors.

I walked through the crowd, stopping every so often to shake a hand or avoid a magic performer on stilts. Finally, making my way through the crowd, I headed up the stairs into the silence of the second floor down to the house.

What had I just done? Aslynn and I were about to hang out. I started thinking that it would probably not be a good idea in front of politicians and the royalty present. Hell, not to mention Ned—or, as I now had it stuck in my head, "Daddy," according to Aslynn. This was work.

After deliberating on the night's actions so far, I swore to myself, walking into the office, to find Kim and ask her for a drink. Not like I needed another one.

I quickly grabbed the bottle and headed back to the main house entrance to pay my toll to the Mouth Man, Man Mouth, whatever, still thinking of Aslynn.

After five minutes of wandering around, I walked up to the two men, still resolute in their duties. The Ambrosia was from Gramps's stash. He had twelve bottles, and I was giving away one. To put it into perspective, one bottle from, what I gathered, could fetch $5,000 on the open market. Nectar of the Gods, when you drank it, the thirst-quencher turned into your favorite flavor and would change the instant your mind decided to; you liked grape better than cotton candy—boom, done.

As I held out the bottle, Terrence smacked Mouth on the arm. "Shit, I lost. I thought he wasn't good for it."

Mouth grunted his approval and reached for the bottle, grabbing it in his large hand and sliding it into his jacket pocket.

I looked over, saluting the two men, turned, and left. I

thought I heard a high five being given but didn't turn to verify.

Arriving back into the ballroom, I saw the party was still in full swing. Looking down at my castor, I saw I had been gone around thirty minutes. "Damn," I said to the white noise of the room, looking around for Aslynn or, for that matter, Kim. Of course, I found Phil. He saw me first, running up with Jamison in tow.

"Bruther, where the hell have you been? Aslynn got all huffy and left not five minutes ago," Phil said as Jamison, obviously having more to drink that me, just pointed at Phil, smiling.

"What he said."

It hit home that she was Jamison's sister, and I had the sneaking suspicion he was the reason she left. I was about to say something I would later regret when Ed walked up with Kim.

"Right, we need to go to the crucible room. There's been an incident," Ed said loudly as the roar of the crowd was picking up.

The three of us cut through the horde again, heading to the offices, Kim not letting me get in step beside her. It was a short walk, all of ten steps outside the double doors, as the spaces were beside each other. Jenny, Dr. Freeman, Frank, Angel, and Carvel stood there as well as a group of security I hadn't met before.

It was time to sober up and fast. Good thing I wasn't on security tonight.

The door closed behind us, completely cutting off the noise only a few feet away. Talk about good engineering. I guess with the building usually being empty, you don't notice these types of things.

Frank walked into the crucible room, the eager group

following. I saw Carvel look back and smirk. Yup, he was up to something, and I bet it had to do with making my life significantly more complicated.

"Everyone quiet down," Frank said over the murmurs in his monotone yet edgy voice. "I understand that phone and electronic devices were disabled via a ward minus a few devices, so I apologize for the delay. Everyone in this room is aware that the president was supposed to gate in via the Postern after the Planes Drifter show. That didn't happen."

The group all looked confused at the same time. Phil sat his drink down.

"As most of you know, Leon was supposed to gate her in. He went missing, so we used a stand-in gate Mage just as good. Gilbert also went missing with a special gate stone just after the show. There was also a reported spike on the E-Relator that read black," Frank said as he let the room take in what he had just said.

The room turned to look at me all at the same time in various levels of obviousness. Apparently, that meant a demon showed up and not Belm. He, even though tolerated, was not on the cleared list and not in attendance tonight. The list was one of the many things the Transitions Office did. It cataloged people and things. What they are and/or were, not to mention what they could do. The congresswoman from earlier obviously was staying away from things not fully explained on the nice list.

"When did this happen?" Carvel asked, stepping forward. "Is this president person all right?" he asked, making it out like he was more important than the president of the United States.

"She's fine. The president will just not be here till tomorrow. It happened right after the band's set was over," Frank said, turning to the screens.

"I saw Max running out right after the show," Carvel said, pointing right at me, gesturing to the two armed guards at the door.

Ed lightly held up his hand; the men froze as if they had been turned to ice. I could tell he was using some type of casting. Seeing him use his powers was impressive. Carvel also stopped talking. While not under whatever it was the two men were, he knew not to push Ed.

"You come to my place of work, and you threaten my staff. Then the minute something happens, you accuse them of being involved. I can assure you Max was not involved, and you would be wise to focus your efforts on the actual issue at hand," Ed said in finality. If you took a breath in the room, you wouldn't get any air out of it. Ed had drawn the line in the sand, and everyone knew it. The question was what side of the line everyone else was on.

I looked over at Kim as she glanced at me, almost as if the night's prior events were not even registering. It's easy to forget how powerful people are until you see them taking a stand. I was proud to call him a friend and boss.

Brushing it off, Carvel turned to Frank. "Where did this all take place?"

"In Jacksonville, in an area called Fleming Island to be exact. We have a safe house there they gated her to. She was then to gate here using the only activated gate," Frank said as Angel zoomed in the map on the big screen.

The tension in the room was thick as molasses in January. Ed was still eying Carvel as the old man turned and stormed out of the room, the two guards slowly following as if they didn't know who or where they were.

As Carvel reached the main door, he stopped and turned the two guards flanking him. "Max, we will be talking tomorrow. Do not stray too far from the area," the old lanky man said with the noise of the party filling the air before the door closed behind him.

"What a dick," Phil let out as he made some weird gesture I hadn't seen before followed by a solid middle finger. Ed looked over in a sigh of agreement.

"Well, that's that. You all know where we stand now. Max, he is serious. I talked to a few close contacts of mine today. We have enough support to push back but only by a string. On top of that, as you can see by the message on the screen, we are to support the CSA defense teams here to help figure out why two very prominent gate Mages have gone missing."

I looked over, surprised to see Kim standing right next to me. "Hey, I've been looking for you all afternoon," I said as the group started breaking out into separate conversations.

"I just needed a break, oh, and you smell like a brewery," she said, not giving anything away. For all I knew, she had been in the garage making out with Ben or whatever that guy's name was. "How was your date?"

"My date?" I said, taken back and realizing that I was not only close to full-on drunk but had in fact been all over Aslynn.

The president of the United States was sitting in a house in Fleming Island, a suburb of Jacksonville, and this was the conversation I was having.

"Yeah, she kind of left," I said, rubbing the back of my neck, letting my bow tie loose to hang down on my shirt.

Kim snorted, looking out of place with her still-amazing outfit. "You're still batting zero there, big guy. Better luck next time," she said as she walked over to Ed.

I couldn't tell if she was flirting or making fun of me. Perfect.

"Right, everyone," Ed said to the group. He was getting ready to put a plan in motion. "Frank and Angel, you're on watch here all night. Dr. Freeman, you're good to go for the afternoon. Phil, Jamison, and Max, you guys go sober up, then we will talk first thing in the morning. The meetings start up at 11:00 a.m. Be here at nine. Kim, I don't think we will need you specifically. Your people are doing fine, and I believe you're staying here tonight. Breakfast will be served at eight o'clock."

That was it; Ed had given the team its marching orders. Jenny had stayed out of the conversation and left directly after Carvel.

Phil and Jamison immediately headed back toward the party as Kim was adjusting her dress in the window reflection of the crucible room.

"Hey," I said, walking up beside her reflectively. "Want to grab a drink? I have a feeling it's going to be the last chance for a day or two."

"Sure, sorry if I was being an ass earlier. This dress, these people. I just don't feel like myself."

"You know," I said, standing up a little taller. "I've enjoyed not feeling like myself the past year. Let's go do it some more."

Kim cracked a smile, her red lips catching my eye. Not to mention the lipstick all over her teeth. While she was something else dressed like this, she was still Kim.

We settled on the alcove reserved for the Pixies, as it wasn't as loud. While Petro made sure to introduce us to everyone and also make us join in on a few traditional Pixie songs, the setting was actually rather cozy. Kim and I sat on a plush couch covered in velvet with a table in front overlooking the floor. While I had gotten used to the new drinks not available for regular consumption, Kim was still a classic. We ordered two old-fashioneds, and finally—after Petro had to stop a group of Pixies from taking their clothes off—got a chance to talk.

"You think all these politicians are going to be as friendly tomorrow when they find out that Vampires are real?" I asked in a reflective tone, Kim nodding as if she was holding the same thought.

"Politicians are never friendly, and no. You've seen the way they are. See how they have been looking at the Pixies—they're terrified. If it wasn't for Trish's calming drinks and their ability to relax people, I think a few of these folks would have run out the door on first sight," Kim said, taking a sip of her drink.

"Agreed. You should've seen a few of them checking in. Hey, I need to ask you something," I said, getting nervous for some reason I couldn't explain. Kim just nodded, sipping her drink.

"Up until a few weeks ago, you wouldn't even talk to me. Now, well...here we are," I said, hoping I wasn't reading too much into things.

Kim shuffled, taking another sip. "Look, as much as this is all new to you, think about how I, and for that matter everyone else, feels. I'm a normal person. I don't have superpowers or can make a sword shoot fire. It's scary what some of you can do. I know some of the Ethereals would rather wipe most of us out and just take over things. Scary thing, I think they could come close."

There it was; she said it. I had already realized the divide and maybe jealousy of the regulars would be in play. Kim was, for some reason, telling me more than I thought I deserved.

"Three years ago, I would be lucky to get one OTN call every six months. You show up, and next thing I know, I'm arresting a man for trying to lick his butt in public just to watch him turn into a cat and take off. Things are changing, and in some ways I'm like our favorite inspector, Dick. It's just complicated, and it's going to get more so."

I sighed, sinking farther into the cushions of the couch. I was hoping for an explanation of her affection for me coming to fruition. That wasn't going to happen, or maybe I was just reading too much into things and just looking for love in all the wrong places.

"I'm still trying to figure this all out. The past few days have been crazy. Hell, I feel like an outsider," I said, being honest about the demon thing.

Kim let out a light giggle, spilling some of her drink on the floor. "You're a train wreck, and you know it. Hey, I'm going to call it a night. I'm staying over in the dorms. Good night, Max," Kim said, standing up.

Standing up, I looked at her and smiled. I leaned in—for what I don't know—ending up with an awkward hug. The type you give someone you never met in a room full of people that knew each other giving each other hugs.

My offer to walk her back was declined, and I watched her stride away.

It was close to midnight; looking over, I saw Phil laid out on a couch in the opposite alcove. Guessing that the party was coming to an end soon, I stood up. Looking around for Petro but not seeing him, I saluted the room and headed off to bed.

CHAPTER 9

*I'll Gladly Pay You Tuesday
for a Favor Today*

The steam in the bathroom was just the way I liked it. I was sipping my morning coffee, trying to read the news on the foggy screen of my phone. The smell of mint and cedar stuck to the moisture in the air, making the room resemble a private sauna. The dark-tiled walls and floor helped with the process that had become my morning ritual.

Just when I scrolled to the article about a large police presence south of Jacksonville, a text popped up on my screen. I sat there on the small wooden stool beside the shower letting the water run before I got in and sighed.

Max, I want you to meet a few folks before the meetings start, Ned sent, obviously already up and running around the building.

What I hadn't noticed was the text from Kim that came in at 3:00 a.m. *I'm still up* was all it said.

Was that her inviting me over last night or just seeing if I was still up working? I knew she was working with the security team and may have some information on yesterday's disappearance.

Of course, I texted Kim first, telling her I'd meet her for breakfast and that I'd just gotten her message. *Fair enough*, I thought. I figured Ned would find me in the dining room; he knew the drill.

Getting cleaned up with Phil's ever-famous hangover potion plus a solid cup of black coffee, I was ready to face the day. As I threw on my castor and official work clothes, all the events that transpired last night still hadn't fully computed. I needed to talk to Petro but first needed something to eat.

"Maxxxx." The cool, slithering voice came from behind my desk, followed by the distinct smell of pepper. "Spent enough time in the shower as always, I see."

It was Devin, or as I had figured it, the devil himself, Lucifer or whatever you wanted to call him. Erring on the side of caution, as I had learned to do around these types, I opted for a joke.

"Spend a lot of time paying attention to my shower routine?" I asked, figuring that would at least get his attention. Devin, like Belm and Bo, cared very little for those he spoke to in most cases. Directly addressing what he stated always helped drive the conversation.

Devin let out a smooth laugh. He held one of those black cigarettes Trish had picked up yesterday, smelling of burning rubber and flowers.

"You would be surprised. Looks like you had a fun party last night, everyone having a good time getting acquainted," Devin said as if he was trying to make a point. He also had his black book sitting in front of him. That meant business. He had popped in a few other times to do nothing more than talk or tell me some weird piece of information.

It usually didn't add up to much more than me knowing that Phil went to church and passed gas. What I did know is that he had a habit of spending time like this with Gramps, and I, as his de facto grandson, took on that role.

"It was. There was a little issue last night, but I think they are getting it sorted out," I said, taking a seat and looking at my castor to check the time. I needed to be downstairs for breakfast.

Belm had explained the rules of dealing with demons and the like. Unlike Fae, they could be a little looser with the facts, making sure if they gave you something, they took something. The funny things was, the day prior, thinking about this, I wondered if Bo, and Belm, actually both owed me something.

Devin sighed. "I know you're on a time crunch, so I'll just slow that down a little. I'm here, as you probably know, on business."

Did he just say he was slowing time down? "I'll be fine," I said, knowing that leaving was not going to be an option anyways. Then the thought hit. *Petro.*

"Oh yes, your little friend. I understand he has a mate now and did not take the liberty of bringing any associates today. He is down eating with everyone. He talked to you just five minutes ago when he came in here."

I didn't ask and just relaxed into the seat, figuring he had convinced Petro to leave. He opened his book onto a page with only two lines written on it.

"As you know, I wouldn't be here with my book unless I thought there was something to give or take, and a balance needed to be claimed."

I nodded my head, agreeing, letting him continue upon my visible approval of his statement.

His suit was so immaculate and pressed that it made me

feel underdressed in the shirt, blazer, and slacks I had on. After all the president was coming in later.

"Today I am going to leave an open note here, and I'm not expecting anything in return. I need you to understand and agree. If so, I'll close my book, and we can talk."

I sat there computing what he had just said. He was asking me to do him a favor without anything in return. It would be nice if he just stated it that way. It sounded backward, but that's what he truly meant. There were rules, however, and Belm told me to never question them. So I didn't.

"OK, but I can't promise that I can help."

"Fair enough. You're perceptive like Tom. At least you're not drinking. He would be, even this early." Devin stopped, raised his eyebrows and getting a closer look at me, obviously taking it back that I wouldn't do the same.

"You've met Bo. He is, shall I say, a loose version of what most of the things that I work against are. You should be concerned, not as much about what he will do, but about what he has done."

"Has he done something that I need to be aware of?" I asked, getting tired of the topic over the past two days and figuring it was about to get more piled on it.

"Oh, yes, he's incredibly old and has done some very nasty things. That being said, nothing that truly pertains to you and your current situation. Just him paying you a visit. Let me ask you. What do you think the Transitions Office you work for, that you registered Bo through truly is or does?"

"Well, Mages, Ethereals, and the like come in and register. It's like registering to vote in a way. You want your voice heard, you have to register. That's how it was explained to me by the Council. Plus, most of these folks don't even have an ID or a Social Security card, for that matter."

"Wrong," Devin said, lighting another cigarette and offering me one as I held my hand up in placation. "Did you know the office was set up by the Council, not regulars as most people assume? No, you didn't, did you? It was set up by the Council and groups sometimes loosely tied to them. Lobbyists, special interest groups, and so on."

I sat up a little straighter, realizing he was telling the truth.

"I see I have your attention; let me continue. Do you wonder where or, more importantly, what that information is being used for?"

I shook my head, not truly knowing, and as noted, was planning to investigate. Ever since Bo's visit, the Transitions Office hadn't sat right with me.

"Here is the good part, Maxxx. What if I told you that the information was being gathered to form rosters of a sort, and being used or purchased to identify and collect certain individuals?" Devin asked with a tang of anger in his tone finishing the sentence.

"You mean like when someone sells your identity to a marketing company and you get a bunch of adverts in the mail?" I asked, trying to pinpoint where he was going with this.

"No, Maxxx. Leon and his backup were both kidnapped and detained by some of your friends from last year. They got their information from you and the Transitions Office registrations directly. Also a few factions in the regular governments are using the office to identify high-value targets. I am sure from your army days you know what that is."

"This can't be true. It's just sorting out who's here and who isn't. From what I understand, it's also to help control the amount of traffic to and from the Plane. The regulars are concerned about the Fae," I said, seeing the expression on his face harden. He didn't like pushback. Oddly enough he relaxed, taking another drag from his cigarette.

The poor reaction the congresswoman had to seeing Petro and the other Pixies at the party the night before came to mind, setting off all kinds of alarms. They had referenced a roster after seeing them.

"Maxxx, you need to listen to what I'm saying closely. It's being weaponized, I believe the new political phrase is. The people in the regular government may not be that regular. That's all I can say about that. What I will tell you is to check on the status of all the gate Mages that you specifically have registered to date."

"All right, but…" was all I got out as Devin stood up.

"Maxxx, be careful. Politics and our world always lead to bloodshed." As Devin disappeared, his book was the last thing to dissolve into nothing.

I sat there for a minute looking down at my castor, realizing not even a minute had passed. It took me a moment processing everything Devin had said, and in one shining moment, it all clicked.

The Transitions Office was a front for targeting people, or whatever. My stomach started to turn. I needed to get to the box and check out the other registrations.

After I took a brisk walk to the main entrance, the sounds of a building full of people appeared. I quickly turned into the dining room, avoiding the large group huddled and talking in the hallway.

"Ah, Max, good morning," Jenny said, walking over and actually smiling as she handed me a folder with what I supposed was my assignment for the day. I guess her work was done after last night, and we had our trusty Dr. Simmons back.

I looked around the room to see Dick, Kim, Phil, and Petro

all at the table flipping through their own folders and eating.

"Good morning, everyone," I said, looking over at Kim, getting a read on her mood.

"Hey, boss, you changed clothes and smell different. I thought you got some new smell good juice," Petro said with a screwed-up look on his face.

"I'll explain later," I said, looking over and giving Petro a slight nod. "Thanks, Jenny. Is this the agenda for the day?"

"Correct. Everything you'll need is in there. You're doing pretty much the same thing, starting at 11:00 a.m. for the Council and regular government members, getting them checked in. Ned insisted you be done by noon so you can attend some of the meetings," Jenny said, picking up her cup of coffee.

"Bruther, you'll notice that it's a different crowd today. Last night was mostly midlevel folks and bootstrap hangers. The heavy hitters will show up today. The primary will be here at eleven thirty. It's all situated after yesterday," Phil said as he stuffed a doughnut in the side of his mouth as an unlit smoke hung out the other. He followed this up by a loud slurp of coffee. The guy had style.

"Morning, Kim," I said, sitting down and reaching for a small bowl of fruit. "Sorry about the late response. I was passed out last night. You not get any sleep?" I asked, hoping she had, in fact, wanted me to pay her a visit. I was wrong.

"Sorry about that. I figured you may be awake with everything going on. A few of my people found some information on the box that was of interest. We'll have some time after we eat. I asked Ben to stop by to brief us in a few hours."

That was it; there was nothing there. She wanted to show me what her new boyfriend, Ben, had found while I was passed out.

"Sounds like a plan. I have a few things I want to look up anyways," I said, looking over to see Ned walk in on cue.

"Max, there you are. I have a few people that I want you to meet before you get back to work," Ned boomed as he pulled his long, straight gray hair back.

He was dressed in an odd pastel-yellow suit with a long flowing jacket that almost looked like a cape. Ned was in full on Fae mode this morning, the gold medallion around his neck signifying his position on the Council. He was a good man, or whatever, a politician, but the right kind, actually trying to make a difference.

I stayed seated as Ned stood there waiting. "Looks like a rain check," I said to Kim, shrugging my shoulders. "I'll text you when I'm done."

"You'll have plenty of time," Ned said, grabbing my arm, pulling me in to talk as we walked.

Kim let out a sigh. "Typical, oh, and looks like there is going to be plenty of rain and wind the next few days" was all she said.

"Did you see the weather forecast?" Ned asked, looking me over, making a grunt of approval that I had actually showed up dressed for work.

"According to Kim, rain," I said, getting in stride beside him as we headed to the ballroom, and what I was guessing were the meeting rooms that the dignitaries were set on using.

"A tropical depression showed up out of the blue. Not completely surprising, it being hurricane season. It's going to start getting nasty today and stay that way for a week or so. Flooding and winds up to sixty miles per hour for the next few days. Obviously, you haven't stepped outside yet. It's already starting to rain. It looked like the sun didn't come up for an extra hour this morning."

Just as the words rolled off his tongue, a boom of thunder reverberated around the main entrance that you could feel in your feet. Ned stopped before we walked through the doors.

"Max, I'm introducing you to Councilman Darkwater. Nicholas Darkwater, to be precise. He's an Earthborn Mage who showed up out of nowhere earlier this year. Very connected and an independent of sorts. We're working on some gate legislation together, and he wants to meet you. Plus, I owe him a favor. You know our kind and their favors."

"Fair enough, as long as you're not selling me into a life of servitude."

Ned let out a light, uneasy chuckle. "Look, I know Councilman Darkwater mostly by reputation, what of it there is. Earlier this year he helped my son Jamison out of a tight situation and has called his marker. That just happens to be meeting you."

A rumble of thunder finished his sentence as I started to think that being an apprentice wasn't as easy as I thought it was going to be.

We walked up the stairs to see Marlow Goolsby walking out of the door. Marlow glared at me, slightly nodding his head toward Ned but not saying a word as he walked past us. He walked with a purpose, generating a slight breeze.

"What crawled up his ass?" I said lightly as Ned knocked on the door, shaking his head in disapproval not responding.

The door opened as Mouth stood there raising an eyebrow, or maybe it was more like half his forehead, letting us in.

"Where's your partner?" I asked, having the notion that I was much safer with Terrence around.

Mouth let out a grunt as Councilman Darkwater stood up. "Ned, Max, welcome. Come in. Have a seat. Coffee for our guests," the man snapped at a woman in the corner with her eyes down.

The man was wearing an outfit much like Ned's but dark gray. His hair was overly black, almost to the point of absorbing light, and contrasted with his pale skin, all lending to a rather bland appearance. He stood roughly six-feet-tall, medium build, and other than how sharply he was dressed, he would blend into a crowd. His pitch-black, neatly parted hair was the only feature that made an impression. Well, and maybe his slate-gray eyes that almost glowed. His voice was also calm and soothing. The smell of incense lightly hung around the room.

"Councilman Darkwater, it's a pleasure to meet you again," Ned said in full politician mode.

We shook hands, and as coffee was delivered, I noticed the young girl that had served us. She was in her twenties and seemed petrified. I looked over at Ned and Darkwater, letting them know that I noticed. As soon as I did, Darkwater ushered her out of the room with a flick of his wrist. She left, her hands together in front of her.

"She is a little shy. We're working on that," Darkwater said, the smile never faltering from his face. "So let's get down to business, shall we?" There was a pause as he spoke back up. "Sorry, I understand there are a lot of meetings and other things going on this morning, and your time is limited," he said, pulling back his aggressive attitude only worn by people in positions of utter and absolute power.

"Understood," Ned said as the tension eased out of the room. "It's going to be busy...plus, this storm."

"Max, I am sure Ned has told you something about me. I'm a fairly new member of the Council, an independent, and with that I am finding my place before the Balance. As you understand from your background in the military, even people in charge need a favor every now and then."

"Sure," I said, sitting up in the comfortable chair that had already lowered me to below eye level with the man. "Ned said something about a favor, and you wanted to meet me. Nice choice of security, by the way. That guy gets around," I said in an attempt to see what Darkwater would do.

Problem was, I should have been more concerned with Mouth, as his hand the size of a bear's claw lifted me out of my seat onto my feet. There would be a bruise there in the morning—if he didn't turn me into a pile of broken bones first.

With a light flick of Darkwater's index and middle fingers, Mouth froze in place, dropping me Another turn of his wrist and a light whisper of "*Venia*." Mouth turned and left in a rigid manner, suggesting he was not fully driving the ship.

It was official; this guy was in control. I looked over to see Ned take a deep breath. "I don't think that's necessary. Max was only joking. Those two were working last night together, and Carvel was involved."

"Understood, yes, I don't allow my guests to be harmed. I do my best to follow Fae customs. Mouth works for Carvel, and he is helping me fulfill my obligations while my apprentice and staff are away working on another issue. Anyways, as I was saying. I would like Max to run an artifact to Savannah for me. Not too far, but it can't be gated and could potentially draw some attention," Darkwater said, tapping his fingers.

Ned spoke up, cutting me off. "What is this artifact?"

"That is irrelevant. It's sanctioned and is to be transported via normal means as it's too risky to gate. We are concerned gating could mean it being intercepted. I'm just asking Max to transport an item, nothing more or less, in return for my marker."

"I know you're playing by the rules. Just remember, Max

is my apprentice and will need to know what it is he is transporting. His life will be your responsibility, especially if he is not informed. Also remember that," Ned said, playing the game of chess that appeared to include my safety.

The conversation would probably make anyone else crawl behind a piece of furniture and hide. In this world it seemed normal when negotiating a favor, or marker, as they called it. Devin, while not as aggressive, was just as assured when he was balancing his scales. I hated sitting there like the monkey in the middle.

"It's settled then. The artifact is a navigator, one of three that I am aware of."

Ned let out a breath and tilted his head. "I see. Yes, Max will do it. Max, a navigator is a powerfully enchanted item. It's from the Plane and almost at the level of the Fountain. It works like one of those simple tracking spells. Much more powerful, though, and does more than just help you find things. It can bring things to you by means that are considered…well, let's just say outlawed."

"I can see all this time around the Atheneum has helped your knowledge of rare items, and from what I understand, the Fountain is no longer in existence. Anyways, the artifact shall be secured, and you will have an escort from my team."

"I could use a road trip," I said. The two gentlemen, not seeing my humor, decided to ignore me. "When do we go?"

"Perfect," Darkwater said as a smile actually appeared on his face. "A week should do. I still need to make some arrangements for the pickup."

"Great, that's settled. We will discuss this further before you leave," Ned said as he stood up in a manner suggesting I follow.

Mouth and the woman from earlier were no longer in the

room. Darkwater stood up, leading us to the door. We made small talk on how my training was going. The meeting was just as Ned had explained these often went: a mixture of intense bravado and methodical posturing.

Rounding the door back into the main hallway, Ned stopped and looked over, a scowl on his face.

"He's an ass. Only been on the Council for a year and probably not even over fifty Earth years old. I don't trust him, but he has never given me a reason not to."

"I was going to ask. He seemed a little high-strung. Seems like he's just building his contacts up," I said, clicking my tongue.

"You're catching on. Issue is not many others have done work with or for him. He helped me through his civilian contacts when Jamison was in a spot of trouble. Enough of that; time to get to work. I'll see what else I can dig up on him, as I'm not sure why Mr. Goolsby was there," Ned finished as he walked off.

I had the feeling Ned was not happy about the meeting but in the same breath also not going to be owing this Darkwater guy anything. Ned's statement led me to believe he would not be asking him for another favor and would be checking this delivery out before it was time. Phil as well as Petro told me that most Ethereals and Mages would hold onto markers as if it was a bar of gold, in some cases, waiting dozens of years to use them. According to Ned he had only been on the hook for a year. Thunder boomed again as wind started echoing off a window somewhere. The neutral light from outside fading to dark gray.

I hadn't noticed until it was blaring outside with a storm how quiet the place usually was. That and the hundred or so other people now in the building.

I texted Kim, and much to my surprise, she responded

almost immediately with *Meet me in the crucible room.* I also noted a text from my folks telling me they were heading out of town for a few days till the storm conceded.

The recently updated offices were packed with people working as the president was showing up in two hours. For all the planning, our team had been released from security duty. *Bummer*, I thought, shaking my head. I wasn't complaining, but it felt odd in the place I called home.

I made my way to the crucible room full of monitors and radios. Kim stood at the far right hunched over the box with a fit, square-jawed man standing over her shoulder, one hand leaning on the back of her chair. I could only guess that was Ben.

"Hey, guys," I found myself saying in a snappy tone that garnered Kim's attention.

"Meeting not go well?" she asked, looking over at Ben. He was smiling and reached out his hand.

"Nice to meet you. Name's Ben. I'm new to the marshal's OTN team," he said in a slight southern accent that I placed somewhere between Tennessee and Kentucky.

I shook his hand, holding it slightly longer than necessary and generating a raised eyebrow from Kim.

"You two know each other?" she asked, looking skeptical.

I snapped out of it right on time. "I thought so for a minute. Sorry, I'm Max."

"That's all right. I was in the army for a few years as well and do the same thing all the time," Ben said, letting the slight tension out of the air.

Do I know him? I thought. He was the type of person who was immediately likable. So I chose not to.

"Great. Ben, tell Max what you found last night," Kim said,

typing on the keyboard and reaching over to the printer to hand me two sheets of paper.

"Well, I was looking in this fancy computer and found two other reports of missing gate Mages, as you call them. Not nearly as important or big time as the one that caused all the fuss yesterday but still, nonetheless, missing."

Standing there, I felt a sinking feeling form in my stomach; I already knew who the two other Mages were. Looking at the printouts confirmed it. I had registered the two other Mages three weeks prior. Leon, the missing gate Mage, recommended that the two register at our office with the hopes I would get some time to take them to the Postern. I hadn't, and in all actuality, I hadn't paid much attention to them, the goal being not to turn into a tourist attraction. There were already enough of those in town.

"Max?" Kim asked, noting I was standing there staring at the papers.

"Nothing. I just don't think this is a coincidence," I said, deciding on keeping the details to myself until I could get some time to think. I was at that moment sure Carvel was already foaming at the mouth if he had this information. Or maybe he didn't yet. Either way people were missing, and I was standing there just thinking about myself.

"Agreed," Ben chimed in.

"Let's get this to Ed before we talk to anyone else," I said as Kim cocked her head, looking confused. She had not been involved in yesterday's conversation.

"This is important, Max. I think we need to get this information out," Kim said as she eyed me skeptically.

"Look, I'm just saying there's enough going on today as it is. It would be better to spend quality time looking at this. That's all," I said, honestly believing myself and walking back my prior selfish thoughts.

"You're right. Let's plan on getting this over to Ed after the final meetings wrap up tonight," Kim said as she took the papers from my hands, standing up. "They're starting soon anyways, and from what I hear, we are all on the bench for the day."

Kim smiled, walking out, Ben following behind looking like a lost puppy. Or maybe I just thought that. It was time to bounce a few things off Petro while everyone was freaking out about our VIP's arrival.

I grabbed the charm hanging from my neck, whispering for Petro. It took a few minutes, but as always, he came flying into the room. He had a slight smirk on his face, and when he landed on the desk, I could clearly see lipstick smeared on his cheeks.

"Hey, boss, how's it hanging? Let me tell you what I got—"

I cut him off at the pass. "I need to bounce a few things off you. Let's head to the office. Are you also off duty?"

"Sure am. We don't do to well in the bad weather anyways, and the Pixie delegation is already here. Funny thing is, I'm the only one here from the Plane, probably a good thing. What's up?"

"Let's get to the office—too many ears around," I said as we walked through the crowd.

Getting back to the office, I spent the good part of thirty minutes rambling over the details with Petro. I walked through all the events of the past few days out loud, not in my head, making the whole odd situation seem connected.

"Seems somehow connected to me, boss," Petro said in affirmation.

"That's the thing. How? It's too much for it not to be. Bo, Devin, the missing gate Mages all tied to our office, Carvel, and then to top it all off, this Darkwater guy. Just not sure how," I said, sitting back in my chair while Petro leaned against the computer monitor, lightly dusting the desk.

"Well, boss, it all seems to have something to do with you. Like you said and already knew, Devin pretty much confirmed that the Transitions Office was up to no good. That would at least make four of those things line up. Plus, Devin tricked me. Why? That doesn't happen often," Petro said, biting his small bottom lip.

"I need to talk to Ed, Jenny, and Phil about this tonight after most of everyone has left. It may even have to wait till tomorrow."

"Can it?" Petro asked, making a good point.

Carvel didn't seem to be the type to sit on something or let it play out. If he had more information, he would act. If he knew about the other Mages, I was betting he would already be here taking me away to some dank cage. Carvel was already trying to convince everyone that I was responsible for the missing gate Mages and for the demon showing up already.

"You're right. Let's head back; the VIP should be here in a few minutes, and I want to get a good seat to listen to her speech before the meetings start up," I said as Petro flew up, landing on my shoulder along for the ride. I could tell by the look on his face that our conversation had sobered him up, and he looked concerned, deep in thought. We walked to the main ballroom in silence.

"Where the hell have you been?" Phil's voice boomed through the crowd as we waded through the mob in the main hall that had solidified since we left.

"Issues" was all I could muster without spitting out the details.

Three months prior Phil and I had joked about "issues"

we both had after a long night of drinking at FA's. Since then, when something was up, we would use the word "issues."

Phil squinted his eyes as we both nodded. I could see him reaching for a cigarette, only stopping, figuring it wasn't a good idea with the crowd around. "Well, that's that. I'll round the team up after the last meeting."

"Let's keep it in house," I said, referring to only the group that stayed in the facility. That was that as the three of us made our way inside the large room.

The initial plan had been to have the speech last night while everyone was in the ballroom. From what I understood, some people didn't show up because of the president's absence. The room, while not fully decorated, still had the stage Planes Drifter had played on set up. The crowd was a sea of people mostly standing with a several rows of chairs in front of the stage that had already been occupied. We opted for the cheap seats and situated ourselves by the door.

The lights dimmed, calming the crowd into silence.

"The president of the United States of America!" came booming through the room speakers. The crowd erupted into a loud round of applause. I scanned the room, noticing a few patrons not joining in on the adulation. Typical politicians. Looking up, I saw that on the second-floor balcony, Councilman Darkwater stood next to Carvel, neither moving nor applauding.

As the crowd's applause subsided, a boom of thunder and flash of lightning showing through the windows kicked off the speech. There were no cameras or phones permitted, the annoying glow of phones absent allowing for a clear view. Amazing how cell phones ruined most concerts.

"Good morning, everyone. Thank you for hosting me and being flexible in your plans for today. I understand how important these meetings are for each and every one of us here." The smooth yet commanding voice of Rebecca, the US president, came out through the speakers.

"We are all about to set forth on a journey together that will forever change the way we look at each other and the worlds we live in." There was a slight pause, allowing for a spatter of clapping. I noticed the delegation from the Plane remained mostly unmoved by the speech as again a boom of thunder reverberated through the hall.

"There are many people here from their respective governments that are just now learning about the depth of this initiative. If you are here, you are already aware of the intricate layers that make up our fragile world; I can assure you this is needed. There are things and problems only we as a team together can solve, and with this Balance, we can achieve anything," she said, again with the pause allowing for clapping.

The rest of the speech was much of the same, talking about togetherness and the need for acceptance. Funny thing was, I wasn't exactly sure who was in need of acceptance. There was something alien about the message. Almost like something was going on that I wasn't in the know about. Phil looked content, giving his penance to the applause as did Petro and, for that matter, as did I.

By the end of the speech, it was clear by the crowd who supported the Balance and coming out to the regular world.

"Time to go," Phil said as he popped an unlit cigarette in his mouth, only to have it yanked out by Mouth, who had positioned himself at the door directly behind us.

Phil looked at the beast of a man with hate in his eyes. I knew that look and how strong Phil truly was. If he wanted to, barring any abnormal strength Mouth had, Phil could throw the hulking man to the other side of the entrance or, for that matter, tear his arms off and use them as drumsticks.

Terrence interjected, handing Phil his unlit smoke back as the crowd started piling up at the door, pushing us down the hall like a surfer on a wave.

The door to the dining room had been closed and an access pad added to keep others out. We punched in our code and walked into the room, only to see Dr. Freeman and Jenny sitting behind a computer looking at a weather update.

"I hate that big slothy-looking, troll-smelling, sausage-fingered mutt," Phil exclaimed as he finally lit up his smoke. In most cases Jenny would throw a fit. The dining room was not a place for smoking, but I had a feeling she was not going to push his buttons.

After a few minutes, Phil spoke up. "Sorry, all. That big oaf Mouth is out there being an ass because he knows I won't start any trouble here."

"That's fine. I'll let it pass this once. I'm sure you two will sort it out," she said, shaking her head. "This storm's getting crazy. It will be a hurricane before long, and looks like it will be sitting off the coast just spinning for a few days."

"The Council's doing?" I asked, knowing that they sometimes did things like this to cover up odd happenings. That's right—they could make things like a bad storm happen. It didn't happen often, but it did happen. I wonder if they had told the president about that yet.

"Honestly, no. I wouldn't rule anything out, though, with all the people here. It actually looks like a few dignitaries are leaving early due to it. Security has agreed to open some of the gates this afternoon after a few VIPs have left," Jenny said as Dr. Freeman chimed in.

"They are saying it could churn in the Atlantic until it hits a category 5 then head inland. They aren't sure where yet. Better go buy out all the bread and milk you'll never drink now," he said in light jest.

"Where's Ed?" I asked.

"He's escorting the leaders down to the meeting rooms. They're about to start. Ned came by and asked that you stop by around 2:00 p.m. They're having a break, and he wants you to listen in on a few things. Probably take notes while he goes out and politics by the coffee maker," Jenny said, finally closing the laptop and sighing.

"Oy, family meeting tonight," Phil said. "Max has issues."

Jenny looked in understanding of our little code word game and just shook her head. Dr. Freeman lived in the Atheneum. He was not always around when we were socializing, often missing some of the inside jokes and nuances of our conversations. He spent most of his time in the stacks reading or helping the tech folks catalog the books to digital.

"That's going to be hard to do," Jenny said. "Ed's set to gate back to the Council chambers this evening and won't be back till tomorrow. The Council is having a private meeting separate of the regulars."

On that note the decision had been made. Phil, Petro, and I would go to the office and drink. It would also give me some time to prep Phil on the events previously explained to Petro.

Before heading off to find Ned and then to the office, I made it a point to find Kim, explaining the plan for tomorrow morning.

"Sounds good. I need to head to the store and get a few things before the storm gets too bad. Mostly some bread and milk," she said, as I tried my best not to let out a snicker.

"Look, if you need to stay here, just let us know," I said, hoping to get her to agree. Again, it didn't happen.

"We'll be fine. Ben and I are planning on setting up in the office if the storm does hit," Kim said, patting me on the back.

We. She used the term "we." What was I doing even thinking about her? For some reason I couldn't help myself and awkwardly returned the pat on the back.

Kim and I headed down to the converted range, making small talk, mostly about the storm.

"Ned's over there waiting on me. Probably to show me off some more. If something changes tomorrow, call me," I said as we parted ways, Kim getting in a final dig.

"Show you off? To whom?" she said mockingly as she walked over to Ben standing at the end of the hall.

"Max, there you are. I was getting worried. There are a few people I would like to introduce you to, and they are about to discuss the Transitions Office," Ned said, clearing his throat.

I was still watching Kim and Ben, not looking over.

"Unless Kim has taken up with dating her cousin, I think you still may have a chance," Ned huffed out, ending in a lopsided grin.

"I'm not, it's not…" I decided to shut up and smiled back, immediately changing my mind about not liking Ben. He was smart after all, finding out that information last night. Not to mention that meant Kim was still single.

We both let out a noticeable breath walking into the meeting room.

CHAPTER 10

Check, Please

The next morning, I awoke to find calm taking over the bustle of the past few days. It wasn't as if I could hear the main building; it just felt quieter. Petro, Phil, and I had met for our evening drinks, going over the events of the prior couple of days. Ed was gone till afternoon, and there was a shift to cover at the Transitions Office. We played a heated game of rock-paper-scissors after no fewer than five rounds of drinks, landing on Phil and Petro going in for the morning shift.

While Petro and I usually did about everything together, it was a chance for me to get some time to myself. The morning Zen was, of course, interrupted by a group text from Ed. *Be back at 4pm meet in the dining room.*

As the ring reverberated around my small room, I grabbed my castor and lurched into the shower for a steamy thirty-minute-long session of standing in the water staring at the dark tiles.

I finished up putting on my favorite pair of jeans and the PD T-shirt that Abby Normal had left me.

"Good morning." The voice of Leshya floated in eerily as I sat down at my desk looking through emails. There were several from the local authorities on the storm, a handful from Kim, and one from Ed I decided could wait about our annual cyberawareness training.

The storm was getting worse; by now most folks had left the Atheneum that weren't supposed to be there. When the gates were finally opened, folks streamed out of the facility like rats off a sinking ship.

I could hear the wind pushing on the stained-glass windows while the constant roll of thunder delivered a slight vibration to the room.

"Leshya, how are you holding up?" I asked, not seeing her for most of the event.

"Good. I wanted to see if you needed anything and to drop off a note Ned left for you while you were preoccupied last night."

Leshya handed over a handwritten note. *Fae are always so old-fashioned*, I thought.

> Max,
>
> *I talked with Kim before I left. Carvel will be finding this out soon enough. We are looking into it. Don't let it get to you. Councilman Darkwater has asked that you meet him for lunch. I gave him your number, so be on the lookout for his call. I will be traveling for the next week and will be out of touch. For the next two days, work on your blending, and we will look at your project when I return.*
>
> *Thanks,*
> Ned

Guess that was that, and I could relax. Truth be told,

relaxing was the last thing I could do. Everyone around me seemed to be shielding me from whatever was going on. Or, at the least, assuming I already knew. It was time to go on the offense. I looked at Leshya; on cue, the paper lit and burned itself out of existence.

"I think you should take the Judge with you," Leshya said in a momentary flash of insight.

The Judge was a gun that Gramps left me that was, well, the Judge. It used special ammunition, and if you were to shoot someone with it, the weapon would, in fact, figure out if there was a reason to either stun, knock out, do nothing, or kill whomever it was aimed at. I had yet to try it out. It was an enchanted item and, like my sword, a fabled weapon from the Plane. In fact, I figured some of the attention on me was due to these items. It was like driving a supercar in high school.

"I'll do that," I said, looking over. She always seemed to know what was going on. With the knowledge that Gramps was still alive, I was positive he was somehow feeding her information. Hell, maybe he was driving the ship.

Leshya smiled, leaving the room as silently as she had entered it.

I walked through the main house, still seeing people that I didn't recognize. As noted, a few new faces were working in the offices on security, mainly from the marshal's office.

It was noon by the time I got a call from Phil that the day was a bust. Usually there would have been at least a handful of people come in; today, zero. I thought maybe it was the recent missing Mages and everyone knowing that our office was somehow tied to them; however, for my sanity, I ended up figuring it was the storm.

We decided to meet at FA's for a late lunch, as it was easy to gate into the office from the Postern. As luck would have it, FA's was next door.

I walked through the gate, catching the two watching cartoons on Petro's tablet we had put on the desk for him to use. It was old *Tom and Jerry*. Petro was dusting at a scene with Tom having an iron dropped through his mouth and weighing him down as he rounded a corner, the iron swinging around to flatten his face. I found myself standing there, joining in.

"Time for a drink, boys," I said as the two looked over, obviously not having taken their eyes off the screen for some time.

"Damn straight, bruther," Phil bellowed as Petro flew up to the door, looking out.

"I'm gonna need a ride," Petro said as the storm was pressing leaves and rain on the windows.

The storm was getting worse, and I really hadn't put much thought into getting anything together. It was as dark as night in the middle of the day. A roar filled the air as I threw on a raincoat hung up at the door. Petro zipped inside the protective yellow-rubber covering.

The walk to FA's was roughly five feet but enough to soak Phil. He was playing it cool and didn't bother with a jacket. He looked like a wet rat with all his hair and long beard sticking to his face.

"Look what the cat drug in," Trish said from behind the bar, the wind and noise following us inside.

"I think we have the wrong place. I'm not in my Sunday best," I said, everyone chuckling, knowing it was exactly where we wanted to be.

By this time Trish had our orders down: Phil with a tall glass of Jamison, Petro a cap of spiced rum, and what I had been trying to use to replace my need for water, Vamp Amber. Sitting in our normal places, I looked around; the place was oddly empty.

The thing about the Fallen Angel is that it's not really in one particular place. You could walk in from several different locations: New York, Chicago, and a few other select spots.

"What's with the small crowd? It can't be storming everywhere," I asked, seeing Trish flash her eyes at the door. We heard the sounds of the door opening and closing behind us. Phil, Petro, and I stood up instinctually.

I could hear the leather on Phil's castor tighten as he flexed, as Petro flew directly up to the ceiling. He did this to get the lay of the land.

"Hey, boss, there's three of them, and they don't look happy," Petro said loud enough for the now-quiet room to hear.

The three figures stopped, looking directly at us, not giving anything away.

The other thing about FA's is that it's what's called warded. As soon as you walk through the door, you're about as normal as the rest of the patrons. The ward somehow dampened magic as you walked through the threshold. Jenny tried explaining to me that it somehow shut off the Etherium in the person walking through. She said the one at FA's was extraordinarily strong and uncommon due to the power needed to maintain it.

Trish was not one to mix words or actions. When she looked over our shoulders and didn't respond, it was an easy signal to read.

"Hey, we can move over if we are in your seats, seeing that the rest of the bar is open," I said, finally getting my footing and squaring off with the group.

The trio consisted to two large men and a lean yet agile-looking woman. No one stood out in the group as a leader. After a slight pause, making the other few patrons go silent, it was clear they weren't here for a drink.

"All right, where's the boss?" I asked, figuring out these were the lackeys. I kicked back the rest of my beer in one pull, letting out a low belch that warranted a snicker from Phil.

Trish, at that moment, yelled toward the kitchen. "Amon, we may have trouble." Her voice was assured and final, making the already-stopped group freeze in place further as well as our crew. Petro even dropped down.

In the sustained silence, a noise from the kitchen started to flow out of the narrow food-service slit. Amon was taking a break from cooking and getting ready to play bouncer.

The sound was that of steel on steel, like a blade getting sharpened or sword being pulled from its scabbard. The thing that got everyone's attention further was the noise continuing for roughly five seconds, followed by the solid thump of a blade dropping to the floor, lodging itself, with the follow-up spatter of material hitting kitchen equipment.

"Jesus," Phil said as he completely turned his back on the group and looked toward the kitchen.

I had never seen or met the cook at FA's, but had been warned that if he ever came out of the kitchen, it would be best to be in another zip code as fast as possible. The small slit serving the food hid the cook; every time I tried to look all I could see was a hulking mass moving, and plates appearing. The food was intricate and top notch. Amon was no slouch in the kitchen.

"Enough," a voice came from one of the tables, as we all shifted our focus to a short older Asian woman that appeared out of nowhere.

Trish spoke first. "Ying Yue, this explains a lot. It's a pleasure. Can you please have your people relax? I can promise this group is no threat," she said as she motioned a slight bow of her head, showing earned respect.

"All right, now that's out of the way, mates," Phil said, picking up another glass that magically appeared and downing it in one swig.

"Patricia, my apologies for the entrance. I understand you are vouching for our safety and accept," Ying said, walking over and motioning her team to stand down. As they did, you could still feel tension in the air.

"Ying, been a while. Phil, you may know Ying. Max, Ying Yue is the head of the Gate Guild. The organization that oversees the gate Mages as well as Ethereals. Kind of like a union, before you ask," Trish explained, pouring us all another round of drinks and sitting a glass of red wine in front of Ying.

She ignored the three others. You could see the disappointment in their faces. *Hah*, I thought. *That's what you get in my watering hole.*

You could hear the sound of a large blade being pulled out of the floor with a crunch, followed by the long slink of it being sheathed again.

"Sorry about the distraction. You can understand, due to recent events, our teams have been on edge as of late," Ying said, taking a sip of her drink.

I looked at her without picking up my drink. "What events?"

"Don't be coy, Max. We all know several gate Mages have gone missing lately, and they all seem to have one thing in common." Ying paused; she was theatrical. "You."

While Phil and Petro also worked at the Transitions Office, gate Mages had a particular interest in visiting that site due to my overseeing of the Postern. I figured this is why she left the others out.

"Everyone needs to clear out. We are shutting down for the evening," Trish said for what I had to figure was the first time.

A few stragglers left the bar; we all stood there in silence. While Trish was on edge, you could tell she was not overly concerned. As the final person left, Trish spoke first.

"I think you two need to talk. Ying, you have no enemies in here. Max is on the right side of things. I vouch for him."

The statement must have carried weight as Ying visibly relaxed, letting the tension out of her stance. "So, Max, tell me what I need to know."

As soon as she relaxed, the three goons calmed down, walking up to the bar and sitting down. Trish finally served them.

"Sounds like you know about as much as the rest of the folks I've talked to over the past two days. I don't believe Bo is involved," I said, watching Petro fly off to the bathroom to place a call as we did when something off happened.

"Bo?" Ying asked, looking around.

"The demon."

"Ah, yes that," she said, shaking her head in understanding.

"I think that's why people are tying this to me. He's shown up close to the areas the gate Mages went missing," I said as Petro flew back and winked before landing.

"They have names," the woman from the goon squad said. Ying lifted a hand, calming her down.

"No disrespect meant. What I strongly believe, after some well-placed information, is that both of your associates registering has more to do with this than anything," I said, probably giving out more information than necessary.

I looked over at Trish, seeing her nodding her head in cautioned affirmation.

"The Transitions Office?" Ying asked, raising an eyebrow. Obviously, I had struck a nerve.

"Yes, they both registered and soon after went missing. I honestly don't know how Bo plays into this. It's just a gut feeling."

"A gut feeling? You willing to stake your life on it?" Ying said, obviously using some Vampire humor that I recycled on Frank every chance I got.

"Bruther, I think we need to talk about the rest of this when Ed gets back," Phil said, sliding his finger off his nose, telling me we had given up a lot of information without truly receiving anything. I figured she was just feeling me and the others out.

We spent a few more minutes talking about the Balance and made formal introductions to the goon squad, Phil and the stern, slim woman spending more time talking than needed.

As the group prepared to leave, Ying walked up, reaching out her hand.

"Use this wisely. It will ensure that any uninvited guests are no longer an issue. Thank you, Max. I believe you. Just don't let anyone else know that," Ying said, pulling me in for a light kiss on the cheek and handing me a small silver coin that was obviously a gate of some sort. She smelled like mint and sunlight, reminding me of Trish in some ways.

The door opened, with sounds from the storm filling the air. They were staying in the area. My phone chirped as the door closed behind the group with a message from Jenny stating Ed was back early and needed to meet with everyone.

"Trish, thanks," I said. The three of us finishing our drinks hurriedly, sitting out cash on the bar to hopefully cover the expense.

"You three be careful. The storm's getting worse, and by

that, I mean both of them," Trish said, referring to the missing Mages and literal storm outside.

"Trish, there's no one else in here except us, right?" I asked just as we were about to step off.

"Nope, just us."

"Tell you what. Let me pick that cash back up and ring Ed to see if they want to come here. After all, you saw what happened. It may be good for us to talk this through. That is, unless you're closed?" I trailed off innocently.

"Private party it is." Trish's face lit up. She walked to the back, then over to the door. I could hear her giving the cook instructions for food.

After a quick text, Ed and Jenny appeared through the front door, again reminding us there was a raging storm going on outside.

Jenny's hair was pulled back in a ponytail, flowing out the back of a Jacksonville Jaguars ball cap. Ed wore a long raincoat that suited him well. His hair, as always, looked to be manicured to perfection, even after being outside in the blender the storm was becoming.

"Right, perfect idea," Ed said. The two walked up, Ed taking Jenny's coat and tossing it over a chair. "I see the closed sign. Not too often that's up. You may just cause a riot."

"Hey, it will give me a chance to get caught up on a few things after catering the ball, and I needed an excuse. This reminds me of the old days when you and Tom would come in here asking me to close down so you could have some type of meeting."

Trish was enjoying the attention and soon walked over three trays full of various appetizers, including a handful of sandwiches and her famously expensive Fae honey cheese dip. She spent a few minutes filling the others in on the visit by

Ying Yue. Ed didn't seem concerned.

"Lass, this is great," Phil bellowed as the group dug into the platters.

Trish was strategically using the time to fill us in on a few changes at the Fallen Angel. "There are some changes coming. With the Balance and challenge of keeping this place manageable, we've decided to close down a few locations."

"Locations? I thought there was only one, and it's not anywhere," I said, packing an amazing stuffed mushroom in my mouth. The earthy smell mixing with sausage.

Ed let out a chuckle as he always did when he knew something others didn't. In case you were wondering, ever since I told Ed about Gramps still being alive, he was again able to read my thoughts. After a few tests, we figured it was another of his timed spells tied to the will. Gramps wanted me to keep some secrets from Ed during my initialization.

"Well, the location in St. Augustine is the original one. All the others are just empty warded buildings that gate the patrons here. With everyone that will more than likely be coming and going after finding out about this place, it will be nearly imposable to manage. There have been a few folks who walk in one location and out in another. That usually takes some effort to correct. Especially if they are regulars," Trish said, getting out the information she wanted to the group before Ed went into work mode.

"Right, so there have been some developments since we last talked from the Council," Ed started, wiping off his hands and laying his napkin on the bar top.

"Carvel has already linked the other missing gate Mage to the Transitions Office next door. With him being in the position he is, Max is being suspended from working with any further registrations," Ed finished, sitting back for questions.

It was obvious he already knew the information I wanted to share with him tonight, and I wondered if Kim had called him ahead of time. She had reservations about not going directly to him; however, it had only been roughly twenty hours.

"So that means?" I responded not knowing the full ramifications of the statement.

"You can't work in the Transitions Office. You are fine with your primary duties with the Postern and the Atheneum," Ed countered.

"What about me?" Petro spoke up from his plateful of shrimp, looking as if he had fought them off and was eating his prize.

Jenny interjected in a tight voice, "They don't think you matter as a Pixie, so it has no effect on you. Plus, they don't know about your life debt, and I suggest we all keep it that way."

She wasn't happy, and Petro relaxed, flying over to my shoulder.

"This is shit," Phil started in his thickest accent. "Bunch of knobs. No clue what's going on. I bet that dust bag has something to do with the disappearances."

"Relax," Ed chimed in. The conversation was getting heated. "I think Carvel is just embarrassed from your little prank. You know, the one that got delivered to his mother that just happened to be in the main house that his gate was in. Not to mention she had company when she read the note."

We all chuckled, including a rumble from the kitchen that reverberated around the bar.

"This is a good thing," Ed continued. "Max, it will give you time to do some legwork on the missing Mages and talk with Belm in the meantime. I also understand you are meeting with

Councilman Darkwater. Running some errand for him. Truth be told, I already have your replacement."

"That was fast," I said, shaking my head without noticing that I had drunk my third Vamp Amber in five minutes.

"Dr. Freeman will be helping in the office till things get settled. I think this is a good opportunity to separate Max from something he is obviously not a part of. Plus, get the good doctor finally on the official payroll," Ed said, sipping his Magnus. "Here is where things get interesting. The Transitions Office was not something the civilian governments came up with. It was our own Council. Two of the major Council members pushing this are none other than Carvel and Darkwater."

It was clear the intent was to put a facade on the office and its dealings.

The team sat there, taking in the new details. It didn't make sense. Mages and Ethereals didn't want the world knowing their business. They only agreed to three Council members being regulars, including Marlow Goolsby. The United Nations would take on several seats from our community. In all fairness there were already several Mages in positions of power in the regular world. The deck was stacked.

Jenny looked over at Phil, Petro, and me. "That means that certain members of the Council are more interested in our own kind than the rest of the civilians are."

She was right. It was suspicious at best. *Why gate Mages?* I thought to myself, knowing there was an audience.

"Because, Max, think about it." The group was used to Ed's chiming in on a thought and didn't blink an eye. "All these changes and the one thing that both groups will use. Gates. We already know they tried to gate over a fully powered Ethereal last year. You control the gates, you may as well control everything. I'm not so sure if this is all completely connected, but I bet that there are people on the Council involved."

It was always politics at the end of the day. People wanting more power.

"What about those Thule folks?" Petro spoke up with a slight twang to his voice.

"Yes, that," Ed said, obviously saving this for last. "There was a reported sighting of Chloe late last night. Another gate Mage went missing, and a CCTV feed caught her face profile in the area."

I leaned back in my chair, knowing Ed was holding this back. This meant that things were about to get busy—and fast.

"Wait a minute. Why are you saying there may be Council members involved? Why not say this about Chloe up front?" I asked, truly not knowing the depth of the Council.

"Max," Trish spoke up, saving Jenny and Ed the hassle. "The Council is large and to think that there are not members, or in the least people, tied to the Thule society would be naive."

She was right. I knew it. So did the others.

"Got it. I see why you're good with me being pulled from the Transitions Office. It makes it less obvious that I'm doing something else," I said, finishing my fourth beer.

"Precisely," Ed said, finishing his drink. "Plus, it may take some of the spotlight off you for now."

We talked about the other gate Mage who had just gone missing for about thirty minutes. She was a young, promising Mage from Canada who specialized in diverting gates. While not as publicized, it was important, and you guessed it. I knew her from a few weeks ago when she came into the office.

Diverting gates, according to Jenny, was the act of changing one or more locations of an established gate. The physical moving of items and people was starting to make a little more sense. One could divert a gate and send people to a less-than-desired location.

I was still sidetracked by Bo and Belm being out of the picture the past couple of days. Either way things were starting to get interesting.

Jenny and Ying were friends, and when she talked about her, it was without reservation, someone I could trust. After all Ying did tell me as much. I was convinced that I was the wild card making people nervous. I didn't blame them after last year, and had kept a fairly low profile.

The rest of the afternoon was spent back at the Atheneum figuring out who all the new faces in the building were and making sure they needed to be there. Ned, working with Kim, made sure all the new workers were vetted and badged. She was oddly gone by the time we got back. I needed to ask her why she talked to Ed first.

In total there were around two dozen new people doing various things around the facility. This included a person to work the old computer at the desk in the evidence room and a few people to work the entrance, much like the Dunn in London, including a couple of actual marshals doing their OTN training.

Belm had even been given access to the facility. That was a new one hot off the presses, we found out about when we arrived home. Of course, he wasn't there. This was actually against the wishes of Ed; however, his decision was trumped by someone up the food chain. If I had my guess, Devin had someone else's name in his book owing him a favor. I might ask the rest of the group if they had actually ever met him.

CHAPTER 11

Time to Make the Doughnuts

The next morning, I met my first truly old vampire. It was immediately evident why none of them were at the ball, or meetings for that matter.

The smell was the first thing that hit me walking into the conference room. The team had obviously avoided this assembly happening in the sacred dining room. If you've ever been to a house with more than one dead body in it, the owners in many cases attempt to mask the smell with perfumes and air fresheners.

This usually leads to the scent of rotted fish and flowers. Or as many people do, use the bathroom and spray air freshener, only combining the scent to create literal poopourri. Take your pick; for me I'd rather one or the other, not the nauseating combination.

Davros had a dead-fish-flower smell seeping from his body. It hit you even from five feet away. While not horrible, it caught and demanded your attention. He was the father of Circes, the vampire that had been killed last year, and he was a close friend of Dr. Freeman's. The two were at the table talking as I walked in.

To finish off the scene, he was dressed in a sleek, dark suit with a black silk shirt. It wasn't buttoned at the top, and he wore a cape covering most of it. His hair, as I thought it would be, was slicked back like oil on his head. Davros's skin was delicate and thin with the look of paper. You could see the veins and muscle under his flesh. Phil was right; meeting a truly old vampire was nothing like the young ones. His eyes were even pitch black, and when he opened his mouth, fangs showed through the smile.

"Max, I would like to introduce you to Davros," Ed said, realizing I had been standing there staring for a moment too long.

How do you introduce yourself to an old vampire? "Great to meet you. I'm sorry about the loss of your son," I said, looking over and also noticing Frank in the room.

"This one actually has manners. Not like your grandfather at all," Davros said with a toothy grin, looking genuine. "Thank you, Max. I understand you had a great deal to do with dispatching his killer. For that I am in your debt."

Frank, Ed, and Dr. Freeman all looked over, shocked by the statement. During the past year, I learned that an owed debt was something not to take lightly and many times was taken to a person's grave.

I wish Phil and Petro didn't have to cover the shift this morning. In all fairness I had a feeling Phil knew Davros was coming and left way before he showed up. After we got back last night, we all went our separate ways. Petro spending time with Cacey.

"It was a team effort," I said, deciding on cutting to the chase. Apparently, I also had gained a reputation for getting to the point rather quickly. "To what do we owe the honor?"

"To the point, as stated by others," Davros said in a silky yet strong voice. "I'm here to meet you for myself. As you know Carvel has pulled you from the Transitions Office. I am part of the security branch and a senior Council member. If a vote occurs, I have a voice. Like others I have never met you and needed to do so."

Ed, looking apprehensive, spoke up. "I can assure you Max is on the right side of things."

Before I could speak up, Davros started back. He commanded the space. "Possibly. As I stated I have a voice; however, I am in your debt. Take that as you will. Do know that certain factions on the Council are moving to have you expelled."

"Expelled?" I asked, seeing the looks on the others' faces.

Davros let out a light chuckle. "Expelled."

That was the last word he said before standing up, bowing his head and moving toward the door. The entire time Davros was in the room, Frank had kept his head down in a sign of obedience. I heard about this and how the younger vampires respected their elders, even if they didn't like them.

After Davros left the room, we all stood there looking at each other. Dr. Freeman escorted Davros out to the front gate.

"What the hell was that all about?" I stated louder than needed.

"That was you gaining another ally," Ed said, shaking his head positively. "It seems Council members are taking notice of current events, and it appears they are choosing sides."

"All right, enough," I said, getting heated. "I'm not a child. This is foolish. It's not a game. We need to figure out what happened to these gate Mages and get Belm's ass here now."

Ed let out a breath in approval. I obviously had said what he was thinking. "Yes, it's time we chatted old Belm up again.

I think he's hiding something or at least not sharing. Listen, having Davros on your side is a good thing. This means the V's are likely to vote in your favor."

That was it. I lost my composure. "Petro!" I called loudly to the charm. It took ten seconds for him to appear.

"Ed, I'm sorry, but either you tell me what's going on with this voting or Petro and I are leaving now."

Petro picked up on the mood, knowing my current opinion of things, and took position behind my shoulder. He looked concerned but, as always, had my back.

"Right, calm down. I understand why you are frustrated. Listen, you are new to all this and out of nowhere show up as Tom's grandson with all this crazy power. With the Balance on the line and everything happening recently, everyone is on edge looking for an escape. Some see you as just that. We have been working to keep your powers under the radar. It's not working anymore. Some people know you can use hellfire, and that's not all…" Ed said, trailing off.

"I get that, but what is, or might be, getting voted on?" I asked, stepping within a few inches of Ed, looking him square in the face.

"Your life, or in the least what to do with it," Ed said in one breath, pressing his already straight lips.

That was it. The cat was finally out of the bag. Then and there I decided to take fate into my own hands.

"Ed, you didn't think I needed to know any of this?" I asked, raising my voice, drawing everyones attention. "I've had enough of these games. I'm having lunch with Darkwater today, calling a meeting with Belm, then deciding if I want to be part of this clown show."

I had made up my mind. If the Council and working under them was going to be this crazy, I was going to go at it on my own. This was the first time being an independent Mage had crossed my mind and in doing so leave the Atheneum behind.

Petro hovered in the air. I looked over to see him looking sad yet determined with my words. I nodded and walked out of the main offices, heading to the old house.

"Hey, boss, what was that all about?" Petro asked as we walked up the stairs.

"You know how I said no more games last year? Well, the issue is that others are playing games."

"I don't think Ed is," Petro said, walking into the kitchen of the house.

"Doesn't matter. He's moving up to the senior Council this year anyways. Look, everyone seems to think they don't need to let me know what's going on. Trying to protect me, from what? Thing is, I'm making important choices based off a lack of knowing."

We stopped in the kitchen, looking at each other, Petro lightly dusting the counter.

"You're right. I think we've outgrown this place, boss. Plus, with all the new people. The others care for you, but things are changing," Petro said, putting the nail in the coffin. I was moving out. Maybe not today but soon. I still had to figure out what was going on first and how to pay rent.

I texted Belm; he responded he would be over later with some information that may come in handy. He followed it up by some animal emojis. *Demons*, I thought walking into my office.

I needed some time to think, as I walked over to the desk, hitting the button to open the bar down to my lab.

Sitting on the worktable was the short staff I was working on. The plan was to put a handful of spells into it to release when needed without having to pull power, or specialize in the specific type of magic used. I sat the gate stone Ying had given me down, figuring Petro could take a closer look at it later. She said it was a onetime thing. It must be like the smoke charm Trish had given me the year prior.

The staff could hold five spells. The first, I had decided, would be a stunning spell. This happened to be complete and ready for me to load. The next would be a shield; third, a freeze spell; fourth, a light; and last but not least, a small homing beacon. My intent was to have Petro help get it finished in time for the run I was about to do, or as everyone liked to call it, "the favor."

The stunning spell had to sit for a few days in a freezer. The freezer itself was from the 1950s. Dark, dirty with age, and barely keeping step. Opening the door, I found the potion that would become the stunning spell sat in a small copper pot.

Binding it to the staff was simple. Making it wasn't. Petro had done most of the legwork while I watched and learned.

I pulled out the small pot, opening a book on the table to the page marked "blending" with a yellow Post-it. Sitting the pot on the table, I put the end of the staff into the silvery substance and said the incantation, holding my palm up to the pot, pushing my will into it.

With a muted pop of ozone and slight tremor in the staff, the spell seeped into the first set of markings. This slot was shaped like a triangle surrounded by various runes.

Did it work? I thought to myself, figuring I would see if Phil would let me try it on him for a bottle of whiskey.

After thirty minutes of cleaning up, I had cleared my head and texted Ed a light apology, also saying that I would be around later to see him after lunch. As soon as the text was sent, another came in from Darkwater saying that he was in town and the only place open due to the storm was FA's.

I closed the lab and got presentable, as another hour passed. I decided to gate into the Transitions Office to see how things were. While I wasn't supposed to work there, no one had specifically told me I couldn't go there.

Gating into the building, I saw there were a few extra people working. Kim stood there with what looked like one of the marshals from the house.

It threw me off seeing Kim. Phil and Petro knew I wanted to talk to her about going to Ed. You could see the looks on their faces, as if they had been caught with their hands in the cookie jar.

"Hey, everyone, looks like I missed the party," I said in a semi sarcastic tone. Kim cocked her head sideways as the other marshal was talking to an elderly woman signing a registration form.

The thought of anyone signing these made me sick to my stomach. Kim walked over and leaned in. "I talked to your friends. Let's go in the back for a minute," she said, leaning close, the heat of her breath tickling my ear, the light smell of expensive perfume lingering.

We walked to the back room while Phil and Petro attempted to look busy.

Before I could say anything, Kim spoke up. "Sorry, Max. I know you wanted to wait to talk with Ed together. When we got word of another missing gate Mage, I didn't have a choice but to report it. Well, you know Ed; he figured there was more. I was so busy that I forgot our conversation and told him what I knew. I'm just so damn tired and stretched thin."

She was being sincere and for the first time apologized, looking for my understanding. Dammit, a woman in distress. My weakness. I let the tension out of my body and any thoughts of irritation as the wind started to howl against the outside wall, breaking the silence.

"Hey, it's all right," I said, seeing for a second what I thought was a mild tear forming in her eye. "I've felt the same recently. I even got in an argument with Ed earlier. Listen, we're friends, and nothing will alter that. I know things are changing with everything about to happen. I just need to know who has my back."

Kim perked up, seeing that I wasn't upset but just wanting to know what was going on.

"You're right. Everyone is stressed out. I had a tough conversation with Inspector Holder as well."

"You know everyone has trouble handling Dick sometimes," I said before the words got out of my mouth about Inspector Holder. Too late; we were both laughing out loud. I could also hear two nosy friends of mine snickering under their breath.

"All right, guys, I know you're at the door," I said as the two came busting in.

"Hey, sorry, boss. Kim came in and was all worried, and we know how you've been, so figured we would try to help out," Petro said as Phil raised an eyebrow to make sure I wasn't mad.

"Phil, for the love of God, if you stopped drawing pictures of the male anatomy every time Inspector Holder was around, I'd stop making unknowing jokes," I said, patting him on the back. He was chewing on an unlit cigarette, as he often did.

With that out of the way, there had been more than just a handful of changes. The marshal's office would now have someone present at the Transitions Office. Since most of them were new to the world, I was guessing it was generating some issues or maybe light PTSD. Most interesting was Ed ordering all registrations from our location to be stored until he, Jenny, and Ned could figure out what was really going on. That made me feel a little better for the old lady out front.

"Time to make the doughnuts," I said, letting out a slim smile as Kim reached out, patting my back as we walked out of the back office.

I walked into FA's with the wind on my back and the rain still pounding the side of the building. Councilman Darkwater sat at one of the far booths, raising his hand and motioning me over. I nodded at Trish, who gave me a solid smile and wink as I strolled over.

He was dressed much like before in a neat suit, wearing the same generic look on his face hiding his striking gray eyes. The light scent of incense came from him as he stood up. It must have been some expensive cologne that at the end of the day smelled like the old, cheap aftershave one's dad would use. The kind as a kid you would splash on your face, about making it melt off. It cost money sometimes to smell cheap. Or maybe he smelled nostalgic?

"Good afternoon, Max. Have a seat," Darkwater said, motioning me to sit opposite him in true politician style.

"Good to see you again. What's for lunch? I'm starving," I responded, looking down at the absence of menus or cocktails, for that matter. This was business.

"I ordered before you arrived. Trish stated she knew what you would like."

"Fair enough; as long as it's Fae honey tacos, the day can continue. I appreciate you asking me for lunch. What's the catch? There's always a catch."

"Your reputation precedes you. As you know another gate Mage went missing," Darkwater said, leveling his gaze.

"Just found out a little while ago. Does this have something to do with the delivery?"

"Yes, it does. The whole point of us driving the artifact to Savannah is to avoid any issues that gating may create. It's a short drive, but as you understand, distance does not mean much to some people. It might as well be three feet or one hundred miles. The issue is that I am planning on you running the errand for me tomorrow."

"Tomorrow? I thought you said a couple of weeks."

"I did. That information is new as of the minute you sat down. We believe that someone is after the artifact, and, as you obviously are figuring out, that person or persons is more than likely part of the Thule Society. Ah, our food." Darkwater huffed as Trish brought out two plates followed by a round of waters.

Darkwater had a filet and fingerling potatoes. No greens. Sighing at the lack of alcohol, I had, as one would guess, Fae honey tacos. I beamed at Trish as she sat the plate down. I thought to myself, giving it away on my face, *Only a politician or cheesy salesman would eat steak for lunch.*

Picking up on my judgment, he sipped his water, not touching the cooling meat.

As I bit into my first of two tacos, he watched. He could let his steak get cold. I figured the man wasn't going to eat it anyways.

Much to my surprise, tilting his head, Darkwater cut into the filet. After all Amon had made it, and it smelled amazing. The look on his face was one of happy surprise as he chewed. He had never eaten at FA's. The mild, delightful shock wore off his face as he noticed my grin. He followed suit.

"This is amazing. I see why you like this place. Of course, I've been in here but never to eat," Darkwater said as he nodded to Trish.

The food let the tension out of the air as we both sat and ate in silence for a few minutes.

"Councilman Darkwater, this is the second time I've heard

the Thule Society mentioned today. Listen, I have enough heat on me right now. Plus, this storm—I'm not sure if this is the time or place."

"That makes it the perfect time. Everyone thinks you're probably hiding out with Carvel chasing you mindlessly around. He's a handful, enough of one to cause you a headache. I'm on the intelligence committee. I don't deal with the security piece. I know things. For example, I know you don't have anything to do with the demon that showed up other than blindly registering him, unbinding the creature. Yes, I know all about that," Darkwater said as Trish walked over with a glass of red wine, sitting it in front of him.

Trish looked over as I shook my head, needing to be focused. I was not going to let my guard down. Well, maybe in a few minutes.

"I'm not looking for any more trouble. I'll help Ned and get that package delivered. We may need to check the weather," I said, having a gut feeling he was being honest with me for the most part.

"Perfect, and here I thought this would be difficult. The weather is stalling south of Daytona overnight, and the drive north should be safe. I have arranged for you and my escort to gate back to the Atheneum."

"I think I'll gate on my own," I said, reminding myself to grab a gate stone from the Evergate in the Postern.

"Of course. Well, either way. The weather looks good heading north tomorrow. It's settled. I'll have a car to pick you up at 11:00 a.m. sharp. I'll call Ned after we wrap up here."

Running an errand was easy; I had other questions. "Why was Marlow Goolsby in your office? He came out in a huff," I said, figuring this would be my chance to see where Councilman Darkwater stood with things.

"Ah, yes. Mr. Goolsby. Not the biggest fan of yours. He respects you, though. You are very forward. Tell you what. You are making this run easy for me, so I'll tell you something, and you can share it with your friends."

I didn't like the way he said "friends." That meant he didn't see Ed and the rest of the team as such. He did, however, respect Ned as a peer. He respected power. I knew the type from my time in the military. I was just a tool. He wanted to have lunch and make sure I was cognizant enough to make a special delivery for him. I nodded my head, and Darkwater leaned forward, lowering his voice.

"The Transitions Office that is causing you so much trouble was initially a project Marlow Goolsby was asked to work on as a bridge between the regular and Mage population. Did you know that?"

The look on my face answered his questions. "Goolsby is a thug. Why would they want him involved in anything?"

The slight huff Darkwater let out told me that I was once again not fully seeing the big picture. "What he does is a service to both worlds. Like it or not, he is one of the few people in the world that works in both spaces. His business dealings since the death of his brother have become more distant. He is now on the board of Mags-Tech. Soon to be one of the biggest companies in the world when it comes out."

"All right, I get it. Let's get to the point," I said, thinking he was having fun stringing me on.

He drew back and grinned, the smile not reaching his eyes. "The Transitions Office four weeks ago was pulled from him. He was shut out of the workings of the office. Given a pat on the back and seat on the new Council. What you need to know is that he was not very happy about it. I'm sure you have heard about his hidden temper by now."

"Again, the point," I said, sharpening my voice.

"It's not that it happened, but the why. A program getting taken over from its founders is not out of the norm. The Council pulled the management of the program from the civilian governments. The thinking is that it can be weaponized by the civilian governments and used for targeting. The information is too important to just hand over to anyone. That's not the point, though. The point is what the information will be used for by the Council or who gets it. Goolsby was not happy to get rid of it, and when it went live, the implications became quickly obvious. You know, pass the bill and read it later. Three of his clients who had registered went missing soon thereafter. Much like your gate Mages." Darkwater took a sip of his drink. "How ironic, an office developed by the Council to be ran by regulars, only to be taken back over by the Council and used for the exact reason they worried about."

He said it again: "Your." I had a feeling he felt separated from the situation. It was also a way people spoke when they had an interest in the subject.

"I get the danger of the office. Most Mages and Ethereals that I've talked to don't like it. Why don't you just shut it down?" It was a valid question.

"The Council is much larger than you think. You saw a piece of it. While Mages and the like are not as prevalent as you would think, the world and the Plane are large places. Anyways the recommendation went up this morning to shut it down. You will hear about it soon. It came up after Carvel pulled you from duty," Darkwater said as he let out a breath.

"How are the registrations being intercepted?" I asked, having trouble figuring this piece out.

Councilman Darkwater nodded his head, his slight grin finally reaching eyes. "Intercepted? Novel thought. That is the part of this that I'll leave with you. Maybe talk with Goolsby."

That was it; the lunch was over, and we were standing up, shaking hands. The overall meeting was not what I thought it would be. I went to meet about doing a job for Ned and came away with some information.

I walked over to the bar as he left. Mouth, who had been standing at the door the whole time, smirked at me.

"That was interesting," I said as Trish walked over. I sat at the far end of the bar and pulled out my phone as she leaned over.

"I can't get a read on him," Trish said. "He seems nice enough. Noticeably young for a Councilman."

"That's the thing. Everyone keeps saying the same thing about him. I need to get with the team. Can I get a coffee to go?"

Trish walked over, stirring a packet of Fae honey into the cup as I showed my pearly whites, smiling at her. "I could kiss you," I said, winking.

"You'd fall in love, and I'd fall asleep," Trish countered, leaning over and giving me a light peck on the cheek. She smelled like sun beaming down on fresh-cut grass.

I had finally started getting a paycheck around Christmas last year; Gramps had left me an account as well. The two allowed me one paid cup of Fae honey coffee per month. Trish would ever so often sneak me a cup free of charge.

The phone call I made to Ed was needed. I apologized and told him Belm was stopping by later, plus the information about Goolsby.

Ed had a way of deescalating things. He said he understood and jokingly said he didn't like it when he was fired from his first job either. I don't think he had ever been fired from anything. I needed to get out of the Atheneum for a while, and between talking with Kim and having lunch, I was feeling better.

The group text went out, this time having everyone meet at the Transitions Office. The weather had proven for another slow day. I sent a text to Belm as well to see if he could meet us early. He replied, as always, with an emoji, this time a cat followed by several music notes.

An hour later the team met in the Transitions Office: Frank, Kim, Belm, Phil, Ed, Jenny, Jamison, and Petro. Dr. Freeman stayed at the office to make sure nobody touched anything.

The storm was blowing outside, and I was feeling drained from gating so much lately. I needed some of that snake-oil potion of Phil's to wake me up.

"Right, Max, fill us in your lunch date," Ed started, generating a snicker from the team. Petro was perched on my shoulder wearing a thoughtful look on his face, not saying much.

I filled the group in on everything. Most of it was old news, but some of it perked the ears up of a few people. When I let Petro know I was leaving in the morning, he said he was going to work on something for me with the other Pixies and took off.

"Bruther, so you're saying Mages or some daft Ethereal is doing this kidnapping," Phil bellowed as he stroked his beard.

Belm spoke up in his raspy voice. "Seems to me that you have two problems that are related. Bo being summoned and showing up at the wrong places at the wrong times, and the actual kidnapping of the gate Mages. I talked to him this morning. As much as he can hold back information, he can't lie, especially to me. He has nothing to do with their kidnapping. I'll tell you what I did find out. Whoever summoned him here works with the Transitions Office. He figures since the Gate Mages being kidnapped are somehow linked to the Transitions Office, if he can find the next gate

Mage to get yanked, he can more than likely, through whatever means necessary, find a way to his summoner."

"Why is it such a big deal, and why can't he just go find them like he finds everyone else?" I asked, clearly seeing why demons were not at the top of everyone's Christmas card list.

Belm hacked up a laugh as Jamison rolled his eyes, speaking up. "Whoever summoned Bo is immune to his tracking and various other sources of his influence. If Bo manages to kill his summoner, then he is free and unbound. You just freed him up with the registration to do other things. He is still tied to his summoner—I found that out today. You may want to get that information to the Council, tell them to calm their tits about Max."

"Another thing," Belm rasped. "Anyone talk to Mr. Goolsby yet? His name came up, and I'm not sure why. Something Bo said about 'one of them.'"

Ed raised an eyebrow, looking over at Jenny. "Max, you said you are leaving tomorrow. I think Jenny and I will be paying Mr. Goolsby a visit."

The rest of the group mumbled approvingly over the rumbling of distant thunder. Frank was oddly quiet and gated back to the Atheneum after Belm finished.

"That reminds me," Kim spoke up, having walked over sitting beside me. "I'll check the weather and road reports for the morning. Maybe let the state police know you will be driving through the area, just in case."

Honestly, I hadn't thought about backup or any help with my run tomorrow. "Sure," I said, seeing the calculating look on Ed's face.

"Max, you do know there are people who want that artifact. Plus, it is tied to gate magic. You should probably be on your toes tomorrow. If you weren't under Councilman

Darkwater's safeguard, I would insist on one of us going along," Ed said as the rest of the group slowly nodded in affirmation.

"Sure, I'll be in the dining room at 10:00 a.m. getting ready. I'm taking the Judge with me." That elicited another round of head nods. To Ed's point of being under Darkwater's protection, it meant he was bound to not let any harm come to me of his own will. When Ned agreed to my use, they both bound a spell to the paper that noted the marker. Just like going to one of those sleazy prepay-check car title shops, however much more elegant and lethal.

After talking about my trip for a few more minutes, we landed on using the linked communicators in case something happened. I also noted to the group I was taking a stone from the Evergate.

We all said our goodbyes, going separate ways through the gate, Jamison and Belm heading to FA's. *Lucky bastards*, I thought heading home to get some much-needed rest and practice in. After all, I still had homework...

CHAPTER 12

A Medium-Size Favor

I walked into the dining room to see the group sitting around the table working. The bag I had slung over my shoulder clunked on the table, getting everyone's attention.

"Is someone eating curry at 10:00 a.m. in the morning?" I asked, smelling the strong aroma of spices.

Dr. Freeman, who spent most of his time in the stacks or crucible room, pointed his short, pudgy finger at Phil. Upon closer examination a yellow streak was sitting on his beard, obviously being saved for later. He looked like he hadn't gotten much sleep last night and was having dinner-breakfast.

"Morning, bruther. Oy, I'm paying for it also. My stomach's in knots. Just took some of that pink stuff. Pepto something. That's a strong potion," Phil said as I shook my head, watching him clean the mess out of his beard.

"Anyone see Petro this morning?" I asked. He wasn't at breakfast, and I guessed he was on a hot date last night.

Jenny walked over, smiling and holding out a long towel.

"Here. Petro and the girls stayed up all night finishing your staff. It's done and just like you wanted. They used your notes. He said to call him before you left so he could show you how to use it, and I also think he's planning on tagging along."

I opened the towel and held the staff in my hand, feeling the raw power coming off it. "Damn. If they used my notes, then I should be able to figure it out."

I sat it next to my bag, opening it up and pulling out the Judge and Durundle, the famous flaming sword of the First Coast Riot that almost burned down Marlow Goolsby's restaurant.

I was already dressed in my enchanted blue corduroy blazer that I had received from the team on my re-birthday last year. Yes, that's the year that your body either does or does not start doing magic. The Mage community called it your re-birthday, and it always landed on one's thirtieth birthday. The blazer could hide things and had a mild protective element to it. When I was shot in the shoulder last year, only the tip of the round broke my skin.

The holster for the Judge, while concealed underneath, had some weight to it, not like the enchanted sheath for the sword that magically made the blade appear and disappear. The only thing I had hanging off the modified pistol strap I wore that you could see or feel, was the sword handle and hilt. It took up as much space as my service pistol.

"Looks like you listened last night," Ed said, sipping a cup of tea and standing over Jenny's shoulder as she typed on her keyboard. "We're heading to see Mr. Goolsby as soon as you leave. By the way, Kim called and said the weather is going to pick back up this evening, so you should get back as soon as possible. She also wants you to stay close to your phone. I have a feeling she may be in the area just in case. The storm is likely to become a category 4 or 5 hurricane and is heading this way. We will need to take some precautions at some point."

"You mean like get bread and milk," I said, being a smart-ass.

"No, Max. Storms are strong natural occurrences." Jenny cleared her throat to correct Ed.

"All right, usually natural occurrences. It will have some effects on the wards around the property, and as stated, it sometimes covers for more nefarious things as people generally leave or are evacuated. A good portion of Jacksonville and most of St. Augustine are to be evacuated by noon tomorrow if you live in the coastal area or a flood zone," Ed said, walking over and looking at the Judge.

"Got it. I'll be back. I stocked up on beer after the ball. There was a bunch left over, so I grabbed it." Phil smiled at my statement, as did Ed.

"Petro." I breathed into the charm as he came zipping around the corner in his leather armor.

"Hey, boss" was all he said. There were two things I had learned about Petro. First, if he didn't ask and just came, I couldn't say no, and he played that game well. Secondly, he knew that I had seen the staff and was waiting for a compliment. He was squirming and dusting, waiting to hear my opinion.

"This is amazing. I don't know how you did it," I said, picking up the staff and seeing a grin spread across his face. "Is it just like my notes?"

"Yes, sir, everything down to the invocations. The only thing we had to work on was the tracker. We couldn't get a charm to work well enough over distance, so you will have to either touch it to the object or shoot it with the invocation," Petro buzzed as I added it to the inside pocket of my blazer. "We tested it on the smart lady—I mean Jenny—this morning."

"What he's saying," Jenny said, "is they would have

needed to cut a piece off the staff in order to make it work. That would have broken the enchantment on it originally. The girls told me this morning the thing is enchanted. Couldn't explain how or what. Just that it is."

"That's another thing, boss. Like she was saying, it seems to have something else enchanted into it. It's harmless unless you know how to invoke it. We'll figure it out later. It may be nothing but extra power storage like your castor."

"Fair enough. Thanks. This means a lot, Petro. Jenny, tell Macey and Lacey I owe them one. All right, my ride should be here any minute. I'll keep the communicator on," I said, seeing Petro acting like he was ignoring the situation.

"Yes, Petro, you can come," I said, the dust from his wings floating in front of me. "Listen, I don't want anyone to know you're around. Can you keep out of sight?"

"Sure thing, boss. Consider it done. I was planning on it anyways."

The sound of the newly installed buzzer vibrated the room. Got to love technology. The alert actually sounded like a cheap gong from a 1980s video game. It went off anytime someone pulled up in front of the building.

"Shall we come out and meet your date?" Phil asked, standing up. I knew he was going outside anyways. Jenny snickered as Ed shook his head. I looked around, noticing Petro had already disappeared.

Out front sat a large black SUV, much like the ones important politicians or the marshals used. It was obviously armored and made for transporting significant things and people. What happened next set the tone for the rest of the trip.

The door opened as the vehicle rose a couple of inches. Mouth stepped out and grunted. Every time I saw him, the sheer mass of his body took me by surprise.

Phil let out a breath followed by a quick laugh as he lit up a cigarette.

"Hey, Mouth, where's the better half of the power couple?" I asked referring to Terrence, Phil's old guild friend and the man's apelike partner.

He stood there looking at me, the overhang of his eyebrows shadowing the look of irritation on his face. He let out a low, growling grunt, pointing to the passenger side.

"This is going to be great," I said, looking over at Phil and Ed.

"Be safe, and call if you need anything," Ed said, watching as the hulking man got back in the driver's seat.

The doors closed as the whisper-quiet interior of the vehicle took over. I thought I could hear his stomach making odd noises. He smelled like wet dirt or, as I would call it, mud. Earthy yet raw.

Reaching over, turning on the radio, I found the local rock station and turned it up slightly to fill the soundless void.

Mouth didn't like this, ramming his fist through the touch screen of the radio. His paw was the size of my head. Much to my enjoyment, the demonstration of strength only stuck the radio somehow on easy listening. A Lionel Richie song started playing.

The entire episode occurred before we even pulled out onto Highway 16. That's when the unexpected happened.

"I don't like you," Mouth said in a voice that sounded like the rumbling V-8 of an American muscle car. "You keep that face of yours shut, do the job, and we go our separate ways." It took him a rather long time to get the entire sentence out.

"You don't work for Darkwater, do you?" I asked, figuring

out he was not happy to be here and was also clearing a marker for his boss. Mouth just grunted again, ramming his fist into the hole where the radio used to be in an attempt to finally kill it, only to have it switch to a local country station.

We both let out a sigh and said, "Shit" at the same time. I held my hand to the crater he had made in the new dashboard and pushed a little will into the space as the radio took its final breath. Mouth let out a snort of approval. We drove up I-95 in silence.

The fact that I was unnervingly relaxed about the run should have been the first warning sign that things were about to go very wrong. It never fails when I'm given a normal job or task that it would more than likely end up in something catching on fire or worse.

Turning off I-95, we headed west, north of Fort Stewart. I knew the area well, spending most of my time in the army here. We were driving out to the middle of nowhere down a two-lane road covered in trees, the branches swaying cutting through the air.

Mouth rumbled up out of nowhere. "I don't like this" was all he said.

"You know where we're going?" I asked, actually glad he had said something even though it wasn't good.

"Yes, the Repository. It's north of the base," he growled. "The artifact is being secured with help from the civilian government, that's all I know. This is the back way to get th—"

The initial blast came out of the tree line, pushing the large SUV off the road, sliding on the damp pavement. The storm was large, the rain reaching the Savannah area as well. Mouth corrected the spin of the vehicle, pushing the accelerator hard on the road and avoiding a large tree. The side street we turned on was unpaved and red with clay, the truck sliding as he gunned the large engine, pushing the button to engage the four-wheel drive.

"You think it's good going off the route!" I screamed, the sound of trees cracking coming from behind us.

"Doesn't matter. If you have a gun, get it out," Mouth said. I could hear the strength of his hands gripping the steering wheel. This wasn't some elaborate show. He was trying to get us out of the ambush and didn't know what was going on.

I touched my ear, talking out loud into the communicator but only hearing static.

"Not going to work. The truck's warded against magic, or I would have already called," Mouth said, followed up by what I believe was some type of insult to my intelligence.

"Petro," I yelled as the eight-inch hero came flying out of the hole in the dashboard. "You've been in there the whole time?" I asked, shocked. There was the loud crack of a tree falling beside the SUV as we drove.

"Yup, and I thought I was a goner for sure. Your pal here knew I was back there and did that on purpose," Petro said, jumping on the dash and looking around.

Mouth snorted. "I hate Pixies."

"I thought we had a moment, and here you go trying to kill my friends," I said, pulling out the Judge and seeing an actual grin come across his face.

"Hey, boss, there are two or three Mages. They're gating in and out all around us shooting spells. Not sure how they're doing it," Petro said. He was good at figuring out what type of magic was being used, almost like a bloodhound.

Mouth started to grumble again. "Your cell should work. It's not magic, is it? You idiot."

At the end of his sentence, a large rock the size of a small car dropped out of thin air onto the hood of the SUV, slamming it to a sliding halt in the wet clay. Petro, while able to fly, hit the windshield hard, creating a small crack, knocking him out momentarily.

Mouth had the steering wheel in his hand bent in half, the airbag covering his face. I tasted blood in my mouth. There wasn't a passenger side airbag, and if I were to guess, it had been removed for some upgrade.

It felt like an eternity when in reality, the whole ambush had lasted only a couple of minutes. A few seconds passed before my head started clearing.

I felt a large hand pulling me out of the shattered passenger side window. On instinct I pulled up the Judge and squeezed the trigger. Nothing happened. Was it broken?

After a handful of seconds, the fog in my head completely dissolved. Mouth was standing there with an MP5 in one hand and the other on my shoulder. "Stupid" was all he said. I glanced over to see Petro still unconscious.

I looked down, figuring the pistol had judged Mouth to be on my side.

"You ever point that thing at me again, and I'll kill you," he said pointing the MP5 into the tree line, letting out a bark of rounds, *tat, tat, tat, tat,* in several controlled trigger squeezes. He knew how to handle a weapon.

With his threat, the Judge would probably go off next time, I thought to myself. Getting in position behind the rock, we both sat there for a few seconds letting the silence tell us our aggressor's position. I figured Petro was in the armored vehicle; it wasn't on fire, so I opted to focus on the immediate problem.

"Hello," I whispered into my communicator. Mouth was doing the same thing into some type of hand radio.

"I can hear you. Where are you?" Phil's voice came over

the radio. "We can't get a lock on your location."

As I started to talk, a bolt of lightning streaked above our heads followed by two loud thumps of spells hitting the SUV.

I reached in my pocket, ensuring the Evergate stone was still there. It was.

A spatter of gunfire came from the MP5 again as I reached over the hood looking for a target.

"Hey there, big guy. I have an idea."

Mouth looked over, pulling out a boomerang from under his coat. He blew out as it lit up. The following throw was impressive. The sound of the weapon cut through the air.

"I have a gate stone. Let's get in the back, grab the artifact, and gate back to the Atheneum," I said, finally seeing one of our attackers step out from behind a tree.

My heart sank. It was the shooter from last year that had worked with the Eater, whom Belm had impaled and Chloe had shot, and whose body went missing. It started to line up. Pearl was the one throwing the lightning. It was the Thule Society.

Rage filled my thoughts as I pulled up the Judge. The man was distracted by something in the other direction. I pulled up the pistol and fired. The boom was so loud that the rest of the scene went silent. Mouth raised an eyebrow and looked as the man exploded into dust. The Judge had made up its mind. Death—not the type that lends itself to mourners but total destruction.

The cadence of Mouth's MP5 started back up as lightning hit the rock, chipping away at it. A cloaked figure was coming out of the opposite tree line, exposing us to the spell about to leave their hands. I then saw what had distracted the now-dead shooter, as we called him before.

Petro came streaking out of the tree line like a laser, sword out, sticking it into the person's face like a lawn dart. It was the eye thing I had heard so much about. I was about to throw up when a large hand grabbed my arm, snapping me back to reality and away from the body Petro was flying from. He must have gotten up during the confusion and gone to work.

I was losing track of time. Pulling out the staff, I released the stunning spell into a dark patch of bushes that was moving, generating a muffled "Omf."

There were more spells coming at the vehicle, and it appeared the number of our attackers was growing. Mouth lurched me over to the vehicle, cramming me through the front passenger door. He was right behind me as I crawled over to the back seat. Petro was already inside. The artifact was in a wooden and iron crate the size of a mailbox.

The SUV was warded, and the spells hitting it, while making dents, weren't getting through. The front driver's and passenger side windows were shattered, allowing us to see out and return fire. Mouth was leaning forward shooting at random targets. I was more calculated, lining up a few precise shots, landing one more with the same results as earlier.

Before I could start wondering where the boomerang was, it lodged itself in the seat in front of Mouth covered in blood. "Jesus," I said, fully understanding our situation.

The smell of ozone, burnt copper, and gasoline filled the air, overtaking the odor of the burning submachine gun barrel. I was used to the smell of carbon and guns being fired. It was comforting, but not in the back of an SUV surrounded by angry Mages.

A loud boom shook the vehicle as the back windshield shattered into a thousand pieces. Petro flew to my hand, and I pulled out the Evergate stone, grabbed Mouth by the arm, and put some will into it. Nothing happened. This was supposed to work. Mouth looked over at me, taking a deep breath, the realization that things were getting worse setting in.

He pulled out another clip, growling, "Last one."

"Petro, the tracking spell in the staff. You tested it on Jenny, right?" I asked, having an idea. Phil was talking in the background, still trying to figure out our location.

With the front windows shattered, both the communicator in my ear and Mouth's powered by Etherium were now working inside the SUV.

Mouth's radio was also chirping with voices. The people had been talking to us; however, we had been too busy fighting to notice.

"Sure did. We tested it on the..." Petro trailed off, flying into my blazer pulling out the staff. "*Sequor*," Petro yelled, holding the staff as Mouth started back up, firing in single-shot mode to conserve ammunition.

Jenny's voice came over the radio. "Locked sending location."

Petro had linked the staff to Jenny, and when activated, it only took seconds to triangulate our location. It must have worked both ways. He was going to get two boxes of Golden Grahams when we got back. If we got back.

Pearl stepped out of the tree line as the last empty click of the MP5 resonated in the vehicle.

Mouth huffed, reaching to grab his boomerang. He wouldn't last in front of Pearl.

Just as Pearl raised his hands, several gates opened all around the vehicle. There was the thud of a body landing on the roof.

"Kiss my arse, powder boy," came the voice of Phil as the distinctive sound of two fully automatic shotguns filled the air. I could smell the lit cigarette he had hanging out his mouth. Pearl loosed a bolt of lightning, only to be stopped by the shield Ed threw up in front of Phil.

Frank took off into the trees in a whirlwind of blurring speed. Mouth, as if he'd planned this, burst from the SUV rejuvenated, the door flying off in his rage. We were back in business and on the offense.

They had used a combination of the Evergate and the tracking beacon to find and gate to us.

Ed lifted his hands, forming a spell, when a green ball of light came out of a dark spot in the tree line, hitting him in the side. His shield dropped as Phil jumped off the roof dropping the shotguns, landing on the ground with a glowing sledgehammer in his hands. The boys were back in town.

I mustered the last of my resolve, jumping through the hole in the vehicle Mouth had created, pulling out Durundle and yelling, "*Ignis!*" The blade roared to life, the same as it had at the Blue House. It was the first time since then it had done so.

Phil charged Pearl as the hiss of another green ball of goo slammed into the tree behind him. Phil was glowing, having fully charged his strength. He was strong, the type of strong that could knock down a building. As he was about to make contact, Pearl simply vanished, leading Phil to slam into the trees, knocking several over.

Mouth had found someone, and by the sounds of the crunching bones, he was doing fine. I heard several other pops as the attackers were gating out of the fight.

The green spells were still coming from a dark spot in the tree line as the person throwing them finally noticed me, sending two in my direction. I lifted the sword, the blade taking the first blast while the other flew overhead, missing me by inches.

Ed was on the ground, alive but injured. Petro stayed in the vehicle, having done enough. The sounds of police sirens echoed in the background as I pointed the sword at the tree line, willing it to throw fire at the void space.

Bloodred flame erupted out of the blade as it met its mark. Frank, also seeing the attacker, distracted them long enough for my shot to land. The screams of a woman filled the air as Frank came flying through the air toward the vehicle.

The thing about hellfire is that it sticks to everything it touches, not like normal fire where if something doesn't catch, it will fade out. Hellfire burns till it's done, like napalm.

In the now-lit space flailed the figure of a woman pulling a burning cloak off her head. It was Chloe. She looked up, the rest of her body engulfed in flames as she disappeared through a gate.

The silence that followed was accompanied by the settling of falling trees and the crackle of fire on damp wood. Petro buzzed out of the truck, flying over to Ed, who had finally sat up.

Mouth came pounding out of the tree line holding a man's arm and throwing it on the ground. Did he have blood on his mouth? Where was the rest of the man? I had questions.

Frank stood up, dusting himself off while Phil cussed up a storm in a pile of trees that had crashed down on him after his impact. The scent of burning wood and gunfire filled the air. The spells cast by Chloe lent a strong sulfur smell to the air.

I stood there taking in the chaos of the scene. The area was destroyed. The SUV was cratered as the engine finally started smoking. The rock that had fallen on the vehicle was covered in dark marks from Pearl. During the excitement I hadn't noticed the side we had been fighting from was also covered in spell scores of various types.

I was starting to feel set up again and further resolved to figure out Chloe's part in this. Seeing her after all this time had shocked and also focused me. The gatecrystal was obviously connected to the missing gate Mages. The Thule Society was behind the disappearances. I was sure of it. They were using the Mages and the gatecrystal, to do whatever it was without detection and quickly. The Thule Society must have been moving large quantities of equipment or people.

A tree went flying by, Phil finally standing up and walking out of the mess. He was covered in clay and grime, pulling out a bent cigarette and trying to light it.

Mouth was on the radio taking instructions from what sounded like Darkwater. "Yes, it's secured, yes, no" was the last thing he said.

Three black SUVs like the one we had arrived in pulled up with the lights on. The marshals had arrived. Kim and Ben both jumped out of the trucks, looking around in shock. Good thing they never saw what we actually did to the Fountain of Youth and just heard about it.

I wasn't sure how they got here so fast, but I was starting to think they had been staged in the area. As always, I was the last to find out about it. I reached in my pocket, pulling out my phone, flipping the ringer off silent. The phone chirped happily with text messages, several from Kim telling me she was coming up and would be in the area and another stating that they received a call of heightened Etherium levels in the area.

I had shut my ringer off by accident. *I wasn't the last to know after all*, I thought to myself, walking over.

"Let me guess; you didn't get my messages," she said as Ben looked around speechless.

"Yup" was all I got out.

Kim shook her head and directed the other marshals to sweep the perimeter. They carried some type of custom submachine guns with dark-blue clips in them.

"New fall colors?" I asked, finally patting myself down and taking stock to see if I had any injuries. Of course, I did. Looking down, I saw there was a dark-red patch on my jeans looking like melted skin.

Kim grimaced as the pain started to set in. I could still walk, and the wound must have been some type of superficial burn. I had been hit by a stray bolt of Pearl's lightning; a full-on hit would have been catastrophic. It was easy to see why Ed had been cautious last year.

In all the excitement, I forgot that Ed had been directly hit in the side with one of Chloe's spells.

We all converged on him at the same time. Mouth was still by the SUV.

"Ed, you all right?" I asked, seeing the look of subdued pain on his face. He was hurt but too proud to show it.

"Nothing a few cocktails and a warm shower can't fix," Ed chuckled lightly, deciding on not doing so again. The spell had hit him directly in the side of his chest, his ribs looking out of place and blackened. The smell of burnt flesh stuck to him.

"Bruther, give me the Evergate stone. I need to get him to a hospital and to Jenny," Phil said as Petro hovered over Ed, lightly dusting the wound. Earlier in the year, I had cut my hand learning how to use a sword. Petro did the same thing, soothing the wound, his dust acting like a mild pain reliever.

"A hospital?" I asked, figuring he would just take a potion and be fine.

Phil looked over, shaking his head. "Can't magic blood, and he looks like he is giving it out like candy on Halloween."

I handed Phil the Evergate stone without question as he scooped up Ed, walking through the gate back to the Postern and the Atheneum. You could hear Jenny on the communicators in the background. She was waiting for them, yelling at Phil to get his ass moving. I shut my communicator off.

Petro was breathing heavily; he had a slight char mark on his wing. Standing on the hood of the SUV, he was checking himself out and giving me a thumbs-up while making a smelly face and pointing at my leg.

Frank came over next with the two other marshals. "The area is cleared; they're gone."

Kim looked at the two men holding a bag of what looked like jewelry and a few handguns. "This was all we found, ma'am. Whatever hit those two over by the large pine tree evaporated them except for what's in this bag, mostly the metal stuff," the taller marshal said, handing it to Ben.

"Yeah, about that," I said, pulling out the Judge and checking the chamber; it was empty.

Kim raised an eyebrow and pointed at the gun and then the two piles of gore.

"Yup," I said, motioning Mouth over.

"What do you want?" he growled, obviously not in a good mood. For him I was guessing this was a super-not-good mood.

"Let's pack that thing up and get out of here," I said, looking at the arm sitting on the ground behind him.

"We still got a delivery to make. Since our inconspicuous trip was found out, we might as well have an escort," Mouth said, looking at Kim for approval.

She slowly nodded, looking over at me and rolling her eyes. Did Mouth just use a five-syllable word?

"Max," Kim said as we got out of earshot. "You look like hell. Someone knew you were coming and your route. From what I understand, that vehicle, once the doors are closed, isn't traceable by magic."

I stood there for a minute, watching as Mouth unloaded the cargo, walking it over to the SUV. Frank had walked up behind me and, in true V style, made me jump.

"Sorry, Max," Frank said in his smooth yet overly normal voice. "Couldn't help but overhearing," he said as Kim and I huffed, knowing vampires have amazingly heightened senses. "If what you are saying is true, they must have been using magic. You can't just pop in and out of gates like that, even using the latest e-tech. I bet someone got their hands on that vehicle or something one of you owns. Hell, it could be the artifact. I can smell it from here."

"That's the thing," I started. "The whole point of doing it now was to throw everyone off just in case. Plus, with the storm, Darkwater was assuming no one would be paying attention. It was planned for next week."

We talked for a few more minutes trying to solve all the world's problems when Mouth walked back over. "You ready, cowboy?"

Cowboy? I thought. *Was that a compliment?* I grinned as he followed up the sentence with affirmation that he did, in fact, not like me.

"I want to get this delivered so I don't have to look at your ugly face one more minute. It would make me happy to punch you in the face," Mouth drawled out, the entire conversation taking way too long to have any lingering effects. I could hear his fists closing.

Kim and I talked for a few more minutes as Frank and Petro jumped in the SUV with us. The marshals would follow along. I asked if it was OK for anyone to drive one of their SUVs. Apparently Council business was officially…well, official. She cleared the scene, tagging the destroyed vehicle for pickup.

The rest of the drop off was as smooth as we hoped it would be. The facility was bland and indistinct. There was a mix of military and CSA agents waiting on us; I made sure to thank them for their lack of help. That at least got a smirk out of Mouth.

Frank and Petro rode back with Kim; the smell from the wound on my leg was not sitting well with the two. It did have a strong odor; I needed to get it looked at. Maybe a drink first, though.

Passing I-295 south of downtown, my phone rang. It was Phil's ringtone. He had left a message several months ago while he was highly intoxicated at some bar in Miami while I was helping with a case. He had sung the first verse of "Friends in Low Places," by Garth Brooks, in his thickest drunk Irish accent. I had recorded it. It was a real crowd pleaser. Mouth didn't think it was funny.

"Bruther, Ed's stable, and Jenny's waiting on you. There are also a few people here to see you of the Council type," Phil said, letting me know to have my game face on. "Ed's out, so Ned is here as well. It's that Darkwater fella and Carvel."

"Thanks. Make sure there's cold beers in the ice bin. See you a few," I said, making kissy noises to really piss Mouth off. Phil, as he always did when I made those noises, called me some weird Irish cuss word and hung up.

People who have never served in the military, or police for that matter, oftentimes are lost on humor like that. At the end of the day, everyone's one big family, like it or not. Mouth grabbed the steering wheel, making the plastic under the leather crack.

CHAPTER 13

Gates and Gravestones

"You listen to me," Mouth said, the tires of the SUV crunching on the gravel drive in front of the Atheneum. "We aren't friends. Let me ask you a question. Why do you think those people attacked us today?"

"To get the artifact," I said, taken back by Mouth's sudden outburst of conversation.

"You are stupid, aren't you?" he growled, bringing the vehicle to a stop.

The day had worn on me, and I was tired of the insults. "Listen, I've had enough of you calling me stupid. Either you spit it out, or we have a problem on our hands."

Mouth raised an eyebrow, letting out a deep breath through his nose. "At least you have some type of backbone. About time."

I was starting to think all he respected was brute force and violence. Then I realized he was trying to tell me something. He just didn't want me to think that it meant anything.

"The reason we were attacked today was not because of some stupid artifact. It was actually delivered an hour earlier. They came for you."

"What do you mean the artifact was delivered earlier?" I said, looking over at Mouth, his eyes locked on the front of the building.

"You are daft. We were a diversion. I figured it out when I got in the vehicle. An artifact as powerful as the gate crystal would make the hairs on your arm stand on end. The little stick, sword, and gun you carry is enough to make my skin crawl. It makes you a showy beacon," Mouth said, trudging through the conversation as the other vehicles started pulling up behind us.

"I didn't think about it, but you're right. I must have been ignoring the lack of support or interest in the shipment," I said, putting the pieces together. "Do you think someone set this up to have me killed?"

"That's the second most reasonable thing you've said all day" was the last thing Mouth uttered as he cut the ignition. You could see the imprints of his hands on the steering wheel.

Terrence was standing there with a tense, disheveled expression on his face. He looked like he had just received bad news and wasn't happy about it.

Mouth walked up to his partner as they both looked back at me still in the SUV. I was texting Phil, thinking he would be outside.

My texting was interrupted by Petro hovering outside the window, dinking his sword off the armored glass.

"Hey, Petro," I said, finally stepping out after not seeing a response from Phil. "Where's Frank?"

"He's all vamped out. Frank's not getting out of the SUV

until Angel gets here. She is gating in shortly," Petro said, motioning me to hold out my hand so he could land. The wind was picking up, and, as Kim said, the weather was going to truly start getting bad.

"Gents," Kim said, making me jump from behind the vehicle. She stood there with Ben and the two marshals from earlier, one holding the bag of what was left from the ambush. "Where do you want this?"

"It stinks," Petro gasped. He had an excellent sense of smell and blood or anything close to that made him ill. It seemed to throw him off. He didn't ride back with me due to the smell of the injury on my leg. Oh, yeah, about that...

As soon as the thought crossed my mind, the burnt, crisp area on my upper leg started to howl with pain.

"Just take it inside to the evidence room," I said, distracted by the pain now riding up my leg. "You sticking around?" I asked Kim.

"No, the weather's getting worse. We're heading to the field office in Jacksonville before the bridges are shut down. You need to get that leg checked out," Kim said, taking the phone out of her pocket and shaking it at me to ensure I let her know what was going on.

While the sound of wind and rustling trees filled the air outside, the shouts of Phil occupied the main entrance. It was coming from the back offices. The new security personnel had set up a desk, motioning us over to check in.

Petro flew over to the short, thin man's face. "I'll dust you so bad you'll fart sand for a month. Get out of our way," Petro said as I nodded, walking by.

I think the man was trying to figure out what the hell type of job he had landed. I made a mental note to stop by later and get the guy some coffee or a drink.

Mouth and Terrence stood outside the offices as Phil's voice boomed again. Terrence shook his head. "I wouldn't go in there."

I ignored the two goons, opening the door while Petro perched on my shoulder like a parrot. Phil, Carvel, Darkwater, and Ned all stood in the conference room. Ned was standing between Phil and Carvel.

"I'll beat you like your mother did" was the line in the sand from Phil that forced Ned to react.

"Enough. Phil, you will respect members of the Council, or you will not work for the Council."

I could tell while Ned was trying to cool the situation, he was a man of principle, and I couldn't argue with his logic. "What did I miss?" I asked, walking into the room as Phil marched over to the opposite side of the desks, taking Ned's advice.

"Max, I heard you were injured. Jenny will be back in a few minutes and needs to check you out," Ned said, looking down at my leg. In all fairness I was a mess. Mud on my blazer and pants. Bloodstains from the wound, and my boots were also caked in filth. Funny thing was, Mouth didn't appear to get an ounce of dirt on him the entire time.

"Yeah, I'm going to need to get this checked out soon. Carvel, Darkwater, to what do we owe the pleasure?" I said, looking at Ned to make sure I was good. He slightly nodded. If he didn't approve, he would have started talking.

Carvel spoke up first. "We had a report of a large battle not far from here. Spells, gates, and the death of several Mages, a troll, and apparently someone ripped the arms off a full-blooded Fae. You just happened to be there, much like when everything else in this part of the country goes bad."

"How do you know all this?" I asked, genuinely interested.

"We had a team from the repository check it out. They are working on getting the area secured and cleaned up," Carvel said as Darkwater relaxed his posture, showing his odd lack of concern.

"Hmm, right, you just figured all this out," I said, looking around.

"You, Pixie," Carvel spit out, his obvious dislike for Pixies showing. "How many people were there, and how many did not make it out? Oh, and do not spare the details on the type."

Petro, surprising me, spit out the information with pinpoint accuracy. I often took for granted how powerful and sensitive Pixies are to the environment. After all, he could smell me opening a box of Golden Grahams from the other side of the house.

"All right, I get it. Why are you here?" I asked, seeing the look on Carvel's face darken.

"I'm here to ensure you no longer are a threat to this establishment. If it wasn't for Ned's place on the Council, you would be having significantly more issues than you currently are. I think you tipped someone off to the shipment," Carvel said as Mouth and Terrence walked in.

"You don't have the authority," Ned spoke, putting his hand on Phil's chest as he started walking back over. Petro was oddly calm.

"You good, buddy?" I asked under my breath as Ned and Carvel continued to spit at each other, egos filling the room like fog off a warm river. Ned wasn't budging.

"Ah, whatever, boss, I could care less. Probably better off not dealing with these crazies," Petro said gently, actually not caring. I chuckled at his lack of worry, calming me down; a grin spreading across my face. That got everyone's attention.

Darkwater took a deep breath letting it out slowly. Carvel

started talking, his voice growing louder. "You smirk now. You have something to do with all this. That same group of Mages you staged that ambush with are also responsible for several robberies and recent assassinations by means of newly unregistered gates. All persons somehow tied to you. I find it odd you seem unscathed by the little tiff you just left."

I looked over at Ned. They hadn't told me this. Ned filled the silence. "Is Max under any clause of the accords that would make your statement valid?" Ned was going full boss mode.

Carvel looked over at Darkwater, who said, "I'm not part of this. I simply came by to check on everyone and to close my marker with Ned. I have no issue with Max. He did as asked. How and what happened in between, I could care less. Just that the end result was achieved," Darkwater said, wearing a neutral expression. He might as well have punched Carvel by the expression on his face.

"Max, Darkwater set your trip up so attention would not be paid to the main delivery. With every Tom, Dick, and Harry watching you, he knew that you doing something like this would draw everyone's consideration away from the true delivery," Ned said, nodding over to me.

"Correct assessment. This will conclude our business," Darkwater said as he handed Ned a gold-looking coin, a pop of ozone filling the air. "Gentlemen," he said, bowing his head and walking out of the room.

Carvel followed Darkwater out, turning before walking out the door. Phil didn't move and forced him to walk around. "We will be seeing you soon. This isn't over."

As the door shut behind the two men, all four of us just looked at each other. I passed out...

What seemed like a few seconds ended up being an hour. I could feel the breeze from Petro's wings on my face as the voice of Phil boomed, "Wake up, bruther, nap's over. Jenny just left.

You'll live to drink again. With me, that is, maybe."

"That was fun," I said as Petro landed on the back of the couch sitting in my office. "What happened?"

Petro made a ticking noise. "You passed out, and Phil brought you up here. I think he touched your guitar."

Phil looked over at Petro with the death stare. "Anyways, I don't think that Jenny and Ed got to make the trip over to see Mr. Goolsby."

I sat up, seeing my leg was lightly bandaged and I was wearing a plaid pair of tight shorts.

"These yours, Phil?" I asked, standing up and realizing my leg was still sore but supporting my weight.

Phil just grunted, snickering, as they were obviously too tight on me. Between my black Planes Drifter T-shirt and tight shorts, I looked like I was heading to a frat party.

"Your stuff's over there on the chair," Phil said, flinching at a loud clap of thunder.

"So Goolsby's still probably expecting them," I said out loud, going over, grabbing my blazer, and putting it on over my T-shirt. I walked into my room, grabbing a pair of sneakers and not taking off the shorts.

"Uh, you didn't hurt your head, did you, boss?" Petro asked, buzzing over.

I grabbed Durundle and put my castor on, looking at the two. "We're taking a little field trip."

It was a short walk from the gate under the Gate Bridge to Riverplace Tower. Phil was trying to talk me out of it or at least get me to put on some decent slacks.

Petro was in my blazer due to the weather. It had picked up, starting to lightly rain. A hurricane would do that. The wind would blow and thunder boom with no rain. The outer bands were firmly taking hold of the First Coast area.

"Bruther, I bet they aren't even here," Phil said loudly over the wind and thunder, the sounds of light rain starting to spatter on the pavement.

"Looks like they left the lights on to me," I said, pointing at the building and stepping into the street, mall-walking at top speed.

We walked through the side entrance only to find the security guard sitting at a table looking confused.

"Ed and Jenny to see Mr. Goolsby," I said, seeing the misperception in the man's face as he looked at Phil. I knew from last year that Goolsby's security system was top notch, and he more than likely already knew we were in the building.

The man didn't move as we walked over to the far elevator reserved for the Blue House. Goolsby's office was on the same floor. We walked into the elevator, hitting the thirteenth floor. Like before, the elevator lurched to life, going up more than thirteen floors. As the doors slid open, four heavily armed guards stood at the hostess stand, staring at us.

I repeated myself. "Ed and Jenny to see Mr. Goolsby." The men moved in on us, the tallest touching his ear, obviously being talked to.

The tall man let out a command as the others stopped. "Mr. Goolsby will see you. Please follow me." The man was over six-foot-five, much like the bartender we had encountered last year who just happened to be working tonight. The look on his face was stoic. I was betting he was a V. Lean, strong, and commanding.

We walked past the kitchen to a door as it opened. A woman in a suit was leaving the room. *Funny thing—you could hardly tell I about burned the place down last year*, I thought to myself. It was also odd to see people dressed up with a hurricane heading this way.

"Max, Phil, and?" Goolsby said, somehow knowing Petro was in my blazer.

"Come on out, Petro," I said as the tall, slender man ushered us the rest of the way in, closing the door.

"If you are going to come into my establishment against my wishes, you should at least abide by the dress code, Mr. Sand," Goolsby said in his stern yet smooth business voice.

"Yeah, well, things have been a little crazy today, and I think I'm one of them at this point," I said, not taking my eyes off the man. Phil looked uncomfortable around Goolsby, and I had never figured out why. Petro flew down, landing on a small table sitting beside the two chairs facing the desk.

"Let me be clear. I understand Ed was injured today. I agreed to meet with him and Dr. Simmons this afternoon. If it was not for that first fact, you would not be here," Goolsby said, setting his absolute authority while in his establishment. I couldn't argue the point after last year.

Seeing my understanding, he walked behind his desk, taking a seat, Phil and I following. Come to think about it, I did look ridiculous. I don't think I was fully awake or had planned this out prior to coming. I had a feeling Phil and Petro would get a laugh out of this later. Not thinking this completely through, I decided to throw out a softball.

"I take it you understand why the team wanted to talk to you?" I asked, taking a neutral tone.

"During a hurricane that is turning and heading our way, I have no clue. Obviously not to check on my well-being."

"I'm going to cut to the chase."

"As your reputation dictates," Goolsby followed.

"I had lunch with Councilman Darkwater yesterday. He

happened to mention your involvement in the Transitions Office." I decided to leave out the details he mentioned about his initial involvement to see how much Goolsby would give up.

Goolsby leaned back, opening a drawer and pulling out a bottle of scotch. I hated scotch. On the other hand, I noticed Phil sit up. Goolsby was opening another drawer, pulling out three glasses, looking back, and pulling out what looked to be a small cap. He was prepared for everything, even Pixies.

Without asking he poured the three glasses and cap with a few ounces of the top-shelf liquor.

"Mr. Sand—"

"Max," I interrupted.

"Max, you have yet to surprise me until today. I was waiting for your team to start figuring this out. I just didn't think it was going to be you."

I didn't know if that was an insult or a compliment, so I landed on the latter. He wanted to talk.

"What's the story? You know the Council is looking at shutting them down."

"Ah, yes, the Council," he said as he took a sip of the scotch, the three of us following suit. Phil let out a sigh. I had to admit for scotch, it was good. "First you have to understand what the name of the program that started the office truly was. It's something that has been around much longer than all of us. Something the Thule Society based all its crazy fanatics on."

"So you're saying you have nothing to do with that crew?" I asked, figuring I was about to hit the jackpot.

Goolsby laughed out loud, losing his composure for the first time. "I've spent my entire adult life fighting the very core of what they stand for. I may not be the most respected person in some circles, but even I have a moral compass. The office was based on a part of the old accords from the Plane called the Purity Law."

That got Petro's attention as he dusted lightly.

"Ah, your friend knows of it. The initial idea of the Transitions Office was to register and better understand the world outside of our own. The governments wanted to know who and what was out there. It was agreed upon by both parties to record and register everyone. Hell, we do it ourselves. Driver's licenses, passports, loans, even college admission. You have to have some type of history or record. Most Ethereals and Mages aren't exactly part of normal society. With gates and well…magic, not all these things are needed. When the Council approached the five major governments, this became an immediate threat to normal society, or at least a threat that was already there that many had not planned for. Some countries knew, however, and let the Council manage its own. This was possible mainly due to the small size and lack of public display. I'm sure you know that has all changed over the past several years."

"I get all this. How does the Purity Law come into play here?" I asked again, trying to get to the point.

"I'll get there. The United States led the way with the registration planning and process. A select handful of Council members were picked to work with the government and group of prominent people that dabbled in both worlds. With my brother's death, I was in charge of Mags-Tech. That is how I got involved."

Phil spoke up, finishing his drink and placing the empty glass in front of Goolsby. "Why the history lesson?" Phil asked, putting an unlit cigarette in his mouth. Goolsby looked at him, daring Phil to light it. Phil didn't.

"Don't be ignorant. You know my involvement in the

Order Society. We are here to preserve mankind's interests. What we do or how we do it is up for debate, but do not fool yourself about who is on the right side of things. The Council does the same thing for Ethereals, Mages, Fae, et cetera…Mags-Tech was created to help bridge that gap by my late brother Ezra without having to butcher who we are as a species. The Council for the most part is the same. The Thule Society is hell-bent on making a new master race of unstoppable monsters."

That got my attention. "You know, it's always the ones saying they are right that often find themselves on the wrong side of things at the end of the day," I said, garnering a nod of Goolsby's head. He didn't disagree.

"As I was saying. The Council does not like human involvement in correcting issues in this space. That is why there are oftentimes disagreements and at other times understanding and cohabitation. To finally answer you, when the Transitions Office was set up, a group of persons including myself wanted to know what exactly is out there. At first the Transitions Office sounded harmless. Then incidents started to happen almost instantly. The Council kept the occurrences from getting out. People and types of Mages that had never been realized before came out of hiding in hopes of acceptance. The first was a gentleman named Randy. He was a Mage of sorts, born to a half-Fae and human family. Except he was also a shifter and able to do both at the same time with little effort."

Phil let out a whistle as Goolsby poured him another drink.

"Precisely. Needless to say, he was found dead three days after registering. The issue, however, is that he somehow survived for over two hundred years prior to his visit to the office. This happened three more times. No one ever knew these incidents occurred. So people kept on, and are still, registering. I am sure they are continuing to also disappear. The Council figured it was the civilian governments hunting these people down and, to put it bluntly, killing them. The office and the running of it was pulled from our team, and that leads us to wonder why. Even though both parties created it."

"What does this have to do with the Purity Law?" I asked as Petro spoke up.

"Sounds like something a hi-Fae would do on the Plane. They do that kind of stuff all the time. Get rid of things they don't understand."

"Correct. The Thule Society, however, thrives on making these types of anomalies and using them to gain power. I would think they would keep the subjects rather than kill them," Goolsby said, sitting back in his chair.

"You said civilian governments. Does the Council honestly think the human population is capable of doing this?" I asked.

"Yes, and I can assure you they are. You know from last year that while strong, when a Fae or Ethereal crosses over to Earth, they lose a little bit of their power. It's that little bit that makes them mortal. The Fountain of Youth was the answer for getting around that. You ensured that is not an option. The Council wants to keep its secrets, but knows it must work together with the civilian governments. The civilian governments are the same. The Thule Society, on the other hand, wants chaos and to prevent the parties from joining. The Purity Law on the Plane is a death sentence if you do not fall into certain categories. Sound familiar?"

"The Nazis during the war. Hell, the Thule Society sprung out of that group," I said, showing off my historical knowledge.

"Wrong. The Nazis sprung out of them. The Council doesn't want to go up against a new threat, and neither does the civilian government. They look at anything not registered as the type of threat the Thule Governance, as we should be calling them, brings," Goolsby said, putting the cap on the scotch. "Or something none of the parties want the others to know about."

"I see, all three parties in their own way are wrong. Two sides coming together maybe to fight what they don't know and a third making the unknown. Dammit, this is all over the place," I said, finally starting to figure it out. The Council's dirty little secret. They didn't want anomalies, like myself to a point. Neither did the civilian governments. All the while the Thule Governance, as I now call it, was using this to their advantage. "I still don't understand why the Council took over the office."

"I believe it's because the Thule Governance has its hands in the Council. They do in the civilian governments. Think about it. The Council sets up this office with some help as a show of good faith, then lets the civilian governments manage it. Then something goes wrong, which may have been on purpose. It then makes since to give it back. That is what my organization often works to address. You do realize, the Council has been around thousands of years before the United States was formed. The gate Mages are a means to an end. After all, unregistered gates are being shut down, and illegal gates are being used to carry out actions based on information gained from the registrations," Goolsby said, standing up and bringing our meeting to an end.

"Wait, why are you telling us all this? We came here because we believe you are involved in this, and in the least it appears you have skin in the game," I said.

Goolsby chuckled, taking a sip of water. "Of course I do. Look, this is my city, and I have a significant business interest in the Transitions Offices."

"I find anything you told me not to be true, I'll be stopping by again," I said as Phil again looked uneasy.

The tall security guard opened the door, Goolsby motioning us out. He was not going to shake our hands, and I had the feeling we had overstayed our welcome.

"Max, please respect my prior statements about your presence in this establishment" was the last thing Goolsby said.

The storm was picking up as we walked back to the bridge and gated to the Atheneum.

"Gods and graves, can someone explain to me what the Purity Law is?" I asked as Phil handed out drinks in my office.

"It means that if you're different, then you're not part of the greater good," Petro said, speaking up. "An undesirable. On the Plane that part of the Accords has been taken both ways. Either the normal Ethereals are of pure blood, or it's everyone else that is. It's what makes the class system tick on the Plane. Also, why many Fae and older Mages don't consider Pixies to be productive members of society. We're not up to their standard of pure," Petro said, obviously not happy with the phrase.

Phil finally spoke up. "Bunch of bigoted mumbo jumbo, but I'll tell you that there are those on the Council, the Fae mainly, that really believe in that stuff. Ned is an exception, as are a few others. This is all just thoughts and prejudices. Every society has them. It's just a smokescreen. The Thule Governance is trying to create something new, and the Council is working to take out things they can't explain or haven't been able to find over time. Total shit."

I had to agree with Phil. "I'm not disagreeing. It's just that something's missing here. It's like all this information is floating around, and we're missing something staring us right in the face," I said as Petro looked down at his phone.

We worked with Mags-Tech to get him a miniphone that he could text and call on. It was slightly smaller than one of the new-style smart watches, and he carried it in a small bag slung between his wings. When he landed, he usually dropped it on the ground.

"I got to go, fellas, hot date tonight!" Petro said, grinning.

"Petro, every date you and Cacey go on is a hot date. Pretty soon we will either have a house full of Pixie babies or a wedding. Phil and I are taking bets," I said, getting a grin out of the group.

Petro looked up. "Really? A bet?"

"Aye, as of right now," Phil said, smoothing the foam from his beer out of his beard. "Bruther, you think that the demons have something to do with it?"

Petro buzzed out of sight.

"Yup, what I do know is something Bo said to me keeps floating around in my head. From the sounds of it, whoever called him here didn't know it was Bo that they were specifically summoning. It's like the person was just sending out a call for your local neighborhood demon to show up, do some particularly nasty work, then either leave or cause a scene. Issue is, Bo likes it here and, from what I gather, is looking for whoever brought him here."

"That means Bo has to find the person and get them to release him. Smart move on him coming in. He has it halfway figured out. The person can't summon him now; however, Bo can't hurt or directly find them either. If someone else was to, though…" Phil trailed off. I figured he was about to recommend us try to summon him.

"He's not helping with the kidnappings; he's trying to figure out who the hell is doing it and going to get someone else to do his dirty work and find his summoner, I bet. Bo's literally trying to help in his own sick way. He can't tell us who it is because he's bound to them."

Phil and I both bottomed up our beers, burping in chorus. Phil tapped the tip of his nose, lighting up a smoke.

After a few more beers and making unflattering jokes

about Phil's lack of respect for trees, I called Jenny.

"How's Ed?" I asked, putting her on speaker with Phil giggling lightly in the background.

"He's better. It looks like he will be on light duty but will be on his feet tomorrow. He's staying at my house tonight due to the storm. Which by the way, will be a category 4 making landfall just south of the city around Palm Coast. Everything will be shut down. We will have time to go over everything tomorrow. I'll head over when the sun comes up. I'll take the tunnel over," Jenny said as Phil grinned at the mention of the two staying together. "Phil, wipe that shit-eating grin off your face. I can hear your leathery skin from here." She hung up.

"Tunnel?"

"The lass has a tunnel that stretches underground from her house to here. Comes out somewhere in the stacks."

Finishing our last beers, Phil headed out. I walked over to my room, passing out still in my clothes.

CHAPTER 14

Did Anyone Order a Monster?

Walking out to the office after my morning grooming ritual, I found Leshya standing there holding the Judge in her hand.

"Morning, Leshya. Can I ask why you're standing there with my gun?" I asked, not nervous; however, I was more concerned with her lack of emotion while holding a weapon.

The storm overnight had picked up, much to my surprise. It was already to the point of blinding, the wind and rain outside making its presence known. The Atheneum was not only warded but apparently shielded, being stronger than most normal structures. The stained glass behind my desk was being smacked by a handful of branches that would have shattered most.

"It's needed elsewhere," Leshya said in her monotone cadence.

"I signed for that," I said, remembering how important signing for things in the army was.

"You are released from your obligation. The papers are on

your desk. Can I get you something to eat?" she asked, the gun still hanging in her grip.

"No, thanks, I'm good," I said, always remembering to not eat her food or, in that case, allow her to cook. "Let me ask. Is this needed by someone important to me?"

"Yes" was all Leshya said as she walked out of the office. It took a minute to digest the scene. The wind howled on the outside walls, sounding like a train passing close by. The lights flickered, and I noticed the cool smell of fresh rain hanging in the air.

"Morning, boss," Petro said as I sat down at the island counter in the downstairs kitchen. We had a morning routine of having Golden Grahams together every morning before we left to the main house. Recent events had caused a break in the routine. After all, who was going to pass on breakfast?

Gramps's old place was large, having a full, fairly outdated kitchen. In all fairness, I never really used or went into many of the other rooms in the house. It was a sizable space, roughly four thousand square feet. Other than the kitchen and main hall, I never went to the sitting or living room downstairs. I just went up to the office and my little room attached to it. Gramps's room had been sealed when he disappeared, and after a few failed attempts, I gave up trying to get inside.

"Morning. Sleep good?" I asked, pouring a bowl.

"Hell no. It's too loud with this storm. We tried everything. I ended up going to sleep finally with some music on twenty minutes before my alarm went off," Petro said, dusting on the table. He looked tired.

"How's Cacey?"

"She's fine. Same thing. All the noise kept her up, too, and let me tell you, she's not in a good mood this morning. Anyways, I guess it's a good day to just relax."

"Pretty much. Jenny and Ed are meeting us in the dining room. Phil and I were thinking about working on casting hellfire spells. Not with a blended item, sword, or whatever."

"Big-time. I'll go down there with you. If you can get that nailed, people will be hard pressed to pick a fight with you. A Mage that can throw around hellfire," Petro chirped proudly as we both put our bowls in the sink.

The new front entrance desk looked as out of place as a nun at a bar. James, one of the new security personnel, seemed to be pulling most of the shifts. My guess was he was single, needed a place to stay during the storm, and wanted the overtime.

James was thin, of medium height, and black. His hair was short and had obviously been cut by one of those barbers that took more time than needed making all the lines perfect. His eyes were a darker deep brown, and his radiating smile usually faltered when James tried to stop one of the crew, checking for identification. I had promised to stop by and say hello after yesterday.

"Morning, James. How'd you get stuck here today?" I asked, walking up, Petro landing on his desk.

"Morning, Mr. Sand," James said in a light yet professional tone.

"Call me Max. That's the second time I've been called Mr. Sand in the past few days. Most people call me by my family name now, Max Abaddon."

"Understood. It's what's listed on your badge."

"Badge?" I asked, raising an eyebrow.

"When the storm passes, all employees of the CSA, NCTS, and Atheneum will have to wear a badge in the building while working. It's different than your CSA badge."

"Good luck telling Phil that," I said as he let out a light, amused breath. "Anyways, I just wanted to say sorry about yesterday. Things got a little crazy. Hey, I hear you went to the FBI academy?"

"I did. Then one day a group came in having this hush-hush presentation about a special new marshal's task force. Most of us were not interested in working with the marshals; it's considered...well, let's just say all but two of us walked out."

Petro looked up, just as interested as I was. James was very well spoken and in fact had graduated the academy at an obviously young age. He looked to be twenty-one at most.

"Then this guy walks in and starts doing magic tricks, but these weren't tricks. When he was done, a woman walked in. I've seen her around here, Angel, I think her name is. She then proceeds to show us her fangs and jumped on the ceiling. The girl that stayed with me—I think her name was Tiffany—passed out. They carried her out; I never saw her again. Let's just say I had to see more. The rest is...hey, I'm still trying to figure this out."

"You and me both. Where you from?" I asked, genuinely liking the kid.

"College Park, south Atlanta. It's a rough spot. I was good at math and worked my way into a scholarship at Georgia Tech. Next thing you know, I'm joining the FBI at eighteen. I think that's how I got selected. Tiffany was younger than the rest of the candidates as well."

"Tell you what. I am guessing by the storm outside and the looks of that bag you have over there you're staying the night. I'll stop by later; we can grab a drink," I said, nodding for Petro to get up.

"That would be great. Yeah, I'm staying here; my apartment's near the beach and pretty sure I'll not be going back for a while. Ben's supposed to stop by later and give me a break. Before I forget, Ben and Terrence, that guy that hangs around the ogre, left you something. Ben was going to take it to the evidence room. Terrence said he would handle it, then just left it here, telling me to give it to you to when I saw you. Here," James said, handing me a box.

Inside were the leftovers from yesterday's ambush. A few pistols and some odd items left from the bodies that had been "judged." I loved thinking that. *Typical*, I thought, closing the top on the box and not touching the effects. *Leave it up to me to do all the work.*

"That box stinks," Petro said, wrinkling his nose.

"Let's go. I can hear the rest of the mystery gang in the dining room," I said, giving James a nod and light solute.

Phil had beaten me down, and I was guessing he obtained more of his "magic snake oil," as I liked to call it, back in. As if reading my mind, there was an extra tube sitting on the table in my normal seat.

"Morning, Ed. How's the ribs?" I asked, seeing him sitting rigid in his chair obviously wrapped in bandages. I sat the box down, nodding to Jenny, who was looking like an overprotective mother hovering beside Ed.

"They've seen better days," Ed said with a light strain in his voice.

"Also worse," Phil chimed in, smothering a plain bagel in cream cheese.

"Good morning, Max. How's the leg?" Jenny asked, looking over at me.

"Actually, much better. I'll have a scar without a doubt. It's still sore. I don't think I'll be running any marathons anytime soon," I said as she walked over, sticking her finger in my wound.

"Ouch! What's that all about?" I whimpered as Phil, Ed, and Petro let out light coughing laughs.

"Odd. It should still be healing or in the least still show signs of tissue trauma. It's almost completely healed." She had insisted I drop my pants and show her. So I did, proudly displaying my floral boxers.

"Max," Ed spoke up, "remember the conversation we had in the labs about you having some odd ability to slightly mimic other Mages' power if they use it on you? I bet this has something to do with that."

"Bruther, keep your mouth shut about that kind of stuff." Phil reiterated that it was our little secret, and one Jenny was wanting to study.

"Right. I hear you three paid Marlow Goolsby a visit. You have guts, I'll give you that, or you're as stupid as an ogre," Ed said, obviously happy with our move.

"Either way, let's hear it. We're glad you did. Everything's moving fast, and with the storm we hopefully have some time to come up with a plan. Angel and Frank are in Jacksonville, and Dr. Freeman flew to Atlanta. It's just us," Jenny said at the wrong time.

A pop of ozone filled the air as Bo appeared, sitting at the end of the table, dusting water off his shoulders.

The group froze. Ed and Jenny looked tense as this was their first time meeting this particularly polite demon. Phil looked indifferent, shaking his head and popping a smoke in between his lips, sitting the bagel down without taking a bite.

The facility was heavily warded. Devin as well as Bo, as it seemed, were not affected the same as everything and everyone else. There had to be a reason, and I would find out. Maybe it was something Gramps had done before he disappeared. I had heard too much about the wards for it to be a coincidence.

Bo was still dressed in the same tacky red-velvet suit that

was at least two or three hundred years old. The round rose-colored glasses sat firmly on his face as his long nose pierced the void. He still looked as if something was crawling under his skin; however, the pungent smell was now replaced with the scent of cloves.

"Hello, darlings," the demon said in his smooth, congenial tone.

Ed spoke up first. "I think we've met before."

"Indeed, we have. That looks like it hurts. You should be lighter on your toes next time a Mage slings a plasma ball at you."

"How do you know that?" Jenny asked, standing up, doing so when she felt defensive.

"Oh, I was there watching only of course. I may have accidently tripped on the undergrowth and knocked a few bad guys out, but it wasn't on purpose," Bo said, grinning showing a mouth full of an impossible number of razor-sharp teeth.

"You took out that Mage or whatever that was slinging spells at us from the other side of the vehicle when we were exposed," I said, figuring out how we got into the vehicle without getting hit.

"Me? No, must have been an accident. Anyways, I came to hear this little story you're about to tell," Bo said, looking over at the box and squinting his eyes.

We all looked over at the same time.

"What's in the box?" Ed asked as I walked over to it.

"Not much, just a few guns and some stuff left over after using the Judge," I said, opening the box lid.

"Don't touch—oh, never mind; this will be fun. You already touched it anyways," Bo said, leaning back as a loud bang and vibration rattled the room.

"That's not outside," Phil said, standing up, walking over to the box and pouring its contents onto the table with a clatter of noise. In the middle was a bracelet just like the one I had given Chloe last year, connecting the two of us and resulting in the ultimate demise of her partner, Vestulie.

"Shit" came out of at least three of our mouths. The muffled rumble of the storm was interrupted by a loud crack from the main hall. Either we had a run of bad luck or, as I was guessing, the bracelet had been put there on purpose.

Phil grabbed the two pistols from the dead Mages, slamming a clip in each and handing me one. When you're at home or in one's place of business, people often let their guard down. The Atheneum was well warded, and patrons rarely walked around with weapons. This was the exact reason I needed to learn how to cast actual spells. While Phil was extremely strong, he didn't have the ability to cast spells. Most, if not all, Earth Mages such as Phil fell into the same category.

The wards had proven to have limits. Demons, Devin—whatever he was—and certain gates were the only things proven to break through its security. Even then it was hard. Ed once told me that at least three to four times a day they got an alert of something trying to get into the facility.

Ed wasn't moving, and much to my surprise, he reached under the table, pulling out an odd-looking disk, throwing it toward Bo. With a snap of ozone, a protective circle sprang to life around our uninvited quest. Did I ever mention the chairs in the dining room have silver circles inlaid in the floor? There was more than one reason the dining room was used as much as it was, and it even had internal defenses. We'll get into circles later.

Bo sprang to his feet, howling in anger, spittle coming from his mouth, ruffling his elegant demeanor. There was the demon I'd heard so much about. Ed trapped him inside a circle, ensuring he wasn't getting out. After a glance from the group,

Bo sat back down in his chair letting out a breath, crossing his legs.

"Right, calm down. I'll let you out when this gets sorted. In the meantime, you and I are going to have a little chat," Ed said, obviously not up for the fight that was about to take place.

"Bruther, when I open the door, let it rip. We'll figure it out from there," was the last thing Phil said as he lit the cigarette hanging in his mouth, charged his body with crushing strength, a light gray mist coming from his hands. He pushed the doors open to the main hall.

The scene was as I expected. A monster and, well...James. It stood over ten feet tall at the far end of the hall, obviously having burst from a hole in the floor. A light haze of dust filled the air, reaching the front entrance. The smell of crushed rock and what could only be described as a wild-animal scent filled the space.

It was built like a large gorilla without hair, carrying itself on legs that looked like they belonged on a large cat. Perched on top was a head that melted into its neck that was oval, looking like the Cheshire cat out of Alice and Wonderland. It didn't have lips, just rows of pointed fangs disappearing inside its mouth, which happened to almost reach its broad pinned-back ears. It was hard to compare the creature to anything else, so I finally decided that is was just a plain old large scary-ass monster. Topping it all off, its tail was slightly up its back and split into three long spiked appendages that had obviously caused most of the cracking sounds we heard.

James was by his desk, holding an odd-looking submachine gun. Most Mags-Tech weapons had transparent magazines with colored ammunition, signifying their use against Mages and Ethereals. This was such a weapon. Goolsby had made his underground weapons trade legitimate as CEO of Mags-Tech. I'm sure he was cashing in. As Goolsby said, he had more to gain than lose from the Balance.

The *rat, tat, tat* cadence of controlled bursts started not soon after I took in the scene. James was absolutely trained. Phil and I let loose a handful of well-placed shots, trying to see their effect on the monster. Moving, the creature took hunks of black marble out of the floor.

Much like the soldiers who dealt with the giant scorpions we ran into last year at the Fountain of Youth, handheld weapons were useless against this creature. I saw the look on James's face as he backed into cover.

I dove behind the closest column, as one of its tails swung through the air, cracking the pillar in front of me. James ducked behind his newly found desk.

Phil—well, Phil was standing in the open flipping it off, pumping more useless rounds into the monster and still gumming his lit smoke. You must give the guy a nod for style. To point, he was drawing its attention away from us so we could find cover.

Petro had at last joined the battle, flying to the ceiling, taking his position and reporting down to the ground team. I ran over to the desk.

"Well, I guess drinks are out tonight," I said to James as he clapped another magazine in the weapon, smoke pluming from the hot barrel of his gun.

"That thing didn't even flinch," James said, shaking his head. "What the hell is that?"

"A monster," I said, thinking of a plan.

"Yeah, what type?"

"A big one," I said, reaching down to my charm and calling Petro. That was how it worked usually.

"Hey, boss," Petro said, flying down, landing on the floor, and shaking dust from his wings. The air was getting thick.

"And?" I asked, raising an eyebrow.

"Yeah, that thing came straight from the Plane. Someone gated it here. Looks like a chimera. Not like the ones you read about here. This is a real one. They can be a few things, mainly a mess of different types of creatures all rolled up into one. This one's mad," Petro said in rapid succession.

A loud boom shook the room as Phil had landed a crushing blow to the creature. It would be a minute or two before he could work up another. There was a crash and throaty howl, the creature smashing into the back wall that separated the stacks from the rest of the main entrance hall.

I was still wondering what Ed, Jenny, and Bo were doing in the dining room. *Tea*, I thought, cracking a smile. James looked at me, confused.

"I have an idea. James, shift over to the double doors leading to the other wing. When I give you the signal, get that thing's attention. Petro, go to my room and get that coin Ying gave me the other day. Before you zip out, let Phil know I have a plan and to keep that thing moving until James opens up." Petro nodded at my instructions and flew off.

"Now?" James asked as I smirked at him.

"Yeah, now. Just wait for the signal to start firing," I said, peering over the desk and giving him the all-clear signal to move.

The creature was getting up from the rubble, shaking dust off its back as Phil stood roughly twenty feet in front of it with a large iron bar he pulled out of the broken column. He was as strong and tough as it came. Phil could funnel Earth magic into his body, toughening himself up and making him superstrong. He could stand toe to toe with things several times his size. Phil's main issue was he could only keep it up so long. Without his gear and ability to use other items, he was draining his reserve.

I saw a flash of dust as Petro delivered the message and took off. In all fairness, the whole sequence of events had lasted only a couple of minutes. Petro would be back within seconds, and all Phil had to do was hold off the creature. It suddenly dawned on me; I didn't know what to do with the coin from Ying.

As the creature shook off the dust, it picked up a large chunk of rock, slinging it at Phil, who only batted it aside.

Petro buzzed down, dropping the coin and taking flight back up to the ceiling. Phil went flying over my head, crashing into the front door with a cracking thud. A few boards broke loose as the sounds of the storm outside started to fill the space, echoing off the stone walls and marble floors.

"Shit," I whispered under my breath. I could see Phil's face; he was bleeding from his mouth, nose, and ears. Leaning over I gave James the signal to start firing at the creature. While the rounds didn't affect the monster, it did grab its attention. The cadence of gunfire took over the noises from outside.

The creature was still behind the water fountain, looking in the direction of the dining room. I was betting on Bo or something else having drawn its attention. It let out an angry howl of irritation.

Looking at the newly formed crack in the door, I could see water trickling in, mixing with the dust generated by Phil's graceful landing and creating gray mud at the foot of the massive doors. Phil stood up, shaking his head.

In a flash of brilliance—or stupidity, depending on how you look at it—I pushed my will into the crack, pulling the water from it. As I practiced in the shower, as soon as the water started to swim around my hand, I dug a little deeper, pushing the hellfire out as far as I could.

While I couldn't throw the hellfire yet, I could push it out several feet. The combination of hellfire and water let off a hiss of anger, sounding like a steak hitting a hot pan full of oil.

I had tried to move the water in the entrance fountain before, but whatever that stuff was didn't ever want to play.

Steam filled the air to the left of the creature in a rush, cutting off its ability to focus on the dining room or, for that matter, me. Looking closer, I saw that the monster had grown at least two more feet tall. While the steam would cover a limited space, the area in the main entrance was massive, and I only had one shot at whatever it was I was about to do.

Staring at Phil and taking a final breath, I stood up, as the scent of lavender filled my nostrils. Looking over, I saw Jenny smiling at me, her hands glowing green.

"Bingo," I said as Phil took a deep breath, leaning over to pull a short knife out of his boot and flicking his finger off the end of his nose. Phil charged the beast again, letting out a howl of anger.

Jenny leaned over, touching my shoulder. A light-green tint covered my body. An odd effect of Jenny's shield is it also had a calming property, making you feel like everything was going to be all right. I was sure she did that on purpose so guys like me wouldn't have an accident in their pants.

I rolled out, charging the creature from its left side under the cover of the steam. As soon as Jenny's shield took hold, my ability to produce said steam disappeared. I was guessing I had ten to twenty seconds.

Its head whipped around, Phil drawing its attention and James pushing through the double doors, taking position. The crazed hipster jumped in the air, landing on the bottom steps of the staircase. The creature swiped the now-empty space with its foot-long claws. By the time the monster turned around, Phil was on the catwalk in midair holding out the dagger.

Phil landed on its back, plunging the blade as far as he could into the monster's hide. It was much like one of those mechanical bulls at a cowboy bar that all the drunk people ride on. Phil went sailing through the air. He looked like one of those people you see in Pamplona getting flung around like a rag doll.

The monster's tail whipped. This gave me a clear view of its side, and I noticed its deadly appendage slamming into the spot James had just occupied.

I let out my own howl of frustration, running full speed at the exposed side of the monster.

Yeah, it was much larger and scarier up close.

Phil was already back up, and the two were in a type of circling standoff like you see on the nature shows. I moved with the creature, trying to figure out what to do with the coin in my hand.

The beast struck first, slashing out its front claws and tail at the same time, sensing me. I was in the air. Its tail caught me off guard, me forgetting the two others it had. I landed directly in front of and underneath our visitor's broad chest. Being so close, I could taste the musky scent the creature was letting off.

It was still focused on Phil as a gob of drool the size of a baseball landed on my face with a gloopy spatter. I immediately started retching, which just happened to get the chimera's attention. It looked down, not seeing me under its torso but backing up enough to grasp something was under its chest.

"Hey there, fella, nice kitty, snake, whatever," I said, seeing the light-green glow of Jenny's shield strengthen. She was giving it all she had. No wonder its tail hadn't snapped me in two.

It let out a breath, smelling like a mixture of iron and

copper, lending to its recent dining on raw flesh. It may have eaten James; I couldn't really tell in all the excitement. I figured the lack of blood coming from its mouth was a good thing.

Phil lunged at the creature again, jumping higher than a natural person could by drawing on his power. The monster followed suit, obviously not thinking I was a threat but taking another swipe at me with its tail. I slid to the other side of the hall, the green shield slightly faltering.

There was a distinct crashing noise as the monster rammed Phil into the stone wall. From my perspective it looked bad.

I was still on my back when Petro dove down out of sight toward the wall Phil had been smashed into. If Petro was coming down, he must have seen something bad.

Much like last year at the Blue House, I was done playing games, and yup, there it goes—my temper. The thing may have just crushed Phil.

"Hey you, that's my drinking buddy, and I'm the only one allowed to slap him around," I screamed out loud, noticing it was still growing. Pretty soon it wouldn't be able to fit in the entrance.

The monster whipped around. The dust cleared, and I could see Phil lying there in the pile of rubble that was once called a wall. It looked like the damn thing was about to eat him. I screamed again, getting its full attention.

It let out a screeching howl, spittle flying through the air. I did the same, charging the beast for a second time, hoping Jenny's shield would take the impact.

The green shield was still glowing around my body as I slid on the ground directly beside the chimera, grabbing its front leg and pulling myself underneath its belly. I noticed it took issue with seeing or knowing something was directly under it.

The coin was still in my hand as I channeled all my will and rage, igniting its leg in a blaze of lava-hot, sticking hellfire. The creature shrieked in pain, its flesh melting away. Hellfire was like napalm. It burned whatever it touched until it was done. The smell of rotted, burning flesh filled the air.

I had only a second, ensuring the coin was deposited and shifted as the front claw of the chimera launched me through the air.

I landed on my back, the shield no longer active. I took a second to orient myself, as blood trickled from my side.

There was a heavy sucking sound, followed by a loud pop. The creature disappeared into itself, leaving behind only dust and a light outline of its body in the space it had just occupied.

The room immediately went silent, again giving purchase back to the sounds of the storm raging outside.

Jenny ran over, propping me up. "What the hell was that?" she asked.

"A gift from a new friend. Go check on Phil. I think he's hurt," I said, reaching down, calling for Petro.

It took a few seconds as Petro came walking over instead of his normal flying.

"Hey, boss," Petro said, shaking dust out of his hair.

"You OK?"

"Yeah, I just can't fly. Too much stuff in the air. Phil's all right; he's pretty banged up. Smells like you are too," Petro said, commenting on the odor of blood coming from my side.

"What about James?" I asked, looking at the caved in hall entrance.

"He's OK. I think he's stuck on the other side of the door. I can smell his cheap aftershave. I like him," Petro said, walking closer and sliding down the side of my leg to sit on the floor.

I proceeded to pass out for the second time in two days.

CHAPTER 14.5

Bubble Boy (Ed and Bo)

Ed looked over at Bo as Phil, Max, and Petro stormed out of the room. The door slammed shut as the team rushed the chimera in the main hall, the sound of muffled gunfire erupting on the other side.

The dining room was warded and heavily fortified. The circles under each chair were an example of how thoroughly the space had been considered.

Ed, Jenny, and Bo looked at each other.

Bo spoke up first. "You do remember me, darling. I believe Germany, winter, 1942. You, Tom, and that team of mercenaries came looking for the Nazis' occult artifacts." The rumbling yet soothing voice filled the space, Bo grinning at Jenny, his sharp teeth changing the tone of his face.

"We weren't mercenaries, and if memory serves me correctly, you actually were one of the reasons we made it out alive," Ed said, leaning back in his chair, a loud bang reverberating off the walls. The name alone was not enough to connect the two.

Jenny looked over. "This is all well and good, gentlemen; however, I think the boys could use a hand." She stood up as another loud crash shook the room.

Jenny opened the door, dust floating in as the sounds of gunfire and Max shouting came in just before the door closed and sealed itself off, leaving Ed and Bo alone.

Bo stood up as much as the bubble would allow. "I wouldn't go around spreading rumors about me like that. People may get the wrong impression."

"The first and last time we met, Tom and I walked into a room that was covered in gore. Blood was dripping from the ceiling, and you had a man in your hands torn in half," Ed said, the thought of the scene making him shiver lightly.

"Tsk, tsk, I was just hungry, and well you know. Those fellows weren't up to anything productive, so I had a little snack," Bo purred, sitting back down. You could tell the memory delighted him.

"You killed and dismembered twenty senior Nazi officers and scientists. You then proceeded to disappear. What were you doing then, and what the hell are you doing now?" Ed asked, getting to the point.

They had in fact encountered each other for a brief time. Mages often met more people with their extended lives than they could remember. Ed had always remembered the face and way the creature was dressed that day in Germany during the war. That memory was nightmare fuel. Tom and Ed spent countless days trying to figure out who or what Bo was. They had figured he was a demon; however, they were not sure why he didn't attack them.

"Who's counting? Anyways, I'm here because someone summoned me here. To be more precise, someone with the same blood that called me here last time. I'm still bound to them, so what I can say is limited, but I can tell you this. I have a feeling it's the son or daughter of whoever summoned me last time. I ate them," Bo said, raising an eyebrow, as the sounds of someone screaming filled the silence.

Ed knew enough about demons to know that if they hadn't eaten you, or at least tried, you had something they wanted. Bo was different; he didn't seem to want to hurt anyone. Or at least, no one on the team.

"I don't think any of this is by chance, Bo. Tell you what. I'll make a deal with you." Bo perked up at those words, Ed realizing the gravity of what he had just said.

Thing is, Bo was three for three on helping the team, and Ed was hedging his bets that it would be in their best interests.

"I'm all ears," Bo hissed.

"You answer my question. Not any of this 'leave out important details' bullshit; promise me you will not harm anyone on our team, and I'll ensure my assistance in tracking down your summoner. When we do, I also ensure that you are allowed safe passage and an audience with the Council. We did it with Belm; my word is good," Ed said, snapping his finger and dissolving the bubble around Bo.

"Ah…trust, how quaint. OK, deal," Bo said, taking in a deep breath. "I'm not like many of my kind, as you know. I am more of a collector of things and not some hellion general. Those are the types the Council and your group mostly know about. Belm, your little friend, is the son of the overlord. I think you know about some of that business." Bo raised an eyebrow. There was something about that statement that hit home for Ed, forcing him to take in a deep, calming breath.

"Right. Get to the point," Ed snapped.

"Thing is, I've been here a little longer than you are aware. Your satellites only register one of us if we gate or use magic. I have done neither until recently, biding my time confined to a small cell. As you know, a few years is nothing to me. Anyways, I never met who summoned me other than what I told you already about them. What I can tell you is that I was summoned before your team's little trip under the bridge last year. Lilith, as I am sure you are aware by now, was absolutely part of all this and came to talk to me about the Fountain as well as the gate crystal. All with the same purpose. Power and being able to gate or bring whatever they like back from the Plane or wherever. Lilith groomed Chloe, was responsible for all those deaths, and even though failed last year, from what I understand, still got what she wanted." Bo took a break, the sounds of another loud crash filling the space.

"So Lilith has been using you?" Ed asked, cocking his head.

"Not really. Just making deals much like this one for information. Back in the under, I'm known for my collection of things or knowledge of them. That nasty piece of work of hers, Chloe, was particularly open to making deals. Anyways, to my point, I was in my nice little condo underground when I overheard the team going after the gate crystal. Not any gate crystal but mine. Thing is, it was secured."

Another loud crash filled the air as Bo winced. "I believe that one is going to leave a mark. So, as I was saying, I figured the true reason I was summoned was so that the people so politely taking care of me could steal my things," Bo trailed off, rage filling his voice, commanding the room. Just as quickly as it had appeared, his temper dissolved.

"It makes sense. They would never be able to come to your home or wherever and get these things from you," Ed said, getting the bigger picture on how Lilith and the Thule Society were operating.

"They want a world filled and run by monsters, some 'new race of creatures' gibberish. I can see it in your eyes that you already know this. They asked me how to get to the Fountain. I was unfortunately the one that told Chloe how to use the journal to find the back door. The gate crystal. Those wretches stole it from my home. How, I don't know. When I find them, I will be sure to ask them as politely as possible while I decorate the space with their entrails."

"So why these two items?" Ed asked.

"Simple. The Fountain, as you know, is used to come over as a full Ethereal or, as it was used, to make a normal human a Mage. A powerful one at that. The water wasn't fully charged; however, it also has another interesting effect. That is why it was hidden away."

Ed let out a huff of understanding, not knowing this.

"As for the gate crystal. You can see by your uninvited guest outside why. I just came by to say hello, plus I have a nose for when certain-type gates are being used. Wonder how they got through your wards. Not me, in case you're asking,"

"Who has the crystal? It was delivered and secured."

"Was it? Hmm…couldn't tell. Seems to me someone used it to make a bunch of link bracelets. I bet there has been a good amount of people gone missing to make those. Sacrifice and all. Oh, Max…" Bo trailed off, snapping his fingers and sneezing, the smell of burning flesh filling the room.

"Tell your underling next time he jams a gate coin in a monster to activate it. I accidently sneezed and set it off. I think this will conclude our visit. I just need to see where that creature gated from. If you get an idea where they are holed up, please let me know," Bo said, standing up, snapping his fingers, and disappearing.

CHAPTER 15

All Clear

The smell of hot coffee and freshly toasted bread filled my nostrils. I was lying on the couch, eyes closed, in Jenny's small house tucked away in the woods behind the Atheneum.

Jenny's house was small and homely, cozy, being at odds with the doctor's scientific personality. Comfortable furniture filled the space with pictures hanging on all the walls. The lights burned a dull yellow, casting the house in a relaxed mood.

Phil and Ed's voices could be heard discussing the attack. For the first time in days, I could hear an eerie silence, forcing me to believe the storm had passed.

"Morning, boss," Petro said, the light breeze of his wings on my face.

I cracked my eyes open, letting out a stale breath. My mouth felt as if it had been cemented shut.

"Gods and graves, how long was I out?" I asked, Jenny

walking in with a tray of coffee and toast.

"Long enough. Two days. The storm's passed," Jenny said, sitting down in the chair opposite Phil and Ed walking into the room.

"Bruther, you look better," Phil said, leaning down to pick up my coffee. Jenny sternly smacked his hand. Phil had a black eye accompanying his right arm in a sling.

"I feel better. How about the storm?" I said, telling the truth. The past week had been a nonstop roller coaster, feeling much like last year when everything started to happen.

"Right. It hit pretty hard on the coast. It took an odd curve and went back out into the ocean before things got too bad. Typical flooding and downed trees. It wasn't a natural storm, or at least its turn wasn't," Ed said, looking over at Phil.

"What happened? Why are we all here?" I asked, starting to regain my faculties and sitting up.

"Well, boss," Petro started, landing on the table, "the Atheneum got pretty messed up by that freak. Right after the storm turned, a full squad of CSA agents showed up looking for Bo. For some reason Ed here convinced them it was the chimera. There was enough burned flesh to confirm it. They're still there to see if anything is missing and also cleaning up."

Ed looked over, taking a deep breath. "The last thing we need is for a demon showing up anywhere close to you and the team. Look, Max, we learned some rather valuable information. Bo believes the small amount of water Chloe took from the Fountain was used to make a regular person a Mage. From what he says, it can happen overnight and is one of the reasons the Fountain was secured over time. While we already know some of this, do we know anyone that fits that bill? New mysterious Mage with a large amount of power no one knows anything about?"

"Councilman Darkwater?" I said, scrunching my face. The rest of the group settled already, obviously going over this while I was passed out, reliving the moment for my benefit.

"We have a smart one here," Phil chided.

"Precisely. Jenny did some more digging, and we pulled Frank in as well. There is literally nothing on him prior to being assigned to the Council. The kicker is, we are having an issue figuring out how he was even placed there," Ed said as the big picture was starting to line up.

"So transporting the gate crystal...the meeting's all a ploy?" I asked, not fully buying it.

"To a point. We believe that while Councilman Darkwater 'walked' into his power, he is just doing what he can to gain status. I'm not even sure if he knows how dangerous the Thule Society is," Jenny said, motioning me to eat the toast.

"I say we go and get some answers from the man," Phil said, putting an unlit smoke in his mouth, earning a death stare from Jenny.

"All in time. I think that would be a mistake. The question is what's going to happen next. We need to figure out where these gate Mages are—and soon. According again to Bo, the bracelet that allowed that creature into the Atheneum was made using the gate crystal recently. He is working to find out where. I talked with Ned. He's looking into the chain of custody on the artifact, trying to keep it under the radar," Ed said.

"Don't bother," I said, the warm sensation of the coffee filling my throat, clearing my mind. "They never really had it. Well, at least it was never delivered. I'm sure they got something, but not this."

"How do you know this?" Ed asked. Jenny walked in with a cup of coffee and handed it to him. Phil blew out air, looking at her as Jenny let out a snicker, walking back to the kitchen and bringing out a cup for Phil in a pink mug, pronouncing the drinker a "princess."

"Something Mouth said to me in the car. I don't think they ever truly had it. If Darkwater owned it, why would he make it look like someone attempted to steal it? It's because he still has it and or has given it to someone else and needs it off his hands whenever the shit hits the fan. I think the gate crystal was a tradeoff for the water out of the Fountain," I said, standing up, realizing my leg was still sore and I had a bandage on my side.

"That was our assumption as well. I believe we are all on the same page. Ned told us to sit tight for a few days in case something comes up. He will let us know when we need to take this to the Council. I believe he is trying to figure out if there are any other players in this," Ed said, also standing up.

"Seems like an awful damn lot of hands in the cookie jar," Phil said, shaking his head.

"It is. We just need to figure out which hands to slap," Jenny said, looking over at Ed.

I noticed while Ed was still stiff, he was moving around and almost back to normal. My side and leg, on the other hand, were still front and center.

"She's right. We know who the true enemy is here. Darkwater may just be a means to an end. We understand he's power hungry, but that's nothing new on the Council. We need to find the gate Mages," Ed said taking a deep clearing breath.

"Where are you going? The three of you look like zombies. I'm betting they want you all out of commission as well. Whomever sent that chimera knew it would not take us out," Jenny said, giving us all that motherly look.

"I'm going to check on the rest of the house and see if everything's in place. I also want to talk to Leshya for a few minutes," I said as Petro took flight and Phil stood up.

The three amigos back together again. I could almost hear the sound of music fill the air. By the looks of us, though, it was more like the three stooges.

We walked into the main entrance, or at least what was left of it. The place was trashed. Large holes dotted in the walls. The fountain was the only thing that appeared to be unharmed. Gouges covered many once blank spaces on the floors. The space had been cleaned up for the most part as a team of workers standing outside taking a break had been working.

"Hey, guys, I'm going to…" James trailed off.

"See some ID. Well, you can ID deez—"

I cut Phil off. "James, you OK, man?" I asked, seeing him calm down. I don't think he fully recognized us at first.

"Sorry about that. It's been crazy. There's been so many people in and out of here over the past two days. I'm fine. You guys?"

"Ahh, we're good. Thanks for the help the other day. You can sure handle a weapon," Phil said, actually giving James a compliment. James's smile lit up as I shook my head, signaling to keep his smiling to a minimum. I could tell Phil was giving James his stamp of approval.

Petro flew over, putting his fist out in a motion to bump knuckles. James did, as Petro went flying back a few feet. It was clear that James didn't know the proper Pixie fist-bumping technique. We started chuckling.

"Hey, man, anyone come in here the last two days from the Council?" I asked.

"Yes, Carvel and Darkwater. They came in with the first wave of security. Left soon thereafter. Asked me if I had seen a demon. Besides, whatever that creature was, I honestly hadn't seen anyone else," James said, looking at the group of workers walking back through the entrance.

James was in fact telling the truth. He never saw Bo in the dining room.

"Catch you later for that drink," I said as we wound our way to the office and, more importantly, the bar.

"Hey, boss. You just woke up from being passed out for two days. You sure you want a drink?" Petro asked, all the while motioning for me to pour him one.

"That's exactly why" was all I said.

Phil sat at the chair directly across from the desk as Petro took his position between us on a stack of old cork drink coasters.

I fired up the computer, seeing a list of emails from Kim and one from Ying. I scrolled through them, Kim sending several reports of incidents with odd gates popping up. Her next note was a triangulation of the gates to a central point. While I didn't think this meant much, I printed it out on the small printer I had purchased sitting on the edge of the desk. Clicking and clanking, the printer finally spit out the paper.

The note from Ying was to call her. I bet she had figured I used her present. That was furthered by the next email, noting a chimera had gated into the Council halls, causing "issues."

Great. One more thing for them to blame on me.

"Bruther, what's up?" Phil asked, taking a pull from his Vamp Amber.

"It's Chloe and these bracelets. If they can use them to gate here, why can't we use one to gate to them?" I asked, trying to put some semblance of a plan together.

"That's a great idea, boss. Thing is, I don't think they're here anymore. I can't smell them. Those are made by black magic and smell to high heaven," Petro said as Phil and I looked at each other, saying at the same time, "Carvel."

The bracelets didn't theoretically gate you; rather, they pulled you by a leash. Carvel, as well as Terrence and Darkwater, had been there and had access to retrieve them with little to no supervision.

"Phil, call Ed and let him know. Maybe he can get with Ned and figure out what happened to the evidence. It's not totally strange, them taking evidence; we just need to make sure we can get to it. If not, we know we have an internal problem," I said, downing the rest of my beer in one pull.

"A plant?" Phil said in contemplation.

"Something like that. Look, trust me on this. Like we said before, I think we have a few different things going on and need to make sure we are looking at this from all angles. Someone could be helping Chloe and not even know it," I said, watching Petro finish his cap of rum.

It was time to go on the offensive. I needed to make sure I didn't end up with a death sentence in the meantime because of demons. I was already in enough trouble, according to everyone. For a minute I had the fleeting vision of me riding in the back of a car during a ticker-tape parade, celebrating the team, saving the world. That visualization left as soon as Phil belched.

Phil and Petro left after another round of beers. Petro was going to check on Cacey, who had left with Macey and Lacey a few days prior to the storm. Pixies and high-wind events don't mix. From what Petro had told me, they thought he was brave for staying. I guess it's all just a matter of perspective.

My phone chirped as I walked out of the steamy shower, a towel wrapped around my waist below the fresh dressing on my side. It was roughly 10:00 a.m.

"Kim, I was about to give you a call. I got your emails," I

said, looking at my face in the mirror, stroking my light beard.

"I know. I put read receipts on them, as you are well known for your ability to open emails on time," Kim said, letting out a cute snort.

"Ha, ha. Hey, I'm getting better. Anyways I'm getting cleaned up. You want to meet at FA's for a few? There's a new book I want you to take a look at." Kim was silent for a second. Telling someone there was a new book you wanted them to look at was another code phrase we used. It informed the other person to meet face to face, keeping prying eyes or ears off.

Kim let out a sigh. "It's not a date, and I would prefer some pancakes. The diner by the winery?"

"Why, do you think I wanted it to be?" I asked back, enjoying this new attitude Kim had taken up with me over the past few weeks. Passive flirting is what I liked to call it. Since I figured the new man in her life was in fact her cousin, all bets were back on, and I wanted to see where this went.

"Funny, Max, I'll be there in an hour."

Kim didn't want to meet at FA's, telling me she thought the place was compromised. That, or she really just wanted some pancakes.

Grabbing my service pistol, I looked over at all the stuff I had accumulated over the past year sitting on my nightstand. I glanced at the short staff, realizing what Mouth had said. The less the better. I picked it up, putting it in the sling I made for it. Petro explained how to recharge it, and I had actually taken the time to do so the night before our uninvited guest.

I jumped in the Black Beast, heading toward town with Planes Drifter roaring in the background. Leaves covered the road as pieces of downed trees cut by linemen sat stacked in piles at various intervals. I started reflecting on the things I could affect.

In a flash of thought, I yelled out, "Bingo!" banging the steering wheel before lightly apologizing to the old girl.

Carvel and a few other Council members insisted I have my system access revoked until this was sorted out. That was the one thing that I had proven myself to be well above any standards the Council may have toward technology—hell, regulars for that point.

Someone didn't want me in the system looking around. Funnily enough, I could probably use someone else's access. Typical Council, not thinking that regulars could actually help with something.

"Kim, hey, you wouldn't happen to have your computer on you by chance?" I asked, calling her, forcing me to turn down the radio. I committed a sin.

"Yeah, sure, I don't leave home without it. I'll bring it in," Kim said, hanging the phone up before I could say another word. The drive for me was about fifteen minutes.

I forgot it was a longer drive for her. It gave me some more time to think. I sat for the next twenty minutes thinking about ways to mine information that could be helpful.

What if I started looking at how the Council knows when a demon shows up? I thought to myself. It made sense. It was obvious Mags-Tech invented technology to track Etherium spikes. Maybe it could do the opposite. Bo was looking for whoever summoned him. He knew who it was; he just couldn't really act on it. It is fairly obvious they were tied to the Thule Society and had the gate Mages, due to Bo always showing up. Maybe if we looked for the opposite of a spike, we could find the locations.

Kim knocked on the window. I was staring into the distance in deep thought as I flinched at the noise.

"You OK in there?" Kim asked, rolling her eyes.

"I'm fine. I think I may have an idea, and you, not being on the Council's radar, may be just the person," I said, getting excited for not only being at the diner with Kim but actually having a plan before Ed or Jenny.

We sat at a booth beside the kitchen. The smell of eggs, coffee, and syrup filled the air, making my stomach do cartwheels. The place was crowded. Looking around, I saw it was mostly full of workers cleaning up after the storm and a few cops.

"What will be it, loves?" the waitress asked. She was short and round and looked as if she had worked in the place for years. Fact of the matter was, she had, and I recognized her as waiting on me last time I was in.

"Pancakes with a side of bacon and coffee," Kim ordered, knowing what she wanted.

I ordered the two eggs sunny-side up, bacon, and hash browns smothered with cheese. With a half bottle of ketchup, you had a lifetime of drunk memories all in one eclectic place.

I went over my thoughts with Kim as we both sipped coffee, my mouth watering at the smells filling the air. It was nice being in a normal place. I had one day a week where it was a no-magic zone. I would have to come back here.

"And you thought about this while sitting in your truck?" Kim asked as our food arrived, us both attacking our plates like crazed animals.

"Yup, orf...umff," I said, food coming out of my mouth as I talked. I took a drink of water, clearing my throat. "Yes, I think all we need to do is figure out how to access the system that tracks every time a demon pops up. See if it tracks other events. Which I bet it does, to an extent. Do a search for gates or other events; then do a reverse search. I bet we will get a few leads. From what I understand, gating and demons are about the only two things traceable by these type automated systems. Locations that have a mysterious recent lack of gates or happenings," I said as a drop of syrup went down Kim's chin. She caught me staring.

"When? Things sounding like a bad social media news story about tracking your every move?" she asked, finishing the last of her bacon.

"Now, fire that thing up." I was good at finding data. From what I was told, Kim's system was the same as the portable laptop I had. It wasn't at the level of the box but had access to all the major tracking systems. The box also had a global cross-reference database. Yeah, I know, I'm a little bit of a closet nerd.

Kim stood up, making me scoot over in the shallow benches, taking a seat beside me. "Here you go."

For the next twenty minutes, we searched reports, tracking down the last notification from when Bo showed up. Not the most recent. We decided that big brother may be watching. We found a file labeled "Bo-Chicago" and clicked it.

"Bingo," I said, clicking the report link.

The file had a report and link to a file folder. After a few more minutes, we landed on the main page for the CSA's GPS/GMRS tracking systems. It was buried, and unless you knew what to look for or had direct access to the terminal, one would never find it

"You see that?" I asked in the form of a statement.

"Designed by Mags-Tech. Of course," Kim said as I clicked a few more keys.

Once we were in, the system was easy to navigate. There were files all labeled for what I guessed was the assigned tracking event. There was a file for demon that, over time, changed to Belm, then to Bo. There were also a few files that had odd names that I was guessing were code for something. We even found a few files on the Vale Project. Great. Fun times.

"That looks odd." Kim pointed out looking at a folder labeled "Transfer" with yesterday's date.

"It is. Look at this. See that extension? It automatically deletes itself after it's accessed or downloaded. Someone's in here gathering data," I said. "Ah, here we go." We scrolled to the bottom of the page, finding an input box.

"What do we put there?" Kim asked, sipping her coffee, moving closer to me. She smelled like bacon, syrup, and the light perfume she had obviously sprayed in the car before coming in. Good luck fighting that back.

I opened one of the normal-looking files, copying the extension followed with the word "gates." We entered the same pattern, using different terms, the previous ones disappearing, obviously being input to the main system. After about ten entries, we stopped.

"I don't want to flood the system. Call me tomorrow morning. Let's see if there's any new files in the system. Hey, you want to go grab a drink?" I asked, feeling brazen after my conquest of the chimera.

"I have to go. We are having reports of that large cat showing back up around town, and it was just classified as OTN by the local police. I have to get back and see what's up," Kim said, smiling at me.

I looked back at her; we were inches apart. Was this it? Was something about to happen? A kiss?

Kim cleared her throat. "I need to get out of the booth there, sunshine," Kim said as I snapped back to reality and moved out of her way. "I'll call you in the morning" was the last thing she said, walking out the door, leaving the bill on the table.

Getting back in the truck, I about jumped out of my skin as my phone started ringing in an odd loud tone. As do most people my age, everyone had a ringtone. Phil's was his drunken Garth Brooks impersonation, Jenny's was a light harp, Ed's was the sound of two cats fighting, and Petro's was the theme song from the old TV show *The Facts of Life*. This was an unlisted number.

"Hello, Max," the smooth yet stern, strictly business voice of Marlow Goolsby said on the other end.

"I haven't set anything on fire for a whole two days. To what do I owe the pleasure?" I asked, thinking the timing was odd.

"I see you and your friend Kim have been pulling satellite data from the CSA, Mags-Tech satellite. You are smarter than everyone else says you are."

"Thanks, I guess…" I said in the form of a statement. The familiar knock of Kim on the window grabbed my attention, making me jump again. She was holding up her phone, shaking it, obviously receiving a call from the same number.

"I need you and Marshal Kimber to meet me in thirty minutes at the address I'm about to text you. Come alone, and no, this is not a trick. Let's just say we may be able to help each other," Goolsby said, hanging up, the text immediately following.

I cracked the window open. "Going my way?" I asked in the cheesiest John Wayne voice I could muster.

"I looked up the address. It's not far from here, just a little north. Oh, and I grabbed some cash out of my car. Here, I almost forgot," Kim said, handing me a crisp ten.

I had the feeling she was playing games, but, in all honesty, she had one hell of a poker face.

"Thanks. I was about to text you about that," I said, obviously lying.

Kim walked over to the passenger side, taking out her

pistol and checking its action. "You planning on trouble?" I asked, getting ready to do the test of all tests. This was, after all, the first time Kim had been in the Black Beast officially.

What test, you may ask yourself? Well, it's the test that, if you know me, I believe has changed the course of history. Relationships gained and lost. Houses divided and crimes committed. Yes, it was time for the classic "Will she say anything when I crank up Planes Drifter on the radio?" test.

"Anytime you're around lately, there's trouble. Or haven't you figured that out yet?" Kim said, sliding into the seat, lifting herself up by the handle. "You think we should call this in?"

"Goolsby's a lot of things, but if he says he thinks we can help each other and to come alone, that's good enough for me. At least for now. He didn't say anything about telling anyone. Just to come alone. He knows we would catch that. I say let's see how this plays out. After all, we basically just hacked into the Council and Mags-Tech satellite system from a diner. I'm sure this has something to do with it," I said, leaning over and turning up the radio slightly, giving Kim a chance to balk.

She didn't. The lighter song "Pale Grinder" came on, and Kim started bobbing her head. I think it was the first time I never truly cranked up the radio.

"All right, so it looks like we're going to Matanzas National Park. The address is to one of the beach houses on the other side of A1A," Kim said, looking over at me grinning.

"What's so funny?" I said, the grin spreading to my face.

"Well, you finally figured out a way to get a woman in your truck. Congratulations," she said, letting out a slight chuckle.

The stereo in the Black Beast was a newer addition. It had a touch screen that had various controls for the vehicle, many not working due to the vintage of the truck. The one thing it did was show who was calling when attached to Bluetooth.

The grin on Kim's face washed away like the tide on the other side of A1A when Aslynn's name appeared on the screen, followed by her special ringtone. Kim raised an eyebrow at my selection.

"Cute. Do I have a song by Queen as a ringtone?"

Funny thing was, I hadn't given a ringtone to Kim. She was never really nice up until recently, and I hadn't gotten around to it. I rolled my eyes, thinking it was time to grow up and stop with the ringtones.

We rode in silence for a few seconds, and I eventually sent the call to voice mail. This was not shaping up to be a good week.

"That looks like it up there where that black Mercedes just pulled in. I think we can pull around the back," I said as Kim checked her pistol again, nodding.

I think the call actually got on her nerves. She, after all, knew who Aslynn was from the ball.

The crunch of gravel came from under the truck turning in. The house was an older two-story beachfront property that was separated from the surrounding residence by a couple of lots. The gravel drive turned into a solid concrete slab with a two-car garage around back. If I had to guess, the house was built sometimes in the '90s. While the front of the house facing the road was built to look like the entrance, the parking and drive were ocean side. It was painted a creamy white with well-maintained stucco and reflective windows, screaming *snowbird*.

Goolsby was already standing outside of the car and oddly alone. It was the first time I didn't see any hired muscle around him. Kim and I looked at each other.

"Hey, Marlow, long time no see," I said, trying to hide the

stiffness in my side.

"I think we already know you are a smart-ass. Let's get to the point. I don't trust many people, and after last year how about you?" Goolsby asked as Kim looked over shaking her head.

"Not many. The usual suspects. Not you," I said, making sure there was no love lost between the two of us. Kim was neutral from years of having to put up with Goolsby before he went public and supposedly cleaned up his act.

"The feeling is mutual, I can assure you," he said in a calmer tone that expected. "One person I happen to trust is Edward Rose, your boss. Not in the way that we tell each other secrets, but in the way that I trust I know how he will react to the actions of others," Marlow said, looking over at Kim.

"Mr. Goolsby, I don't think we came here for a lecture on friendship," Kim interjected.

"Of course. There is a point, however. There are a handful of systems that are run through the Mags-Tech mainframe that I get personal alerts on. The GPS system you accessed happens to be one of them. Don't be shy; I know what you just had for breakfast," Marlow said, making Kim and I glance at each other.

"Are you physic? Or maybe come upon some unexplained power recently?" I asked, thinking about the water from the Fountain. Was he a Mage now?

"No, I triangulated your coordinates when you accessed the system. Plus, one of you smells like cheap bacon and the other like syrup. I can smell the two of you from here," Goolsby said, taking a breath that told us banter time was over.

"Nonetheless. As I was saying, there is one other person I used to trust that is no longer as of…" Goolsby looked at his watch. "Let's just say no longer employed."

Kim shuffled, understanding the inference.

"OK, we get it. What do you want?" I asked, standing up straight.

"As you figured out, this specific GPS satellite system has a Mags-Tech upgrade that tracks surges in Etherium. Much like an e-meter, it can tell us in most cases what kind. Not the small stuff. Just the big stuff. I received a notification. This time it was for dozens of signals. The alerts you set. I went to ask my IT lead that works directly for me what was going on, only to find him rapidly dumping files out of the system. I just happened to be watching from my tablet." Marlow stopped, flipping open the laptop on the hood of the car. It was an oddly shaped, larger-than-normal system. The container it was sitting in had two slots, each holding some type of tablet. Goolsby starting punching keys.

Kim shuffled her feet, taking a deep breath. I was with her. Goolsby was taking too long.

"Is there a reason this is taking so long?" I asked as Goolsby popped out one of the tablets from the case.

"Yes. I was downloading the data. As I was saying, when I confronted this person, they froze, and I could tell we had a data breach. After some direct questions, we gained some valuable information. For example, do you now that someone had given our IT person a code to dump the alerts when a certain demon was gating or working magic? Also, but most importantly, to hide certain types of events in certain concentrations," Goolsby said, holding out the tablet as Kim took it.

"Two things to understand. First, this is a revenue stream for the organization. In all fairness probably one of our most lucrative. I checked; over the past year, profits have been down 45 percent. This also had been manipulated not to raise suspicion. You can understand that with the Balance coming, Mags-Tech will go public; our books can't appear to be inaccurate. We will be fine now that we have found this discrepancy," Goolsby said coolly.

There it was: money and power. I had just helped Marlow Goolsby with a serious problem twice in over the course of a year. Killing his brother's murderer and now saving face for his company. I still hadn't figured out how he ran it from the board and not the CEO position he relinquished.

"Ah, I can see the realization in your eyes why we are here talking now," Marlow said, Kim looking concerned. She was smart, but I had a feeling the full picture hadn't landed yet.

Kim interrupted. "We looked at that data just a little over an hour ago. All this has happened since then?" Kim asked, genuinely having the million-dollar question.

Note to self: Be careful what I watch on my work phone, I thought, smirking.

"Secondly, I know what you're looking for and believe that information is on this tablet. Yes, I know you're looking for those Thule Society fanatics. It's bad for business, and I still haven't cut the head off that lion. You helped cut its claws," Marlow said, closing his laptop and walking to the driver's side of the car, taking out his keys.

The sound of waves and seagulls filled the void.

"That's it? You're just going to leave us with this tablet?" I asked, Kim taking a step toward Goolsby as he froze, staring at her with calculated precision.

"Don't," Goolsby said, slipping into the front seat, starting the whisper-quiet engine and pulling out.

Kim and I stood there looking at each other, holding the tablet.

"Should we turn it on?" Kim asked, shrugging her shoulders.

"Let's get it back to the team. I want Jenny to take a look at this thing. You coming or still need to head to Jacksonville?"

"I need to get back. You better call me tonight or else."

We drove back to the diner talking about Marlow's semicryptic message. Both of us decided that it was, as always, in his best interest, and we were about to do his dirty work.

Driving off I figured there was only one way to cap off an eventful morning—a trip to FA's.

CHAPTER 16

Hangovers and Heartaches

After several rounds of top-shelf old-fashioneds, I called Phil to come pick me up. I can say with all duplicity that gating while intoxicated can be adventurous and at the same time not so fun. I had yet to gate after drinking a good amount without finding myself being extremely sick on whatever was on the receiving side of the gate.

Trish, and the rest of the bar, was busy, and she had somehow acquired my keys. The storm was over, and all the travel from the ball had subsided. At some point Trish came over and explained that most folks knew St. Augustine was the main location and, due to the storm, figured the place was closed. It didn't make sense, but I went with it as she carried on.

It was roughly four o'clock by the time Phil came in. He had simply gated through the Transitions Office; however, he was late working on tracking down the bracelets from the chimera incident.

"Total shit, bruther. We have to open the place back up, business as usual. Of course, you're not allowed and all," Phil said as he started pounding gin and tonics like it was his full-time job.

Within thirty minutes we were singing Styx songs at the corner of the bar where, much to everyone's surprise, Trish had installed a jukebox. She apparently watched some bar rescue show and was under the impression that adding a jukebox could possibly raise profits something like 200 percent. It was awesome, and everyone was surely enjoying our rendition of "Mr. Roboto."

By 7:00 p.m. we both took a breath long enough to notice the dozen or so text messages we had both received.

Ed came walking through the door with Jenny not looking happy. Phil and I leaned over, acting like we were fine. Phil snorting was probably the first sign that we were in fact hammered and not going to hide it.

"Gents," Ed said, looking at us, trying to size up the level of issue he was going to have the rest of the night. "Trish called and said I needed to get you two home."

Phil was so red in the face he finally burst out laughing, causing me to follow suit. "It's Mr. Roboto and company," I said, not realizing the words coming out of my mouth.

Ed shook his head and smiled as Jenny walked over to the bar talking with Trish. "Right, well if you can't beat them, join'em," Ed said, pulling up to the bar and wincing as he sat down.

Phil and I motioned for another round, only to be met with glasses of water, while Ed got a glass of Magnus served neat.

We sat at the bar for another two hours talking about everything but magic. Jenny joined us to be the voice of reason, including scolding me for not calling my parents.

The next morning was rough. I was still sore and

hungover. Petro fetched some of Phil's magic snake-oil cure-all. After I downed the elixir, things started to come back into focus.

I needed to get with the group and go over the details from yesterday. The prior night was needed to center my thoughts and the team's collective sanity.

"Man, you look rough, boss," Petro said as I finally made it down to the kitchen table. He had even pulled out a bowl for me after dropping off the potion. He was being a little too nice.

"Thanks, Petro. How was your night? I noticed you didn't come out with Ed and Jenny. Missed you, man," I said, filling my bowl. Yes—cereal first, milk second.

"Well, the old lady wanted me to stay in last night and watch a movie. I think she wants to move in," Petro said, looking at me in a manner suggesting he was asking permission.

"What does that entail?" I asked, seeing him come to life.

"Well, first we need to get what you called married. We call it 'joined' back on the Plane. Then we can live together and start raising a family," Petro said as milk permeated his majestic mustache.

"This is deep for an early morning hangover conversation. If you're looking for my blessing, you have it. Hey, you know that sitting room downstairs? I never go in there, and it would be a great spot for you two," I said, enjoying the normal conversation.

"You still thinking of moving out?" Petro asked. It was a good question. A week ago, I was primed and ready to move. This morning it wasn't even a thought.

"If you're asking if you can have the house, the answer's no. If I do move out, I promise you will have the run of the place. After all someone will need to keep an eye on things for when…" I choked out the last words, about to refer to Gramps as the binding spell took hold, not allowing me to speak about him being alive.

"You OK, boss?"

"Yeah, I'm fine. Hey, when are we planning the wedding?" I asked, gruffly changing the subject.

"Well…I kinda have to ask first," Petro said, rubbing the back of his neck.

"Sounds like you got some work to do there, playboy," I said, Petro hovering over to me.

Petro started gyrating his waist, letting me know he did plenty of work already. We both chuckled and headed to the dining room. I texted the group, letting them know we needed to meet.

I saluted James sitting at the security desk, entering the main entrance hall. It was moved due to the cleanup and only a few feet away from the dining room.

"Morning, sunshine. Looks like you all had a great evening," Kim said in a snarky yet playful voice. She beat me to my own meeting. I noticed she had some light scratches on her face that were not there yesterday. I wonder if she had found the cat man.

"You OK—" I started, being cut off by Phil walking in and closing the door behind him.

"Morning, bruther. That was a pisser last night," Phil said, slapping me on the back and bowing his head toward Kim. He smelled like fresh soap this morning and, as always, sweet tobacco. Not the bad, musty smoke odor, but that of an old pipe full of some exotic flavor. I made a joke about him using Irish Spring soap, and now I thought he used it to brush his teeth.

"Right. I think we all know each other. Kim was filling us in on yesterday's events. Did you bring the tablet?" Ed asked as I sat it in front of Jenny. She already had her laptop on, punching buttons faster than Petro could tell jokes about my dating life or, well…lack thereof. Note to self: Call Aslynn back.

"Let me get this straight: you two figured this out while eating pancakes?" Jenny asked, smiling and confirming the story she knew was true. I think she was impressed.

Kim and I both grinned, looking at each other.

"Not everything is solved by magic. I think this is a lesson for all of us. We have technology and might as well use it. Some of those old goats on the Council would be wise to do so as well. Great work," Ed said, looking around the room. Him calling the Council "old goats" caught us by surprise. "Jenny, how long do you think it will take to pull the data Max isolated?"

"Probably a few hours. Long enough for Max to work on his castings. Ned just sent me a note. He's not making it over today. Inspector Holder is with him in meetings," Jenny said as Phil and Petro volunteered to help.

"Next order of business. As you are all now aware, the Transitions Office is back in action. The Council has taken over all operations openly. We all know it was under the radar. Now it seems like they are helping instead of other nefarious reasons. Optics and all, before it was for a reason; now profiling Mages and Ethereals is justified. The regular government is fine with it as long as they have access to the data. Honestly, I don't think they know what to do with the data fully yet. All in the name of safety. The thought according to Ned is that only the Council will be able to help with any issues that may come up," Ed said, sounding mildly annoyed.

"With that we are no longer pulling duty in the office," Jenny chimed in. "The Council is sending a group specifically trained to manage 'the administrative center,' as it's going to be called. One Mage and one Ethereal, be it a V or a Fae. I think the statement for the office in town was 'Not any of us.'"

Phil let out a chuckle, putting an unlit smoke on the table. "More time for us to get into trouble."

The room all looked around at each other nodding, basically echoing Phil's sentiment.

"Phil, what did you find yesterday about the link bracelets?" Ed asked as Phil sat down the jelly doughnut. The strawberry jelly burst out the other side as the group looked over at him, white powder covering his beard and mustache.

"Omff...moff," Phil said as he finished chewing his bite, taking a sip of coffee, and popping the unlit cigarette back in his mouth. It helped him think.

"So after our little party with that damn beast, James took that evidence box downstairs all proper to secure it," Phil said as it dawned on me to send James a text. After all, he was just outside the door.

"I confirmed this..." Phil stopped, looking over. James walked in appearing nervous; all the eyes in the room were on him.

"Hey, man, have a seat," I said as James relaxed and sat at the chair closest to the door. Jenny nodded in approval.

Hey, give the guy some credit; we fought a monster together.

"Anyways," Phil started back. "James checked in the evidence, as is procedure. Here's where it gets interesting. Those goons Carvel and Darkwater showed up the next day, including Terrence in tow. We know this because James checked them in. Terrence now works for Councilman Darkwater. There was some type of agreement, and he is now under his employ. I went to check out the evidence room, and no one checked the stuff out. It was gone," Phil said, taking a break to sip his coffee, the smoke rolling to the corner of his mouth. I didn't smoke, but watching the guy was art.

James spoke up. "No one other than someone in this room or a member of the Council would have access to that part of the Atheneum."

Kim looked over, letting a breath out through her nose. "Right. Like keeping that monster I keep hearing so much about out of here."

"Close, lass," Phil said. "Thing is, we have something that everyone seems to ignore. Pixies are a smart lot," he said as Petro lightly dusted the table.

Macey and Lacey spend most of their time in the labs. They were basically in-house scientists and very smart. Jenny, a few months back, told me a handful of stories about them doing some fieldwork and the aftereffects. Those two apparently liked to use rather creative potions to solve their problems. Not to mention if you mess with one, you then truly had an issue on your hands with the other.

"The ladies"—as Phil called them—"were in the labs when I went down and happened to be in there when that lot showed up as well. They took the box of goodies and left. So I called Terrence. He was hesitant at first but stated that it was checked into the Council evidence keep that same day. Wrong!" Phil exclaimed, followed by the sound of a horn like a buzzer at the end of a basketball game. "Jenny checked. Someone logged them in minutes after our call. Long story short, I gated over and picked one of the bracelets up and put it in a grounding box. It's down in the lab," Phil finished.

A grounding box was made of silver and iron, two elements that had drastic effects on Ethoturgical items.

"Macey and Lacey have it down in the lab running tests. I want to see if we can get some type of tracking or reverse spell to work on them. For some reason, by the time we got the bracelets, they were neutral. Almost like someone didn't want them traced. Or perhaps they were made that way," Jenny said, looking up from her keyboard long enough to get her point across.

"I'm not buying it. Something's off about those folks," I said, thinking about Terrence. He had shown up at a few key odd times; however, he didn't seem to have any skin in the game. I started thinking back to when Mouth dropped me off. He was obviously doing his job, but Terrence seemed to be present, all the while being deliberately removed.

"They'd say the same about you," Ed said, making a point. "Politics is a nasty business, but we need proof, not conjecture."

The rest of the room agreed, including James. He chimed in. "Oh, and Dr. Freeman will be back today. He called the front desk."

"Great. I need him to do some research on this gate crystal. I hear he's moving back on campus at Flagler College, taking up a new position. Things are too cramped for him around here," Ed said, standing up. "Jenny, when you get the data, send out a message. Talk to everyone shortly, and, gents, no day drinking today."

Kim walked over, her phone already up to her ear. "Hey, Max, I have to go. I'll be back later."

I nodded, watching as she walked out of the room in a one-directional conversation, telling someone when and where to be. I wanted to find out about that scratch on her face. *Oh well*, I thought. Target practice time.

Phil, Petro, and I walked down to the shooting range. James had to get back to work, and this time we promised an evening of drinks. Phil even patted him on the back.

The shooting range was in the lower levels, underground and carved out of rock. I had yet to figure that out as there was not much underground but sand and water in Florida. It had some odd properties, one being that if you shot a firearm, there was next to no noise. Other noises echoed loudly off the walls. The space was the size of a tennis court, and the Council had used it for meetings during the ball. Everything was back in order. The room, as always, was cool and smelled of damp stone.

"Remind me again how you are going to help me, Phil?" I asked, as he couldn't fully cast without a blended or enchanted item. He could still light small flames and do a few odd tricks but nothing that truly projected.

"It's just like me projecting my strength. For me to light a candle, it takes about as much gas as it would for you to sling a ball of hellfire." Phil was right. I had recently been working on collecting the element in my hands. I had gotten to the point of being able to do it with water to create steam and project it out, but the reaction pretty much did all that work.

Petro chimed in. "Let's try this, boss. Try to collect as much in your hand as you can. Use your hand that you wear your castor on."

I had been practicing this. My issue was setting everything around me on fire and controlling it. To date, I had been able to effectively do this through the use of an item that allowed me to focus. The sword, rod, or even the Judge, to a point.

The red glowing ball started forming in my hand, hissing as it did in protest. That is one thing Jenny had commented on. My ability to also work with water, even though much lighter, seemed to generate the hiss.

Phil and Petro watched as the bloodred flame took shape slowly calming down. I took a breath, concentrating on the shape of the flame and not the end result. According to Ned and Belm, once I had a ball in my hand, all I had to do was throw it. While it would have a little more kick, it was still the same concept.

As I held out my hand, the flame started wandering up my arm. It still amazed me that it didn't burn my skin. Clothes, yes; skin, no. After realizing I wasn't getting the ball of hellfire this go-round, I shook my hands off, flinging the sticky flame onto the stone floor. Phil and Petro hopped back, avoiding the little pieces bouncing off the floor.

We spent the next hour doing the same exercise. It wasn't until Phil started making fun of my dating life that I finally concentrated.

I looked down at my hand, frustrated yet motivated at the same time. Thoughts of the past week started to come into sharp focus. The ball, Carvel, the ambush, Bo, everything. I took a deep, calming breath, pushing my channeled focus into my hand. I could feel the castor warm up; the normal burning-red flame engulfed my hand.

It was more concentrated, and for once I could actually hear the whisper of the flames lick the cool air. Not the sticking, flowing flame that I used to burn into the flesh of the Eater or the chimera—it felt solid almost like a liquid. I made a fist again, focusing on trapping the flame in my hand.

A tight pulling sensation in the chest took my breath for a second. I opened my fist up, exposing the burning, angry, bloodred ball of flowing hellfire in my palm hovering in place, begging for direction. The flame crackled under my control.

"Holy shit, bruther!" Phil yelled.

I excitedly slung the small ball of hellfire at the targets, setting them on fire. The ball shot from my hand with more force than I had used, taking me again by surprise.

Petro jumped on Phil's shoulder as he hopped up and down. I found myself doing the same, minus being on Phil's shoulder. My hand was red and sore from trying for the past hour but otherwise fine. On my third jump I settled down, feeling drained from the effort, not to mention my side and leg.

We sat and watched the flames dance on the target and stone wall behind it as Phil lit up a cigarette.

"Well, I guess you passed that class," Petro said, nodding his head. He looked proud. I felt proud. Or maybe it was the magic hangover elixir in my system.

After a few more light attempts, I had the basics of it down. It had taken some gas out of my tank, and I still had a few things to get to.

The crew walked me back to the office, us all eying the bar but erring on letting it be for the moment. I needed to call my folks.

"I'll be down shortly. I'm betting Jenny's about got that data pulled," I said as Petro made a whooshing noise, acting like he was throwing a ball of hellfire.

My mom picked up on the second ring.

"We could have been swept away, and you would have never known." The voice of my mother sternly came over the line.

"Well, you were in another state, so I figured that was a slim chance unless the Marriott was flooded due to a pipe bursting," I said, pushing my luck.

Mom chuckled. "Just messing with you. I heard you've been busy."

"You seem to always know a lot," I said as I could hear the phone clicking to speaker, my mom yelling for Pops in the background. I hated talking to old folks on the phone.

"Well, dear, your friend Kim stopped by last night. She was out looking for someone and found Oscar. She was in the area, so she dropped him off. Told us you have been busy," Mom said, as if she knew more than she was letting on as my dad joined us.

My father had his mind erased before I was born, protecting my mother and her unborn child—that's me—from an attacker after Gramps. Ever since then he has not been a fan of, or really accepted the magical community. He thought everyone was weird. Jenny, Petro, and I had actually been working on a spell to bring his memory back, or at least a part of it.

"Yeah, that cat is a handful, always wandering off. Coming back days later. Plus, the thing eats as much as I do. Don't even get me started on Oscar. I still haven't figured out where he goes to the bathroom. He never uses the litter box. Gramps and his cat," my dad chided, and again I noted even my parents called him *Gramps*.

"I'm planning on stopping over for dinner next weekend. I haven't seen Oscar in forever," I said, letting them know I would come around soon and hopefully getting them off my back for the next few days while we tracked down leads from the tablet.

"That would be lovely, dear. I have a few things for you also," Mom said as my dad cleared his throat.

"We found some old things of yours in the garage. I was going through some old boxes. Well, I didn't want to throw them out. You can pick up your stuff. See you then," Pops said. I could hear him walking off.

The phone clicked off speaker. It was just Mom and me. "Be careful. I heard about what happened at the Atheneum and about Ed getting hurt. I'll make a lasagna."

"Yeah, about that…" I said, realizing that she had not heard about my injury. Kim had done me a solid. I also think I was starting to figure out how she got that scratch. Wonder why she didn't tell me about last night.

"Just be careful. Call me Friday. I may have you pick up a couple things for me to, you know, work with."

That was my mom's way of telling me she was basically going to get a cauldron out and make potions. She was, after all, a witch.

"Love you too, Mom" was the last thing I said as we both hung up, the line clicking.

As if the great text gods knew I was off the phone, a ding, vibrate, and zip notified me that Jenny was ready to go over the data.

After a few seconds of reflection thinking about the phone call and Kim's encounter with Oscar, I called into my charm, for Petro.

"Hey, boss," Petro said with a grin on his face.

I raised an eyebrow, taking in his smirk. "Either you just won the lottery, or you just bumped uglies for the last ten minutes," I said, shaking my head.

"Wrong and wronger," Petro said, landing on the desk and dusting the space. This was something different. I knew when he was excited about girls, but this was different upon further inspection. "My brothers are coming to visit in a couple of weeks!"

"Treek and crew?" I asked, hoping I remembered the names correctly.

"You bet. Treek, Gran, and Bosley. They said they're bringing the Evergate stone back. Treek figured since there's ten stones in the Evergate to use, you wouldn't notice one missing. He was wrong, as always, and they have a surprise," Petro said, overcome with excitement. I know he missed his brothers. The Plane, not so much. "We got to have a party."

"All right, all right, wild man, calm your wings. Let's get through today first. We'll plan something. I guess they'll be coming through the Evergate," I said remembering our initial encounter.

Petro and I walked into a full room. Frank was even there, nodding and giving me a toothy grin showing off his fangs. Dr. Freeman was also in the room, and true to her word, Jenny had added James to the list of trusted people. For now.

Kim walked up and smiled. "Call your mom yet?"

"Actually yes. You should have mentioned that you visited my folks. Did Oscar give you that scratch?" I asked, wanting to get the conversation out of the way.

"No" was all Kim replied with.

I stood there, cocking my head looking for more.

"All right, the report of the cat person came in close to your folk's house. We went into the woods, and I walked into a grove of what had to be at least twenty cats in an abandoned house. Going through the house, a cat jumped down off a half-collapsed bookshelf and scratched my face. After that, I don't remember much. It's embarrassing. I think I passed out. Anyways I wake up to find Oscar licking my face. Ben was outside and didn't realize I had passed out or whatever. That was it. Ben walked in, and I took the cat and went to your folks' house. It was about two hundred meters from the tree line. I asked your mom about the house, and she said it was abandoned after a drug bust years ago. She said Oscar prowls around there due to all the stray cats that have taken up there. I filed a report, and animal control is going to clear it out," Kim said, lightly smiling, lifting an energy drink to her lips.

"You know those things will kill you..." I said, realizing I drank potions frequently without reservation. "I know that house. When they moved in a while back, I could see it when the leaves dropped in the winter. Glad it worked out" was all I could say. The whole story seemed suspect; however, she believed what she was telling me. I thought it was time to check up on old Oscar. I was starting to suspect there was more to the cat than met the eye.

The rest of the team stood around looking at Jenny as she rolled out a freshly printed map on the table.

I walked over to Phil, bumping him with my shoulder. We both stood there with Petro perched on my shoulder.

"As everyone knows we have been given some data that may pinpoint the location of the missing gate Mages. Ed believes this information needs to not leave this group. He has reported this to Ned and was given the same opinion. Here is what we know," Jenny said, looking over at Frank.

Frank was dressed as most other Vamps during working hours, in an immaculate manner. Today it was a suit with no tie. An extra button left undone. Tailored to be functional as well as classic. His hair was slicked back on his head, and his pale complexion somehow worked with his chiseled, soap opera–like features.

"There are three locations that appear to have any lack of reporting. Each area is roughly twenty square miles in diameter," Frank said in his smooth, casual voice.

"One in Greenland, another in Norway, and the last in, of course, southern Germany. We believe that the gate Mages are more than likely being held in Greenland or Norway due to the gate magic showing up on the e-spectrum before the reporting stopped. It appears Mr. Goolsby—"

"Goolsby. He's no mister anything," I interrupted Frank, not liking the casual show of respect for the man.

Frank smiled. We were friends, and he knew I didn't mean any disrespect. Vamps were, after all, infected Fae. The one thing they didn't take lightly to was being disrespected. They were actually rather protective of the human race due to the codependence. Technology had changed much for the vampire community, and in most cases, they were as normal as the rest of us, minus the superhuman strength, thirst for blood (be it synthetic or real), and an extended long life. Due to recent technological updates, they could even hang out during the day.

"Can't disagree with you there." Frank started back up. "The data was pulled in six-month intervals. Max, I believe you and Kim did that piece. Goolsby just isolated it. We believe this data breach is contained. When I say data breach, I mean we don't think that the Thule Society or whoever may be on the payroll on the Council knows this yet. The data is not awfully specific. The geographic locations in Greenland and Norway have made is simple to locate our possible targets…" Frank continued as I leaned over to Phil

"Where is he getting all this other than that tablet?" I asked Phil in a hushed whisper. Others in the room were mumbling, so our sidebar conversation wasn't out of place.

Phil, on the other hand, had two volumes: loud as hell and church-mouse quiet. "The Vs have a private army of sorts. Kind of like their own sub-Council. They police their own and all that rot," Phil said, getting a stern look from Jenny. "The scary thing is the damn private army they control. The CSA, as you know, uses them frequently. Frank and Angel after last year have gained street credit with the leaders of the clan, as they call them."

I shook my head catching the tail end of Frank's review.

"The Devil's Castle is located in Greenland. It's not truly a castle, rather a large geo-formation. There's a research facility that was used by the Allied forces during the war. We project this to be our first targeted location. The footprint is fairly easy to nail down to a handful of locations. It will take a few days to get everything together. Germany is going to be the hard one to narrow down due to the density. Norway will also take a little research," Frank concluded, handing it back over to Ed.

"Bullshit. Let's go tonight," Phil bellowed out followed by a belch.

"Right, everyone, calm down. I know this is the first solid lead we have; however, we need to take this in stride. We are going with the most obvious location first. Lilith understands these types of things, and it will more than likely be the low-hanging fruit; however, it's enough for us to bring to the Council and get their full support after we get on-site and confirm. We aren't going to sit on this but need to be careful. The Council is not aware of this, and we do this, we do it of our own accord. Unless we go and get solid proof, I'd rather ask for forgiveness than permission. We all know the consequences if things go south," Ed said, deadpan serious.

"Where's Belm and Jamison?" I asked, noticing their absence.

"Max, we…" Ed said, looking around the room, "believe it's better to leave Belm out of this operation, and more importantly, as far from you till this Bo thing gets situated. The Council has asked him to locate Bo anyways."

I gave a thumbs-up, shaking my head. There was more to it; I knew it. Ed literally had just said he was involved by proxy. He was smart and chose his words wisely. By now the team that was at the Atheneum during the attack fully understood Bo's involvement in this.

Phil, Petro, and I talked with Ed and Jenny about my casting success. I was exhausted from the attempts, and everyone acknowledged as much. The plan was simple: meet up in the morning, pick a team, and get as close to the first location as we could.

CHAPTER 17

*And the Party Begins
with a Song of Rebellion!*

It was roughly 6:00 p.m. by the time Petro and I made it back to our side of the house. As usual we parted ways at the kitchen.

Walking up the stairs, I took my time looking at paintings of the past proprietors of the facility. More importantly the Postern; for some reason I felt all the eyes of centuries past gazing at me in contempt.

"What?" I said to no one, the sound echoing off the empty hall.

"Hey, Max," Belm's raspy voice came from behind my desk, almost making me lose my footing on the stairs. "Easy there, killer," his voice channeling down the stairs.

"What's up with demons and making it a personal hobby trying to scare the shit out of me?" I said, letting my impatience flow into my voice.

By the time I was in the office, Belm was already walking

to the bar, the squeak of my chair evident. I bet he had his feet on my desk. That's reserved for my, Petro's, and Phil's feet.

"Relax. I think you're going to like this scare," Belm said, pouring himself a glass of Magnus. The smell of cloves filled the air. His tone was one of excited interest. He was either about to tell me he was getting married or that I won the lottery. Both highly unlikely.

I walked over, picking up a glass, but Belm put his hand over mine, lowering the glass and looking me square in the eyes. His eyes were endless pools of black. So dark the light didn't reflect off them. They were both predatory and intrigued at the same time. It froze me in place.

"Have a seat. I think it's time you and I have a little chat," Belm said in his raspy yet now stoic voice. It was like a dad talking to his son about why they weren't getting a puppy for Christmas.

He went back behind the desk, sitting down, opening the drawer that held all the potion bottles that Petro could not even figure out, pulling out a crimson-red one. We had decided to label them "Do not drink"—you know, in case we got hammered one night and ran out of good ideas.

"Call your little hetero life partner. I think he needs to be here as well."

I reached down to my charm, calling Petro. Not ten seconds later, he came flying into the room looking over at Belm. "Dammit" was all he said, easing over to the table and landing. He lightly shook the dust off his wings.

I looked between the two of them, having the sinking feeling that Petro knew what this was all about.

"Petro?" I asked in the form of a statement.

Petro just let out a deep breath and shook his head.

"Great. Now that we're all here, first things first. I have

a gift for you," Belm said, reaching into his leather jacket and pulling out a discolored handkerchief. He clunked it on the desk, exposing an old-style skeleton key.

"What's this for?" I asked, reaching over to pick it up.

"A key to one of the gates in the Postern. The person who wanted you to have this told me to inform you that this is a belated re-birthday gift free of obligation," Belm rasped, clearer than usual. He was getting better at holding himself together, and other than his eyes, he could pass as normal.

It was obviously a gift from Devin, his father. "What does it do?" I asked as Petro walked over to the key. I scooted my chair close to the desk so he could see.

"It will take you wherever you want to go; however, opposite of the Evergate, it will not bring you back. This is the Seekergate. The bonus is you don't have to have been to that location. Even more importantly the gates were built to work together. Never go through the Seekergate without a gate stone from the Evergate," Belm said instructionally, his age and experience showing.

The Evergate is the most used gate in the house. The only caveat is that you had to be at a location to gate back to the Postern, and even then, only if you had one of the ten stones set in the door. One happens to be in the possession of Petro's brothers. You could leave a stone hidden somewhere and gate there from the Postern. It was like setting up an automatic two-way gate. In most cases it was just a one-way ride back to safety, often referred to as plan B.

I sat up straight. "This is amazing. Thank you."

"Don't thank me yet," Belm joked, taking a long pull of his drink. Petro sat there, not giving anything away.

"All right, what is it, and why can't I have a drink in my own house?" I said in a smart-ass tone.

"Well, I think you are going to have a busy night. See, what if I told you there is a reason demons keep showing up around you, and for Devin taking such an interest in you as well?" Belm said, drawing it out.

"I'd listen. I'm trying to figure out that very thing myself," I said, sitting back, leaving the key on the table.

"Devin, as you know, is my father. Have you ever wondered if I had any brothers or sisters?" Belm asked as a lump started to form in my throat.

"Bo?" I asked, seeing Petro shaking his head and smoothing out his mustache. I had to admit, it was epic.

"Well, we are all kind of related, I guess, in one way or another, but no. I have a sister. Your grandfather…well, let's just say your grandfather was close to her at one point in his life."

It landed on me like a ton of bricks at the same time, feeling like the last piece of a puzzle fitting into place after hours of sacrifice. "Liliths, my grandmother," I said, letting out a breath at the same time.

Belm nodded. Petro didn't look in my eyes.

"Petro, you knew about this?" I asked, more intrigued than upset.

"Hey, boss…well, you smell just like a demon and throw hellfire around, so yes," Petro said, looking up to see me shaking my head with an exacerbated grin. "You're not mad at me, are you, boss? For not saying anything? I thought you kind of knew."

"About Lilith, yeah…I knew about that. Belm, start talking," I said, not being as coy with him. After all, he was family. Was he my great-uncle's brother's cousin's nephew? It was slightly jumbled, but I landed on great-uncle.

"We knew you hadn't figured it out yet. With everything

going on, we thought it was prudent for you not to know."

"You mean that I'm, what, 25 percent demon? Or that we are related? Does my mom know about any of this?"

Belm took a deep breath the rasping in his chest moving. "No, I give you my word. She knows nothing of this."

That was that; he gave me his word.

"This is why Devin keeps coming around. You keep showing up, and whoever the hell Bo is has decided to ruin my life," I said, feeling much like I had one year ago sitting in Ed's practice. I still hadn't figured out who or what his partner was.

"Well, this is where things get complicated. Bo doesn't truly know. He kind of just feels the pull, if you know what I mean. With that and the recent issues with Lilith, Devin and I decided to give you all the tools and information you may need to survive."

"Survive!" I said, standing up. "I'm tired of this cat-and-mouse game. You gave me this key and came here for a reason."

"To the point, as to be expected. Well, as of thirty minutes ago, someone beat you to the Devil's Castle. That someone is Bo. He just informed me that there is a gate Mage there as well as a woman that he said smelled like you with a British accent both in cells," Belm said, implying that he had some type of link to Bo he didn't want others knowing about.

"Chloe," Petro said, standing up.

"Calm down, buddy. Let me get this straight. You or whoever wants me to go to this place and do what?" I asked, wondering if I was being manipulated by the devil himself.

Belm let out a laugh, sliding the red potion over. "Drink up. You haven't figured it all the way out yet, have you? Max, you are the by-product of Lilith's experiments to form a superior race of hybrid demons. Demons that could walk among normal society and still be just as strong. Almost godlike. In some cases, maybe stronger. The jury's out on that one. Anyways your mother and Tom was the human part separated by a generation," Belm said, cocking his head toward me.

"You're saying she tricked Gramps into having a child?" I asked, hoping that there was more to the story. Love and war, mistakes made, and all that good bullshit.

"Oh yes. Tom was heartbroken. The Purity Law and that Transitions Office both have the same intent. To catalog and keep the races pure. Sound familiar? Sounds better when you call it something else and compare it to the DMV. The Council has known about this for some time. They don't want something new popping up they can't handle. They're scared of what it may produce. To be honest there's not too many Dr. Frankensteins running around. Just that one..." Belm said, getting sidetracked and trailing off.

"You want me to go there bring back the gate Mage and?" I asked again.

"Be the hero of course," Belm said, shaking his head. "I don't want anything. I need you to go there and leave this box there. It will erase any trace that Bo was there. He said he might have tripped and fell, causing a few deaths. The last thing we or you need is a report that he ripped apart a private army. He did this without my knowledge or Devin's approval. If this waits till tomorrow, it will be too late. The location, I am betting, will be sanitized."

"That's it? I'm not a cleanup service."

"Let me ask you this. Would you rather be feared or prosecuted? All joking aside, maybe a little hero action is just what your reputation needs. Drink this potion; it will bring out the best in you, and, little guy, test these under a full moon. It will yield better results in figuring out what they do," Belm said, taking in a deep breath, relaxing his shoulders, and sliding the potion to my side of the desk.

There it was. Another small wave in a large ocean. I was losing track of all the loose ends faster than they appeared. I picked up the key as Belm tossed a map down.

"Bo is riding a thin line, but at the end, our goals are all the same. To stop Lilith. By now you understand, however, that if she is captured, it will look bad for our type, and she is family. We need to take her back to the under permanently. Max, we aren't all bad. It's not what you think. The over and under, heaven and hell, whatever you call it. There has been a war raging for thousands of years. Things are changing and shifting. Most of us are bad, but we are fighting for the same things as everyone else does," Belm said, finally standing up as well.

"Money and power?" I replied, looking down and seeing the concern on Petro's face. He was avoiding this so we didn't have to deal with it. Petro thought he was protecting me.

"No. Home," Belm said as he popped out of existence, leaving the smell of ozone lingering in the air.

"Well, Petro, looks like we are going to have a long night," I said, bottoming up the potion and immediately regretting it.

Besides the sensation of my insides burning, my senses came into laser focus. My vision, hearing, smell, and overall awareness slapped me in the face at a level I hadn't experienced before.

"Wow there, boss, you're glowing with whatever it is that stuff happens to be. It's like you're radioactive with magic," Petro said, smirking and impressed.

I grinned, listening to Ed talk to Jenny from across the house. "Saddle up. We're taking a little field trip," I said, walking to my room to grab every last piece of gear I had.

"We're actually going?" Petro asked, smiling from ear to

ear. Like I said, the little guy likes action—that or he was simply happy I wasn't mad at him. There was still a long talk that needed to be had. After all we shared Golden Grahams together every morning.

Five minutes later we were both in our gear from last year. I had Planes Drifter playing "To Hell and Back" in the background, setting the tone for the evening. A song of rebellion. I had my sword, service pistol, freshly charged short staff, Evergate stone, and two grenades for good measure. Yeah, I kept those under the bed. You know, in case of monsters.

I felt good, alive, like live energy. It was coursing through my body. "Let's get down to the Postern. We need to be quiet heading out," I said, looking down at the map. "When we get there, send a message to Phil letting him know we will be back soon but not where we are. Put the location in your phone on a delayed send afterward, just in case, to go out after thirty minutes so we can get this knocked out."

The box Belm had left was the size a new watch would come in. He had said to just open it and walk away.

Petro was holding a small rifle and had his ever-trusty sword hanging off his hip. The gun looked like something a GI Joe doll would have. It held darts that would dissolve or dissolute magic.

We looked at each other, both raising an eyebrow as Petro flew up and we fist bumped. "Alexa, music off!" I exclaimed as we walked out of the office shutting of the tunes.

The trip to the Postern was uneventful. For some reason I expected Leshya to stop us along the way, telling us to turn back. It never happened. I could hear the others in various locations throughout the house. I even swore I could hear someone kissing.

We walked into the Postern looking at the gate on the far

right opposite the Evergate. It was a normal-looking wooden door with swirling designs carved into the stained wood. The doorjamb was just as ornate having carved designs.

Petro had taken his position over my shoulder. "You think this is going to work?" I asked, pulling out the key and pushing it into the slot, feeling the immediate flood of Etherium. I turned the key to the right; the lock clicked. I concentrated on the location in my mind that was on the map as I pulled the handle, opening the door and seeing a shimmering wall. I pulled the key out of the door as I walked through the gate with Petro on my shoulder, closing it behind us.

The pull in my stomach was immediate and violent. I took the final step out of the gate, and the feeling subsided to only be replaced by the freezing cold. "Dammit," I said, realizing that Greenland was in fact colder than Florida. Petro must have picked up on the vibe, shaking his head and closing his wings over his shoulder. I hadn't seen him do this before.

It was dark, as Greenland was slightly ahead of Florida. We knelt down behind a rock, looking down on a three-story concrete facility with a satellite dish on top having various security lights filling the dark spaces around the building with light. We could see the Devil's Castle standing resolute behind the facility.

"It's awful quiet, boss," Petro said directly into my ear, reaching down and tapping out a message to Phil, setting up a delayed note with our location just in case.

"Yup, according to Belm, Bo has already been here. I don't think we will be seeing too many people. Wait..." I said, focusing on the building.

The potion was in full effect. I could see a handful of faint heat sources in the building. "Damn," I said, impressed by the newly found short-term boost. "There's at least five people or whatever in there. One looks funny; the other four are, I'm sure, people for some reason."

"Where do you think we should go in at?" Petro asked, shaking off his wings.

"The front door. You smell that?" I asked Petro, knowing he could smell blood a mile away.

"Sure thing. Blood and e-core, lots of it, crafts and people. Yuck, I didn't notice it till you said something. This cold weather has my nose off slightly," Petro said, wrinkling his face.

We slid down the hill, still working to stay as stealthy as possible, just in case. As we got closer, it was obvious that Bo must have fallen several times over. The front door was off its hinges and used to cut the guard at the front door in half. This was a person. I could see light trails of Etherium seeping from the body. A Mage. Bo had killed a Mage.

"Damn," Petro said, zipping around the room; the smell of gunfire still lingering in the air. "There're at least ten bodies on this floor. I can't tell how many crafts."

The building was much like described. It was some type of old outpost and research facility. Cinder-block walls, old fluorescent lighting, various pieces of antiquated equipment, and cheap vinyl flooring. The walls of the entrance room were covered in blood and gray, sludgy e-core.

"That's what I was thinking. There is one person on the top floor. The rest are at least two stories down underground," I said, Petro looking over letting out a light chuckle.

"We need to figure out what that stuff in the bottle is and sell it. We'd be rich," he said, buzzing up to the roof by the door to the stairwell. He put his finger to his lips, pointing up and noting that whoever was upstairs knew we were there and investigating. By the looks of the room, they probably weren't too concerned with popping out and saving the day.

I pulled out Durundle, whispering *"Ignis"* as the blade sprung to life, turning the muted glow of the lights to a dull orange. The sword had a mind of its own or, as I called it, attitude. Sometimes it was all flames and hellfire. Other times it was a glowing-metal blade that looked as if it had just been pulled from a blacksmith's flame. Tonight, for this little adventure, it was in a mood to show off with a mixture of the two. The blade looked as if it was covered in smooth, lava-red flames dancing slightly above its surface. It almost resembled a lightsaber for all those *Star Wars* fans out there.

Petro looked over, zipping out of my way as I stepped forward and poked my head out the door to the stairwell.

A rain of Mage-killing silver-infused lead came flying down the open center as the *rat, tat, tat, chunk* of fully automatic gunfire from an older-style weapon filled the void. I stepped back in the room, looking around to see what type of firepower the person up the stairs had. The heat signature coming off the body was deep red, reflecting that of a human. Don't ask me how I knew; it just felt right.

Lying on the floor was an old-style MP40 from WWII. The German version of the American grease gun. "Great, Nazis. I hate Nazis," I said in my best Indiana Jones voice.

In all fairness whoever the person up the stairwell was, they more than likely weren't a Nazi. Just another lackey for the Thule Society. Taking a deep breath, I looked at Petro, nodding at him to get away from the door. As good as I felt, it was time to throw some hellfire around.

Petro zoomed behind me, holding his rifle as another hesitant burst of gunfire came from the stairwell. This time the gun only made it to the second *rat* before stopping with no sounds of further action. Our friend was out of ammunition.

Extinguishing the flame in the sword, I put it back in its sheath. The potion, whatever it was, still pushing me to the limits, I opened my right hand, cupping a ball of hellfire the size of a grapefruit.

I walked lightly over to the opening, hearing the sounds of a pistol being cocked. I guess our friend was still in the game. Looking around I picked up the first thing that was available—the arm of one of the soldiers—tossing it into the hallway. I still held the hellfire on my hand, the flames singeing the tactical shirt I had on.

The sounds of a low-caliber pistol rang in the stairwell as Petro let out a loud "Yuck," referring to my handling of the appendage.

After six rounds I heard the distinctive sound of a jammed weapon. Clinks of the shooter frantically puling the slide back and smacking the weapon reverberated in my overly charged ears.

I walked out into the opening on the bottom landing, looking up still seeing the heat signature of the body. The man was leaning over the rail frantically slapping the pistol. He didn't see me.

This time I didn't use a throwing motion. I held out my hand and pushed the ball of hellfire as it rocketed toward the man. The sound of the hissing flame caught his attention a second too late, the ball slamming into his hands and chest, evaporating most of his upper torso. I stood there staring in awe.

I had just killed a man without pause. He was trying to kill me, right? This was becoming routine in a way that didn't sit well with my inner self. The hellfire finished melting through the man as the top half of his charred body tumbled down the stairwell. The smell of burning charcoal and rubber permeated the confined space.

Petro came flying around the corner.

"Holy hell, boss!" he exclaimed, smirking yet put off by the scene at the same time.

"One down" was all I said, taking stock in my senses. I was still laser focused; however, I noticed my hearing and sight were starting to fade slightly. I had pushed the potion, whatever it was, to its limits.

We both looked at the remains of the man, seeing his uniform matching that of the others. About that time a text chimed on both our phones. It was Phil with an emoji of a beer. He must have thought Petro's text meant we were out drinking.

"There are four more people below us; at least one's a craft," I said, knowing they heard the gunfire. Only two of the bodies moved. They took position at the door two floors down. I was guessing two more goons.

"Which one's the craft?" Petro asked.

"The one closest to the door."

Petro looked over, raising his rifle. The little weapon thing was cute; I just wanted to hug it. Before I could say anything, Petro darted toward the air duct to our left. It was the old style with large gapped slats that you could move if you had enough hand strength.

Petro slipped between two slats, looked back, winked and took off. I could barely see a light trail of dust coming from him. While the potion let me see most of everyone else, Petro was a big blank. Normal, not crazy, colors.

I moved out into the stairwell, not being able to see the door below, and walked around to the steps leading down, keeping an eye on the bodies for movement. There were at least the bodies of three people and a handful of crafts in the stairwell; I couldn't work out the true body count due to the amount of violence used to dispatch them.

The figure closest to the door winked out of existence. The craft was gone. Petro had shot it with a dissolution round, making the creature dissolve. *Smart thinking*, I thought as the sounds and energy of a spell being cast went off.

"Dammit," I said under my breath, grabbing the rail, swinging my body around, and landing on the bottom floor. Another sound of a spell being cast. I could also make out a round being fired from Petro's rifle. What I didn't account for was the sting in my leg and side sending an electrifying jolt of pain through my body.

While the potion had me on overdrive, my body was reminding me it still needed a vacation. After a few seconds of reflection, I buried the sensation and grabbed the door handle, at the same time igniting my hand in hellfire. I could tell the person's body was facing away from the door.

The hellfire took only a second or two to do its job. I swung the door open, seeing the Mage in what looked like a gray uniform curve his hand, letting loose a white concentrated bolt of energy.

Petro was down the hall, by the looks of it behind an open door. It was cratered, and smoke generated cover as the man had released several spells in a row.

As my presence registered, the man turned, holding not a casting or spell but a fully automatic pistol as I reached out my hand, again willing hellfire under my command.

While in most cases this would have given Petro a clear shot at the man's back, there was so much energy and smoke coming from the hall I could barely make out the man's movements.

With a howl of anger, the man unleashed the weapon. It was a killing machine. Not a deterrent but rather a device for utter and total destruction on the body of its target. My mind slowed as I pushed out my will toward not the man but the weapon.

Tat, tat, tat, tat...tat, tat, tat, tat. The weapon sang, cutting through the air.

What the goon didn't expect me to do was push a column of hellfire the diameter of a basketball directly toward the weapon. The bullets sparked as they met the hellfire, outmatched by the heat, and disintegrated, joining the stream of hellfire as it slammed into his hand and lower torso, creating a smoking hole.

The silence that follows extreme violence is almost calming. I looked in the goon's face, seeing the realization that he was in fact dying. The hellfire, while still burning small parts around the hole in his body, had cauterized the wound. The smell of burning flesh and fabric filled the air.

It was poetic as the body of the man froze, not dropping to the ground but looking at me with complete and total lack of understanding. It was clear that someone had used mind magic on him. His body finally crumpled on the ground, lighting fire as the hellfire touched the unburnt fabric. I walked over, raising my other hand, pulling moisture from the air, and creating a ball of water in my hand that I lightly dropped on the body. Even I have morals.

"Petro," I said in a low voice.

Petro came flying from the end of the hallway. His face was covered in grime and dark ash. He didn't have his rifle anymore.

"Gods and graves, you all right?" I asked, seeing that he was shaking.

"Yeah, boss, that was crazy. I about didn't get out of the way. Whatever it was that you threw at that guy went through him, the door, the wall, and I believe there is an opening to the outside now by the drop in temperature," Petro said, flying over and taking position on my shoulder. He had been fighting for only a few minutes, but anyone that has ever been in a real fight will tell you it feels like an eternity.

"Sorry, buddy. I think we need to get out of here. That other text go out yet?"

"Another two minutes. We've only been here about five," Petro said, looking down at his miniature phone.

What had I just done? Better yet, why was I doing it? I felt like something was driving and pushing me to do more. It wasn't the potion either. The ease at which violence was coming to me sent conflicting messages, especially knowing my lineage. Pausing, I looked down at my hands; the power coming from my body was more than I had seen many others use. No sword or castor, just me. That came directly from me.

I needed to take some time off and get away from all the craziness that had happened over the last couple of weeks.

"All right, the other two are to our right down another flight of stairs. They aren't moving and look to be injured. Let's get this over with," I said, the weariness coming through in my voice as Petro let out a huff and took flight. As if on that thought, I started seeing the effects of the potion wearing off. My hearing started to muffle, presumably from the gunfire, and the body signatures were looking more like globs. "Petro, this stuff is wearing off. We need to get moving. Plus, I'm freezing," I said, letting out a breath and seeing it crystallize in the air.

"Oh, now you say you're cold," Petro said, lightly chuckling. "I'm freezing my wings off. Think you could use some of that hellfire to warm us up?"

"I'm not sure that would be a great idea down here," I said, my teeth starting to chatter, not thinking before that I could use my body as a possible way to keep myself and others warm. Note to self for later.

We walked around the corner and down the stairs, passing several piles of e-core representing the remains of several crafts. I noticed the lack of human bodies the farther down we went. We finally walked to a hallway that had doors on either side with locked openings at eye and waist level. A slot to see the prisoner and one to push whatever muck they were served as food. These were prison cells and the location of the final two inhabitants of the facility.

"Last two doors at the end of the hall on either side," I said, Petro taking his spot on my shoulder. We both decided that silence was the best tactic to take. The last of my enhanced vision leaving..

I looked over at Petro, smirking and raising my shoulder with indecision. Petro nodded to the door on the right.

I slid the view slot open, but the only things visible were the feet of the occupant. Petro perched on my shoulder, leaning forward and smelling the air.

"Hot damn!" Petro screeched, flying up to the roof and pulling his sword. That was the position he took when there was immediate danger to report back.

I jumped back pulling out Durundle, yelling *"Ignis"* for the second time in one night, no longer caring if they knew we were there.

"Talk to me, buddy," I said to Petro.

"Help..." came a weak man's voice behind us in the other cell.

"Petro, drop," I said as we had practiced. He immediately lowered to my shoulder, lightly dusting the space and looking in the opposite direction.

Petro started talking before I could get a response out. "Chloe's in that cell, boss. She's all messed up. I can smell the power coming off her. I think there is a ward or something around her."

I froze in place, staring at the door.

"Help...my name's Leon. I'm a gate Mage." The voice came again from the door Petro was facing, faint but still alert. He sounded scared out of his mind.

Petro and I looked at each other, not needing to talk as Petro took off toward Leon's door. I took a step forward, hearing shuffling from the door that contained Chloe. The person I had been searching for over the past year. One of the top wanted Mages by the Council and CSA. Considered highly dangerous, she also happened to have led the ambush wounding both Ed and I the prior week.

I could hear Petro shuffling, opening the view panel. I trusted him and didn't turn around. I was hesitant to take my eyes off the door.

Chloe and I had grown close. Too close—at least I thought so. I think I had been, in some odd way, in love with her at one point the year prior. She was a bad seed through and through. Chloe was a plant by the Thule Society. Her actions directly contributed to the deaths of several Mages, Vampires, and the like. She also had shot Jayal in cold blood when we went after the Fountain of Youth.

"Gods and graves," I said under my breath, the sound of the door opening behind me.

I grabbed Durundle with both hands, cutting around the lock to the door like it was warm butter. Did I mention I really, really liked that sword?

The blade hissed on the cold iron. I kept the sword in my right hand as I pushed the door open. It must have been infused with silver, as I could feel the tingle jolt through my body.

Chloe's feet pulled in out of the thin beam of light in the

room. I held up Durundle, lighting the cell in its orange glow.

She was chained to the wall in silver and iron shackles, wearing what looked like a tattered prison uniform that had not been cleaned. Chloe's hair was missing from one half of her head, while the other side was tangled and disheveled. The room smelled of body odor and the fact that she did not have proper space to relieve herself. This was not a prison cell. It was a cage. Even the cold couldn't mask the smell of the space.

While her skin wasn't fully lit by the blade, it was clear she was injured. That wasn't me from the ambush. Sure, I slung a bolt of hellfire from Durundle, but that wasn't enough to do this. Had Bo wounded her? It was obvious she was being punished, or just being used as a pawn in order to get to me.

I could hear the sound of shuffling behind me as Leon, whom I had registered a month ago or so, stood there. While looking rough, he was not nearly in the condition Chloe was in.

"Is this a trick?" I said, looking at Leon, recognition coming across his face and showing instant yet stressed relief.

"She was like that before this morning," Leon said in a shaky voice, letting us know he was probably close to hypothermia. "Whatever happened upstairs never made it down here."

"Hey, boss," Petro interrupted. "I don't think we should get any closer, and in case you haven't noticed, the building's on fire."

The smell of burning building materials started to fill the cold, damp air. We were at least two stories under the frozen ground.

"Shit," I said, pulling out the box Belm had given me prior to leaving. Almost as if it were divined, the sound of Snoop Dogg rapping filled the air. That was Phil's text alert on Petro's custom phone. The damn thing was loud. "Lodi Dodi" repeated three times as we stood there staring.

I knelt down close to Chloe, seeing her eyes come open and look at me as if I wasn't in the room. Whatever was once behind them was gone. What was I doing? That damn damsel-in-distress mode was taking over my better judgment.

"Chloe," I whispered as she shuffled on the ground, trying to focus on me.

As I got closer, I could see what looked like burn marks tracing her veins. Whatever or whoever had done this to her had left it as a message. A message to me. "I get it," I said out loud defiantly. "You're in control, and your people are expendable."

Chloe snapped to attention, obviously being controlled by something other than her own willpower. "Max." The slithering voice came different and distorted from her lips. "I am glad you came," the voice stuttered. Chloe's eyes rolled back in her head as you could see her physical being struggle to support the conversation.

"You have my attention, and I don't think you're going to like that very much. Who are you?" I asked, my breath visible as I held the sword between us.

"Poor boy. You think we are the ones doing wrong here. We are just trying to ensure the future of our kind. Sacrifices will be made. I see you know the truth. It will not be long before the others turn on you," the voice said, getting more solid as we continued.

"Bullshit," I spat out, spittle hitting the flaming blade, making a sizzling sound. The smell of fire and the presence of smoke starting to grow.

"She's stalling, boss!" Petro chirped. I could feel him fly up behind me, the flutter of his wings pushing cool air on my neck.

"Tell you what. Let's say we have a little family reunion, and I'll show you a thing or two about sacrifices," I said, fed up with the scene in front of me, figuring it was Lilith or someone else in close proximity to my background.

"Poor ignorant child" were the last words that left Chloe's lips as she collapsed on the floor in a lifeless pile.

I dropped Durundle on the ground, still lighting the space as I grabbed Chloe's head. The hiss of the flame on the iron and silver infused floor making odd popping sounds.

Her eyes opened again, this time aware. They were tired and sad. The look on her face said everything and nothing at the same time. She tried to lift a hand as I grabbed it.

Chloe squeezed as a tear fell from her eye. That was the last thing she did before taking her last breath, the tension of life leaving her body. I looked over at the chains, grabbing them and setting my hand ablaze with hellfire. The silver and iron burned back, causing a shooting pain to reverberate up my arm, throwing me back.

"We got to go, boss!" Petro shrieked as he flew directly in front of my face. He did something that I hadn't experienced before. He pulled out his sword and stabbed me lightly in the shoulder, snapping me out of it.

Leon had closed the room to the cell. The heat was starting to radiate from all sides, making the cell an oven. I grabbed back control of myself and pulled out the Evergate stone, activating it in my hand.

A shimmering wall of light appeared in the middle of the cell, flickering on the edges due to the iron and silver in the room. I nodded at Petro and Leon as they, without hesitation, walked through the gate. The last thing I did before walking through was push my will into the box Belm had giving me, watching it click open as a stream of light poured over the walls of the room. I walked through the gate, closing it behind me.

The Postern was full. Phil, Ed, Jenny, Belm, Kim, and two Pixies, Lacey and Macey. The smell of fire had followed us through the gate, stuck to our clothes, filling the air. Leon was already on the ground as Jenny's glowing green hands hovered over his torso. In the dull light of the room, he looked even worse.

Petro was sitting on the table in the middle of the room. Kim was pouring a cap of water for him.

"Explain" was all Ed said, obviously in a bad mood.

Belm looked over, raising an eyebrow, checking to see if I had activated the box. I responded with a barely noticeable nod.

Before I could speak up, Belm interrupted in his raspy voice. At the same time, I could hear a faint whisper in his voice flow through my thoughts. *Wait.* "I am partly to blame for this slight deviation."

I had made my own mind up to go. "No, I decided to go on my own. Belm just happened to be at the right place at the right time. Look, I'm a grown boy and can make big-boy choices," I said as Belm let out a huff and light whistle.

"That's not what I mean. What the hell were you thinking?" Ed said, looking like a dad that just caught his son sneaking back in the window after a long night of partying.

"I didn't think this could wait. I'm not like everyone else in here. I have a bunch of people on the Council that want nothing more than for me to be dead from what I can tell. This is connected to me, and I'm going to do everything I can to get to the bottom of what's going on. I would think bringing Leon back is a good start," I said, actually making a rational point.

It looked like Ed and the others, acting like they weren't the room, agreed.

"Well," Phil said, the cigarette he had been smoking hanging off his lips with nothing more than ashes left. "I mean it can't hurt, bruther."

Kim looked over. "Max did find Leon. Jenny, how's he doing?'

"If he had been there much longer, he might not have made it till we showed up," Jenny said, again not in a scolding but figuring tone.

"Belm?" Ed asked, looking over.

Belm just shrugged his shoulders and added in his gravelly voice, "Can't I throw a guy a bone every now and then? Max is due a little good press."

"Dammit," Ed exclaimed, letting out a breath and letting the tension in his shoulders out. "I'm sure we will be getting a call on this soon. Max, tell us what happened. Leon being here in one piece is some good news."

I spent the next thirty minutes going over most of what had happened, leaving out some parts about the discussion Belm and I had prior to leaving and including all the parts involving Bo. For this telling it was just me and the little guy. I had learned that while lying was not accepted, leaving out some of the story could, in the long run, in fact save not only one's own ass but those of others as well.

In total Petro and I had been gone for about thirty minutes. Petro confirmed most of the story, of course embellishing the part where he saved the day with his rifle.

"Right. I think we've had enough fun for one day. Hell, for a lifetime. Everyone needs to get some rest. I have a feeling this will be front and center in the morning if not sooner. Belm, I would recommend you make yourself scarce the next few days unless the Council reaches out. If I can keep you out of this, I would prefer to," Ed said in finality, no one pushing back.

Phil walked over, patting me on the back. "You saved Leon's life. You should be proud."

"Something like that" was all I said, walking off to my room, the weight of the day catching up to my body.

CHAPTER 18

The Principal's Offices

The banging on the door started before my alarm clock, which I had failed to set the night before, would have gone off.

"Jesus, hold on," I said, groggy and still not fully rested from the prior day's activities.

"Bruther, I keep telling you to leave him out of it before he shows up," Phil boomed through the door. "Brush your teeth and put on your tighty-whities. We're going to visit the Council today."

"All right, all right," I said, letting my feet touch the cool floor. I looked over at the old-style alarm clock my mother had given me for my re-birthday. It was the type that had two bells on the top that you actually had to wind. It also had an odd feel to it. When I touched it, there seemed to be more to it than just your ordinary alarm clock. Considering my mother was in fact a witch, it was highly probable.

The clock read 10:00 a.m. I had gotten a good night's sleep after all. Well, minus the dreams, but we will leave that for another time. I crashed around 10:00 p.m., feeling brutally hungover, and I was chalking it up to the potion that had pushed me into overdrive.

I could tell Phil was still in the office. "Hey, stay away from the bar," I said, hearing the clink of glass. The sound of something dropping and a "Shit!" came from the other room.

"It's serious, bruther," Phil's strained voice trailed in the background as I walked into the shower to start my daily routine.

It was odd for Petro to not be the one knocking; I was guessing he was occupied elsewhere.

Based off Phil's statement, I put on my best set of working clothes, figuring I needed to leave all my goodies behind as I looked at Durundle, which I had sloppily deposited on the nightstand the night prior.

I walked out after a few minutes, seeing Phil dressed in the same manner as I was. Strictly business.

"When are we leaving?" I asked, wondering why he was there.

"Look, bruther, play it cool today. This is official. They will have mind Mages there. You need to keep this on the up and up."

I let out a stressed breath. "Thing is, I haven't done anything wrong. Are you here to tell me I have?"

"Not that. Just be careful," Phil said, turning as we started walking out. He stopped, not looking at me in the face. "Max, I know you have figured most of this out. You have demon blood in you. Hell, I even figured it out based off everything going on. Whatever you have to do, keep it to yourself."

We walked to the main entrance, where Ed and Jenny stood talking with James. Petro was still nowhere to be found. "You guys see Petro this morning?" I asked, about to call him from the charm.

"He's not in a very good mood," Jenny said, lightly smiling. "Lacey and Macey told me that he is not invited or allowed to attend the Council meeting today. I think it upset him. Cacey decided to take him out to the woods this morning to have a picnic and talk."

I let out a curt huff, not liking the way the Council—and, for that matter, Mages—treated Pixies. Hell, the Ethereals used them as servants for the most part. "James," I said, finally taking the news in stride. "Let Petro know he can help himself to the bar when he gets back. Not like it ever stops him anyways. Just let him know. It will cheer him up."

"So I get all moody, and I get free rein?" Phil asked, raising his eyebrows and rubbing his hands greedily together in jest, lightening the mood.

"I think you already assume that," I said, knowing full well that the ever-full bar that I assumed Leshya stocked was Phil and Ed's second-favorite room in the house.

"Right, let's get the nerves and jitters out now. Max, you already know this is serious. You are going to be questioned. Just like in a US court but not for a crime. This is like testifying about what happened under oath. Plus, I'm sure you know who called this emergency meeting," Ed said, sniffing slightly as if he had the onset of a cold.

"Carvel," I said, shaking my head.

"Yes, but do know the fact that you came back with Leon and this intel is actually more important than Carvel's little quest to get you out of the Council's good graces. He didn't fully know the situation before he called the meeting, so I am sure there will be some egg on his face when he actually hears from Leon. He is going to be there today. Oh, that reminds me, Ying sent this letter via the messenger gate this morning. I guess we now know one number in the phone book that's still good," Ed said, walking over, activating the gate.

I tucked the letter in my pocket for later. Last thing I needed was another distraction. What I did know was that the message was sent purposefully through the messenger gate to avoid detection. It was confirmed; she was on my side off the books.

The gate in the front of the house led to a handful of locations, the Council halls being one. This would be my second trip to the Council, and I still had yet to figure out where it was located.

The room we gated into was the size of an average master suite. The walls, much like many others in this world, were made of stone and presented decades, if not centuries, of wear.

Maybe the oddest feature of the fortress, that being the only way to describe it, was the lack of any windows or view of the outside world. We could be in a cave, miles underground, or on the moon for all I knew. The smell was distant, however, and pinning it down was hard. The scent of fresh, warm laundry was the closest I could figure. This of course mixed with an earthy smell, much like that of the Atheneum.

Castle Grayskull, I thought to myself, letting out a light chuckle. It did have the feeling of a medieval castle out of some fantasy story. Clean, intriguing, yet elegant and timeless. I looked into the main chamber room on my last visit. It reminded me of the British Parliament. Rows of people on either side with an obvious group of leaders at one end. The guilty party in the middle for all to bear witness and judgment. I was going to hate today.

"Ah," the voice of Ned carried around the corner. He was followed up Ying Yue. "Perfect timing. We can go straight in."

The group exchanged pleasantries as Ying flashed me a wink. "Make sure you read that letter today, but after this," she said, knowing I hadn't. Magic, what can I say?

Ned gave me the same advice that Phil, Ed, Jenny, my mother, Petro, the priest at the local church, Trish, James, the drunk guy at the Waffle House at 2:00 a.m., and everyone else had. "Take this seriously, and just be yourself." Of course, with the added bonus of "You haven't done anything wrong."

I responded in the only way I knew: "Does that mean I need to chug a couple of beers?" The joke was going flat for some reason.

The team walked through the maze of corridors past busy rooms and people from every corner of the map.

Walking up to the main chamber doors, I saw there were two obvious battle Mages on either side. Looking to my left, I could barely make out Mouth and Terrence, with whom I really wanted to have a nice private chat, standing out of eyeshot and lurking in the shadows. We locked glances for a second, both assuming we knew more that everyone else did.

As the doors opened, the Council chambers loomed around the space. It was the size of a large movie theater and dimly lit in a yellow glow. It actually looked like it was designed after the British Parliament's House of Commons. Looking closer, I was betting the House of Commons was a copy of the Council chambers.

The room had seats surrounding the center on all sides with a few tables and chairs in the middle. At the far end was a table higher than the others with three seats.

There was a mix of other types in the room, and I was surprised that I hadn't seen many of the faces during the ball.

The walls were made of wood and stone with intricately carved murals of ancient battles looking biblical. That was confirmed when you looked up to see the painting that looked like a da Vinci. The floor as covered in a large Persian-style carpet that was worn, keeping the background noise down by absorbing it.

What caught my attention was the chair in the middle of the room with a desk on either side. On the back of the chair was an old-style coiled light bulb shaped like a globe, its glass having a yellowish tint from age.

The room was full of conversations and rustling. Some were louder than others; a few groups were looking directly at our team. Ed, Jenny, and Ned walked over to the table as the rest of the team sauntered over to the open chairs by the door.

Jenny motioned me to sit at the table, avoiding what looked like the hot seat from hell. As soon as I took my seat, a loud gavel sounded, notifying the room to stand up. Typical.

The group went silent, as the large man at the end of the room under the three high thrones bellowed the room to order.

There was a hulking, strong black man with a tough, wise face dressed in some type of traditional robes named Titus; a short, intricately dressed blond woman (obviously a Fae) called Lorel; and Anna Vlad. They walked in, standing in front of the thrones. The Senior Council leaders. The man announced in his booming voice for everyone to please be seated.

I always thought that the Council would be all magic and fires. I felt like, while still regal, it could have just as easy been a place to debate my latest parking ticket. Come to think about it, the man making the announcements looked just like Richard Moll, better known as "Bull" from *Night Court*.

As the three senior leaders sat, so did the rest of the room. On the right side of the room sat a table in front of a handful of chairs. Sitting in those chairs were of course Carvel and Darkwater. Two others I didn't recognize also hovered at the ends of the table, both looking like Fae.

"What is the order of the day?" Titus, the large black man, said in a deep voice that would make Darth Vader proud.

"Your honors. Today I bring forward Maximillian

Abaddon Sand to answer questions regarding the event that occurred at the Devil's Castle and also to answer for his recent disregard for our rule of law," Carvel said, standing up dressed in all black like the nice executioner he was trying to be.

The three Senior Council members leaned in, talking to each other as the woman in the middle spoke up. "And who represents Maximillian?" Lorel said in a commanding yet seductive voice.

"I do, my lady," Ed said, standing with a curtsy.

Damn Fae royalty. Who's next—Mab? From what I gathered, most of the royalty stayed on the Plane due to the whole mortality issue. I was starting to think we weren't in Kansas anymore.

Anna spoke up next. She gave the formal swearing-in and made a few general notes on the rules of the house. I felt like I had heard this all before. Anna finished, however, on a chilling note. "You understand that if you bear false witness to this body, it may result in your death and or banishment?"

I answered in the affirmative, taking cues from Ed. He was, after all, a lawyer. Well, at least part time.

Ed leaned over as my response opened the floor to a light murmur. "You will need to take a seat in the chair. You tell the truth, the light will turn green. You don't...well, do your best to tell the truth. The strength of the color red or green will gauge your level of truth as you know it," Ed whispered, putting an emphasis on "as you know it."

I stood, walking over to the chair as what looked like dwarfs walked up, ushering me to sit down. We had been cleared prior to leaving the gate room, so it wasn't to check if I had anything but to make sure I wasn't using any magic or spells to help. I could tell by the pull in my chest some type of enchantment was flowing over my body, the same as walking into a warded room.

Carvel stood up as Ed locked eyes with him, the calculation showing on both of them. I was actually comfortable. The one thing that never failed to amaze me is how often magic types did not value regular humans' ability to be clever. Or their past for that matter. The fact that I was in the intel world and had studied questioning people for years was lost on this group. They relied on magic and other means to figure out the truth.

A thought crossed my mind. I think it did Ed's as well, and he raised an eyebrow. I was going to answer the questions exactly as they were asked. I would leave out any details that had no relevance to me.

Wheel of Fortune crossed my mind as I sat back, getting my thoughts in order, the music from the show lingering. This was a tactic I learned from the start. Give them a few letters, and see if the viewers at home could guess the word or phrase. If they do, oh well, they get a prize but maybe just a piece of it; if not, on to the next word or phrase. You could guess the word and still not win. Plus, I would still be trying to solve the puzzle.

You think chess is a strategy game…

"Order," Bull said as Anna stood up.

"We are gathered to ask questions and hear the testimony of Maximillian Abaddon Sand in relation to the incident that occurred at the Devil's Castle," the smooth yet firm voice came. Carvel stood up.

I noted what she said and let it work in my mind. *In relation.* That meant to me that my responses would pertain to things that I knew as fact and not a guess or tidbit of information given to me in relation to the field trip Petro and I took. Ed's comment "as you know it" also crossed my mind. I was being thrown a soft pitch by both parties and locked in on those two phrases to frame my replies.

Carvel started by asking the normal round of questions gauging the meter, "What is your name? Were you present at…" Green light and so on for about five minutes.

The rules were then laid out. The person who called the gathering was Councilman Icupxyzabc…Carvel. I had given up on pronouncing his name, as had everyone else. He was to ask a question, I would respond, and Ed would have the ability to either follow up or ask his own question. Then vice versa. It was much like watching a hearing back home; however, there was a time limit set. Bull turned over an honest-to-God sand hourglass. The time was set at one hour. Fine with me. I'd just speak slowly. I could play this game.

I looked over at Ed one more time before setting my focus, seeing him looking professional and resolute. He nodded, for once showing no emotion.

"Max," Carvel started in his calmest voice to date. Darkwater was sitting beside him. His face was set in concentration. His lips were flat, and after looking for more than a few seconds, I could swear he wasn't blinking or breathing for that matter. "Did you have prior knowledge of the operation located at Devil's Castle?"

I thought for a minute, taking a pause and buying thirty seconds off the clock. The truth was clear as I knew it. The actual operation and what was going on at that location was unknown to me fully until I arrived. I knew Bo had been there and that Chloe was there. What they were doing or anything about the operation was another story. They could have been baking cookies. "No," I said, looking at my shoulder without moving my eyes to see the faint glow of green. The meter also glowed at different levels depending on the level of truth or my understanding of it. It was much fainter than when I stated my name.

"Max, for clarification," Ed spoke up. "Until the day you went to Devil's Castle, did you know that anyone would be there, or that it was a base for the Thule Society?"

"No," I responded, truly only thinking it was a good bet something was going on there. I paused waiting as the light burned green. Good old Ed; he was in the fight. I let out a slight breath, not relaxing. Darkwater still sat there, not moving or showing emotion.

Ed was making it clear that I didn't have any prior knowledge of the operation at Devil's Castle, effectively removing my attachment to any on-site operation.

Carvel took a deep breath, looking down at his notes. He tried to get me out the gate and was shifting tactics. I sat there thinking that Carvel must truly not have known what happened before or during. Someone else was steering the ship. Worse, he was asking me yes-and-no-type questions, forcing Ed to waste his time clarifying instead of moving the meter in the other direction. The dance was impressive but not in our favor. The questions Carvel would ask in open form would only force Ed again to clarify further.

He was avoiding asking me if I was flat-out involved directly, leaving room for other negative narratives if needed.

"Are you in any way involved in the disappearances of the gate Mages?" Carvel asked, throwing me a curveball. This one was tricky. In reality I wasn't truly part of their kidnapping or whatever. Truth be told, though, it was due to me registering them.

"Yes, but..." I trailed off, and Ed interrupted. The crowd swelled in heated, quick conversation.

"Order!" Titus yelled, shutting the group down instantly. I didn't know the guy but, had a feeling you didn't want to get on his bad side.

"Max, be specific. Why are you involved?" Ed asked in a calm, calculated voice.

I took another breath and let fifteen seconds pass, the room growing impatient. "I registered them. Other than that, I have no involvement in their disappearances." Bright glowing green erupted from behind me. I could actually see it on my skin. The emotion I put into the response pushing the truth reader.

I looked over to see Carvel raising an eyebrow and looking over at Darkwater. His expression did not move. The Councilman took a few minutes to rearrange his notes, going to another tactic.

The sand in the hourglass looked to have moved at least ten minutes.

With the big questions out of the way—or so I thought—the next twenty minutes were spent on mundane inquiries about random events that happened the night I went to the castle, as it was called. I even had to explain it was a laboratory. It was obvious he was looking for any inconsistency that may prove helpful later. That's when the shoe dropped.

"Have you had any interactions other than the registration of the demon you call Bo?" Carvel asked, a slight grin appearing on his normally scowled face.

Realizing he didn't know what really happened, I figured he would bring Bo into the questioning. I paused longer than normal, drawing the gaze of the crowd. Two could play at this game. *Let's see if we can make Darkwater squirm*, I thought, not liking the guy from my prior experience.

"Yes," I said, figuring Ed would follow up as murmurs started to fill the air again being silenced just as quickly. The one thing I liked about this system was that once you asked your question, you were done. No multipart question or follow-up. Straight and to the point. I figured it was due to the truth meter.

"What is your relationship with Bo?" Ed asked, almost

taking my breath away. I couldn't believe he asked. I was through. My head slumped as I gathered my thoughts. I looked up, scanning the room. Ed sat there stoic, not giving anything away. The room was frozen in time, like ice on a windshield before you turned on the defrost on a cold January morning.

Scanning the crowd, I looked to see Ying Yue grinning back at me, shaking her head. What was I missing? The question was clear. Or was it? I took a breath, blinking and looking Darkwater straight in the eyes. The gate crystal…I didn't have to tell everything, just what my relationship was in maybe one instance.

"I'm not really sure," I started the dull glow of green mixed with red showing on my shoulder for the first time. "When I was asked by Councilman Darkwater to transport the gate crystal via ground, we were ambushed. Bo was there and saved not only my life but others' lives and prevented the crystal from being stolen." More green. I looked up to Darkwater. "The crystal as I know it was not the real thing. It was a fake, and so was the other one. The ambush was set up." Glowing green lit the skin on my hands.

I had effectively put Darkwater's reputation on display.

Peering over at Ed his poker face slightly broke, a wrinkle emerging from the skin to the side of his right eye; it was a lawyer's smile. I looked up to see Darkwater break character and pull Carvel into a conversation. The room erupted louder than before as even the Senior Council was conversing.

"Order!" Bull yelled as the room calmed.

"This is not relevant and must be taken from the record. Max is diverting from the question. It has no relevance. In addition, Max's statement is unfounded," Carvel said, the look on Darkwater's face hardening.

I looked over at the hourglass; fifteen minutes left. The rules were clear: one hour, in trouble or not.

Anna stood up. "You asked of Max's relationship with the demon." Thirteen minutes. "He answered. The statement is sustained." The look on Ed's face told me everything I needed to know.

Titus stood up. "Point of order. We will reconvene later on this topic, as the gate crystal is a secured artifact." The bulking man sat back down, all eyes on Darkwater. *Checkmate, assface*, I thought.

The next ten minutes involved questions about the team that I easily navigated, much to my surprise. The fact that I did this on my own was paying off. It was almost like it was set up to be that way for this very reason.

Carvel looked back at me one last time, the room calming and seeing the time running out. "Who is responsible for all the deaths at the Devil's Castle?" He put an emphasis on "all."

I took the checkmate thing back. I sat there, stoic, looking at Darkwater. He had given this to Carvel to ask. I couldn't lie. I wasn't; I also knew Bo was responsible, at least from what Belm and Leon had told me. Could I stretch it? Problem was I believed it. Not just what I was told. Could I pull off all the deaths I caused?

"I was," I said as the light glowed faintly green, allowing me to take a breath. At least they thought I was someone not to mess with as Belm suggested I do.

"Were you attacked first?" Ed asked, knowing the answer as any lawyer would.

"Yes" was all I responded.

Carvel cleared his throat. "Do you mean to interfere or generate conflict with anyone on the Council after this action?"

My throat went dry. I did; I wanted Carvel and Darkwater to be held responsible for what had happened. I all but knew one of them was involved. He didn't ask *who*, just *if*. Ed would clarify. Tell the truth…"Yes," I said hoarsely as the light glowed green. With the recent distractions, I hadn't noticed the last grain of sand flow through the bottom of the hourglass. It was over.

Checkmate…the Council would think I wanted to cause issues with them. It was childish but effective as the light glowed yellow, signifying the end of the questioning. The room erupted.

Guffaws and boos rang through the air. Ed sat there, calm, as did Jenny. I looked over at Phil, finally seeing his face go blank. I hope the main Council didn't think I was against them. It seemed like it, and Ed didn't have time to clarify. I was getting my money back. That is, if I was alive the next day.

"Order, order!" Bull commanded as the room settled.

The senior Council looked at each other, conversing. The next five minutes was nothing but a mixture of loud and muted conversation.

Ed and Jenny sat there not saying a word. Did they not believe me? Did they think I was working with the demons? Even worse, I thought, *Was this just a trick to get me here and take me out?* It was the first time in months that I felt alone. Part of me wanted to just stand up and walk away, while another portion of me wanted to stand up and fight.

Mixed emotions crossed my mind as Anna slammed a gavel down, calling the room to settle.

"Councilman Carvel, as the director of the Council Security Team, what is your recommended action?" Anna asked, deadpan serious.

"To have Max removed from his duties, striped of his apprenticeship, and confined to the reformatory until further notice for action to be taken," Carvel said smoothly. I knew what that meant: death.

Ed sat there not moving. He couldn't be part of this. Could he?

Titus stood up. "Unless there is further objection, the ruling will stand until a vote can be cast. If this carries Max will be detained immediately."

Ed raised his hand. "Point of order." His smooth lawyer voice came flowing into the room. "I have a letter that was dated a couple days ago that I need to read for the Council. I did not deem it necessary unless needed."

Carvel and Darkwater both stood, Carvel speaking first. "This is bullshi—" He was cut off by Anna. Note to self: Buy all her beer—not a couple, all of them—then drink them.

"You will be heard, as Senior Councilman Titus noted. Continue."

Ed pulled out an official letter with a wax seal, pulling it open as he had already read it. "By order of the Supreme Council, the staff employed by the Atheneum under the rule of the CSA in the jurisdiction of the NCTS is hereby put in the control and direction of the Supreme Council." The color, what there was of it on Carvel's face, melted. Darkwater smirked, showing his first sign of emotion.

The Supreme Council was the authority that ruled the chambers and Senior Council. Half living on the Plane and the other half...well, let's just say they had better things to do than be here. It was a little confusing, but I related it to the final boss fight in a video game. Yes, you go through several, but at some point, you land on the HMFIC. For you nonmilitary types, Google that one.

Ed continued. "Any actions taken by this team is under the direct control and authority of the Supreme Council. In the event of conflict, a request for rebuke must be submitted and will be reviewed. Signed, Davros."

The room again erupted in voices louder than any point in the past hour. Looking around, I saw it was clear there was a divide straight down the middle. By the looks of it, however, the Senior Council still called the shots in the room.

"Order!" Anna bellowed, the vampire showing through. Again silence. "We will contact the Supreme Council to confirm. This will take a few days, if not longer. In the meantime," Anna said, the letter being handed smoothly to her from Ed through Bull. She looked at it observingly. "The Atheneum team is free to go." I stood up grinning at the two Councilmen, seeing their irritation.

Just as the group started to talk, Titus gaveled the hammer. "As requested by Councilman Carvel and Darkwater, all information and data pertaining to the actions of Max including the noted material will be turned over to the Security Council for review and action."

Dammit, they were about to get everything. The target locations and the whole enchilada. We already figured the Council had a plant, and chances were they would now know who we had our eyes on. Maybe this whole sideshow was called to figure out if we knew they had been located.

The room started moving at one time like a wave in the ocean. People and creatures moving in every direction. The noise was loud and heated. What had just happened?

Looking at Ed, I saw he was putting his notes in a bag, standing up. Jenny was not giving away anything either.

We walked out of the room to the shouts of others, Phil catching us as we walked out. Out of the turmoil, the one piece I noticed was the absence of Mouth and Terrence.

I started to talk as Ed made it clear we need to put our heads down and leave; I also hadn't noticed Ned keeping up. He must have distanced himself from the proceedings, acting as neutral as Switzerland the whole time and not saying a word.

We quickly made the last few turns to the room we had gated into. The farther we walked away from the court, the fewer people we saw until it was basically us.

"Ah," Ned said in a rather good mood, considering. "Great job in there."

"Great job?" I asked, scoffing. "We just got it handed to us in there."

Ed walked up, putting his hand on my shoulder as the door shut behind us. "Walls have ears. Let's get going."

The gate shimmered to life as Phil raised his hand, activating the portal. "Not coming?" I asked Ned as he stood there, a grin on his face that I couldn't quite place.

"I'll talk to you later" was all he said, turning to leave, swiping his hands down the front of his robes, straightening himself up before going back out into the public's eye. I was starting to think this whole episode was on rails so to speak.

I was the last through the gate, seeing Dr. Freeman, the Pixie gang, and Frank standing there with the others.

"So? How did it go?" Dr. Freeman asked as Petro flew over, giving me the eye he often did to make sure I still had all my fingers and toes.

"Couldn't have gone any better," Ed said walking over to me. "Max, you still have that note from Ying? Hell of a job, by the way."

I was confused. "Hell of a job? I'm…I mean, we're screwed. They have all the data we brought. Plus now they think I am out to get them all," I said in mild frustration. Jenny was also smiling. At least Phil still looked as gassed as I was feeling.

Ed just shook his head. "Drink, anyone? Max, do you care

if we join you in your office? Oh, and, James, care to join us?"

"I guess, hell, why not? Things couldn't get any worse than they already are. I might as well be tanked," I said walking past the crowd and nudging Petro to hitch a ride on my shoulder.

Jenny was still smiling and talking to Frank as he walked off to the crucible room. We marched to the office in various stages of silence. Ed and Jenny, as always, led the way, whispering away to each other. I caught Petro up on what had happened as well, leaving out a few of the boring details. The part about Davros got his attention and a quirk of his lips.

I poured everyone a round of drinks, seeing the motley crew all in the office. In all fairness I don't think they had all been in the office together in some time. Especially Jenny and Dr. Freeman.

"All right, Ed, spill the beans, and please explain this Davros thing," I said, taking a pull of my Vamp Amber in honor of Anna.

Ed took a pull of the Magnus I had just poured him. "Sorry about that Davros thing. I guess that means you didn't know about any of that. Probably for the best. *As you know it* and all," Ed said, smirking, proud of himself.

"What about them knowing the information about the other two sites?" I asked, thinking, as always, Ed was a step or two in front of the rest of us.

"That? I'm pretty sure not ten minutes after you leveled the facility at Devil's Castle, the other two locations were either moved or deactivated. Either way, I'm sure whoever is giving Carvel his marching orders is marching the Council right into a trap. What is really important regardless of the facts, is everyone on the Council will have second thoughts before picking on you in the schoolyard," Ed said, making the point again that today was more of a victory than I had yet to realize.

Jenny spoke up in a smooth yet pronounced tone. "For clarification we were never asked to supply how we received the information and or what it came on, so all we turned over was our notes."

I let that sink in for a minute. They were playing the game. I still didn't understand why they would protect Goolsby other than preserving a back door for later.

Ed spoke back up. "Davros is an old friend of Tom's and, for your complete understanding, happens to be Angel's grandfather or something to that effect, with that related to Circes. The man whose murderer you helped remove from the chessboard last year. Max, that holds weight in our world. Plus, I doubt Davros really gives a shit about any of this."

Damn, Ed had cussed. *He must really be relaxing*, I thought as he took another light pull of his drink.

"All right, I'll bite," I said, seeing Frank smirk at the joke. "What does this all mean and what is going to happen now?"

"We are under the guidance of the Supreme Council, who just happen to tell me that we are to continue on with our regularly scheduled program. Which means find Lilith and the other gate Mages. Oh, and as a side note, when the Council convenes in two weeks, they will be reviewing Davros's request for transfer, which by some odd coincidence will have been revoked by then because he will be tired of hearing about it."

I sat there for a minute as the group took that all in. "Let me guess: you wanted me to flush out Darkwater and the gate crystal?"

Ed smiled as it was clear he had gone full devil's advocate on the Council.

"Yup" was all he said, taking the rest of his drink in one swallow. I cringed, watching as he continued smiling.

"You didn't want to talk about it prior just in case I would give something up. Not wanting to change my mind. I almost forgot," I said, reaching into my blazer that I had thrown over the chair behind the desk. "I haven't read the letter from Ying yet. I guess we can reach her via the messenger as well."

I only knew of two people that could send and or receive message through that gate and one I would rather not. We had spent some time going through a list of names, attempting to send a message that often led to a dead end. Ed was still convinced that the room was more than just a place to pass messages.

Max,

The Blood Stone will lead you. Stacks row TT shelf 12.

I relayed the note to the group. "Blood stone?" I asked out loud, not having a clue where this was going.

"I think I've heard of it before," Dr. Freeman spoke up. "Ed, remember when we first met, and we took that trip to Russia to research the Tunguska event in Siberia that occurred in 1908? If memory serves that is where the gate crystal was found."

Ed looked up, deep thought crossing his face. "Right, we had reports of an extra piece that was reported still there and being used for some type of summoning. That's it, we showed up, and Tom went all native on us. That was the time that we lost…" Ed said, trailing off.

I looked over to see Phil expressionless. Did this have something to do with his wife? I know Phil was younger than the others but by definition still old.

"Petro, take this note and find whatever is located in the stacks," I said as the Pixie crew took flight with purpose together, flying out of the room, dust trailing behind.

Ten minutes later the crew had a stack of papers in front

of us in what looked to be a folder. After twenty minutes of sifting through the paperwork, Dr. Freeman concluded that the blood stone was in fact a piece of the gate crystal that had chipped off when it landed on Earth.

The gate crystal itself was sent here from the war that was raging with the old gods as it was put. No one truly knew, but for all accounts that is what kept the Supreme Council up at night. The paperwork went on to state that it was red due to the blood used on it by a demon trying to summon a legion to Earth, only to be cast aside by the actual gate crystal and sent back to the under.

The story read like something out of the Bible or Greek mythology.

"Ah, here," Dr. Freeman said as Jenny peered over his shoulder. "It says that the two are connected and can be used to locate the other."

"Bingo," Phil said, still not being his normal self after the mention of the old mission.

"Now we just need to find it," I said, looking at the group.

"Right, that's going to be the tricky part," Ed interjected, huffing at the same time. "The blood stone is in the vault, which is only accessible by Tom and has been sealed since he left."

The light bulb came on as I called out, "Leshya!" I was loud and obnoxious. I was sure by now that she was staying in there or in the least going inside to get items often left on my bed. The sword scabbard for Durundle was a prime example.

The rest of the team went silent as two minutes passed. Just as we started working a way into the vault, Leshya came around the corner, stopping in front of the group. I could swear her feet hovered ever so slightly off the ground, generating her silent movement.

"Yes?" she asked, looking at only me.

"Do you have a way to get into the vault?"

"I have this for you. I thought you could use it," Leshya said in her flat yet honest tone.

Leshya pulled out a small box, opening it in front of us, revealing a small bloodred stone that was mixed with crystals. Everyone looked around staring at me. I shrugged, acting the part.

"That's it," Dr. Freeman said, looking at the drawing in the notes.

He was acting the same as he did last year when we found the way into the Fountain of Youth. Not greed or some personal need, just actual educated wonder. I liked seeing him in this mood.

"Right," Ed said, taking the temperature down a few degrees and telling us it was time to get back to work. "Two things. First, as we are all aware, the Council is more than likely sending a large team into a trap, based off the information they collected from the inquiry, thanks to Titus granting them access. All the location data has been turned over. We have warned them of this and have done all we can to help. No more drinking," Ed said, looking over at Phil, Petro, and me.

"Secondly, let's get some rest. In the morning let's meet in Jenny's lab and figure this out. Lacey, Macey, and Cacey, can you please take this down and start to work on a tracking spell?" Ed asked, leaving Petro out as he knew that would leave them all distracted.

The three Pixies moved at lightning speed, grabbing the box and flying out of the room. It was like watching a kid in a candy store; they loved to help and be part of something bigger.

As the group dispersed, I could hear Jenny telling Ed to

take it easy as his wounds hadn't fully healed. Reflecting, I realized I was still a patchwork of bruises in my own right.

CHAPTER 19

You Dirty Rat

Whoop...whoop...the alarm sounded somewhere around four o'clock in the damn morning. James had worked with our Mags-Tech rep to install one after our little visitor to warn everyone in the facility due to the increased staff.

Luckily, I stopped drinking on Ed's advice and actually got some quality sleep. I jumped out of the bed, slamming my hand on the nonexistent digital alarm clock and instead knocking the one my mother had given me for my re-birthday on the floor. The sound of the glass front breaking echoed in the small room.

"Shiiiit," I let out slowly as the sound of Petro bouncing off the door also started filling up the room. "Petro, come on in. I know you have some backdoor way," I said as he came flying from behind my dresser.

"Hey, boss. It's crazy! They sent an entire CSA team in as well as several Council members into a trap last night. Bunch of dead Mages, and Carvel is missing!" Petro spit out at the speed of light. "Davros is downstairs. Kim is on her way. I think she texted you."

"How do you know...never mind. I'll be right down," I said, finally realizing my legs were made to hold up my body and shuffle me to the bathroom. On the way out, Petro smacked on my coffee maker. Remind me to put him in for a raise later.

I rushed through my normal routine getting everything I may need together. The sounds of the team started before I hit the stairwell leading up. That was a first. Walking by the main entrance, I noticed the dining room doors were closed and the noise was coming from the actual offices. Everyone must be in the crucible room.

The team was there, all looking as rough as I felt. Phil had a red mark on his face due to Jenny putting out a lit cigarette that he had tried to light up. Petro was over at the box perched on Jenny's shoulder, the other Pixies on her other shoulder.

Ben and Kim came in roughly a minute after I did, walking up behind me with a smile only a cop or fake priest could pull off. Frank and Angel were in the conference room talking with Davros, who looked at me passively.

"Right," Ed said, walking around the corner holding a steaming cup of coffee. James was following behind, nodding at him as if they had just finalized a conversation. "It happened and the Council is freaking out. Unfortunately, the old adage 'I told you so' is a little cold in light of the circumstances. I didn't think it would be this bad, or they would move this fast."

Jenny stood up, Petro taking flight as she motioned the others out of the way. They were all hovering around, taking up a good amount of space in the room. "Carvel was kidnapped. Eighteen Mages killed and two Vamps. Not only did they ambush the team, but they also made a statement. The amount of firepower they sent in could have taken over a small nation."

Phil let out a whistle, raising an unlit cigarette up to his lips only to stop as Jenny turned to look at him. "Phil, you need to get the gear ready. Heavy ops."

Phil's eyes grew by an inch as he licked his lips. This was a new term for me, and by the looks of Phil, this was letting the kraken out of the cage. Phil stormed out of the room, winking at me with a renewed vigor in his step.

"OK, can someone explain that one to me?" I said, Kim also interested in the interaction.

"Phil is going to get the heavy weapons out of storage. We're going to need them. There's a squad of Night Stalkers downstairs; that means this is ending soon," Jenny said, wearing a concerned face and looking at Ed.

I knew what that was. A six-Vampire team of free blood-drinking killing machines. The team was actually twelve. The other six were human operators, from what I gathered, Delta or the like. They freely gave their blood to overcharge the Vs. Highly dangerous and only reporting to the Supreme Council under Davros's direct management.

"I can smell them from here, boss," Petro added, perching on my shoulder and staring at my coffee as I nodded at him to grab some. Petro scooped his cup in my coffee, taking a sip while standing on my wrist, wiping it out of his mustache, smirking.

We stood there getting an update from Dr. Freeman and Jenny on the rest of the details. Ed was not taking the lead, and I chalked it up to him not having a plan yet.

I was staring at the screen showing satellite pictures of the havoc proceeding the attack when Davros's voice took control of the room. The smell of him hit my senses first. "We believe there is a plant on the Council or working with them. Through divination we have confirmed it is no one on this team. That being said we believe this person has been involved with this team or interacting with it." His smooth, commanding voice floated around the room landing in front of me.

All eyes looked directly at me. "Yeah, I might have mentioned that I thought one of Darkwater's goons was on the take. I can't confirm it, though," I said, taking a gulp of nothing. Davros's presence was weighing down my thoughts.

"You are going to be the one to verify it then. It's only fair," Davros said, looking over at Ed. "Make it fast; you have my blessing." I never thought I would hear a Vampire bless someone.

At that thought Davros looked over. "We all have faith, Max. It's just what you have faith in," he said, turning and walking out of the room. He hadn't read my mind, just picked up on my posturing. "Oh, and take one of my operators with you."

Ed perked up at that. "Max, Jenny, Kim, Petro, dining room. The rest of you, keep an eye out for updates, and keep digging for information. We're heading down to Jenny's lab in a few minutes."

Ed shut the door behind us as we walked into the ever-faithful dining room. "I'm going to make this quick. Max, you, Kim, and whoever will go to Darkwater's office directly and find out where Terrence is. We have reason to believe he is key to this. Once you find him, secure him and get him back here. You have a Night Stalker and Petro with you, so I'm sure you'll be fine," Ed said as Kim and I smirked at Petro, who pushed his chest out at the compliment, stroking his excellent mustache. "While you're gone, we will get the blood stone figured out."

"Already done," Petro said, buzzing over to Ed. "The ladies figured it out last night. Just need a little of that voodoo, as Dick Holder would say."

We all lightly chuckled as there was a knock on the door.

The armored female figure that walked in was jaw dropping. Not in the "Man, she's hot" kind of way, but the way you look at someone looking completely badass.

The curves gave it away as a she. The armor covering the curves of her body was tight and made of some type of Kevlar-infused carbon fiber in all the places that movement wasn't required. It looked like a second layer of skin. You couldn't see the face due to the solid black face shield that was obviously for one-way viewing. Two sleek pistols hugged her hips, as did several smaller magazines. They looked like .22 caliber. I had learned caliber didn't mean much versus what the bullet was made of. On the side of her shins were two long daggers.

On her back were two longer matching katanas. The armor hugging the curves of her chest also held several compartments. Kim and I both looked at each other in awe.

"And you are?" I asked figuring we would at least get to know each other. Night Stalkers were things of legend. Much like the Delta force. Until you actually verified it, one never could truly know if they were in fact real.

"Two," the stern yet feminine voice came out. It almost sounded familiar.

"Two? There are two of you?" Kim asked, not being a smart-ass. For a second the thought of Kim being intimidated crossed my mind.

"No, my name is Two. I have the target acquired," she said, pulling out a tablet and sitting it on the table. Strictly business. "We tracked Terrence to Carvel's personal residence. He was trying to avoid detection due to the unregistered gates he took."

"You figured this out in ten minutes?" I asked, looking at the black façade trying to figure out where to lock my gaze.

"After your deposition, the gate crystal being replaced put

him and Darkwater on the radar of a few people. The one at the repository is a fake. We believe he is working on his own. Until he gated to Carvel's house after his disappearance, we didn't think anything of it other than casual observation," Two said with laserlike precision.

"I swear I know you," Kim said as Petro flew over, inspecting her gear. She reached down into a small pouch and handed Petro his rifle that he lost at the Devil's Castle.

"I could kiss you!" Petro buzzed as Two didn't move, not flinching in the least, handing him some ammunition as well.

"I recommend taking a rain check on that one, buddy. How are we getting there?" I asked, figuring the new gate in the Postern would be best left out of this. Plus, I bet Two already had a plan.

"We are going through a gate in the Council chambers directly to the residence. All Council members have one. Bring one of your gate stones just in case," she said, I guess giving me a look telling me she already knew about all that. "Get your gear, and we leave in twenty."

Kim, Petro, and I went our separate ways, putting on our field gear. I grabbed the usual suspects: Durundle, my service pistol, and short staff. I also picked up the stone Trish had replaced, the same type that Petro pissed on last year, saving our lives. The other Pixies had a song about it. Rather catchy; I hadn't had time to think much about meeting Planes Drifter, but I may just have to get that one over to them, considering I had Abby's cell number.

Putting on my gear, I noticed the shattered glass from the alarm clock I had broken earlier in the morning. I had put it back on the table; however, I noticed the hand was missing. I turned on the tactical flashlight attached to my vest, filling the room with more light than it had seen in a long time. Under the bed lay the hand. Picking it up I noticed a slight tingle in my hand. Pulling it closer to my face, the clear outline of a key came into view.

"Son of a bitch…it's a key to another gate," I said to thin air. I looked at the key for a minute, securing it in a pouch. The book with all the drawings Gramps had in his old lab of the postern included a picture of this key. The way it was attached to the clock, you wouldn't be able to make out that it was a key. As the thought started crossing my mind to go check it out, Petro started tapping on the door.

We took the obligatory five minutes telling each other how badass we looked followed by taking a selfie we would save for later. Petro and I had started a social media page, and while we could post on it, we needed to be careful. Opsec and all.

We all converged in the main lobby, the gate already open. Kim was in her same gear as last year. Her hair was in a tight ponytail flowing out the back of a black tactical cap. She had a modified M4 slung in front of her as well as several flash bangs. I sometimes forgot she was a regular. Petro, picking up on my vibes, let out a breath, breaking my stare. Kim had picked up on that. I often found myself looking just a second too long.

Two was giving us nothing, standing there not moving. Ed looked over. "Right, be careful. We may be moving fast, so get back as soon as you can." He put his hand on my shoulder, nodding at Kim.

I had the sinking feeling that Ed was once again a few steps ahead. Was he getting us out of the way? For some reason I started thinking about Bo.

Two looked over, walking into the gate without hesitation as the rest of us followed. We didn't talk, walking for ten minutes further down into the Council complex and finally reaching a door that had the lock melted.

Two looked down as Kim raised an eyebrow. I guess that

my cue to do something.

I raised my hand, immediately igniting it in hellfire. The reddish-orange flame reflected off the black mask covering Two's face. The melted door lock continued its descent into nonexistence. The metal melting immediately looked like lava flowing down the door, burning the wood. Whoever came through here before was attempting to seal the door. Guess they hadn't planned on mister hellfire.

Petro lowered in the air as smoke started to gather in the small stone hallway. Two reached down, grabbing one of her pistols and pulling it out, then pushing it back down with a click, adding another four inches to the weapon—obviously a suppressor. She pushed the door the rest of the way open, ignoring the splash of melted metal on the floor.

The creature in the room was the size of a large dog and let out a howl of both rage and surprise. Before the rest of us could react, Two smacked three precise rounds through the eyes of the creature, dropping it immediately to the floor. The action was immediate and final. Two walked in, not paying attention to the odd-looking monster on the floor. Its teeth looked like tusks, and it had two oval-shaped black eyes.

The now-limp body was covered in scale-looking armor. Upon closer inspection one round went into each eye and one dead center of the forehead. The glow of green residue from the bullet lingered. The damn thing smelled like raw meat. Petro gave me a lingering look. Kim just shrugged her shoulders, following behind.

Two leaned over, grabbing the collar from its neck letting off a pop of ozone. "Control collar. These fiend hounds are not normally this aggressive."

"Looks mean enough. Well, hope that was no one's pet," I said to cut the silence. No reaction from Two as she activated the gate.

Kim gripped her rifle as Petro flew up beside Two. She seemed to not unnerve him.

We walked through the gate into the crisp, earthy fall air of what I could only guess was Scotland. Kim confirmed this by looking down at her phone.

The gate let out at the end of a tree line beside an old house that was in fact a mix between a Victorian manor and a castle. Two stood there taking in the scene. Petro flew up to the top of the tree line. We had our communicators on, and somehow Two had linked into them. The graying landscape and barren trees lent to the eerie scene.

"Clear. There are people in the house, that's all I know. Can't tell how many," Petro whispered into his communicator.

Two immediately started walking toward the house, forcing us to follow. She moved with purpose and speed, forcing us to take up a light jog. There was a clump of trees leading to the back of the house we mirrored, avoiding the majority of the open space.

Two looked over her shoulder. "Stand back" was all she said. Clicking three small black boxes she pulled from her suit, placing them on the wall. As soon as she stood up, the area around the squares turned to dust, sounding like a puff of light wind. The sandy debris floated off in the wind. That got Kim's attention as she mouthed, "I want one."

Petro flew down into the opening before Two could walk through. I followed as Kim brought up the rear.

Our counterpart reached down, grabbing her other weapon and clicking it again to add the suppressor. "There are crafts here and three Mages. Councilman Carvel is here."

Kim and I looked at each other as she reached down for her phone. I put my hand out, lowering it. "Not yet," I whispered. Two nodded in agreement. "Petro?" I asked, him knowing the drill.

"One on this floor the rest in the basement," Petro said, using his "spidey senses," as I often called them. Pixies were the most underrated beings that came from the Plane.

Two nodded in agreement, smacking her right pistol again down on her suit and attaching a blade to the extended barrel. I just looked, figuring she was blankly staring through me at this point.

Kim walked up, nudging me with her shoulder. We grinned at each other as I felt the weight of my service pistol, a sleek nine-millimeter H&K VP9. I had taken Phil's advice and acquired some "loaded" ammunition. These were like Two's, loaded with silver, iron, or some type of spelled Etherium. Mine had iron and silver in them. In most cases that would neutralize most spells or enchantments; they would drop a craft on the spot. I figured she had enough firepower; I'd use the flashy stuff.

I had yet to mention that I could throw a minor amount of hellfire or water. In all fairness I had used it once outside the range with lethal effect and was not in the mood to gamble.

There was a muffled thump as Petro buzzed in and out of the room with a grin on his face. He had his rifle in hand and was acting like he was blowing the smoke from the barrel.

Two spoke up lightly. "There is no craft on the first floor now."

Petro had taken off, hit the craft with a dissolution round, those being slightly different than the ones I had. You could, in theory, hit me with one if I had been spelled, and I would turn out fine minus a welt.

"Three Mages?" Kim asked, reminding us that we had our work cut out for us.

"Yes" was all Two said in response.

The house was old, yet unlike the Atheneum, it was not decorated in a manner that screamed "timeless elegance." The wall we had punched through led into the kitchen. It was gray, dark, and poorly lit. While Gramps's old kitchen was old school, Carvel's setup took on a whole new meaning. The only modern-looking appliance was a freezer that sat beside a large washbasin with old-style water pipes protruding out of the wall.

The scent of burnt candles hung in the air, mixed with a musky combination of damp cloth and old wood. I imagined this is how the *Munsters*' house from the old TV show would look and smell in person. The house was full of mystery and personality, even if it was on the creepy side.

I walked forward to take point, Two cutting me off and walking like a robot into the main room, pulling open the door leading downstairs. She was whisper quiet. The stairs, like everything in the magical community, were deeper and creepier than need be.

Petro took lead quickly, darting back as we neared a closed door at the bottom. The team didn't speak as Two stood there, not moving and staring at the door.

I nodded at Petro as he landed on my shoulder. "There's a Mage and two crafts on the other side. They don't know we're here yet."

I was reaching out to Two as she kicked in the door, slamming it directly into the chest of the Mage on the other side of the door. The sounds of crunching metal and popping cracks of rock bouncing off the walls echoed in the long hallway.

Kim and I stepped back as Two stood in the middle of the hallway. It was roughly one hundred meters long and eight feet wide with odd-looking enforced doors on either side. What was Carvel up to down here? That was quickly answered by the sounds of the animal that Two put down bellowing in the hall.

As the dust settled, it was obvious the Mage was in fact not dead or knocked out. Matter of fact, he was pissed and making sure we knew it. He was a force Mage. Much like Phil, he was superstrong; however, he could project it.

The door went flying back toward Two as she jumped to the ceiling. I lifted my hand pushing my will into a sphere, slinging a ball of hellfire and lighting the dark space, grabbing everyone's attention for a slight second.

Every time I used hellfire, that seemed to be the result. I paused in reflection on what the hell just happened. The small spot near the wall where my casting landed ate slowly away at the wall, letting off a dull glow.

The pistols the Night Stalker brandished sang, firing multiple patters of silenced rounds. The Mage obviously had some type of shield, creating green dots and ricocheting the bullets, hitting the walls. Petro flew behind Kim as she pushed against the wall, firing a handful of rounds that also bounced off the shield.

Two jumped, running against the wall still firing as the Mage reached up and pushed his will out toward the wall she was running on, making it cave in, sucking her into the dark room.

Kim reached down, pulling out a flash bang as I pulled a smaller ball of hellfire in my hand; we both threw them in sync. We turned our faces as the flash electrified the hall. If you know a flash bang is going off, the noise isn't that hard to manage. It's the light. Mage or not, he was staggered.

No thinking person would believe someone standing ten feet away would throw a flash bang in front of them. These types of people obviously never lived in a military barracks on a Friday night. Mages also had a tendency to ignore normal, everyday things.

The ball of hellfire I threw hit the left side of the shield, burning a hole in it not fully going through. We had accomplished two things. First fully drawing the Mage's attention. Secondly, I just learned that hellfire could damage a shield enough to create a hole, even if I was starting to feel drained.

The Mage stood up behind the shield, looking at us. Kim and I were exposed in the open hall as he grinned, forming a glowing ball in his hands that, if I was betting, was meant to cave in the roof above us. I started to draw more energy together in my palm as the Mage reached out his hands, only to have his head roll off the top of his body, smacking on the ground, touching the shield, and winking out of existence.

Two stood there with the katanas in her hands, flipping them once, shooting the blood off the weapons, putting the blades back in their holders. The Mage's body finally thudded to the ground. It had stood there confused for at least four seconds. Her cut was precise and immediate.

"Just like I planned," I said, standing up and seeing Kim's mild discomfort in the scene as the hellfire winked out of my hands.

The wash of unspent energy flowing back into my body. Two snapped her fingers as two of the fiend hounds took majestic stances beside her.

"Aw, look at that. She made some friends," Petro said, flying over.

"These hounds are very loyal, and taking off their collars bound them to me," Two said as Petro confirmed the theory.

I walked up putting my hand down, only to have one drop a pile of goop in my hand. The sound of Kim lightly retching came from behind.

"Let's go." Kim pushed, knowing this was far from over.

The hallway was longer than I thought with other doors and a few stairwells leading farther underground. Two seemed to know where she was going, and we kept following her.

We took the stairwell at the end of the hall, Two reaching back down and pulling her pistols back out. I looked back at Kim, shaking my head as she clicked the charging handle on her rifle. The two hounds were close behind.

Petro buzzed back, perching on my shoulder. "Hey, boss, they're all at the bottom of the stairs through the door. I can smell magic in the air. They're doing something down there."

Two stopped whispering into her communicator. "They are doing a blood summoning," she said, sprinting down the stairs as the rest of us picked up the pace.

The door, much like the one at the Council chambers, had some type of enchantment, stopping Two in her tracks, looking over at me.

Like before, I charged my hands with hellfire and slung a spatter of it on the locking mechanism. Touching it would ground out the effect, as it looked to be iron. Hellfire, I had learned, was the one elemental type magic that would still burn through the stuff as it neutralized most everything else.

The smell of burning rubber, metal, and ozone filled the air as a light haze took shape in the small entranceway. I knew the minute the doors opened we would be exposed.

"They know we're here now," Petro chirped over the communicators, taking a spot up above head level, pulling up his rifle.

Two, after another second of whining, popping, and hissing, coming from the door, drop-kicked it open violently, stunning the two figures on the other side.

Kim let out a three-round burst from her rifle, the casings chattering to the ground as Two launched herself into the door, firing both pistols into the body on the left, as the other released a spatter of rounds from what looked like an Uzi. Kim and I ducked behind the door as the bullets hissed by, smacking the back wall as Petro let off his shot, tagging the craft in the neck and turning it into a pile of e-core.

The transaction was brief, lasting no more than five seconds. What I didn't immediately notice were the rounds that hit behind us, slinging debris from the wall and hitting Petro in the back as he let off his round. I watched his dust trail fall as he dropped to the ground.

I sprung from my feet, the muffled sound of Two firing her gun coming from the room. I landed on my back as Petro bounced off my chest plate.

Scrambling, I cupped him in my hands as Kim kept focused on the door, also letting off a few rounds. The cadence was off, telling me something was not right.

"Petro, come on, buddy, you OK?" I asked, lifting his wings lightly and rubbing his chest. Petro's tongue slipped out of his mouth in a pant, and he started shaking his butt like a dog getting a belly rub. I dropped him on the ground, seeing him smirk.

"Buy a guy dinner first, will you? I'm OK, just a little rattled. I'm not as big as you lunks," Petro said, shaking the dust out of his wings and waiting a second before taking back off to make sure he could.

He was tough, and the slight hesitation worried me for a second. What really worried me was diving as I had; the wounds from my last two encounters screamed back to life, reminding me that I wasn't yet at full capacity. I stood up, noticing the pain in my right leg was telling me to take it easy. If I was to get in a hand-to-hand scrap, I didn't know if I could hold myself up.

The hounds peered around the corner of the stairwell,

missing most of the action and taking positions at the entrance of the door. I could see the spiked nubs they had for tails lightly wagging. One sniffed at Petro as he flew over and landed on the hound with the lighter-scaled back. "Don't worry, boss, I used to ride these all the time back home. I had no clue you had them here."

"I don't think they're supposed to be here, buddy."

"Max, you better come take a look at this," Kim said. The room was large and sprawling. Carvel's underground lair. In the center was a protection circle much like the one we had encountered last year. Two was standing at its edge, not hiding but staring at the odd scene unfolding in the middle.

Carvel sat in the middle of the circle as Terrence and what looked like another person walked around him. Terrence was holding a book while the other figure held a dagger. "Petro, I thought you said there was only five people here," I said, doing the math in my head.

"That's not a person, boss. That's a V. I can't really tell when they're around."

Something popped in the back of my mind. I knew what they were doing. I stood up walking over beside Two, pulling out Durundle.

"What are you doing!" Kim exclaimed. I motioned for her to stay behind cover, doing the same to Petro.

"Cover us. This may get dicey, and try to get ahold of HQ. I have an odd feeling it might not work, though that seems to be the norm," I said, walking out into the open.

Terrence stopped and looked up as I stood beside Two. He was about thirty feet away, and I could clearly see the pentagram that Carvel was sitting in. Carvel looked up, hatred in his eyes, snarling and wanting to stay something, yet the strap around his mouth prevented him from doing so. The look told me he thought I was doing this. Spittle came from the gaps in his gag; the grunts sounded like that of a wounded pig.

I took a minute, looking around the room and taking in the scene. It was a lab and living space all mixed into one. At the far end sat a fireplace and what looked like a bunch of bookcases chiseled into the wall. To the far right was a door much like the one in the Postern. A messenger gate. This is the one that still worked where Carvel and I first had gotten to know each other.

Two just stood there, not flinching, the guns still in her hands. She was calculating.

"Hey, Terrence, long time, no see. Think you could let Carvel out of that summoning circle before something nasty shows up?" I asked, figuring that I needed to buy some time.

The crusty, old, mean, and hate-filled Councilman was nothing more than a pawn. He had no clue what this was about and had been convinced I was the target, more than likely throwing him off the right scent.

The devil you may know crossed my mind.

"Max, just in time. A little sooner than expected, but nonetheless try explaining your way out of this one," Terrence said in a much harder tone than before.

I rolled my eyes, figuring we were about to get a monologue. I was actually glad that it may just buy us some time. "Yeah, sorry about that. You trying to summon another demon?" I asked, taking him by surprise by the look on his face. Maybe if I got him to admit to Bo, it would call him like a dinner bell.

"Why would you presume that?" Terrence said as the Vampire in the circle turned around. He was covered in armor, close to what Two had on but without the helmet. His black hair flowed below his shoulders; it looked like it was moving on its own.

A look of confusion started to show on Carvel's face. He was doing the arithmetic in his head and quick.

"Didn't like the first one you called up," I said, digging, seeing he was getting irritated with the conversation. Something was going on between Two and the other V, something unseen.

"That fairy demon, right? I'm surprised you didn't pop up instead. Yes, I know your little secret," Terrence said, looking over at his counterpart. "Ignore them. Let's get this done, then you can play with them."

"So you're saying you do know him then. Not too many demons I know have such a dapper fashion sense," I said, knowing that he had just inadvertently admitted to summoning Bo.

The two men started back at the ritual, Terrence mumbling while the V stood behind Carvel, obviously getting ready to use him as a sacrifice. His eyes said it all. An apology and streak of fear all in one expression crossed Carvel's face as he looked over at me after the exchange.

There was a light change in the temperature as a cool breeze swept across the back of my neck.

"Hello, darling." The smooth, growling voice came from behind me, the smell of cloves hanging in the air. Guess he had finally gotten rid of the dead fish smell. I could hear Kim shift as Two looked over her shoulder. The two men in the circle picked up pace, the words coming from Terrence's mouth faster.

"Bo, can I put you down in my book as owing me one?" I asked, keeping my voice low as the tall, slender demon walked up beside me. He was still wearing the red crushed-velvet suit and round glasses; however, he was sporting a new top hat that oddly fit the already ghastly outfit.

"Of course. Maybe dinner sometime?" Bo said, raising an eyebrow. "I get his liver."

"That might have to wait. Can you get us inside that circle?" I asked, quickly figuring time was running out.

"Me, no. You, on the other hand, yes. Being the mighty Max Abaddon Sand and all. Yet to figure it out, I take it. They have no idea what you truly are or what you are capable of. No one does, I'm afraid. I'll give you a hint. Put a little gusto in that sword of yours, and take a stab at it," Bo said, looking at Two and making a V joke. She looked back at the group in the circle, not amused. I could hear her tighten the grip on her pistols. Carvel's expression again changed for the third time in under four minutes. This time it was utter confusion.

"*Ignis!*" I barked, drawing Terrence's attention once again. He, for the second time, looked up from his book, motioning at the V as the long-haired man took up a stance, pulling out an even longer blade. A normal human would have trouble picking it up off the ground. Hell, I didn't even know where he had gotten it from.

Kim came over the communicator. "Comms are out. I have a shot but know it wouldn't do anything, and why the hell is he here?" Kim rattled off a statement, observation, and question all in one breath. I had to admit, it was getting a little chess like down here.

I walked up to the circle as Two stepped in time with me. Reaching out Durundle, I let the blade touch its surface; a hiss of ozone filled the air followed by the blade slowly sinking through its barrier.

"Dammit," Terrence bellowed as I quickly slashed the sword down and up in one motion. Two immediately charged the area I had cut open at lightning speed.

She ripped through the gap with one minor issue. A space that I had not fully cut sliced through the top section of her leg, leaving a hunk of her armor and flesh behind as the two V's collided into each other, letting off a crack and vibration due to the amount of force involved. It pushed Carvel over as Terrence dropped the book, pulling out a wand. Hey, I thought those were only for girls. I had to reset my feet and stood in place, not walking into the circle.

The thought quickly disappeared as he let out a stream of energy directly at the gaping hole in the circle. I jumped to the side, noticing the rest of the circle was fading.

I looked over to see Bo smoking one of those black cigarettes, flicking it out, and taking off his jacket and top hat. He pointed up to the ceiling as a chunk of rock slammed down on the ground directly in front of me.

Another blast from Terrence's wand hammered at the other side. "Oops..." Bo said as he dropped to the ground, shedding the rest of his clothes. Dropping his pants, Bo looked over and winked at me.

"Dammit, Bo..." I yelled as two single focused rounds whistled overhead, only to be met with a portion of the circle that had not dissolved yet.

Let me back up. Belm was scary when he went all demon and whatever else he was. Impressive and massive, a sleek killing machine. Bo, on the other hand, was nightmare fuel. The ends of his mouth opened up to meet his ears as a mouth full of what looked like a combination between razor wire and shark teeth protruded from his once-normal mouth.

His skin melted away till there was nothing but muscle and bone. Sticky and making a cracking noise as the joints on his legs slipped into the other direction, making him almost doglike. His feet and hands turned into claws that would make Freddy Krueger take a few steps back. The whole transformation took under five seconds.

Bo leaped into the air as Terrence slammed a bolt from his wand directly in his chest, throwing the demon several feet into the air. He landed on what was now all fours and stood up, reconsidering the same approach. Belm would have shredded Terrence by now into a pile of gore.

Two and the other V were in a heated battle outside the circle. The sounds of blades clinking at amazing speeds filled the air, sounding like heavy wind chimes in a hurricane. I couldn't tell who or what was on top, but I could tell it was an even match.

I pulled my sword close to the edge of the rock in front of me, only to have another blast from Terrence smash out a portion of the stone. He was waiting for me to move. Bo was walking around the edge as Carvel just lay there, knowing his options were limited.

We needed a distraction, one that would allow me to push on Terrence and open up a path for Bo. "Petro," I chirped over the communicator as another direct burst of gunfire came from the doorway from Kim, also adding to the trifecta of distractions.

"Yeah, boss," Petro said. I could hear him calling the hound a good boy in the background. "Distraction time; don't get too close. He's throwing lightning bolts, and I'm pretty sure he could light up the air," I said, giving him fair warning to stay grounded.

A crash and plume of dust came from the far end as Two was thrown into the unlit fireplace, causing the stone to crumble around her. She launched from the rubble as the clattering of swords began to start back up.

The howl of one of the hounds came out of the opening as the creature lurched forward at full steam, jumping through the air and launching itself over the pile of what was soon to be rubble I was behind. Terrence let loose another round of bolts, hitting the creature in the chest and dropping it to the ground with a final thud beside Carvel.

It was enough; Bo lunged at Terrence from the side as he lifted his wand to react. At the same time, I balled my hand, pulling from my castor, and threw the ball of hellfire directly at him. The ball slammed into Terrence as Bo's maw fully opened and locked onto his head, digging all ten of his claws through the man's chest.

The crunch of Terrence's skull was final and brutal, filling my mouth with bile as I held back from retching at the sight and sound. The howl Bo let out was deafening, the blood flying from his gaping mouth as trails of blood squirted out of several places in Terrence's body. The ball of hellfire I had thrown melted away his legs below the knees. The scene was over the top, like something out of a video game.

As Terrence's mutilated body landed on the ground, a small black rock went rolling out of his fist, landing at Bo's feet.

Bo looked down in confusion as black tendrils started to pour out of the stone racing up the demon's legs. He turned to run as I came out from behind the rock, sprinting toward him but not knowing what I was going to do. Bo put up a hand his body starting to go back to its human form, telling me to stop as one of the coils started to float in my direction.

Bo's voice came into my head clear as a conversation. "I'm going home for a while, darling. Call me later. I owe you one…" was the last thing his voice rang in my head before he winked out of existence—I guess going back home. I reflected for a second, making sure I would find a way to get him back. And on the thought of the vile creature that I just saw rip a man into pieces calling me "darling."

The vampires were still locked in a battle as the circle finally winked out of existence, followed by the sound of three deliberate rounds slamming into the other V as he lunged toward Two.

His right arm exploded, turning him around as the other two rounds smacked into his back, one obviously hitting armor and the last blowing out a chunk of his hair and dropping the vampire on the spot.

Two stood there, blade in hand. It was like they were talking to each other in finality as she raised her blade, taking his head off in one sweeping blow.

I stood there staring as she pulled out a bag from another compartment and put his head in it. I could swear his hair was still moving.

Petro came riding in as the hound saw its companion lifeless on the ground. It walked over, nudging it. The creature was mourning.

Kim walked over about the same time Two did as the entire team converged on Carvel, the blank look on his face not giving anything away.

"You OK?" I asked Two, as there was a visibly missing part of her leg, purple blood adding a sheen to her muted armor.

"I'll be fine," Two said, dropping the bag in her hand and walking over to the book Terrence was using.

"What the hell was all that?" Kim asked after a moment of taking in the utter chaos of the room.

There was blood, gray e-core, body parts, a dead hell hound of sorts, and Bo's clothes all lying around.

"That was Terrence, dirty-ass rat, an all-around real prick who has been calling up demons," I said boastingly, working to untie Carvel at the same time. "About to use Carvel here as a human sacrifice to call up a demon with a little more bite."

Carvel gasped for air as I let the gag loose from his face.

Snot ran from his nose and mouth as his eyes wandered around the room. He and the others, including myself, were taking in the horrific scene of violence.

"Why did you help me?" Carvel asked, rubbing his red wrists, the binding cutting into his fragile skin.

"I keep telling you. I'm one of the good guys. You believe me now, and yes, I'm sorry about the whole mom thing. Can you let it go and, gods and graves, leave me alone?" I said, in mixture of irritation and wit coming out at the same time.

"Yes," Carvel said, taking what looked like his first deep breath in some time, not fully apologizing in his statement of understanding.

"Good. Now we're going to gate back to the Atheneum and figure out what our next steps are," I said, pulling out the Evergate stone and pushing my will into it. The effort took my breath away, as I had used up most the gas in my tank.

"They'll know you're coming, no matter what. They knew when the Council showed up. We sent a group right after we gathered all your team's intel," Carvel said, getting to his feet, wobbling slightly as Petro let out a huff.

Kim spoke up, coming to my defense. "Yeah, we tried to tell you that before all this happened. Plus, I'm pretty sure we're going to be walking into another one. This time we will know."

"Darkwater, we need to talk with Councilman Darkwater," Carvel said, taking another breath that came through in his voice, steadying himself as Two walked through the gate.

"I don't think we need to be telling that guy much of anything" was all I said as Kim marched through the gate.

Petro made a clicking sound as he mounted the fiend hound. "You're not seriously bringing that thing back, are you?" I asked.

Petro nodded his head in affirmation. "Can't let the thing just starve. Plus, old sacrifice here might keep treating her like garbage. My brothers are coming and can take her back to the Plane," Petro said, smirking at Carvel.

"Keep her in the Postern till we figure this out. Carvel, you're coming with us by the way," I finished, seeing the older Mage walking toward one of the knocked-over chairs.

He turned. "You do not get to tell a member of the Council what to do. I need to get some things in order."

"Right, as Ed would say. By order of the Supreme Council, you are hereby summoned to the Atheneum," I bolstered, knowing that privilege was going to be gone soon.

Carvel huffed, straightening himself out and ambling through the gate, cussing under his breath.

CHAPTER 20

Blood Stones and Weary Bones

The Postern had more people in it than we had come back with. Davros and Dr. Freeman stood in the center of the room talking with Two as Petro and I came through. The group stopped at the sight of Petro perched on top of the fiend hound.

Ever see an old creepy vampire smile? Me either. Davros's grin lit up the room with his more-than-present permanent fangs that often stayed in place as V's got older.

"Look at you, little fella," the stoic V said, leaning down. The hound let its gray leather-scaled tongue drop out of the side of its mouth, resting on the two rows of barbed fangs it had. Davros started scratching behind its scaled ear. The friction of his strength sounded like someone sanding wood. The hound made a guttural rumbling growl, followed by a hack, thumping its back leg, or hoof, or whatever it was.

Petro looked over, raising an eyebrow, taking off as Davros continued petting the beast. The rest of us stood there frozen, seeing the display of affection. After a second of silence, Davros realized eyes were melting a hole in the scene. He cleared his throat not out of need but to catch our attention standing up. The scowl immediately took back control of his face.

"I used to have one as a child before leaving the Plane and, well, this," Davros said looking at himself and waving his hands. He meant when he was a Fae, before the curse took hold of him.

"You want to take him with you for now?" I asked, figuring it couldn't hurt for what he had done for us. Petro frowned.

A light smile crossed his face for only a millisecond; if you weren't looking, you would have missed it. "Where did it come from? These are highly illegal by the accords, and even more so if you are breeding them. To answer your question, I'll make sure the beast is taken care of," Davros said.

I looked over at Carvel, sweat beading on his forehead. "One was being used as a guard. We ran into two more at the house. Not sure why they were there. They had collars on. Once removed, they seemed to be rather friendly," I said, looking over at Carvel, not lying but keeping out the details.

"Animals, using fiend hounds as attack dogs. They will get what's coming. Dr. Freeman, time?" Davros asked.

I hadn't noticed initially, but he was blocking the door.

"Three o'clock p.m. our time," Dr. Freeman said in his nasally voice, looking down at his very classy plastic calculator watch.

"Very well. We need to go to the crucible room and talk," Davros said, moving aside, the hound walking in step with him on instinct.

Something wasn't right. *Where's the rest of the team?* I thought. Kim and Petro must have been thinking the same thing, all three of us looking at each other.

I touched my ear, calling Phil on the communicator but not getting a reply. Shaking my head at the two, we all silently followed Dr. Freeman and Davros. Two walked behind us limping slightly, still not giving anything away.

We walked into the main entrance area to see a handful of extra marshals at the front door. James saluted, looking slightly concerned.

Mouth stood outside of the offices scowling, looking at Carvel and acting concerned. Carvel quickly waved him off, and the ape of a man locked his eyes, which happened to be shadowed by his forehead, on me.

The team walked in the door as the massive hand of Mouth stopped me midstride. The body-armor plate I had on pushed into my chest. I smirked, raising a finger and tipping it with a ball of hellfire. Mouth dropped his hand, letting out a breath that moved my hair. I raised my chin, making the flame an unnatural crimson.

"I find out you had anything to do with this..." his throaty voice growled, trailing off as Davros called for us to follow him in.

Kim spoke up first. "Where is everyone?"

Dr. Freeman looked nervous as the sounds of radio chatter filled with combat flowed through the speakers.

"While you were away handling a very important rescue mission, the team was dispatched to our main target," Davros said while Petro darted over to the radio.

"You're telling me Ed, Phil, Jenny, and who the hell else is out there taking on the Thule Society right now?" I said, my chest starting the heave not only in exertion but from the adrenaline starting to come back to life in my body.

"Yes" was all Davros said as I walked up to the live feed, unable to make out the location through the static.

"Where?" I asked, looking at Dr. Freeman. He started looking nervous, staring at his feet.

"Ed said that you were not to leave here. Also, he would reach out if they needed you."

Carvel looked over as I walked to Petro, putting my ear to the radio, trying to make anything out.

Kim stood at the door looking over her weapon, checking the magazines, taking stock of her gear. We were on the same page.

"Davros, can I speak to you in private?" Carvel said in his now-smooth political tone. He was up to something.

"Yes, the conference room, I need to ask you a few questions and get your statement. Everyone else is to continue monitoring the situation. Max, Kim, get some rest," Davros said, motioning Two to follow.

Carvel was the last out of the room, looking back and attempting an odd wink. That old cranky son of a bitch just bought us some time to slip out. I would get rest later and still not break Davros's request completely. See how the game is played?

Mouth slunk in the room after a quick talk with Carvel. "I don't know what you're on about. The boss wants me to help. I hear Terrence is dead."

"Yup, he got ahead of himself," I said, Kim letting out a snicker and then pulling it back as the vision of his mangled body came into focus.

"I still want to beat the shit out of you," Mouth grumbled as I flipped him off. That registered a goofy grin on his face.

"Talk to me, little buddy," I said to Petro as he held his hand up, telling the group to be silent and listening to the radio.

"It's not going good, boss. I think they just requested our help," Petro said, basically making up the statement as an assumption from the garbled talk.

"Really?" Dr. Freeman said, walking up.

"Yup" was the last thing Dr. Freeman heard in his right mind as Petro threw a handful of what looked like dust at his face. I grabbed the balding man as he staggered. Petro and I had practiced this scenario a hundred times. He kept a small pouch of spelled dust on him, being a mix of truth serum and knockout powder.

"I'm really sorry, man, but we don't do it this way, you could get in trouble," I said to the man I respected, laying him down.

"Where is the team?" I asked Kim, watching the door.

"Castle Rock, Antarctica" was all Dr. Freeman said as he started snoring.

We all looked at each other, not having a clue. I pulled out my phone, doing a quick Google search and looking at the map. "It's off the Hut Point Peninsula according to this. I bet it's like this place—more than meets the eye. What is it with all these castle places?" I said, looking at the map and getting a firm grasp on its location. "Petro, go to the evidence room and get the rope we had last year. We may need it. Meet me in the Postern in ten minutes. I need to grab something. Everyone goes out one at a time. Don't look back and just keep walking, like you have to go to the bathroom or something."

The team all nodded, Mouth, the most obvious, walking out first as the rest of the team lingered until the group in the conference room stopped looking at the lumbering form walk out.

I looked at Kim as she left next. Petro was already gone through what I could only guess was one of his secret paths in the building.

It took four minutes for me to walk to my office. I grabbed one of the bottles of overdrive, as I liked to call it, from the desk. Two down, five more left. I still needed to figure out what that stuff was.

"Hello." The voice of Leshya came creeping into the room. I jumped in surprise like a kid getting caught drinking out of his parents' liquor cabinet.

"Leshya, you scared me," I said, figuring there was a reason she was there.

"Here," she said, reaching out and handing me a sandwich.

"Thanks?" I said in the form of a question.

"You will need it. Oh, and the Judge came back today. Here…" she said, reaching out and handing me the weapon. I checked it over quickly, attaching the holster to my belt and moving the pistol to my other hip.

Out of pure respect, I opened the package, taking a bite out of the cucumber/cream cheese/peanut butter sandwich. The mix was amazing. The fresh bread was cooled to mix with the mild cucumber, not to make the peanut butter runny. It was a work of art. I had never eaten her food due to several warnings.

"Leshya, this is amazing," I said as she cocked her head sideways, mildly moving her lips upward. "I have to ask you something. Everyone always tells me not to eat your food. This is great."

She let out a snort that sounded out of place. "I always made Tom the best food I could. Fit for his mood and needs or a king. You need energy, and I thought you could use this. It was our little joke. I would make food for others that was not the best, so people never asked me to make them anything."

Typical Gramps, always playing games. Hell, if the rest of her cooking was as good as this simple sandwich, it was game on.

I left the office, meeting back up with the team in the Postern. Everyone had gotten reset and ready for the next round. Mouth was fresh and stood there with all his gear in order. The other three of us looked as if we had just been dragged through hell, which I was quite sure we had come close to.

"Mouth, how did they get the stone to work?" I asked, thinking about the blood stone.

"That Belm guy showed up. All righteous and crap. Gave them some of his blood, and the thing lit up like a tree," Mouth growled, taking a little too long to spit it out.

"Christmas tr…never mind. We're going in hot. We don't have much time. Everyone ready?" I asked, taking the rope from Petro and putting it out for everyone to grab. Mouth knew what it was, reaching out absentmindedly.

I hesitated. "Did you know Terrence was on the take?"

"That git, yeah, right after our little trip. Didn't know how bad though. Glad he's dead. Wish I could have done him in," Mouth growled, a scowl crossing his face. The look of a friend betrayed.

I pushed my will into the rope, binding it with the team. Anything happened, we would have a one-way ticket back, no matter who in the group gated out. I walked over to the new gate, inserting the key as it sprang to life.

"You have peanut butter in your beard," Kim said, raising an eyebrow, reaching out with her gloved hand, and wiping it off. Not going to lie, her touch put the extra wind in my sails.

Turning I pulled out my H&K, downed the potion from my desk, dropped the flask, pulled out Durundle in the other hand, yelled "*Ignis*" bringing the blade to life, this time in its bloodred flame mood, and walked through the gate.

CHAPTER 21

I Have a Bad Feeling about This...

The violence was immediate. As we stepped through the gate, sounds of rapid, uncoordinated gunfire and spells being cast filled the chilled, dark air.

I hadn't taken the time to realize that Antarctica might be a little colder than Florida; however, the body armor and exertion of the day was keeping me warm. We arrived on a tall tower that surrounded the center of the old facility.

After closing the gate, it was clear that the place was secure. A two-hundred-foot drop-off, the edge of the stone wall greeted us to our backs as a courtyard made for everyday life greeted us on the other side of the four-foot-tall stone wall in front of us.

The place was massive but still contained. You could tell there were narrow passages and rooms spread throughout the compound, lending several places to hide. We sat there looking at each other, taking stock of the situation. I gave Petro the nod as he zinged into the air above the chaos getting the lay of the land. Leaning over to stay out of sight, I noticed Mouth had an MPK5 in each hand. The trigger guards were removed to accommodate his overly sized sausagelike fingers. They looked like toys in his hands.

A barrage of rounds went whizzing overhead, followed by the *whoosh* of a spell. Petro came over the communicator, which I forgot would work with the others.

"They know you're here, boss," Petro let out in a quick, zipping breath. Pixies weren't made for cold weather.

The communicator crackled as Phil's voice came through. "About time, bruther," he said, followed by a few grunts and the *ca-chunk-ca-chunk* of his favorite fully automatic shotgun. The sounds echoed through the air.

"I brought backup. Where's Lilith?" I asked as Mouth peered over the edge, garnering another spatter of gunfire.

"Little busy," Phil came back over the communicator followed by some choice cuss words.

"Far end," Mouth grumbled.

"What?" I asked, the noise and scene taking on all my senses. I was tired and losing my edge.

"Look with your stupid little eyes. They all have their backs to the far end where those doors are," Mouth bellowed, slapping the pistols into action.

The ogre-sized man leaped over the edge of the wall, dropping with catlike grace and unleashing the submachine guns onto the group of goons below.

"And...never mind. Kim, stay here and provide overwatch. I'm getting down there to help the team," I said, hearing three muffled shots coming from her 7.62 millimeter rifle turn two of the goon's heads below into red mist before they could run around a corner, trying to pin Mouth down.

Ed came over the radio, panting for breath. "Stay on the high wall until you're halfway over; then drop down" was all he said.

I looked along the wall to see several CSA agents also firing down on the group. We had the high ground.

"Hey, boss, there's a big cat down there. I think it's on our side, but you might want to avoid it. Looks to be a lion with bigger-than-normal claws and teeth and just, well, it could eat Mouth," Petro relayed, having a bird's-eye view of the fight. He wouldn't be able to stay up there much longer. It was obvious the Council had sent its heavy hitters. As soon as Petro spat out the message, an unnatural roar came from the center of the courtyard.

Running behind the other agents, it was clear there were several partitions below lending cover for both parties. Looking down, I saw Phil unleashing hell on the black-clad new-age Nazis.

It was stunning. I stood there a second, rounds landing in front of me, watching as he unleashed a fury of fire rounds from his shotgun. He followed them up with pummeling blows from the sledgehammer in his other hand on the goons.

It was like watching an artist paint a picture you knew would withstand the test of time or a musician hitting that one chord, asking if the crowd was ready to rock. The scene overwhelmed me, as a rush of adrenaline filling my system, flooding me with energy supported by the potion I chugged prior to walking through the gate.

Letting out a guttural yell, I leaped over the wall, dropping twenty feet into the action beside Phil. The potion was driving, allowing me to land unharmed. The blade of Durundle burned hotter, lighting up the dark sky around us, turning everything into a shimmering bloodred hue.

I let loose a cadence of rounds from my pistol, not close

enough to touch anyone with my blade. Phil, stopping, lifted his head to the sky, letting out a howl. The tattoos on his neck looked alive. He slung the shotgun down, grabbing the other sledgehammer from his back, and ran toward the wall the goons were hiding behind. One leaned over to have their head disintegrated by Kim on the upper level.

To hell with it, I thought, charging as well. We came around the corner to a split group of goons on either side. They started raising their weapons, no longer focused on the upper level. The crunching sound of Phil ramming through the group sounded like popcorn being made on a late Friday night, bones cracking and skulls crushing under the swift blows of his hammers.

I swerved left to find two of the Thule guards running off. I caught one with a full burst from my pistol. The other dodged right, falling as I swept my blade down, cutting the poor man in half. These weren't craft; these were people.

The flame from my blade cauterized the wound, filling the air with the stench of burning flesh.

It looked like they had the Mages by the door on the other end as spells kept flowing from that direction. There was a pause of silence as Phil ran over, a wild look in his eyes.

"Bruther, this is it," Phil said, popping a smoke in his mouth and picking up his shotgun.

Petro came over the comms. "Ed's by the door. He's in a mess."

"Petro, see if you can help. We're coming!" I yelled as the sound of Mouth's submachine guns sang in front of us. I looked up to see tracer rounds from Kim whistling through the air, knowing they were leading to someone's death, cutting Mouth a pathway.

Phil looked over, flicking his cigarette unintentionally on

the body of one of the downed goons. We looked at each other, taking off in the same direction. The roar of a large cat again filled the air, sending a chill up my spine.

Bodies came flying through the air over the wall ahead from the general direction of the roars, landing in front of us and stopping our movement. "Gods and graves," I said, looking at the mangled bodies.

Phil looked over grinning. "Big cats."

We turned another corner to see Ed on the ground with Jenny standing in front of him unleashing a green wave of energy at the Thule flunkies in front of us. We were at least a hundred meters from the far end and still had ground to cover.

"Ed!" I yelled, dropping down beside him. His face was burned, the wound on his side open again.

He opened his eyes, shaking his head and nodding toward the fight. Rage filled my body as I dropped my sword and pistol. Flames erupted from my arms, bloodred infernos again lighting the air. They engulfed my hands, forming streams of flame in front of me as I charged past Jenny.

"Stop!" she yelled.

I slammed through the wall, ripping through it like paper, my hands in front of me burning the path. I kept running as bodies dropped around me, their screams reaching my memory, which would save them for later.

I lashed out, slinging the sticking flame to everything around indiscriminately, pausing only to see Mouth and Phil run up beside me unleashing hell as well.

Our charge was stopped as a crackle of lightning filled the air, knocking us all down in one swift motion. Pearl. The burns on Ed were from Pearl.

I looked over, trying to get up, seeing Phil and Mouth both struggling to their feet as another wave of bolts covered us like spiderwebs. The air hummed with electricity. Mouth grunted, dropping his guns as Phil curled up in pain.

"To the left," Mouth bellowed, motioning us to the wall under a walkway to our left. On instinct we all crawled shambling to cover, as rounds from the CSA team and Kim whistled toward where Pearl was standing.

The three of us sat there, our backs to wall. I could see smoke coming off the other two.

"The hell was that?" Phil asked taking a breath while talking. He reached down, pulling out a flask, downing a few swigs, and passing it around.

"Pearl," I said, taking a pull then reaching over to Mouth, but he shook his head, rejecting the drink.

"Hey, boss," Petro came over the comms. "You guys are good for a minute or two. The Mages at the door are shifting; a few of them went in. That big cat I think might have eaten one or two before they knocked it down. Not sure where it went. I'm coming to ground."

Petro buzzed down, landing at my feet and shaking frost off his wings. He looked blue. I reached down, lighting a small flame in my hand and letting him walk over to warm up. "Not too close. It will burn you," I said, taking a breath.

Kim came over the radio. "We're going to unleash. When you hear us let up, you can move on the Mages. There's only a handful left. Pearl went inside."

As the words came out of her mouth, lightning lit up the sky from the top of the highest wall, slamming into the area the CSA agents and Kim were. Pearl was not fleeing; he was repositioning.

"Change of plans," I said, seeing the other two still winded from the encounter. I looked over the wall, seeing a handful of goons shifting. "I'm going to—"

A black rolling smoke emerged over the barrier on the opposite side, like someone had poured it over the wall. The distinct odor of burning tires filled my nostrils.

"Oh shit," Phil let out.

Jenny came over the radio. "Close your eyes—don't look at it."

Phil, Ed, and Petro, obviously knowing what this was, already had their eyes closed as I followed suit.

The next five minutes was hard to explain. It started with an eerie silence. Then the shuffle of bodies moving from all directions. Jenny again came over the radio telling us not to move or open our eyes. I felt like I was in the scene at the end of *Raiders of the Lost Ark* where all the Nazis' faces melted off.

More shuffling sounds followed by something bumping into my leg that came and went. I stayed the course and didn't open my eyes. Petro had curled up under my arm. I could feel him shaking from the cold, not fright.

I started feeling a light vibration, the smell along with the cool air slowly receding. For some reason I was holding my breath, letting it out and gasping for clean, fresh air.

"Max, you can open your eyes now," the manly, gruff voice of Gramps said, a hand reaching down and pulling me up.

Opening my eyes, it took them a second to focus. They had been shut so tightly my vision had blurred. The figure in front of me was wearing an older style set of fatigues. His gray hair combed over neatly, the aged stubble on his face from a few weeks' worth of not shaving. It was Tom, my Gramps. He looked much younger, maybe a youthful sixty, but it was, in fact, him.

We stood there looking each other in the eyes. I could feel the gaze of the others on my back. The last trail of the black fog seeped into his hands, as he spread his fingers, taking a deep breath.

"Anyone down there?" Kim came over the radio. The others were silent, also knowing who had shown up and what he had just done. Gramps was a necromancer. Ed once told me he could talk to ghosts.

"Yeah, lass, I think we're gonna need a minute," Phil cut in. The sounds of the once-raging conflict hushed in the air.

"There's no one down there but you. They're all gone," Kim said, confused. "Just gone."

Without saying anything, I walked forward, wrapping my arms around the man and hugging him. Not out of appreciation but out of the flood of emotions that was coursing through my body. Confusion, admiration, anger, need—all coming together at the same time.

Tom stiffly lifted his arms, patting my back. "I'm here, I'm not going anywhere" was all he said. The smell of burnt hickory filled my nostrils. I didn't want to let go.

Our moment was interrupted by Phil. "You old son of a bitch," Phil said as he came rushing in, taking his piece of the moment.

"Phil, I see you have good taste in friends," Tom said, letting go and grabbing Phil by the shoulder.

Mouth sighed, shaking his head. "Can we save this? We have business to attend to."

"Way to kill the mood." Petro buzzed over, looking Tom in the face.

"Ice-freeze warrior. Pleasure to meet you," Tom said, holding out his hand for Petro to land.

"Yeah, nice to meet you and all. Does this mean we have to move out?" Petro asked.

The brevity of the comment relaxed the tension; we all let

out a light chuckle except Mouth, who was picking up his guns.

It was shocking to see the aged youth in his face. He must have been faking the old act. Of course, when I saw him last year after drinking the potion Sarah gave me, I did remember him looking much younger, but I was not fully able to grasp the vision.

Jenny came over the comms in a low voice. "I'll ask later. I can see the traces of people, Mages, below on the e-meter. There're still bad guys behind that door. A few just gated out. It's odd, like they keep gating in and out. Taking something. I'd hurry."

I picked up Durundle and my pistol, staring at the man who had affected my life more than I could have ever imagined.

"What was that you did back there?" I asked, also seeing Petro's rifle on the ground and putting it in a vest pocket.

"Something I'll have to pay for later," Tom said, a worried look on his face as he pointed down at the Judge, changing the subject. "Ah, I see Leshya got this back to you to bring along."

I reached down, unlocking it from my belt and handing it to him. "Guess so. She does have oddly good timing,"

"That she does." Tom looked around the group. "Lilith is down there, as are several young children. We have to save as many as we can. There are also a few gate Mages down there I believe you are looking for. I can't vouch for the mental state they may be in."

He finished by ushering Phil in front of us to do his thing. Phil's thing was ripping the doors off their hinges, throwing them several dozen feet through the air behind us.

The entrance hall was cleared out; there was another set of doors obviously leading underground at the far end. We stepped forward, Mouth raised his hand signaling to stop.

"You go. I'll take care of our company," Mouth exclaimed as another mammoth ogre dropped from the catwalk with a tooth-rattling thud. The floor cracking and begging for relief under its massive weight.

The group skirted to the right side of the room as Mouth charged the other man, letting loose a flurry of rounds. They appeared to have no effect on the creature as we reached the far end of the room.

Mouth let out a howl as the crack of wood on bone rang in the air. Phil punched a hole in the door as we poured into the stairwell.

The sounds of thumping and crashing stone echoed in the tight space. Tom looked down the dark walkway. "Pixie..."

"Petro," I interrupted.

"Petro, how far are the others down here?"

"Not far, about a hundred meters. That electricity guy is down there, and then there's..." Petro trailed off, looking over at me. He could smell the blood relation.

"Listen closely. Max and Phil, go after the children. If Pearl wants a fight, give him one. Draw him away if you can. He's not invincible. A little water and he goes to ground," Tom said. A grin crossed my face.

"Bruther, here." Phil threw his canteen over. We had talked about this before; every bit of water helped. It wasn't like the hellfire that came from me. To work water, I had to have a source. More than likely I could pull some from the moist walls but not enough to get a full casting off.

"I'm going to pull what I can from the room. Phil, if you can, get him to stand still; I'll see what I can do. I just need him to be stationary for a minute," I said, looking down at Petro. "I need you to get back to Kim and Jenny and let them know what's going on. There too much radio traffic. Get Jenny down here as soon as you can. She can help with the kids. I'm not sure what's going on, but I think we're about to find out."

Tom grimaced slightly; he knew. It would be a long discussion later if we all made it out alive. Another thundering crash coming from the main room snapped the group to attention.

The plan was slightly changed from most of our party-crashing entrances. Phil, instead of pushing the door in violently, causing general mayhem in the room, would pull it off the hinges so we could use it as cover if needed.

As all plans, things go wrong. The door didn't have any handles. It was fused into the wall. The walls exploded outward, knocking us back against the stairwell entrance. Phil stood his ground, glowing a dull gray. Tom and I went flying backward with no regard to the stone wall.

The potion was still in the driver's seat, pushing me up immediately. Tom took a few seconds to steady himself while the dust still provided cover.

The sound of Phil slamming his sledgehammer into flesh rippled through the air. Bone-crushing thumps echoed as the dull gray surrounding him moved forward out of sight.

Bolts of electricity lit up the dust-filled air, clearing out the space almost immediately. I jumped up bringing Durundle to life. "*Ignis!*" I yelled, jumping up and launching into the room, veering right off instinct.

A cloud of black smoke came in behind me, streaking left.

The room was two stories inside. The top floor was full of medical equipment and small partitioned rooms. Dull lights hung from the ceiling. Below a group of Mages shuffled into a gate opened at the far end of the room. They were pushing what looked like babies in medical containment carriers. The top floor still had several that had yet to be moved.

The room was the size of a large moving theater. You could see down from the entrance as the partitions surrounded the side walls. It was gray, dark, and clinically sterile. The smell of light bleach caught in the air.

Lilith wasn't trying to fight us topside but was buying time to move what was important. We had caught her off guard.

Pearl was on the far edge of the top floor. He had obviously moved back to position himself better to cover the door. I could see his gleaming-white bald head pop up, unleashing directed bolts of energy versus his usual spiderweb type of casting. He didn't want to damage the merchandise.

Phil jumped left, a beam of electricity slamming into the metal support beam beside him and arching electricity through his body, once again dropping him to the ground.

I leaned over the rail, seeing Lilith for the first time. She was tall and elegant. Her posture was perfect. She was dressed in a black leather suit that was not for combat but to make a statement: I am in charge here. Plus, I had a feeling she didn't need anything other than herself in a fight.

Her hair was black and flowing, pulled back in a ponytail showing off her chiseled features. My grandmother was a looker. Lilith's face was almost angelic. The look on it, however, told another story; she was determined and irritated.

I had taken too much time looking at the scene, giving Pearl an oppurtunity to launch a bolt in my direction, blasting the wall to my front and propelling me backward. I tumbled over the lip of a side stairwell leading down, finally taking control of my momentum and stopping halfway down.

Tom was still not moving. The sound of two more people going through the gate filled the room. A Mage on the floor below saw me, let loose an energy spell, and slammed a portion of the stairwell to the ground. Through all the excitement, I still had Durundle charged. I was a beacon with a blazing-red sword in my hand screaming, "Look at me!"

It was a clear shot. Pointing the blade, I pushed my will into the sword, letting loose a tight ball of hellfire that landed directly center mass of the Mage. The goon stood a few seconds before falling to the ground. That got Lilith's and, for that matter, everyone else's attention. Hellfire isn't very tactically useful. It stands out in a crowd.

Tom was still not moving and, from what I could tell, had not been spotted. Phil lurched up, this time with a small revolver in his hand, letting out a chirp of gunfire from a fully automatic pistol.

The stone wall Pearl was behind exploded in the corner. Phil had nailed a perfect shot. The sound of muffled irritation came from the area.

"Max." Lilith's buttery yet firm voice boomed through the air. She was projecting it around the room, as I started feeling pressure behind my eyes. Lilith was trying to compel me to come to her.

I looked over to see Tom gone, a wisp of black smoke in the place he once stood. Neat trick.

"Why don't you and your friends come down here, and we can work this out in an orderly fashion?" Lilith commanded still in a subtle yet convincing tone. I wanted to do just what she asked.

Phil was back up on his feet behind the beam, nodding at me in affirmation. He was going to take another go at Pearl. I shook my head, calling him off. There was a confused look on his face. Gathering my will, I pushed a single word into my thoughts toward him. *Tom.*

I wasn't good at the whole instant mind-messenger thing like Ed, but could pull off a smaller-scale version.

Standing up, Pearl peered around the corner. Blood covered the left side of his face where the debris from Phil's shot had lodged several small pieces of stone in his smooth pearl-white skin. The red liquid was a stark contrast to his pale complexion.

"I'm coming down," I said, grabbing what was left of the old metal stairs and pulling myself to the floor. Pain immediately shot up my injured leg, sending jolts of electricity through my body. The potion was wearing off, and my body was collecting its toll.

Taking a deep breath, I focused on the rest of the room. Several carts with babies and a few younger children lined the sides of the wall, shielding them from the chaos above.

Two other Mages beside her pushed their carts to the side, taking up position, each raising a short staff, much like the one I carried. Another thud came from above. Lilith looked at the two Mages as a small gate opened on the side wall, the main one still shimmering. They both jumped through, presumably to join the fight upstairs. Mouth was about to get some more company.

I scanned the room looking for any signs of the dark smoke Tom was moving in. The cover shielded him from detection.

Pearl launched himself to the floor below, landing with a slight pause before hitting the ground beside Lilith. I needed to learn that trick.

Phil peered over the edge of the rail as Lilith lifted a finger. I never heard Phil in real pain before today. Sure, cussing and grunting, but the sound coming from him was pure pain.

"Stop," I demanded, still figuring that any time I could buy would be one less child taken through the gate.

Lilith lowered her hand, Phil crumpling to the ground. "I

can be reasonable. You come into my home and expect that I do not defend myself. That would be petty of you," she said, taking a step back toward the gate. Lilith stood in the full light of the room, her figure glowing as the gate shimmered.

"You wanted to talk to me, so here I am."

Pearl was scanning the room for something.

"Nice try, Max. With an army? I'm afraid after the last two days, both of our resources have been strained. It took me decades to build my strength and team. It is unfortunate that I will have to do so again. Let's just say I will be much more selective the second time around."

The sterile smell of a hospital room filled my nostrils, and I took a deep breath, steadying my nerves relaying pain to my brain. "Why the children?" I asked, looking to see her right arm wrapped in a gold chord. She was clutching the end in her hand. It was a rope, much nicer and woven like the one we had used not only at the Fountain but in coming here as well.

"I'm not going to stand here and talk about my plans with you, grandchild," Lilith said, Pearl looking at her with blood pooling in his left eye. He hadn't wiped the wound yet to clear the thickening gore on the side of his face.

The room was silent, echoing every movement, the gate letting off a low reverberating hum. There was a rustle of wind, the sound of papers falling, lingering just a second too long. To me it was a sign of Tom moving. I wasn't sure about the others, or they acted like they didn't.

"I'm going to ask you this once. Then I'm going to bury this complex into the Earth from which it came." Lilith paused with a slight raise of her eyebrow, searching for something that wasn't there.

"OK" was all I said, keeping the conversation moving, drawing her focus. Dust fell from the roof as more muffled bangs came from above.

"I want you to come to the Plane with me. Let me show you what it is I have done and explain why. Being a dark Mage, or the enemy as you call it, is all a matter of perspective."

"So having a room full of children, babies for that matter, is supposed to mean something to me?"

Lilith clicked her teeth. "It should mean everything to you."

The pieces started to fall into place as the Purity Law landed in my mind like a ton of bricks. I was an experiment. Belm had told me as much.

These children—the children were like me. Quarter Fae, quarter demon, and half human. The perfect race, capable and carrying the best attributes from all three species. I knew that others were scared of me. Hell, no pun intended, I knew Ed was to a point. I was capable of more than most Mages and Fae could ever dream, all the while being grounded and able to blend in with the civilian population. A new pure species capable of not being caged.

The thought of just letting go, of joining her, crossed my mind. Feelings flooded my body. It was her; Lilith was trying to get into my head again. I focused my will, pushing her out; I couldn't let her know Gramps was here. It had been enough, though; Lilith saw my thoughts and that I did, in fact, not have a plan. She saw my curiosity and final understanding of the children. Lilith also reacted slightly in surprise to me pushing her out.

I slipped the small cord of gate rope behind my back, holding it in my hand. A light breeze flowed over my back. I could feel a nimble tug on the rope as well as the light smell of ozone and burnt hickory. I coughed lightly, clearing my throat.

A smile curled up on the edges of Lilith's face as she saw

my understanding. "Yes, home, Max. Time to come home—" She was cut off.

Pearl went flying through the air, shot through the gate with such violent force that his face didn't have a chance to register what had happened. The blood-covered Mage disappeared into the shimmering void. A sucking sound followed. While actually doing my assigned homework several months ago, I learned this meant the gate was a one-way ticket.

Black smoke dissipated from the area Pearl had once occupied. Lilith turned, letting out a snarl, hunching forward, and raising her arm with the gold cord around it. The spell she let out blasted the air with what looked like glitter for a brief second. My eyes blurred as I stumbled, almost knocking into one of the carriers.

"Hello, Lilith," Tom's voice rang as he walked forward now in plain sight, flecks of glitter lightly fading.

The shock on her face was real but immediately followed by rage. "You will not stop me this time," Lilith lifted her arm as the containers carrying the children started to glow. She was gating them out.

I looked down to see my body also starting to glow. The flame on Durundle flickered out, all control of my senses fading. I had bought Tom enough time to position himself.

Tom launched himself again as the pillar of black smoke slammed into Lilith, pushing her through the gate. The effect was imitated on the carriers as they all settled. My eyes cleared, looking up to see Tom standing half in the gate, half out, a look of confusion on his face. I limped up to him.

"Stay back; she's trying to pull me through." The strain on his face was evident. It was ripping him apart.

"I'm not losing you again, Gramps," I said, lifting my leg

up and kicking him through the gate.

The gate snapped out of existence in a pop of ozone. I looked up to see Phil still down as the babies around me started crying. It started as one, then two. Before long, a chorus of screams and cries filled the air. She was controlling them. Lilith was a monster.

A light rumble shook the room. Radio chatter started blazing through my communicator. "I'm here. We're gating back. Everyone needs to leave now," I ordered, looking around the room filled with cries.

Several affirmations of understanding came over the communicator, including the mild grunt of Mouth. He was still alive.

I reached in my pocket, pulling out the rope and the gate stone. "This better work," I said before clicking my heels together, remembering I had bound Tom to the rope, willing the gate to open and stepping through.

CHAPTER 22

Wounds

Mouth carted in the last of the carriers as the facility collapsed in on itself. The Postern was full of crying and loud voices. The gate rope would forever have a place in my collection—of course, after I figured out how to steal it from the evidence room.

I pulled the team through the Evergate back to the Postern. Mouth was covered in bruises yet was still intact. Phil was alive with his back on the wall smoking a cigarette, his hair standing up and fingers pitch black from the voltage. Petro was hovering over a group of captivated older children, telling the story of his heroic action at the Fountain of Youth while brandishing his sword. Lacey, Macey, and Cacey all danced around him, humming a tune in the background.

Kim was, of course, holding a baby that was crying louder now that she had been removed from her warm bed. Tom, leaning over and taking a breath, was holding Lilith's arm in his hands wrapped in cloth.

I had pulled Tom along with us. In doing so while they were gating, he had brought Lilith's arm with him as she tried to pull him through the other side.

For once, I had gambled and won. The rest of the team used Mags-Tech gates to get out in time. The operation wasn't without casualties. Over the last two days, twenty Mages and ten marshals had lost their lives.

I called Jenny to let her know our status; she was tending to Ed, who was still unconscious from his wounds.

"Then I grabbed the stone..." Petro started as I cut him off.

"I don't think the kids need to hear that. Kim, any word on getting some help down here?"

"The rest of the marshals and a few local police are on their way. Most of the local law enforcement are still doing hurricane cleanup and security. I almost forgot about it with all the excitement."

Mouth lumbered over as a baby started giggling at him. "I've got to go. Boss is calling," the lumbering ogre said, shifting sideways and squeezing out the door.

I took note that he hadn't threatened my life or flipped me off. I think we were making strides in our friendship.

"Max." Tom's voice cut through the noise. Startled, I turned around to see a rustic smile on his face. "That was a close one."

"I'm not sure I'm ready to get into this now. All I can say is you're calling Mom in the morning."

The lines on Tom's face grew as he nodded his head in affirmation.

"That was amazing work you did back there. You saved a lot of lives."

"Well, I didn't save them all, did I?" My temper was taking control as it often did, even after I did the right thing.

"Lilith's out of the picture."

"How do you know that? She tell you?"

Tom unwrapped the cloth. Lilith's arm wrapped in the gold cord was sitting there. The cut was surgical from the gate.

"She's stuck on the Plane or wherever she is. It's not on Earth. We will see her again but not for a long time. You in the mood for a drink?"

I took a breath, wanting to do anything but be in the office with Tom for some reason. I think it was all too much. My body and mind were exhausted. "Sure. Phil, you OK?"

Phil looked up, flipping me off, his charred black fingernail garnering a chuckle as smoke came from his mouth.

"Rain check. Petro, make sure the medical team gets him to a hospital."

The scene was that of pure yet tranquil chaos. A room full of babies and battle-hardened assholes.

"Oscar, let's go, boy," Tom called as the small orange tabby cat strolled out from under the table in the center of the room.

I looked as the two of them strolled out of the Postern.

Ten minutes later after working through the crowded entrance, we made our way to the office. I assumed it was no longer my office. Tom walked in, clicking open the bar and grabbing us both a Vamp Amber.

We both headed to sit down behind the desk. I gave way, walking around and taking a seat in Phil's assigned chair.

"So ask," Tom said, opening the top drawer with the potions in it and pulling them out one by one.

I sighed, taking a pull from the ice-cold beer. The sensation ran down my throat, telling my body it could finally relax.

"Where have you been? It would have been nice to have you here."

"Max, I was gone because I had to be. It's not that simple."

"Not that simple," I asked in the form of a statement, letting the words linger. "I just saw you turn into a cloud of smoke and wipe out a damn army of goons. People have died; we needed your help, and about that…"

"Think about everything that has happened over the last year. Do you think me being here would have changed any of that? Me being here would have put you all in more danger. With me gone certain people stopped paying so much attention to this place."

"That doesn't answer my questions. Gods and graves, are you some type of diviner as well? I've had my fill of those."

Tom sighed, taking a deep breath. "Max, I left because I was looking for something that in the end will become clear. During this I realized the person who had asked me to do this knew that I needed to be gone for your safety. I was in a way lost for several months not having a way to get back. Give me that at least."

"Devin. It was Devin. I know Lilith is my grandmother, and I happen to have had my fair share of drinks with Belm. What is it you were looking for?"

"I can't tell you now. I promise I will, and yes I did find it."

"What about Sarah and that night? Seems to me you could pop in and out."

"That was a one-time thing. I thought I would be back in a couple of weeks, but then I got stuck. No way to get back. Look, there are other places. Places you can't imagine where people like me aren't as strong as they are here."

"The Plane?"

"For some time, yes. The rest I will need to tell you, just not now. I see you figured out how to use the Postern and a few of the Gates?"

I leaned back seeing the look on his face. It was a mix of regret, irritation, and truth. Oscar jumped up on the desk, looking at me, sitting down, and licking his front paws.

"All right, let's shelve that for now. So what's next?"

"Well, I agree. I need to make a few calls. Other than that, I'm curious to see what you've figured out about some of the other gates, what Devin's said to you, what you've been up to, the Balance, just everything." A tear started to take purchase under his eye, quickly being pulled back in by will alone.

He was serious; he had been out of touch for some portions of the past year. Tom started pouring the potions into the bin beside the desk.

"Hey, what's that about?" I asked, knowing I may need more of the enhancer.

"This stuff is a drug, Max. I left it here in case you needed it. I think you're far enough along to figure it out on your own."

I sat back down, shaking my head, knowing he was right.

"Oh, I almost forgot. That smoke and situation. I called in a little favor. Well, a big one. I can still do that, just on a minor scale, but let's save all that for later."

"Does this mean I need to move out?" I asked, wondering if in fact I would have to.

"No, God, no, I hope not. You always have a home here. I am, however, moving back into my room, and we can work something out in here."

"How about the lab?"

"The lab? How do you know about that? It was sealed decades ago after…"

"Devin told me all about it. Said he sealed it up after a little disagreement you two had, guessing that was Lilith. He opened it up, and I've been using ever since."

"I guess that means it's yours. I work out of my room anyways. That reminds me..." Tom reached over, flicking his wrist, the bookcase on the far wall dissolving into a door.

Oscar looked up, sprinting toward the little side opening made obviously for him. "He's been in Jacksonville most of last year with your parents, and I'm sure he wants to get back to his stuff." Sounds of banging came from behind the closed door.

"The Postern," I said, seeing Tom's eyebrows rise. "The way I see it, you don't know how to use all the gates. What is that place?"

"Correct, I don't. The room is here and nowhere at the same time. No one really knows who built the thing originally. I think it was the old gods, and to answer you fully...a weapon, I believe."

"Weapon? I get how some of the rooms can be used for the wrong reason, but a weapon?"

"The journal I left you was a collection of notes on the gates. The drawings are a little more than just doodles. From what I gather, if you get all the gates working and under your control, you can do or go anywhere. When I mean anywhere, I mean the above and below. You know, heaven and hell or whatever you want to call it. Other worlds, other times."

I reached down, pulling the key from the clock my mother had left me sitting it on the desk. Tom cocked his head. "Son of a bitch. Where did you get this?"

"Mom. It was a gift for my re-birthday. I guess I don't fully understand, but after the last year I've had, I'll buy what you're selling. Oh, and I also have this," I said, going to the shelf and picking up the purple box with the stones fitting the iron dragon head on the door.

Again, Tom looked surprised. "My boy, you have been busy. Let me guess. Devin gave this to you."

"He did, no strings attached. He said something about it not being an easy thing to acquire. What can you tell me about this stuff?"

Tom sat there, shaking his head. "Plenty. Let's get a few things situated first. We will have time later. Let's see how Ed and the rest of the crew are doing. Can I use your phone? I need to call to Ned."

Word of Tom's return from death spread faster than high school gossip. My phone was buzzing while he was on it.

"Max, we are going to be getting some visitors in the morning. Tell me everything you know about Councilman Darkwater," Tom said, already wanting to get back on the trail. He was leaving a whole lot of things on the table to discuss later.

I told him everything I knew. The gate crystal, the meetings, everything. I mainly pointed out his connection to Terrence and the access he was given. He had been passive during the deposition, which still bothered me.

Tom sat there, taking it in. A year of the space being mine had spoiled me. I wasn't sure what to do. Go to my room? We sat together for several long minutes.

"I'm going to get some rest. I recommend you do the same. It's going to be a long day tomorrow. The political type," Tom said as he opened the door to his room. The sounds of Oscar purring louder than a cat that size echoed as the door shut.

I reached down, pulling out my charm and whispering Petro's name. It took a few minutes, but as always, he came flying through the door.

"Hey, boss, what's happening?" he asked. I handed him a small cap of rum I poured.

"Here, you earned this one. Crazy night, right?" I wasn't really wanting to talk but just make sure I was seeing things correctly.

"I didn't think we could beat last year," Petro spat out in a fast cadence, slowly drawing off. "But we did! Cacey's a little pissed, but she will be fine. The girls were helping clean up for a Pixie friend they have in Jacksonville after the hurricane. Made a mess near the coast. Flooded most of downtown St. Augustine. They think it was someone steering it. Ben gave us a ride there and back." Ben was now on the friend list after I found out he was Kim's cousin and not a love interest.

"Yeah, you piss in the bushes and downtown floods. Good thing my brothers aren't coming for a few more days. What do you think about Gramps being back?" I truly valued his opinion. Even if what he said was off the wall, it always seemed to make sense.

"You know all that stuff about moving out? I think it may be time, boss. Let's see what happens; give it a few days. Trish still has that place available. For some reason I think she is saving it for you, well, us…" Petro trailed off.

"You kidding me? I wouldn't be safe without you around," I said, seeing him perk up rubbing his mustache. "I'll talk to her when we get some time."

"Hey boss, one more thing. That cat. Can you keep it away from me?"

I raised an eyebrow, giving my word. Petro had mentioned the issue Pixies had with cats.

CHAPTER 23

*That's Why They
Call It the Blues...*

The next morning came early. My coffeepot started as I walked into the bathroom, steaming it up. I could hear loud, victorious singing coming from Tom's room, even with my door closed. The shower drowned out the rest.

"Halls of Montezuma, to the shores...." came the old song of wartime glory.

Standing in the shower, I finally took note of all the bruises and bangs on my body. My leg had obviously been damaged again somehow. The scar stuck out a little too much for comfort.

I turned in the mirror before jumping in, seeing my back covered in dark-purple-and-yellow bruises. My shoulders had what we used to call in the army "strap rash." Bruises from the weight of my vest and the gear had worn red grooves into my shoulders.

A portion of my beard had been singed off. I hadn't realized; I looked like I had mange and guessed everyone was doing me a favor not telling me. My forearms were red from burning parts of my uniform, the fabric melting close to my skin. I looked like hell on wheels. The scars had finally started to pile up.

Another twenty minutes and I was dressed, walking out into the office to find Petro and Tom talking.

"Hey, guys, anything new?" I asked, figuring the lack of messages or texts meant no.

"Not yet, boss. I heard the girls saying a bunch of people are coming here this morning. Good thing you're wearing pants this time," Petro said, laughing. Tom grinned; he did that when he wanted to learn more.

"Later. Let's get down to the dining room. I want to find out how Ed's doing."

We walked to the dining room to find the new normal, dozens of agents and people buzzing around the once morning lake calm of the Atheneum. James was at his desk, looking tired but giving me a thumbs-up.

I reached my hand up to the newly installed keypad to keep people out, finding the amazing smell of bacon, eggs, butter biscuits, and sausage gravy. It filled the air, all coming together in a chorus of reasons to be alive.

Phil was already at the table with a plate that looked as if it had lost the fight. Gravy covered the bottom portion of his beard as he smiled. "Morning, bruther. Bloody amazing food. No idea who made it."

Tom grinned. "I think I know. Don't get used to it."

We all sat down, digging into the feast. Leshya had outdone herself.

Jenny walked in ten minutes later, looking at Tom sitting there, a mix of knowing and disbelief on her face.

"Jenny," Tom said, wiping off his chin, standing up, and getting a running hug from the good doctor. This was followed by a cracking slap.

The room went silent as Tom shook his head. "I know" was all he said in response, followed by a longer hug from Jenny. I was betting this had more to do with Ed rather than her own feelings. She loved Ed; it was clear.

I cleared my throat. "How's Ed?"

"He's still unconscious. The doctors said he will be fine. I checked him out; it seems that he will heal. He got hit by some strong stuff over the past week. The one thing we aren't sure about is if his body will fully heal," Jenny said, also taking in the feast with a confused look on her face.

"Arse, he's all brain anyway," Phil said, reaching for a biscuit, his fingernails still charred.

"Anyways, a bunch of Council members are coming soon. We need to get ready. Shit's about to hit the fan. Tom, I think you may need to talk with them first with Ed not here," Jenny said, rolling her eyes in delight as she took a bite of the gravy.

An hour later after we had all caught up on things, James came in, letting us know our company was gating in and he was leading them to the sitting room on the east wing. The main entrance and doors to that area were still a mess from our little run-in.

We walked as a group to the sitting room, getting high fives from various people I didn't know. Petro was burping, having eaten too much, as was Phil.

Titus, Davros, and Anna stood at the door, all reaching out to shake Tom's hand. I peered in, seeing Darkwater and Carvel sitting with Ned and a few other Senior Council members. The heavy hitters were in fact here.

Tom and Jenny went in as they shut the door. "Why do

you think they're talking to them in private?" I asked, looking over at James and Phil. Petro was perched on my shoulder.

"I bet they had that old codger doing something for them, and he's reporting on it. Jenny because she is in charge till Ed gets better," Phil said, rolling an until cigarette in his mouth. He was nervous. "That Darkwater guy in there had his hands in all this. Mark my words."

The three of us stood there, nodding in agreement.

Twenty minutes later the doors opened, Anna's warm smile greeting us. "You can come in now."

Tom and Jenny looked over at me directly. Titus, the large black man from the Supreme Council, spoke up in his deep, accented voice. "The Supreme Council has met. With newly acquired information, and guidance from the security and judiciary branches, Max, you are no longer under review."

The man stood there, looking for me to respond. It was clear they had already been briefed on everything that had happened. I looked over at Carvel, receiving a slight nod.

"What does that mean?" I asked, looking around the room, still noticing the look of indifference on Darkwater's face. He was actually scowling. Something had him in a bad mood.

Anna spoke up. "Max, you are not only in good standing with the Supreme Council. You are also receiving a field commendation for saving the life of a Senior Council member."

Ned was beaming. This was also good press for him as well. "Thanks," I said, still not truly knowing what this meant.

Davros spoke up. "Oh, your powers granted under the Supreme Council are hereby revoked; your team is now returned to regular duty."

Understood, we knew this would happen. It still meant something. Darkwater grinned slightly. Not enough to notice, but there was enough giving it away to a keen eye.

"I request that Max be held—that is, until further details of Terrence's access to certain information is ascertained." Darkwater was waiting on the protection of the Supreme Council to be lifted.

He was trying to shift the focus off him. We all knew he was somehow tied to this.

The sound of Phil tightening his fists caught in the air.

Davros stood up, walking over to the man in his calm yet controlling voice. "You were responsible as his master. You, Councilman Darkwater, were in charge of the gate crystal, and you alone are the one that we will need answers from."

The room was silent. Phil released his grip. Davros had sucked—no pun intended—the air out of the room.

"Carvel?" Darkwater asked, looking over at the man for affirmation.

"I don't have any say in this," Carvel responded, pulling a Switzerland.

Davros stared back. "You will be restricted to the Council chambers until further notice." Without giving Darkwater time to respond, two Mages came in, walking up behind the man. A cool, calming look came over his face as he looked at me.

I wasn't sure what that was about; however, I knew that his story wasn't over. He had an ace up his sleeve.

As Darkwater was escorted out, the mood in the room lightened. Anna promised me a case of Vamp Amber, and Carvel, while not apologizing, shook my hand.

"I left a package for you in your office," Carvel said in a raspy tone. He looked like hell as well, the signs of the prior day showing.

I looked confused. "Thanks, I guess. It's not going to kill me, will it?"

"I don't think so. It could under certain circumstances," Carvel said, walking off.

I noticed Tom and Titus laughing, both men catching up on long-lost memories. After another thirty minutes, Jenny spoke up.

"I just got a text; we can see Ed now. Then might I recommend a drink later? I'll call Kim and see where she is," Jenny said, the group not missing a beat.

We left the Council members, walking out to jump in Ed's car. We even talked James into coming. Tom gave his supervisor a stern look and gained his permission.

The hospital was, well, a normal hospital. Ed was still in the ICU unit, and we could only go in one at a time. He was a mess. Tubes ran in and out of his body as machines beeped to the rhythm of life. The sterile smell of hospital was becoming all too familiar. While we knew he would be OK, seeing him in this condition was jarring.

We did hear a nurse saying something about a surge in abandoned babies en route and figured we could at least take that off the things-to-do list for the evening. That road would be a long one.

Tom spent the most time with Ed. He came out looking sad yet determined.

"I need to check on a few things," Tom said as we all stood there silent in the hallway. "Six o'clock, FA's?"

The group agreed, leaving Ed to rest and recover. Jenny stayed behind as I figured she would.

Six o'clock came fast. Most of us had spent the afternoon resting. Tom, on the other hand, went to Jacksonville to get sorted with my folks. I would wait till he had a few drinks in him to find out how that went. Mom had texted to call her later.

The team all converged at FA's at the same time, Kim pulling up as we walked out the front door of the Transitions Office.

Before gating over while checking emails, I found the office was going to be moved to another location. They would also be comanaged by both groups. Not one or the other, and the information gathered would change. No longer a way to data-mine Mages, but just who and what you were. Belm had even lobbied successfully to leave that space blank to fill in.

As the group converged on the bar, Trish lit up like a Christmas tree. Drinks were served, food was laid out, and laughs heard. Everyone was surrounding Tom as he told as much as he was willing to share about his adventures over the past year.

"Trish," I said, pulling her aside as another group came into the bar. "That apartment still available?"

She grinned; it reached her eyes. "I've been waiting. Plus, with them moving the Transitions Office out, you can have the whole place to yourself."

I looked at her, taking that in. With the space I could start a business or, better yet, have room for someone else to move in. We talked for a few more minutes, shaking hands and sealing the deal. I never asked her how much rent was, and she never told me.

"What was that all about, lover boy?" Kim chided, walking up and nudging me on the shoulder.

"I'm getting my own place," I said, holding my chin up and winking at her. A slight blush swept across her face.

"Maybe now you can take a girl out on a proper date," Kim replied as she winked, the straw of her drink dancing on her lips.

"Maybe. You know any?" I said as she rolled her eyes, smacking me on the back before walking back over to the group.

Petro came whizzing over before I took off to the bathroom. "There's someone in there. You know," Petro said, pointing down. This was his hand signal for Devin.

I walked in saying his name, the smell of pepper filling the air. "Devin, I hope this isn't a hookup," I said jokingly.

The bathroom stall on the far end opened up, revealing the tall, slender man dressed in his usual dark suit.

"Maxxx, nice to see you in one piece. I see Tom's back. We'll have to have a little chat later."

"Where's Belm?"

"He's busy. Family business. I know you understand."

I smirked at the statement, figuring he was either dealing with Bo or maybe Lilith. Devin's smooth, affirmative voice slightly echoed off the walls.

"So…"

"To the point. Yes, I have some information and a gift for you. First, you need to focus on the rest of the gates in the Postern. I'm sure Tom will be more than glad to help. Secondly, take this," Devin said, handing me a small wooden box.

"What's this?"

"I hear you're moving out. It's a housewarming gift. Take something from the lab, and place it in there. When you move to your new home, open the box and leave overnight."

"What is it?" I pushed.

"I love surprises—well, at least most of the time. So should you."

"You know the Postern is a weapon, don't you?" I asked, actually needing to go to the bathroom.

"Of course. One that will be needed soon" was the last thing Devin said as I walked over to the urinal, hearing the click of the door. The smell of pepper dissipating.

Walking out, this time under three minutes, was a new record for me. I knew things would change soon.

"Max, you said you wanted to tell us something," Phil said, chugging a beer in one gulp.

"Yeah, you did say that. Oh, and what did Carvel leave you in the office?" Kim asked.

"His mother baked me a blueberry pie and left me a thank-you note," I said, winking at Kim; again she blushed. I was starting to think it was the booze.

I looked over at Petro as he nodded.

"I'm moving out, and I quit."

Elton John came over the jukebox Trish had installed. "That's why they call it the…"

EPILOGUE

"Please stay tuned for a special announcement," the TV droned dully. The plan was simple. Wait until everyone had one more normal Christmas and on December 31, there would be a new version of New Year's Eve.

The Council and civilian government called it New Dawn's Eve, a celebration of the beginning of the Balance.

All channels and social media had the same message: "Please tune in December 30 for a special global announcement." The date was strategic. Most people would be off work, while others would be occupied with other things.

A good many conspiracy theorists got it right. There were those, of course, that went to their overly expensive bunkers, but on a whole, the event was set.

December 31

"Ladies and gentlemen, the president of the United States."

The announcement came as Rebecca took the podium. No pomp or circumstance left to the imagination. Surrounding her were politicians, military leaders, titans of industry, movie and music stars alike. Athletes, a few V's, a couple of Mages, what looked like a large dog, and Tom.

"Today a new dawn arrives. While many thought this may be a warning, it is the opposite. It is a homecoming. Throughout history we have all shared our world with things and creatures we know nothing about. The fish at the bottom of the ocean, a spider in the Amazon, or the smallest organism frozen in ice. What we have also shared our world with is magic." There was a dramatic pause as several of the recognizable people behind the president stepped forward.

Not everyone in the magical community was very well tucked away. They needed jobs as well for the most part. The persons stepping forward were all moderately familiar faces to the general public.

"Today we honor our promise of transparency to the people of this country and the world. I am here to tell you that there are those among us that are different, capable of extraordinary things. Doctors who have cured disease, your favorite ballplayer, and those with the ability to do magic." There was another pause as the well-known actor who had stared in many hero films lifted off the ground, hovering two feet off the ground. Another person called the Musician stepped forward, opening her hand, forming a perfect ball of water before pulling it apart, establishing a perfect circle around her figure.

The crowd around the president all clapped. The faces of the people at the bar on Jacksonville Beach froze. Celebrations cut short. Everyone's phones in the entire country buzzed with the alerts and a message of peace.

Max sat at the end of the bar. He flicked his wrist, letting a spark of flame on his finger linger as he lit the cigarette of the women standing behind the bar, nerves and the news justifying her smoking on the job.

"Drinks are on me."

The bar erupted in cheers.

Anna Vlad took the podium next. Her eyes were pitch black as she let a little fang show for the camera. For the next thirty minutes, she described our world and what we have to offer and the peace that will come out of this. It would be one of the most viewed speeches in history, even outpacing Winston Churchill's, to name one.

Other places, as predicted, didn't take it as well. Certain rural areas and already sensitive inner cities saw days of looting, riots, and general chaos. Smaller, less-developed countries fell into dictatorshiplike rule out of fear. The plan was, however, to ensure this was corrected with the might of the new combined worlds. At the end of the day, the plan worked.

One thing that wasn't predicted was the massive surge in religious communities. Faith was not just an abstract anymore. While not everything was laid out to the general public, it was enough. This would cause issues later, but for now, there was peace.

—

Ed sat down the remote control, grabbing his cane. The speech was over. He was finally out of the hospital after a couple of months and able to move on his own. While his mind was sharp, his body was not able to take the punishment. He had moved into the house in the woods with Jenny, cementing their relationship.

"What time's Tom coming for dinner?" Ed asked. The smile on Jenny's face was radiating.

"Calm down. He will be here soon enough."

The doorbell rang as Ed got up, waving Jenny to sit down. He wanted to show his old friend he could walk.

"Can I help you?" Ed said, opening the door. The two men laughed as Tom threw his coat over Ed's head.

"Thanks," Tom said, motioning for Jenny to be quiet as the distraction allowed him to pull out the surprise.

Ed slammed the coat to the floor, acting like he was going to swing at Tom but freezing in place.

Tom was standing there with an official sash and seal from the Senior Council.

"Congratulations. Looks like they're planning on keeping you around for a while." Tom beamed, seeing the pride and joy on Ed's face.

—

In a deep dark cave on the Plane, Lilith and Mengele stood watching the announcement. Lilith's missing arm was wrapped in a cloth capped in leather. On the table sat a mechanical arm still being constructed.

The computer they watched the announcement on sparked as the screen crackled.

"It's done," Mengele said in a throaty voice. The space they were in was secluded and empty. Eclectic furniture adorned the room.

"Is it?" Lilith said, walking over to the far end of the room and picking up the crying baby. "I think it's just begun. The Thule Governance will not sit idle long."

"You know what will happen if others figure out whose child this truly is?" Mengele said as Pearl walked in, bowing his head.

"Yes, and I hope when they do, they come for her," Lilith said, sitting the child back down.

Pearl looked over, waving his hand toward the door.

"Guest" was all he said as Councilman Darkwater walked into the room.

ACKNOWLEDGMENTS

Special thanks go out to all my family, friends, and the authors that still inspire me to do more.

To everyone who has supported Max Abaddon through book one, cheers! I know the editing was tough the first few rounds.

To my family, my wife, and two sons. This book is part of my legacy to you. When I am but a memory in time, you will always be able to pick this book up and remember what a nerd I really was and, well, still am...

BOOKS BY THIS AUTHOR

Max Abaddon And The Will
Book 1

Max Abaddon And The Purity Paw
Book 2

Max Abaddon And The Gate To Everwhere
Book 3

Max Abaddon And The Dark Carnival
Book 4

Max Abaddon And The Crystal King
Book 4

The Sinking Man Series Parts 1-3 Box Set
Parts 1-3 Box Set

Sheltered

Part 1 of The Sinking Man Series

Printed in Great Britain
by Amazon